Homecoming

Ellie Dean lives in a tiny hamlet set deep in the heart of the South Downs in Sussex, which has been her home for many years and where she raised her three children. She is the author of the The Cliffehaven Series.

To find out more visit www.ellie-dean.co.uk

Ellie DEAN
Homecoming

arrow books

1 3 5 7 9 10 8 6 4 2

Arrow Books
20 Vauxhall Bridge Road
London SW1V 2SA

Arrow Books is part of the Penguin Random House group
of companies whose addresses can be found at
global.penguinrandomhouse.com.

Penguin
Random House
UK

First published by Arrow Books in 2020

www.penguin.co.uk

A CIP catalogue record for this book is available
from the British Library.

ISBN 9781787462793

Typeset in 10/12.5 pt Palatino
by Integra Software Services Pvt. Ltd, Pondicherry

Printed and bound in Great Britain by Clays Ltd, Elcograf S.p.A.

MIX
Paper from
responsible sources
FSC® C018179

Penguin Random House is committed to a
sustainable future for our business, our readers
and our planet. This book is made from Forest
Stewardship Council® certified paper.

This entire series is dedicated to the men and women who sacrificed so much during wartime to ensure that we could live in a more peaceful world. From the beleaguered housewives battling on the Home Front, to the evacuated children and the men who fought so bravely in the theatres of war, may their dedication to the cause never be forgotten.

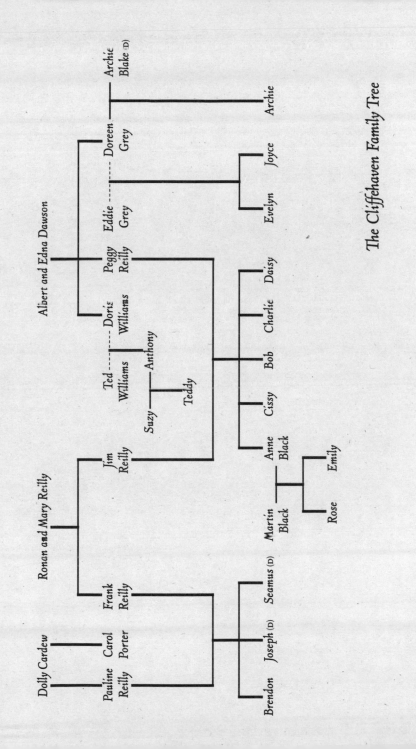

The Cliffehaven Family Tree

Dear Reader,

Well, here we are at the end of nine years and eighteen books! When I first began this series, I was thinking it might stretch to six books, so was delighted to be able to expand it beyond my original ideas, and really steep myself in the Reilly family's comings and goings during the most frightening period in our history.

It's been a joy to get to know the Reilly family and all of Peggy's chicks, and now I must say goodbye to them with a heavy heart. They have become my family and I've come to love each and every one of them – even Doris and Pauline – and although Cliffehaven and all who live there are purely fictional, I know I shall miss them dreadfully.

Many of you have wanted me to carry on into the fifties and sixties with this Cliffehaven series, but I came to realise it would have been too painful to watch our beloved older characters become frail and pass away. Surely it's best to remember them as they are in *Homecoming* – at peace, fulfilled and with the assurance that they will live on for ever in our hearts.

But all is not lost, for there is to be a new series in which we will meet Ron and Dolly in their youthful years, and follow their exploits before, during and after the First World War. There's a lot of research to cover before the writing starts, but I'm hoping that the first book will be published towards the end of this year.

So, this is not goodbye, but adieu for a little while, and I wish you health and happiness in this new year of 2020, and hope you continue to enjoy reading about the trials and tribulations of the Reillys.

Ellie Dean x

Acknowledgements

No author works alone, and long before a book is published an army of people have shared their wisdom, told their stories, and given their advice on the history and ordnance behind the scenes of the tales I've constructed.

Paul Nash has been tireless in his help regarding the history of the RAF during the Second World War, and has cheerfully guided me from making too many mistakes when I've had the wrong aircraft in the wrong time or place!

Jean Relf has generously provided me with the transcript of her father's diaries and letters to help me understand Jim's time in Burma.

Many extraordinary women have enthusiastically related their memories of doing their bit during the war, from ambulance drivers, land girls, Wrens, factory girls working in munitions, to drivers and mechanics – I salute them all, and fully understand why these wartime memories are still so very much alive, for it was an exciting and fulfilling time even though they lived in fear of air raids and life was precarious.

Teresa Chris, my agent, has been with me throughout the journey of this series, and I thank her once again for her tremendous support, and unfailing belief in me and what I can achieve.

My editors at Arrow have changed during the nine years of writing this series, and I want to thank them all for their dedication to ensuring that the books are the best they can be – Georgina Hawtrey-Woore – who is sadly no longer with us – Viola Hayden, who was absolutely on my wavelength and knew exactly what I was aiming for. Jenny Geras, who steered me gently through the editing. Last but never least, Emily Griffin, who picked up the reins brilliantly and with great enthusiasm helped me on the last lap of this long journey.

I want to thank Valerie, Oonagh, Ann, Tina, Linda, Amanda and all my other wonderful girlfriends who provided wine, chats and giggles which saw me through the tough times – and to my sons and daughter who've been unfailing in their love and support.

And finally to my darling husband who never once let me falter and who is always my most stalwart fan, and best friend. I love you.

Prologue

Burma, August 1945

Second Lieutenant Jim Reilly was stunned. He wasn't the only one – his best pal Jumbo McTavish, their fellow officers and all the men of the South East Asia Command who were still in Burma were stunned, too. The Americans' atomic bomb had virtually obliterated the city of Hiroshima, and yet the Japanese High Command were refusing to surrender. When the second bomb erased Nagasaki three days later, it was a long five days before the news came that Japan had finally agreed to surrender unconditionally.

The great joy and relief that greeted this announcement was tempered by the memories of all the comrades that had been left behind in the jungle graves of Burma and throughout the Far East. The cost of winning the war against Japan had been brutally high – not only to life and limb, but to Jim and Jumbo's peace of mind which would for ever be fractured by what they'd seen and heard throughout the Burma Campaign.

The army padre had held a service on the day the Japanese had surrendered, and although Jim had never been a religious man, he'd earnestly and sincerely thanked God that he'd survived and would be going home when so many others hadn't been given that blessing. He'd also given thanks that the planned Operation Zipper to invade Malaya and capture Port Swettenham and Port Dickson in early September would not now take place, for none of the men had the stomach for more warfare. With the certain knowledge that their fighting days were over and they'd soon be boarding a ship for home, Jim and Jumbo had set their minds to thoroughly enjoying their leave.

The beaches of Ramree Island that had seen such fierce fighting were peaceful now, and the all-weather airbase that had cost so many lives to build and defend was running smoothly with almost daily flights bringing in fresh provisions, construction materials and tools, and on their departure, transferring the more seriously ill patients from the field hospital to the larger, better equipped ones in India. The pale golden sand stretching from the edge of the dark green jungle right to the shore of the turquoise sea made a perfect playground now the monsoon was over.

Having time on their hands and the wherewithal to make their camp more comfortable, Jim, Jumbo and the other sappers had put their skills to work on building accommodation huts, a mess hall and a large recreation room that was open to the skies but for a canopy of mosquito netting, to garner the cooler air of evening and provide a place for the men to watch the films being brought in, listen to the comedy shows on the wireless, or hold dances.

The natives, free at last from their Japanese persecutors, had put up makeshift kiosks of bamboo and canvas above the high-water mark to sell their lethal rice wine, tasty snacks wrapped in banana leaves and curries delicately flavoured with coconut and fragrant spices. Their small, slender and beautiful women had finally came out of hiding, as untouchable and remote as ever with their shy smiles and lowered eyes, but adding beautiful colour with their bright longhis and jingling bracelets.

Once the building work was completed, and his time was his own again, Jim had bought a hammock from a Burmese pedlar and strung it between two palm trees where he had a good view of everything that was going on around him. Stripped to his shorts and barefoot, he'd spent a good deal of time languishing in the hammock, a crate of beer close to

2

hand in the shade, his sweat-stained hat shielding his eyes from the sun's glare that occasionally speared through the palm fronds.

The heat was debilitating and he'd been too lazy to talk, even to Jumbo, who'd taken to sprawling his great length in a nearby planter's chair beneath a vast umbrella to read a copious number of books he'd found in the hospital library. Jumbo's red hair and fair skin were perfectly suited to the northern climate of the Isle of Skye, but the tropics had done him no favours, and although he burnt and peeled, he never went brown, unlike Jim, whose olive skin was now as dark as polished mahogany which made his eyes an even deeper blue.

Jim had slept and dreamed of Peggy and home – of his daughters, Anne, Cissy and little Daisy, and his sons, Bob and Charlie – of his elder brother, Frank, and his father, Ron, and the town of Cliffehaven where he'd lived all his life until two wars had forced him to take up arms and leave those familiar and much loved surroundings.

Those dreams echoed the sadness that had plagued him ever since he'd left Beach View, for he'd been gone for almost four years and had yet to meet Anne's little girls, and the last time he'd seen Daisy, she'd still been a babe in arms. Cissy, who'd always been the naughty one with ambitions to become a star of stage and screen had clearly matured during her time as a WAAF at RAF Cliffe, and was now a business partner in a very successful private taxi hire company in London.

As for his sons, they'd left home as evacuees back in 1940 – bewildered little boys who couldn't possibly have understood why they'd had to be torn from their family to go and live in Somerset with their big sister, Anne. Bob was now a capable young man of eighteen and managing the Somerset farm, and Charlie was fifteen, all set to take his school certificate and go on to technical college to study engineering. Jim had missed so much of them growing up, and there had always been a constant shadow of worry hanging over him that his children, and his beloved Peggy, had become strangers during his long absence – and he to them, for the war had changed him irreparably. If only the army would release him, he could return home and begin to repair his relationship with them all and once again be in the bosom of his family.

As the exhaustion of almost constant battle had slowly left him and the long, languid days had begun to make him feel restless and impatient for news of his demob and passage home, he'd abandoned the hammock and set about keeping busy by joining in the fun.

The hot, sunny days had become filled with shopping in the Burmese markets which had sprung up again, or with swimming and playing games of football and cricket on the sand accompanied by the mouth-watering aromas of barbecued meat cooking on hot coals outside the mess hall. The sultry tropical nights had seen Jumbo leave his chair, book and umbrella to join Jim and take part in dancing with the off-duty nurses from the nearby hospital, or drinking beer while watching a film or listening to *ITMA* on the wireless.

There had been trips along the coast in a convoy of trucks, delightfully crammed in between laughing nurses who wore little more than swimsuits and native sarongs. These outings always involved more beer, swimming and picnics on the beach, and they'd returned to camp satiated with sun and sand and sea to fall dreamlessly asleep until birdsong and the chatter of monkeys woke them at dawn.

It was a leisurely, very pleasant life, and if he'd had Peggy with him, Jim could have stayed on this island for ever – but of course all good things must come to an end, and when it was time to leave for England, he knew he'd be amongst the first to board the ship.

Jumbo had gone off just after dawn that morning to the hospital to get more lotion to slather onto his raw skin – or at least that was the excuse he'd given Jim. However, Jim had noticed how he couldn't quite meet his eye, and had seen the way he'd looked at the pretty little Welsh nurse with the long black hair and lilting voice, and suspected the enormous Scotsman was smitten. If so, then it would be interesting to see what came of this seemingly mutual attraction, for Jumbo had always sworn he'd never tie himself down, and was content to live alone in the glens of his Scottish island home where he tended the deer and managed the forest of the laird's estate.

Jim had been about to leave the hut he shared with Jumbo and two other officers to wander down the beach for an early morning swim before breakfast when the Brigade Commander's adjutant had forestalled him by announcing that their commanding officer had ordered a meeting of all officers in the recreation room within the hour. The young man had refused to answer their questions, but spirits soared, for it could only mean they were on their way home at last.

An hour later, the officers of South East Asia Command streamed out of the recreation hall in numbed silence, trying to make sense of it all before they had to inform the men under their command of the new orders. It had felt as though a huge cloud had suddenly blocked out the sun.

Operation Zipper was now Operation Jurist and would go ahead, but earlier than previously scheduled and on a much smaller scale, having transferred a proportion of its original strength to the new Operation Tiderace. Jim and Jumbo would not take part in Operation Jurist which was under the command of a British Naval Force tasked with liberating Malaya, but were due to join 60,000 infantry on Operation Tiderace's vast convoy of battleships, cruisers, destroyers, Royal Fleet Auxiliary and escort carriers which would set sail from Trincomalee in Ceylon and Rangoon in Burma in ten days' time. They would arrive in Singapore in time to witness the signing of Japan's complete and unconditional surrender on board HMS *Sussex*.

Operation Tiderace had been swiftly organised immediately following the two atomic attacks on Japan, and would retake Singapore and reinforce the British Military Administration that was already being set up there. It was not known how long the mixed brigades of SEAC were expected to stay in Singapore, but their brigade commander had warned them they would definitely not be going home before Christmas – and could very well remain in Singapore well into March 1946.

Once Jim and his fellow officers had passed on this devastating news to their men, the previously carefree mood had soured into resentment and bitter disappointment, and the beach became deserted as the men sought solitude to try and digest what these new orders meant for them and their long-suffering families. Silence seemed to prevail throughout the camp, and eventually a long, muted queue began to slowly form outside the communications hut to send this devastating news to their loved ones at home.

Jim had joined the queue, sick at heart, the weight of disappointment lying heavily in his gut as he tried to decide how to word the telegram to Peggy. She would be as disappointed as he to learn he'd miss yet another Christmas, and although the message would have to be necessarily short because censorship was still the order of the day, he would sit down tonight and write her a long letter to try and explain as well as he was permitted why he wouldn't be coming home. He certainly didn't want her to hear what SEAC were up to through news broadcasts or in the papers, but however much he wanted to protect her from hurt, there was absolutely no way around it.

Having sent the telegram he knew would bring her terrible grief, Jim had pushed his way back through the queue that now stretched all along the beach, and tramped over the sand, his eyes blinded with unshed, angry tears.

6

Reaching the small, secluded cove at the far end, he'd slumped down into a fold of the dunes, wrapped his arms about his knees and stared out at the shimmering vista before him.

But instead of a sparkling blue sea he saw the choppy waters of the English Channel which splashed on Cliffehaven's pebbled beach, and where the sky was bleached by the sun and hazy with heat, there was only the dark grey of English skies, and the gathering clouds of a winter storm.

Jim buried his head in his arms and silently wept.

PART ONE

1

Cliffehaven

Beach View Boarding House stood three terraces back from the promenade, and was one of the many Victorian villas that lined the steep hill on the eastern side of Cliffehaven. Despite its name, the only view of the beach was from the room on the top floor, the others looking down into the back garden which had been turned into a vegetable plot or at the roofs of the other houses.

Three storeys high above the basement rooms, and once quite elegant, it now showed the scars of wartime in the patched roof, pitted stucco and shattered steps which led up to the rather battered front door – but at least it was still standing, which was more than could be said for some of the surrounding villas. A gas explosion had devastated two neighbouring houses at the end of Beach View Terrace; a V-1 had destroyed the house behind, and one cul-de-sac further down had been obliterated by a V-2.

For all the damage and years of neglect because of the war, Beach View was a happy home in which Peggy Reilly had offered motherly refuge to the many evacuee girls who'd come and gone over the past six years, and provided a loving home for her father-in-law, Ron, her small daughter, Daisy, and the elderly Cordelia Finch.

Now that the war in Europe was over and the Japanese had surrendered, Peggy's eldest daughter and young son, Charlie, had returned home with her granddaughters, and now she awaited the longed-for news that her husband, Jim, would soon be demobbed and on his way back from Burma. The girls who called Beach View home were beginning to make their own way in the world certain in the knowledge that their years with Peggy had imbued in them a sense of warmth, love and family which would remain with them for the rest of their lives.

Sarah Fuller closed her bedroom door to muffle the noise of the other girls and have some privacy while she concentrated on getting ready for the evening ahead. Her younger sister Jane was having a bath, but Danuta, Anne, Rita and Ivy were dashing back and forth between rooms in a fever of excitement while their landlady, Peggy Reilly, was downstairs with Sarah's great-aunt Cordelia Finch trying to get Anne's two little girls and her own small Daisy to calm down enough to eat their tea.

Beach View Boarding House was alive with the sound of chatter, laughter and running feet, for it was the eve of Rita's wedding, and they were all preparing for the party at the Anchor to celebrate her last night as a single girl. Their menfolk, Martin, Andy, Ron, Rita's father Jack, and the Australian bridegroom, Peter Ryan, had been tasked with staying behind to look after the three children, and were under the strictest orders to remain sober as they'd already had their bachelor night earlier in the week.

Sarah's smile was wry as she contemplated this arrangement, for she and her sister had been living at Beach View since the fall of Singapore, and she knew all too well that if Ron Reilly was left in charge of anything there would be mayhem, regardless of his daughter-in-law Peggy's direst of threats. Ron was a man who still followed his own path, despite having been recently married to his long-term sweetheart, Rosie, and although he was in his late sixties, he still had the vigour and propensity for mischief of a much younger man.

Sarah was still smiling as she pulled up the zipper on her favourite cream linen dress and smoothed it over her narrow hips. Brushing out her long fair hair and carefully pinning it into a smooth chignon, she checked the result in the dressing-table mirror and was quite taken aback by her startling resemblance to her mother, Sybil. It was something she'd never realised before as she rarely took much notice of what she looked like unless it was for a special occasion. However, it seemed that the passing years had transformed and refined her, and now, at twenty-three, she had turned into something very different to the young and rather naive girl who'd fled the invading Japanese in Singapore with her sister four years ago.

This was no bad thing, she realised with some awe. Sybil had been regarded as a beauty by everyone in the ex-pat communities of Malaya and Singapore, and she had certainly shone with her golden hair, dewy complexion and almost effortless sophistication. Sybil had been the consummate hostess and socialite, adored by Sarah and Jane and equally adored and pampered by their father Jock. Sarah knew her mother hadn't changed much since escaping from Singapore with newly born James to her parents' sugar cane plantation in northern Queensland, for her letters were full of her hectic social round, and the enclosed snapshots showed the same vibrant, attractive woman Sarah remembered.

Sarah looked across at the line of precious photographs that were displayed on the narrow mantelpiece above the gas fire. Some she'd managed to bring with her from Singapore, and others were ones her mother had sent. Having studied them closely, she turned back to the mirror to compare those images with her own reflection.

It was interesting to note that her eyes were the same shape but a paler blue than her mother's; her cheekbones were less defined and her nose was perhaps a little too snubbed to be regarded as attractive in the way her mother's was. She was still very slim but had lost the deep tan of her outdoor life in Malaya, and now her skin had taken on the fresh, rather rosy hue of an English girl. But she had certainly inherited her father's firm jawline, and her hair was not pale gold like Sybil's, but inclined to darken with streaks of honeyed brown and copper during the English winters. There were vestiges of her mother in her face, but Sarah decided she'd never be as beautiful, and was happy to accept the fact.

She turned from the mirror and hunted out the pearl studs and single-strand necklace she'd brought with her from Singapore, and once they were in place, she stepped into her shoes and went to stand by the bedroom window, her thoughts far from Beach View and the rather gloomy vista of Cliffehaven's rooftops and chimneys in the dwindling light of evening.

The news of the Japanese surrender had wrought mixed emotions for her and Jane, for the long years of war and separation from their loved ones had seemed endless. It was said that home was where the heart lay, and although they'd both been extremely happy here with Peggy Reilly, the yearning for that home in the jungle had become more acute – the need to know what had happened after the fall of Singapore to their father and Sarah's fiancé Philip ever more urgent. And for Sarah, it meant having to face the reality of keeping her engagement promise to Philip – should he still be alive – despite the fact she was in love with another man.

She'd met Delaney on the Cliffe estate where she'd been working in the offices of the Women's Timber Corps. He'd arrived with the other Americans to complete their training before they were sent into the fighting across the Channel. The attraction had been instant and mutual, and although she'd tried desperately not to fall in love with him, it was to no avail. And yet their dream of being together had been shattered by a twist of fate, for she'd been on the brink of accepting Delaney's proposal when she'd received proof that Philip was still alive, but now a prisoner of war alongside her father in Changi, and holding her to her promise to wait for him.

Sarah had fought a long and very painful battle with her conscience, but in the end she'd known she'd have to end things with Delaney if she was ever to have peace of mind. She must trust that Philip would survive the Japanese occupation, and fulfil her promise to him, regardless of the cost to her own happiness.

She determinedly blocked her thoughts of Delaney, for they stirred up too many agonising emotions, and focused instead on the memories of the isolated rubber plantation her father had managed for Philip Tarrant's wealthy family in Malaya. She and Jane had been raised in the large, tin-roofed wooden bungalow that jutted from the hillside on stilts above the canopy of trees. Even now, she could almost feel the heat and humidity of that fateful tropical night when she'd stood on the wrap-round veranda and peered through the sturdy mosquito screens to the black stillness of the mountains and the jungle that sprawled over them to the very edges of the plantation.

The Malay servants had lit the oil lamps and the orange flames had flickered in the breeze that still carried the vestiges of the day's heat in its dank, musty breath, the smell almost smothering the delicate scents of the orchids, jasmine and frangipani that grew in wild abandon amid the trees. She remembered how the moths had battered against the screens as mosquitoes whined, and tiny pinpricks of light from the fireflies had blinked in the darkness as the deep bass hooting of macaque monkeys echoed into the night. The war in Europe had seemed to be a world away – the threat of invasion by the Japanese merely rumours stoked by scaremongers who refused to believe that Singapore was a fortress and impregnable.

Now Sarah gave a deep sigh and watched the last of the dying sun spark fire in the solitaire diamond ring she'd taken to wearing again as a reminder of where her loyalties lay. She'd been nineteen and Philip twenty-four when she'd accepted his proposal that night, and he'd slipped this ring on her finger.

In hindsight, Sarah could see now that she had been naively caught up in the heady flush of first love; overwhelmed that such a handsome, wealthy man wanted her as his wife when he was regarded as a real catch by the gossiping, catty cliques of women who had daughters to marry off. She had felt that as the daughter of what was seen as a lowly plantation manager, she'd won an enormous victory over those cats, and with her parents' approval, their future together had seemed set to follow the customary privileged and pampered lifestyle of all the ex-pats who lived and worked in the Far East. She'd gone to bed that night to fantasize about her wedding day and the eventual move into the gracious white mansion that had been in the Tarrant family for four generations.

But her dreams had been cruelly shattered by the news that the Japanese had landed on the beaches of north-eastern Malaya, and just before dawn she'd stood with her heavily pregnant mother and younger sister on the veranda to watch the Japanese bombers on their way to attacking the airfields in Singapore.

Philip and her father, Jock, were members of the local civil defence unit, and had been called to arms, but their main priority had been to get Sybil and the girls on a ship to anywhere that was relatively safe. Sybil had gone into labour during the long, treacherous journey down through Malaya to Singapore, and gave birth to James on the day Sarah and Jane had sailed for England.

That had been the last time they'd seen Jock and Philip, or their mother. They learned much later that Jock had managed to get Sybil and the baby passage to Australia with only hours to spare before Singapore fell to the Japanese. What had become of their father and Philip after they'd been imprisoned in Changi was still a source of huge worry, for the news coming out of that part of the world was of slave labour, vast prisoner-of-war camps and hundreds of deaths.

'Well, you don't look very cheerful considering we're about to go to a party,' said Jane, coming into the room swathed in towels.

Sarah's dark thoughts scattered as she moved from the window. 'I was remembering the last time we saw Mother, Pops and Philip,' she replied.

Jane didn't reply immediately, but rubbed her cropped hair vigorously with a towel, before running a comb through the tangles. 'Yes,' she murmured. 'I've been thinking the same ever since the Japs surrendered.'

She pulled on fresh underwear and rolled on her stockings. 'I doubt we'll hear anything much until things settle, and the new British governors can organise searches for the camps and their prisoners. The Japs haven't been known for their record-keeping, so I suspect it could take months to track everyone down.'

Sarah nodded and bit her lip. 'Mother's still convinced they're alive, but I wish I could be so certain. We've heard such awful things about what the POWs have been through, that it would be a miracle if both of them have survived.'

'It's the not knowing what happened to them after Changi prison that's been so frustrating,' said Jane from the folds of the dress she was pulling over her head. 'And I agree, it would be hugely against the odds if even one of them came through. But there is a way to get to the heart of the matter if you're game enough.'

Sarah frowned as Jane straightened the dress and fastened the narrow belt about her slim waist. 'Game for what?'

'When I was in London with Jeremy yesterday, I went into the Cook's travel agency to ask about passage to Singapore. According to the chap there, British Overseas Air Corporation are about to restart their flying boat service from Poole. With all the necessary stops to refuel, it will take

17

about four and a half days to get to Singapore – much quicker than going by boat.'

Sarah's momentary excitement was quashed by the idea of flying all that way. 'I dread to think how much that would cost,' she said. 'And don't forget, Jane, the money Pops sent from Singapore was declared invalid the minute the Japs printed their own currency. With everything so expensive here, I haven't managed to save very much from my wages.'

She took a breath. 'Besides,' she added, 'neither of us have flown before, and I'm not sure I want to risk it.'

Jane plumped down on the bed and giggled. 'I never took you for a scaredy-cat, Sarah. Flying's much safer than it ever was, and cuts the time of travel right down. Anyway, the money isn't really a problem,' she added airily before shooting her sister an impish grin.

Sarah wondered fretfully what her sister was up to. 'Since when? I'm sure the MOD didn't pay you that well.'

'That's true,' she admitted cheerfully. 'But I didn't have time to spend much of it, so I have quite a little nest egg. And Jeremy promised to help out with the cost on the proviso I came back and married him.' Jane blushed. 'Silly, sweet man, he didn't need to bribe me – I'd have married him anyway – but it does mean we can afford the tickets.'

She paused to take a breath, her gaze fixed steadily on Sarah. 'So I went ahead and booked them for the first post-war flight on the third of September – and sent a telegram to Mother telling her our plans,' she finished in a rush. Her face was alight with excitement. 'What do you say to that, Sarah?'

Shocked that her sister had done such a thing, Sarah sank down beside her and tried to absorb this startling revelation. 'I don't know what to say, or how to feel about you rushing into things like that without talking it over with me first,' she murmured.

Jane took her hand. 'I'm sorry I didn't consult you, but I felt I had to strike while the iron was hot. The tickets were already selling fast, and I didn't want us to miss out – not as we've already waited far too long to get back home.'

'I understand your reasoning,' Sarah said hesitantly. 'It's come as a bit of a shock, that's all, and I'm finding it difficult to take it all in.' Her gaze drifted to the photographs on the mantelpiece. 'The dream of returning to Singapore is something I've clung to ever since we left, but now we have the chance ...' She paused, her thoughts in turmoil. 'I'm almost afraid of what we might find there.'

Jane gripped her hand more tightly. 'I feel just the same, for it's bound to have changed after the Japanese occupation, and it will seem strange to be back after all this time – but we need to know what happened to Pops and Philip.'

Sarah shivered. 'That's what I'm afraid of, Jane. If they're both dead, then I'm not sure I want to know how and where it happened – and I simply can't be like Mother who is so adamant that they're still alive despite everything we've seen and heard to the contrary.'

She regarded her sister evenly. 'I do wish you hadn't involved her in your madcap plan, Jane, for I really don't know if I could bear seeing her hopes and dreams destroyed, and have to witness her falling apart.'

Jane's expression became thoughtful. 'I think that beneath her determination to remain positive, she's actually fully aware of how things really are,' she said quietly. 'Mother was always protective of us – especially with me after I had that accident with the horse – and has merely been trying to bolster our spirits with all her wild schemes for their homecoming.'

Jane regarded Sarah solemnly and put her arm about her waist. 'I know her wedding plans for you and Philip have caused you huge distress, and I certainly have no wish to go and settle in Australia now there's a chance of me and Jeremy working in America. But as much as I try to deny it, there is a tiny spark in me which keeps hope alive that they'll come through.'

'I feel it too,' Sarah admitted. 'Although I'm dreading the moment when I have to face Philip knowing I've broken my promise to him and betrayed his trust.'

Jane took a deep breath and let it out on a sigh. 'That, of course, is something I can't help you with. But you know my feelings on the matter, and my advice has always been to let him down as gently as possible, and then go and find Delaney before it's too late.'

She squeezed Sarah's fingers. 'If nothing else, Sarah, this war has taught me that life is too short and precarious to waste it in chaining yourself to someone you no longer love out of a misguided sense of loyalty.'

'That's easy for you to say,' reproached Sarah. 'Your love life is uncomplicated with Jeremy, whereas mine is a complete shambles.'

'I'm sorry, Sarah. I didn't mean to preach.'

Sarah could see Jane's regret was genuine, but she was desperate now to get away from all talk of her marrying Philip. 'You seem very certain we'll find the information we need in Singapore. Why is that?'

Jane seemed relieved at the change of subject, perhaps realising she'd gone too far in offering her unwanted advice. She stood and ran a comb through her drying fair hair, teasing the natural waves into place. 'Now the British Military Administration is in charge over there, it's almost certain Singapore will become the central hub for the British POWs coming out of Malaya, Burma, Indonesia and Thailand.'

'But they could have been sent to one of the Japanese islands, or even to the mainland,' protested Sarah, 'and could be repatriated in Australia. Remember, Jane, Mother has pestered the authorities over the years with letters demanding they be sent straight to Cairns on their release.'

'If that is the case – which I doubt as they're not Australian – then we'll catch another flying boat to Darwin, hire a car and drive across to Cairns.' Jane squeezed Sarah's hand again. 'We'll find them, Sarah, I promise.'

Sarah regarded her sister with some awe. Jane had been kicked in the head by a horse when she was young, leaving her childlike and vulnerable, which meant she'd been molly coddled by their parents and carefully guarded against anything that might upset her. Sarah had always suspected she was much more aware of things than she'd been given credit for, and had used the accident as a ploy to gain attention and be spoilt.

This suspicion had been proved correct during the dangerous crossing to England, for once out of reach of loving but smothering parents, she'd started to blossom. The transformation had been completed during her time at Beach View, and when she'd left to work for the MOD on some secret assignment, she was a fully-fledged, bright young girl ready to take on the world.

Sarah felt a wave of deep affection wash over her. 'You've come a very long way since Malaya, Jane, and I'm so proud of you. But since when did you become so determined and resourceful?'

'Since I joined the MOD and learned how to get around things from the best brains in this country.' She smiled and looked into Sarah's eyes. 'Try to stop worrying about everything, Sarah. We're doing this journey together, and together we'll meet whatever waits for us and deal with it. Now put your lipstick on and smile. We have a party to go to.'

*New orders * not home for Christmas * letter to follow * Jim*

Peggy was on the point of fainting as she read the telegram again, and she only just managed to stumble blindly across the hall to the chair. Her head swam and her heart was plunged into the deepest despair, for her dreams of him coming home within weeks had been shattered.

She fought back the swirls of darkness in her head, the telegram clutched in her hand, the stark, cruel words still imprinted on her mind. Through the haze of shock she became aware of the bustle and chatter coming from upstairs as everyone prepared for Rita's party and knew she couldn't stay here in the hall. Rita was getting married tomorrow, and the last thing Peggy wanted was to make a show of herself and spoil the happy atmosphere.

It took every ounce of will to force herself off the chair and unsteadily make her way into her hall-floor bedroom. Immensely thankful that her eldest daughter, Anne, had taken the three little girls upstairs and was therefore unable to witness her collapse, she closed the door firmly behind her and sank onto her bed. Desperate to regain her composure, she dipped her head to her knees and fought back the great tide of bitter tears that was building inside her.

Once her head was clearer, she reached for Jim's silver-framed photograph and held it to her heart as the dam finally burst and all the hurt and disappointment flooded out to soak the pillow. Aware that her anguished sobs might be heard, she forcibly muffled them in the depths of that pillow, until she was barely able to breathe, and she held Jim's photograph so tightly the sharp corners of the metal frame dug into her. It was a pain she welcomed, for it seemed to override the awful agony in her heart.

What more did the army want from him? He'd been away from home for years already; survived fierce jungle fighting; been wounded; seen his best friend crippled for life and close comrades killed. He'd come through terrible bouts of malaria and dysentery in the belief he'd be sent home the minute hostilities were at an end – only to discover he was still needed out there. It was the most bitter of blows, dealt to her by a few short words that explained nothing, and left her bereft.

Peggy lost track of time as she huddled on the bed in abject misery; mourning the loss of her dreams for his homecoming, and raging silently against the army for keeping him from her. It was only the sound of the three little girls running about excitedly in the hall that reminded her she was needed elsewhere and couldn't hide in here no matter how much she yearned for solitude.

Glancing at the clock, she took a trembling breath, dried her eyes and put the photograph back on the bedside table. 'Oh, Jim,' she sighed. 'What more do they want of you? Why must you stay on? It's so unfair.'

He couldn't answer her, of course, and was no doubt just as upset about being kept back in Burma, for she knew from his letters how depressed he'd become of late, and how he'd longed for home and family. Realising he didn't have the luxury of giving in to self-indulgent tears and useless raging against the army, she dragged herself off the bed, determined to get a grip on her emotions.

She realised she was still holding the telegram in her tightly bunched fist, and that it was now crumpled and smudged by her tears. Smoothing out the creases, she avoided reading it again and swiftly shut it away in the shoe box where she kept his latest letters.

The sight of so many boxes stacked in the bottom of her wardrobe threatened her resolve to keep the tears at bay, and she had to blink them back, closing off the rising swell of emotion and refusing to yield. Those boxes of letters were testament to the length of time he'd been away, and traced not only the history of his war in the Far East, but the lonely years she'd kept the home fires burning along with the absolute faith that he'd come through it, and return to her the minute it was all over.

Peggy closed the wardrobe door and turned her back on it to regard her tear-streaked face in the dressing-table mirror. Had it only been half an hour since she'd been happily getting ready for the party and excitedly looking forward to Rita's wedding the following day? The telegraph boy's unexpected arrival had swept away all her joy in the instant he'd handed her that brown envelope, and there was little sign of cheerfulness and expectation in her face now – in fact she looked drawn and older than her forty-five years

– utterly weary from the toll that this war had demanded of her. The very last thing she wanted or needed was to take part in a celebration.

Peggy glared at her reflection, then squared her shoulders and reached for the cotton wool and a jar of cold cream. Vigorously applying the cream to wipe away all evidence of her tears, she rallied herself as she'd done repeatedly throughout the war, reminding herself that she had responsibilities to deal with, and must get on with the needs of the day.

Rita was no relation but had been part of her family since she was a tiny girl. Following her widowed father's call-up and the fire-bombing of their home, she'd moved into Beach View for the duration of the war. Now her father, Jack, was home from the fighting across the Channel, they'd moved into the bungalow he'd bought from Cordelia, but Rita had come to Beach View for the night so she could share her special day with Peggy and the girls she'd come to regard as sisters.

Peggy finished cleaning her face of the ruined make-up and began again with fresh powder, mascara and lipstick. It was important to look her best and show nothing of her inner anguish, for like all the evacuees who'd come and gone from Beach View over the war years, Rita was one of her chicks – and always would be, no matter where she was in the world. Regardless of how she felt right now, Peggy was absolutely determined Rita would have her party and the wedding she'd always promised her.

She took a deep breath to steady her hand as she applied her lipstick, vowing to smile and join in the fun – and tomorrow she would do it all again and give little Rita the warmest and sunniest memories of this special time to carry with her to Australia.

The tears threatened again as she thought of how soon Rita might be leaving for her new life with Peter on the other side of the world, but she refused to let them fall, realising they were merely tears of self-pity at the thought of losing her. She would miss little Rita as much as any daughter, but she and Peter were embarking upon an exciting adventure and Peggy was immensely proud of them for being brave enough to do so.

In a way, she admitted silently, she rather envied them the fresh start away from the doom and gloom of a battle-weary and grey England where rationing was tighter than ever and the reminders of war could still be seen in the numerous bomb sites. The idea of such an adventure had made her wonder fleetingly if she and Jim should do something similar once the war was well and truly over.

However, she'd soon come to her senses, realising Jim had probably seen enough of the world to last him a lifetime – and the reality was they were in their middle years and far too settled in Cliffehaven with their family to go searching for adventure beyond these shores. Adventure was for the young, the ambitious, the energetic and free – and Rita and Peter were made of the right stuff to thrive and make a success of a new and very different life under the Australian sun.

Peggy dabbed a last puff of face powder on her nose, nodded with satisfaction at a task well done and clipped on her earrings. She'd had her dark, curly hair shampooed and set that morning at Julie's Salon in the High Street, and the over-enthusiastic application of hairspray meant it had remained rigidly in place throughout her crying jag.

She regarded the result of her repairs with a jaundiced eye and knew she could do no more. Ready or not emotionally, it was time to plaster on a smile and join the fray.

The Anchor was an ancient building squashed between the shops and houses in Camden Road, which ran parallel to the seafront. It had been a hostelry for over two hundred years, its cellars and underground tunnels a perfect escape route and hiding place for the smuggling gangs that used to roam these southern shores. The peg-tiled roof dipped low over the tiny, diamond-paned windows of the upstairs accommodation, and the wattle and daub walls which had slowly begun to lean towards its neighbour were veined with black oak beams. The painted sign hanging over the door was inclined to creak against its iron moorings in the wind, the anchor and lettering now barely discernible from decades of salty air and rain.

Rosie Braithwaite had rather shocked the more staid residents of Cliffehaven when she'd bought the run-down Anchor some twenty years ago, for it was most unusual for a single woman to take on a pub licence – especially a glamorous platinum blonde, who wore clothes that enhanced her hourglass figure. But she'd persevered despite the prejudice, and had run it almost single-handedly and to great effect until it was now a popular watering hole. Romance had blossomed between her and Ron Reilly, and after a long courtship, they'd finally tied the knot just before VE Day.

Rosie had reserved the large table by the inglenook for the Beach View party, and had provided plates of sandwiches and packets of crisps to help soak up the alcohol. The pub was open for her usual customers, so she'd persuaded her barmaid, Brenda, to come in to work that evening, giving Rosie a chance to join in the fun.

However, word must have got out about the party and within an hour the bar was crammed with customers, some of whom were spilling out through the door and onto the pavement. Rosie immediately realised she couldn't have the evening off after all and, with a shrug of stoic acceptance to Peggy, went to lend a hand to the beleaguered Brenda.

The party was almost immediately in full swing, for Ron had somehow found a new upright piano to replace the wreckage of the one that had been committed to a bonfire during the VE Day celebrations and, resplendent in a tight red dress and matching high-heeled shoes, Gloria, the blowsy landlady from the Crown, was hammering out a series of favourite music-hall tunes so everyone could sing along. Earrings swinging and bracelets jangling, her raucous contralto rose above the other voices, urging them to greater effort, and making it difficult to conduct a proper conversation.

Peggy determinedly joined in while keeping a close eye on the elderly Cordelia who was inclined to go overboard on the sherry during such events. But she needn't have worried, for like all of them, Cordelia seemed to be aware that she needed to pace herself tonight in preparation for tomorrow's wedding, and was sipping slowly from her glass.

Peggy's face muscles were aching from all the smiling she'd done since leaving her bedroom, but she refused to allow herself even a second of weakness, for it could burst through that wall of will she'd constructed to keep her tears at bay. This was no time for self-indulgence. She would enjoy this moment and make the best of it, for it was very special, and far too precious to spoil.

As Gloria took a brief respite from the piano to down a double gin, Peggy glanced across to the bar and caught Rosie's eye to share a knowing look. They recognised the signs. Gloria was already well refreshed, and the more she drank the louder she became. She could be the life and soul of any party as long as no one upset her, but the wrong word or look would send her into fighting mode – and that could lead to all sorts of trouble and kill any celebration stone dead.

Peggy watched Gloria to gauge her mood, which seemed carefree enough at the moment, but like the English weather, it could change in an instant. She then lifted the glass of bitter lemon she'd chosen to keep a clear head for tomorrow and took a sip, wishing it was something stronger that might dull the pain in her heart and lift her spirits. Setting the drink aside, she lit a cigarette and wondered where her sister Doris had got to, for it was most unlike her to miss out on a party. Deciding something must have cropped up over her own wedding, which would take place next weekend, Peggy turned her attention to the girls who sat with her around the large and battered oak table.

Ivy had travelled down today with her husband, Andy, from their little flat in Walthamstow, and would be staying with Andy's Aunt Gloria at the Crown – or at least Andy would, for Ivy had insisted upon spending tonight at Beach View with her best friend Rita, so they could share every last minute together before the wedding.

Peggy smiled, for the rather plain little Ivy had blossomed since her marriage to the young fireman, and now she was positively glowing in the first few months of her pregnancy. It was a delight to see her so happy after all she'd been through lately, and Peggy knew she would look lovely in the bridesmaid's dress Sally Hicks had made especially for her. Rita's dress was a closely guarded secret, but Peggy had no doubt it would be perfect and that Rita would make a beautiful bride.

Peggy turned her gaze to Sally, who'd been her very first evacuee. She'd arrived bewildered, half-starved and afraid from London, in charge of six-year-old Ernie, her frail crippled brother. Their neglectful mother hadn't even bothered to see them off, and it had been months before she'd even turned up in Cliffehaven, only to flit off again with some new man.

Away from the slums and the hardships of the East End, and eased from the sole care of her brother, Sally had also blossomed during her time at Beach View, and had gone on to marry the local fire chief, John Hicks, with whom she now had little Harry. Young Ernie still lived with them, but now he was a strapping youth of thirteen and no longer wore the calliper that had been forced upon him following his bout of childhood polio.

Sally's gift of home dressmaking had been sorely missed over the years she'd spent down in the relative safety of Somerset with her brother and little boy, but on her return to Cliffehaven, she'd soon been in great demand, and John had turned their front parlour into a workroom for her so she could fit customers in private and work in peace while little Harry was at school. Rita and Ivy had been very lucky to have her make their wedding finery, but Peggy suspected Sally would have done it no matter how busy she was, for she still regarded herself as one of Peggy's chicks – which she most definitely was to Peggy's mind – and rather touchingly wanted to repay the love and kindness she'd found at Beach View. Which, of course, she hadn't needed to do at all.

Peggy eyed the bitter lemon without much joy and decided a single dash of gin could do no harm. She went to the bar expecting to find Rosie, but there seemed to be no sign of her, so poor Brenda was really struggling. As Peggy patiently waited to be served, Gloria began thumping out 'Ten Green Bottles'.

Peggy watched her chicks joining in with great enthusiasm and once again felt her heart contract at the realisation that this could be the last time they were all together. Ivy would return to London on Sunday; Danuta planned to leave for Poland at the end of the month, and Sarah had told her earlier that she and Jane would be on their way to Singapore at the beginning of September. It was still not known when Rita would embark on her long journey with Peter to Australia, but it would inevitably be sooner rather than later now the Japs had been cleared out of those southern waters.

Peggy's smile was soft as her gaze drifted to her darling eldest daughter, Anne. At least she'd come home at last from Somerset with her children and young Charlie; yet even she would soon be moving out of Beach View with her husband, Martin, back into the cottage they'd bought at the start of the war.

Peggy knew things still weren't really right between Anne and Martin, but they loved each other enough to struggle on, determined to pick up the pieces and repair the damage the war had done to Martin and their marriage. Martin seemed to be coping better with family life, even though Peggy suspected he was still plagued with nightmares from his years in the German prison camp. What he'd experienced there was never mentioned or explained, but he'd found someone in Roger Makepeace, his wingman and fellow POW, who shared his demons and, according to Ron, the two men still met daily at Cliffe aerodrome to sit in deckchairs and slowly put their worlds to rights.

As for Charlie, Peggy rarely saw him. He'd joined the local rugby club, spent hours with his grandfather Ron and Uncle Frank, and quite often went out night fishing with Frank, or spent hours on the beach helping to mend the trawling nets or tinker with the engines. The cheeky little boy who'd left Beach View six years ago was now fifteen, and as tall and strong as a man, with a stubborn determination to follow his own path in life that was the very essence of his father, and his grandfather.

Peggy was roused from her thoughts by Brenda nudging her arm. 'What can I get you?' she shouted above the raucous singing.

'A large gin in that, please,' Peggy shouted back.

Brenda raised an eyebrow, but the gin was swiftly added to the bitter lemon and the glass returned. Peggy thanked and paid her, still wondering where on earth Rosie had got to – and at that very moment she appeared in the doorway next to the bar that led to her upstairs rooms, her lovely face flushed with some inner excitement, her blue eyes sparkling.

Peggy's curiosity sharpened when she caught Rosie tipping the wink to Gloria who immediately began to play 'Danny Boy', but before Peggy could ask what was going on, Rosie had moved from the doorway and the most glorious violin music came from behind her.

Peggy turned, and there was Fran, russet hair glowing in the lamplight, green eyes fairly dancing with mischief as she stepped into the bar and made her way towards the piano.

The crowd parted like the Red Sea and there was an awed silence until Ivy broke it with a joyous screech of welcome before she sent her chair crashing and dashed across to hug her.

Peggy and the Beach View girls followed suit and swooped on Fran who was forced to stop playing as they hugged and kissed her and admired the bump pushing out beneath her maternity smock.

'To be sure, 'tis a grand welcome,' she said through her laughter. 'I'm glad I managed to surprise you all.'

There was an instant babble of questions, and Cordelia pushed her way through the gaggle. 'Let the dog see the rabbit,' she ordered. 'There you are,' she said breathlessly, 'and how lovely to have you home again even if it is only for a while.'

Fran handed the violin to Peggy so she could gently embrace the elderly woman. 'I couldn't be missing Rita's wedding, Grandma Cordy,' she murmured after kissing her cheek. 'And I've so longed to see you all again.'

Peggy fought back happy tears as Fran turned to embrace her. 'Welcome home, darling girl,' she murmured against her cheek as she tried desperately to think where she could accommodate her and her husband. Beach View was full to the rafters.

'Now, you're not to be fretting about where to put us up, Aunt Peggy,' replied Fran, who knew Peggy's thought processes so well. 'Gloria has most kindly rented me and Robert a room for the week, so we'll be just down the road and will get lots of time to see each other.'

'A whole week? Oh, Fran, does that mean you'll be playing at Doris's wedding next Saturday?'

'I could hardly refuse seeing as how she gave me this wonderful instrument,' replied Fran and then laughed. 'To be sure I never imagined the day when I'd see Doris married again.'

'I don't think any of us did,' said Peggy, and smiled. 'Meeting the Colonel was the very best thing that could have happened to her after losing Ted and her home like that.'

Rita gently touched Fran's arm. 'I hope you don't mind me asking,' she began tentatively, 'but would you ...? I mean, could you play at our wedding?'

Fran hugged her tightly – or as close as she could around her bump – and laughed. 'Oh, wee Rita, of course I will. Did you think I'd come all this way and not do such a thing?'

Rita's dark eyes filled with tears as she thanked her. Wiping them away, she suddenly frowned. 'But you don't know the order of service, or the music we've already chosen,' she fretted. 'How will ...'

Fran smiled and patted her cheek. 'To be sure, 'tis all sorted, Rita. Now let's get on with your party and have everyone dancing.'

She reached out to retrieve the violin from Peggy who could have sworn there was still a glint of mischief in her eyes – but what further surprises could there possibly be?

Gloria fetched another chair and abandoned the piano to go and lean on the bar and share a knowing grin with Rosie while Fran sat down.

Peggy held her breath as Fran tossed back her hair and nestled the violin into the sweet curve of her neck. The crowded bar became hushed but for a minor disturbance near the doorway that was quickly quelled. It was as if they knew they were in for something very special tonight, for many of them remembered Fran's violin playing during the later war years which had lifted their spirits and made them forget for a while that the fighting was going on just across the Channel.

Fran met Peggy's gaze and grinned with such cheekiness that Peggy knew something was afoot, for she'd seen that grin before. But Fran merely ran her bow smoothly over the strings for two beats and then began to slowly build the tempo.

A movement in the surrounding crowd caught Peggy's eye and she gasped in disbelief as Mary slipped onto the piano stool and began to accompany Fran in the hectic Irish tune which immediately had everyone tapping their feet and clapping in time.

Peggy couldn't take her gaze from Mary, whose fingers danced with such speed and skill over the keys, for although they'd corresponded often, she hadn't seen her since she'd left Beach View in 1942, and it was as if the years had melted away, for she was still the same pretty girl, with her dark hair and eyes, her softly curved figure and sweet smile.

Mary had come to Cliffehaven in search of her birth parents after discovering that she'd been adopted. Her quest had revealed the truth eventually, but it had brought her little joy and caused ripples of unease and regret to reach out to Peggy and those who'd been involved so long ago and had kept their vows of silence in the matter. For the childless Rosie, it had dredged up painful memories of her nefarious brother's deceit and wicked manipulation which had betrayed Mary's natural mother and snatched away Rosie's one chance of adopting the baby she'd come to love. The only good thing to have come out of those dark, hurtful revelations was the close friendship Rosie and Mary had forged.

Peggy knew that when Mary had left for Sussex to enrol at teaching college, she'd found the missing pieces of her life and was content to leave the past behind and look to the future with her sweetheart, Jack Boniface. And yet that future had been marred by tragedy, for shortly after their marriage, and the birth of their son, Jack Boniface had been killed during a commando raid in Germany.

Peggy's heart swelled with love in the knowledge of how much effort and planning must have gone into this surprise visit, and her spirits rose for the first time since she'd received that awful telegram.

In the light of this new joy, she realised Jim would come home when he could, and until then, she would wait for him as she'd waited throughout the long years of their separation. The war was well and truly over. He was safe. That's all that really mattered.

Ron had realised that the little girls would be too excited by the prospect of tomorrow's wedding to go to bed early, and were therefore in need of something to entertain them. He'd brought Harvey, his brindled lurcher, and had arrived at Beach View in his long poacher's coat and carrying a crate of beer just as Peggy and the others were leaving for the Anchor, and had promised faithfully to keep things in order, not drink too much, and have all three children in bed no later than seven.

And he'd fully intended to keep that promise. Unfortunately, even the best-laid plans could go awry, for he hadn't factored in the age of the children, and how they might react to his surprise.

Ron had closed the door to the large dining room, made sure the other men had a beer and the children some squash, and then reached into one of his deep coat pockets. 'Now, girls,' he said, eyeing each of them fondly. 'Your grandad has a special surprise for you. But you have to be very quiet. Do you understand?'

The three little girls nodded solemnly, their eyes wide in anticipation.

One by one, Ron carefully drew the sleeping ferrets from his pocket and held them close as they drooped over his arms. 'This is Flora and Dora,' he explained softly. 'They're a bit tired because they've been out hunting today, so you must stay still and very quiet and not wake them too quickly.'

Daisy, who would be four at the end of the year, was singularly unimpressed because she'd met and played with

Flora and Dora many times. But Anne's Rose, who was already four, gasped and tried to reach out to stroke Dora's soft fur, and was quickly forestalled by Ron who knew the ferret could be tetchy about being touched when she was half-asleep, and inclined to bite.

Little Emily, who was not quite three, just stared.

Ron held the ferrets against his chest and gently stroked their bellies so they remained calm as they began to wake and take an interest in their surroundings. 'Now,' he murmured, 'keep very still and quiet while I put them down so they can explore.'

Flora and Dora sat on the floor, their noses twitching to scent the air, and then Flora, who was the more adventurous of the pair, decided to scamper towards Emily.

Emily screamed, scrambled to her feet and was still screaming as she ran to Martin and clutched at his legs. Not to be outdone, Rose swiftly followed suit.

Dora fled beneath the table, but Flora shot across the room to sit on top of the gramophone box where she let out a high-pitched screech and a stream of stinking poo.

The smell hit them all, and the two children carried on screaming and would not be calmed even when Martin bundled them into his arms. Daisy folded her arms and rolled her eyes in world-weary disgust at her cousins' behaviour.

Ron quickly got to his feet, deciding Dora could stay where she was, but Flora needed rounding up before she did further damage. He was just reaching to grab her by the scruff when the door opened and Fran's Robert stepped into the room.

'Shut that door,' shouted Ron.

But it was too late. Flora had seen her chance to escape, and before Robert could react, shot like lightning across the room, through his feet and out into the hall.

Ron turned swiftly to find that Dora had disappeared from beneath the table, so had no doubt followed her sister. 'Quick,' he shouted. 'After them.'

Andy, Robert, Jack, Frank and Ron dashed into the hall with Peter limping behind them and little Daisy running to catch them up. Martin, with his arms full of small, sobbing girls, was left behind to deal with them.

There was no sign of the ferrets, and with his heart in his mouth, Ron could only pray that Robert had shut the back door behind him. If they got outside, he'd never find them in the dark.

The door was, mercifully, closed, and Harvey quickly sniffed out Dora who was wedged beneath the large kitchen dresser and spitting venom. Harvey danced on his toes, barking excitedly, as Daisy clapped her hands and laughed.

'Shut up, Harvey,' snapped Ron. 'Go and find Flora. Seek. Seek.'

As the dog galloped off back into the hall, Ron ordered Robert to keep Daisy out of harm's way and shut both doors while he tried to get Dora out of her hiding place. He quickly shoved the table and chairs to one side, and then stretched out on the floor to plunge his arm beneath the dresser. His fingers scrabbled for her scruff.

Dora was having none of it. She didn't want to come out, and as she reversed deeper beneath the dresser, she hissed and spat, her needle-sharp teeth snapping at his fingers, her eyes gleaming with fear and fury.

'Here you go, mate,' drawled Peter, handing him a gardening glove he'd plucked from the top of the dresser. 'I reckon you might need this before you lose a finger to those teeth.'

Ron grunted his thanks, pulled on the glove and eased his arm beneath the dresser again. 'Come on, Dora, wee girl,' he soothed. 'There's nought to be afraid of.'

Dora closed her strong jaws on the gloved hand and Ron swore. Once a ferret got their teeth into something it was the devil's own job to get them to release it – and it damned well hurt. Ron knew there was only one thing for it, and as Peter lifted the front of the dresser to give him more room, he dragged Dora out, her teeth still embedded in his gloved fingers.

Frank grabbed her scruff and held her determinedly until she was forced to relax her jaws enough for his father to get his hand out of the glove. As Ron sat on the floor amid the debris that had fallen from the top of the dresser, to nurse his bleeding, aching hand, Frank soothed Dora by gently stroking her stomach until she went into a dreamlike trance.

'To be sure, Da, that was an eejit thing to be doing. Did ye not think the wee girls might be frightened to see such strange beasts?'

'Aye,' he admitted ruefully. 'I realise now it was daft. But how was I to know Emily would react like that?' He scrambled to his feet and went to wash the puncture wounds beneath the cold tap. 'And we've yet to find Flora,' he added dolefully.

Harvey's barking came distantly from upstairs, so Frank deposited the now calm Dora in his father's deep coat pocket and, shooting him a look of exasperation mixed with humour, followed the sound, the other men on his heels.

Ron realised Martin must have soothed the girls out of their hysterics, for there was no sound coming from the dining room. He dried his hand, hunted out an old tube of antiseptic cream from the dresser drawer and smeared some over the wounds before following the others. The kitchen was already a mess, the dining room stank – and the Lord only knew what he'd find upstairs.

Flora was on top of Cordelia's wardrobe, the floor now littered with the hatboxes which had been stored there. Their contents had been spilled across the carpet, and Harvey was trampling them in his eagerness to reach Flora who arched her back and spat at him.

'Get out of there, ye heathen beast,' stormed Ron, aghast at the damage his animals had caused. He ordered Harvey to sit and stay with such command that the dog squirmed beneath the bed. 'Shut the door, Jack. We can't have her getting away from us again.'

The men quickly removed the hats and boxes from the floor to the bed, and Daisy scrambled up with them to sit amid the chaos and enjoy the show.

Ron turned to his son. 'Right, Frank. You take the left, I'll take the right – and, Jack, you stay at the front with Robert and Peter. She could go in any direction, so be alert and ready to grab her.'

Flora eyed them, gave a high-pitched screech and weaved back and forth trying to decide how to escape. As the men reached for her, she took a flying leap over their heads and landed on the dressing table. Glass jars and bowls went skidding to the floor, hairbrushes, combs and pins scattering in all directions, and as the men advanced on her, she leapt from the dressing table to the bedside cabinet, sending the lamp crashing to the floor and tipping the glass of water over Cordelia's new paperback book.

Ron was sweating heavily in fear of what Peggy and Cordelia would have to say on their return, but forced himself to remain calm as he tried to coax Flora into staying put.

Flora had no intention of staying anywhere she could be so easily caught, and quickly sought refuge beneath Cordelia's pillows before burrowing deep beneath the bedding.

It was a tactical error and one that Ron could now exploit. He lifted Daisy off the bed, threw the pillows on the floor, and signalled to the men to trap Flora in her hideaway while he carefully began to lift away the eiderdown and blankets until only a sheet covered the quivering, hissing mound.

Ron signalled again and they untucked both sheets, until the wriggling, frantic Flora was wrapped up like a parcel and safely back in Ron's arms. She urinated and defecated in protest, splattering Ron's tatty jumper and shirt. But he grimly held on to her as he coaxed and crooned to her to calm her down.

Flora finally relaxed, and Ron unwrapped her from the filthy sheets, stroking her all the while and talking softly to her until she lay supine in his arms. Then Ron eased her into his pocket with Dora, heard her soft mewls of pleasure and knew the drama was over.

'Strewth, Ron,' breathed Peter, regarding the devastation. 'It's going to take all flaming night to get this lot cleaned up.'

'Aye, it will that,' he rumbled before grimacing at the mess all down his front. 'But I'm thinking a strong drink wouldn't go amiss after all the shenanigans.' He pulled a quarter bottle of Irish whiskey from an inside pocket. 'Let's have this downstairs while I put these sheets to soak and clean meself up.'

'You told Mummy you wouldn't drink, Grandpa,' said Daisy with a righteous glare, her small arms folded.

'Grandpa's thirsty,' he replied. 'Mummy won't mind.'

Daisy wrinkled her nose. 'You smell.'

'Aye, that I do, wee girl,' he said solemnly. 'Isn't it time you went to bed?'

Daisy shook her head, and in no mood for an argument, Ron headed down the stairs to the kitchen.

He stripped off his shirt and jumper, dumped them in the sink with a good dose of washing powder and proceeded to wash them through along with the sheets. Wiping down the stains from his old corduroy trousers, he then wrung out the sweater and put it back on, shivering at the unpleasant feel of wet wool against his skin.

Once the sheets and shirt were pegged on the line, he returned to the dining room to find Daisy curled up on Frank's lap, her thumb in her mouth. 'Where's Martin?' he asked.

'Putting his girls to bed,' said Jack, handing him a generous tot of whiskey.

The bottle didn't last very long, but luckily Peter had brought some rum, so they got stuck into that. Martin eventually came down and gratefully accepted a drink before offering to put Daisy to bed. But although she was fighting sleep, Daisy refused to leave, and showed signs of being as temperamental as the ferrets, so they let her stay.

Charlie wandered in from his practice session at the rugby club to find them drowning their sorrows. He cheerfully plucked Daisy from his Uncle Frank's lap and carried her off to her bed, staying long enough to read her a story.

Then it was all hands to the task of putting the house straight – or as straight as they could get it. Because the ferrets were Ron's, he'd been tasked with cleaning up the poo. Peter tidied up the kitchen, and then went to help the others in Cordelia's room. Andy remade the bed while Jack tried to mend the lamp and smooth out the dents in the shade while Martin picked up the scattered hairpins, bottles and jars, and Charlie did his best to repair the hatboxes and put the hats away. The straw hat had been well and truly trampled by Harvey, and there was now a definite hole in the crown.

'I can't mend this, Grandad,' he said, holding the hat up. 'What on earth are we going to do about it?'

'Put it in a box and shove the lot on top of the wardrobe,' said Ron, his wet jumper still clinging unpleasantly to him. 'I'll buy her a new one.'

'But what if she was planning to wear it tomorrow?'

'We'll just have to hope she isn't,' he retorted. He looked round the room, relieved that nothing important had been broken. 'Come on. We've done all we can, and it's almost time for the women to get home. We don't want them catching us up here, for it'll be the wrath of God on our heads if they do.'

He saw his grandson's frown and put an arm about his shoulder. 'Ach, Charlie, it'll be all right. To be sure, Cordy and your wee mam will be fine about it all. You'll see.'

Charlie was clearly not sure about that – and truth be told, neither was Ron. But they'd already missed at least three hours of good drinking time, and Ron wasn't about to dwell on such things.

Peggy had enjoyed a wonderful few hours of singing and dancing and catching up on all of Fran and Mary's news.

Rosie had called time and Brenda had gone home, but the Beach View women remained at the table, reluctant to end the happy evening, even though it would be an early start in the morning.

Anne made the first move. 'I'm going home to check that Martin got the girls to bed all right,' she said. 'They can be a bit of a handful when they're over-excited, and he still finds it difficult to cope with all their noise.'

Peggy kissed her goodnight, and twenty minutes later rounded up the others. 'Time for bed,' she said as the hall clock struck eleven and she noticed Cordelia was drooping with weariness next to her. 'You have a very big day ahead of you, Rita, and Cordy and I need our beauty sleep if we're going to be in any fit state to enjoy your wedding.'

Rita grinned, her brown eyes sparkling, her dark curls dancing above her shoulders. 'Ready when you are, Auntie Peggy – although I don't feel a bit sleepy. I'm too excited.'

Peggy reached across and took her hand. 'Of course you are, love. And quite rightly so.' She pushed back her chair just as Andy and Robert came through the side door to walk Gloria and Fran back to the Crown.

Peggy regarded them sharply, for although they seemed sober enough, they looked decidedly shifty. 'Did you have a good evening?' she asked suspiciously.

'Very pleasant,' said Robert, not quite meeting her eye before swiftly turning to Fran. 'Come on, love, it's late, and you must be tired.'

There was a flurry of hugs and kisses for Fran and Gloria, and then everyone was fetching their coats and saying a fond farewell to Mary, who would be staying at the Anchor with Rosie until Sunday.

Peggy kissed and hugged Mary. 'Sleep well, dear, and I'll see you and Rosie tomorrow at the church. It's so lovely of you and Fran to play for Rita's wedding. You can have little idea of how much it means to her – and to me.'

'It's a real pleasure, Aunt Peggy. I'm just so sorry I haven't been able to visit before now, but with the baby and every-thing ...' She blinked rapidly and smiled. 'But he's older now and bit more manageable, so I felt it was all right to leave him at the farm with his grandparents, who've been utterly brilliant all the way through everything. They dote on him so, but I suppose that's only to be expected after los-ing their Jack.'

Peggy swallowed the lump in her throat and patted her cheek, then quickly hugged Rosie, thanking her for plan-ning the surprise and giving them all an evening to remember. 'I'll send Ron home straight away and see you tomorrow,' she promised before turning away to help Cordelia to her feet.

Linking arms with Cordelia, Peggy and Sarah walked along Camden Road, with Rita and Ivy chattering non-stop ahead of them, and Jane in deep conversation with Danuta tagging along slowly behind. The air was fresh and cool after the fug in the Anchor's bar, the sky clear and starlit, and Peggy was looking forward to getting her shoes off and having a cup of tea.

They crossed over the main road that led up from the sea-front and made their moonlit way along the rough track which ran between the back gardens of the terraced houses and petered out eventually at the foot of the surrounding hills.

As Rita and Ivy ran into the house, Peggy frowned at the sight of the sheets hanging on the washing line. She knew for certain they hadn't been there when she'd gone out, and could only think that perhaps one of the little girls must have been overtired and accidentally wet the bed. At least someone had thought to wash them out instead of just dumping them in the laundry basket for her to deal with.

Shrugging off this thought, she helped Cordelia over the threshold and, to the steady rhythm of young Charlie's snoring in his basement bedroom, climbed up the concrete steps to the kitchen.

All seemed quiet and as she'd left it, so she shed her coat, helped Cordelia off with hers and crossed over to the range to put the kettle on the hob. By the sound of it, Rita and Ivy were already heading for their bedroom – so excited they'd forgotten to say goodnight – and she could hear the familiar sawing of Ron's snores coming from the dining room.

'Would anyone else like tea?' she asked, kicking off her high-heeled shoes.

Sarah, Jane and Danuta shook their heads, and after kissing her goodnight, made their way up to their bedrooms. Cordelia plumped down in her favourite fireside chair and gave a sigh of pleasure as she too eased off her shoes and wriggled her toes. 'Yes, please, dear. A nice cuppa will be just the thing to help me get to sleep.'

She looked around the room and frowned. 'Something's different, but I'm blowed if I can see what it is,' she muttered.

Peggy leaned against the sink and wondered what Ron's mucky old gardening glove was doing on the draining board alongside a mangled tube of antiseptic cream. She ignored them to look around the kitchen and immediately spotted what it was that had changed.

'Someone's shifted the dresser away from the wall and tidied up all the clutter on top,' she said with surprise. 'Now, why on earth would they do that?'

Cordelia shrugged. 'Beats me, dear. Who's to say what men get up to when left to their own devices?'

Peggy thought about those sheets on the line which, now she came to think of it, had come from a double bed, not a child's single or cot. She picked up the gardening glove and saw the fresh bloodstains inside it which might explain the tube of cream, but who on earth would have been gardening at night – and why shift and tidy the dresser? It was all very odd.

'Something has been going on here, Cordy,' she said darkly. 'And I aim to find out what.'

'Oh dear. Don't tell me Ron's been up to his shenanigans again,' sighed Cordelia, still twiddling her toes. 'You'd have thought he'd have learnt by now to behave himself.'

'Watch the kettle, Cordy. I'll be back in a minute.'

Peggy didn't wait for a reply and walked quickly into the hall in her stockinged feet. Checking that Daisy was asleep in her bed, she continued on into the dining room where she immediately smelled the sharp and unmistakable tang of disinfectant.

Puzzled by this, she frowned, and her disapproval deepened as she spotted the empty rum and whiskey bottles and noted that all the beer was gone too. It seemed they'd had quite a party despite everything Ron had promised, and now he was stretched out in the armchair by the hearth, Harvey at his feet, both snoring fit to bust.

Harvey must have heard her exasperated sigh, for he raised his nose from his paws to regard her warily, his ears flattening to his head, his tail moving weakly against the rug in supplication.

Peggy knew that guilty look, and it confirmed her suspicions that something had happened here tonight. She folded her arms and glared at Ron who was still snoring as if he hadn't a care in the world.

Harvey sensed trouble and got to his feet, quickly slinking past her, tail between his legs, in search of sanctuary with Cordelia in the kitchen.

Peggy stood and watched Ron for a moment, noting that despite the warm evening, he was still wearing his poacher's coat over a sweater that looked as if it'd been wrung out and left to dry on him. As she regarded these disreputable items of clothing, something squirmed in one of the coat pockets, and she heard the unmistakable chirrup of ferrets coming from its depths.

That was enough to bring the simmering suspicions to a head and raise her blood pressure. She marched across the room and jabbed him none too gently in the shoulder. 'Wake up, Ron,' she ordered. 'Wake up this minute and explain to me why you brought the ferrets with you.'

Ron slowly opened one bleary blue eye and then the other to look up at her in bewildered innocence. 'Ach, Peggy, wee girl. Are ye back already? I must be off home to me Rosie.'

He struggled to rise from the chair, but Peggy pushed him back and barred his way. 'You're not going anywhere until you've told me what's been going on here,' she said flatly.

'Going on?' he asked, wide-eyed with hurt innocence. 'Why should anything have been going on?'

'Because there are washed sheets on the line; a bloodied gardening glove on my draining board; the dresser has been shifted and tidied up and I can definitely smell disinfectant – and if that wasn't enough, you've been drinking and have got ferrets in your pocket.'

'Aye, well, I can explain,' he replied, his gaze drifting to a point somewhere beyond her shoulder. ''Tis all quite simple, wee girl, and nothing for you to be worrying your pretty head about.'

'Don't patronise me with your blarney,' she snapped. 'What happened here tonight?'

''Tis sorry I am if you think I'm being patronising,' he replied dolefully. He hastily swallowed a yawn. 'To be sure, I'm ready for me bed. Can we not discuss this in the morning, Peggy?'

'No. Out with it, Ron – and I want the truth, not any of your fanciful nonsense.'

He took a breath and focused his gaze on his feet. 'I thought the wee girls would like to meet Flora and Dora. But 'twas a terrible mistake, for Emily took fright and Rose joined in, and their screaming sent the wee beasts scurrying.'

He bared his teeth in a forced smile which didn't quite reach his still wary eyes. 'Still, it's all right now. The girls are asleep, and Flora and Dora are back in me pocket. So there's no harm done, and I shall be taking them home the minute you let me pass.'

Peggy stayed where she was. 'But that's not all, is it? Why the sheets and the blood on the gardening glove? And what had to be disinfected in here?'

'Ach, Peggy, you're a hard woman, so y'are,' he said on a sigh. He looked down at his bitten hand and haltingly confessed to the entire sorry tale. 'I'll be buying Cordelia a new hat first thing on Monday, I promise,' he said into the ensuing silence.

'You'd better see you do,' said Peggy, trying very hard not to laugh at the absurdity of it all. 'You really are the limit, Ron,' she managed. 'You surely haven't forgotten the day Sarah and Jane arrived to utter chaos, when you let the last pair of ferrets loose in the house?'

He lowered his gaze and concentrated on filling his pipe. 'Aye, but I hadn't taken into account the wee ones' reaction.'

'That's your trouble, Ron. You never do think of the consequences. Poor little Emily must have been terrified to have blasted ferrets rampaging about the house.' She took a breath to calm herself. 'I can only thank God none of the children were bitten.'

Ron nodded. 'To be sure, so do I,' he admitted. He lifted his head and grinned. 'But Daisy thought the whole thing was a terrific game.'

'I have no doubt she did,' Peggy said drily. 'But then she's known those ferrets since she was a baby, and is well aware she mustn't frighten them.'

'Ach, Peggy,' he sighed, ''tis sorry I am for causing such trouble. I promise never to bring the ferrets into this house again.'

'I seem to have heard that promise before,' she retorted, still cross with him, and not at all convinced that he was truly contrite. 'But as we have a wedding in the morning and it's now almost midnight, I'll say no more about it. But one more caper like this, and I'll box your ears.'

He chuckled and winked at her. 'I'd like to see you try.'

'Don't tempt me,' she retorted.

They regarded one another with deep affection, knowing this wouldn't be the last time they would draw swords, and as he smiled up at her, Peggy couldn't help but smile back. He was a lovable old rogue, and as always, she forgave him. 'I've left Cordelia making tea. Will you stay for a cuppa?'

Ron shook his head and dragged himself out of the chair. Planting a kiss on the top of her head, he squeezed her shoulder. 'You're a good girl, wee Peggy. I'll wish you good-night and go home to my Rosie.'

Peggy followed him through the hall and into the kitchen where Cordelia was making a fuss of Harvey.

'I hear you're in trouble again, you old devil,' Cordelia said with a glint of laughter in her eyes. 'What was it this time?'

Ron grinned down at her and patted her cheek. 'To be sure, wee Peggy will tell you. Sleep well, Cordy.'

Once the back door had slammed behind him and his dog, Peggy sank into the other chair to drink the tea and share the story with Cordelia – making sure there was no mention of the hat, and thankful that the new one had been carefully stowed away inside the wardrobe.

Cordelia giggled. 'It's a good thing I have another book to read,' she said. 'But I won't tell him that. It'll serve him right to have to buy me a new copy.'

Peggy chuckled. It seemed that Ron's shopping trip was going to turn out to be rather expensive.

2

Rita and Ivy had so many things to catch up on and discuss in their excitement for the coming day, and being together again, that they'd still been chattering long after the rest of the household had settled down for the night. Ivy had fallen quiet and hadn't responded to Rita's latest enquiry, and Rita realised that her friend had gone to sleep, curled like a child beneath the covers of the other single bed.

As the Town Hall clock struck one, Rita lay there staring at the ceiling, and wondering if Peter was doing the same in his boarding house billet along the coast. Restless and still unable to sleep, she eventually drew back the covers and tiptoed barefoot to the window in her soft, faded pyjamas.

Opening the curtain just enough to peek through, she leaned on the sill and gazed out over the rooftops to the moon which was almost full, and reflected in the small sliver of sea visible between the chimneypots, and then looked up to the dark sky to watch the stars twinkling. She wondered if they were the same configuration of stars on the other side of the world, for it would be reassuring to have something familiar to look at so far from home.

She tucked her curly dark hair behind her ears and gave a soft sigh. She had an inkling now of what Ruby must have gone through before her marriage to Mike and subsequent migration to Canada, for she was nervously excited about tomorrow and all the hullabaloo it would entail. Although she'd never been one to take centre stage, she could hardly wait to dress up in her beautiful gown to share her wedding vows with Peter.

Yet throughout all the plans they'd made for their big day – and the even bigger adventure they were about to embark upon – there ran a thread of fear which she couldn't quell. She would be going into the unknown once they boarded the ship for Australia, and even though she'd have Peter at her side, and he'd described so well what awaited them there, it was clearly very different from all she'd ever known.

As she looked out of the window and the bedside clock quietly ticked away the seconds, Rita thought again of all she'd be leaving behind. Beach View had been her refuge after her own home had been fire-bombed, and Peggy had been a constant, loving presence in her life even before her mother had died too young. Rita knew that if it hadn't been for Peggy's love and care, her father would never have coped with the trials of bringing up his six-year-old daughter while he struggled to grieve and support them.

Rita felt the prick of tears and blinked them away. She could barely remember her mother now, for the few photographs of her had been destroyed during the fire-bombing. Yet, in the silence of the night, she could still hear faint echoes of her voice, and feel the comfort of her arms about her in those moments when she missed her the most. The thought of leaving her father behind troubled her, and despite all his assurances to the contrary, she seen the sadness in him when he'd thought he was unobserved, and knew he would be bereft at her departure.

And then there was Peggy, who'd been a mother, confidante and wise adviser during her formative years, and dear old Ron, who'd been a grandfather and font of knowledge about the world. And Beach View, which had been her home; this room shared with Ivy who'd become as close as a sister, and who'd been with her during moments of great fear and deep sorrow, as well as times of fun. Was her love for Peter and the promise of a new life strong enough for her to make such a sacrifice? Or would their adventure together turn sour through her longing for home and those she loved?

Rita took a shallow, quavering breath, knowing their love was indeed strong enough to see them through whatever they had to face – and that although she might get horribly homesick, she was meant to spend the rest of her life with Peter, even if it was on the other side of the world.

'Rita? What you doing there? You'll catch yer death, gel.' Ivy threw the old dressing gown over Rita's shoulders and hugged her waist. 'Not 'aving second thoughts, are yer?' she teased.

Rita shook her head and dismissed the doubts as last-minute nerves. 'Not about getting married to Peter. But I was thinking about you, Dad and Peggy, and this place. It's going to be so hard to leave you all behind, and I feel horribly guilty about abandoning Dad.'

'Then you mustn't,' said Ivy firmly. 'Yer dad will 'ave Peggy and Ron to talk to, and he'll be so busy with 'is workshop, I reckon he won't 'ave time to worry about what you're up to. Besides, he promised to visit you out there when you and Pete are settled and start 'aving kids.'

'I know,' Rita sighed, leaning her head on Ivy's narrow shoulder. 'But I still wish he'd agreed to come with us and set up over there.'

'Jack's a man what knows 'is own mind, Rita, love. He's been away from home right through the war and is too old to be going gallivanting again. I know it won't be easy for yer, but you gotta give it a go, gel. A chance like this don't come that often, and Pete's a good bloke. He'll look after yer.'

Rita giggled. 'You're right, Ivy. I'm just suffering from last-minute nerves, that's all.'

'It's the time of night,' said Ivy, shivering in her thin nightdress. 'No one can think straight at two in the morning, and you're just letting yer imagination run away with yer.' Ivy drew Rita from the window towards the two single beds. 'It's time you was in that bed and sleeping,' she said bossily. 'Come on, gel, or you'll be fit fer nothing in the morning.'

'I am going to miss you, Ivy,' Rita murmured, giving her a hug, and then gasping in delight and awe. 'Oh, my goodness, Ivy. I felt the baby move.'

Ivy grimaced and gently ran her hand over the small, hard swell beneath her nightie. 'Yeah, he's inclined to do that. Usually when I'm trying to sleep.'

'Do you think it's a boy?' asked Rita.

'It would be nice for Andy, but it don't really matter what it is as long as it's all right,' Ivy replied. She pressed Rita down onto her bed and pulled up the covers. 'Go to sleep, Rita, and don't worry about nothing except them big bags under yer eyes you'll 'ave in the morning if you lie there worrying about things.'

Rita slid down the bed and nestled into the pillows. 'Thanks, Ivy. You always did know how to cheer me up,' she said drily before jerking upright again and touching her face. 'I won't really have bags, will I?' she gasped.

'Course not, you silly mare,' scoffed Ivy on a giggle. 'But I will if you don't shut up and go to bloody sleep. Me and the baby is wore out.'

Rita slid back down beneath the covers and closed her eyes. Ivy wouldn't stand for any soppiness, but at this moment, she could have kissed her and told her she was the very best friend and sister a girl could have.

On that comforting thought, Rita drifted off to sleep and dreamed of floating down the aisle towards Peter in the fairy-tale dress Sally had made for her.

Peggy had slept surprisingly well considering that Daisy had crept into her bed sometime during the night and was rather restless, and it was barely light when she rose from her bed, eager for the coming day. As she quickly dressed in an old blouse and skirt and tied the wrap-round pinafore over everything, she could already hear that the rest of the household was up and about. They'd clearly caught wedding fever too.

Peggy left Daisy sleeping off her late night and went into the kitchen to prepare breakfast, only to find the porridge already simmering and the table all but cleared. It seemed that everyone had already eaten, but for Anne and her family

As she stirred the porridge to keep it from sticking to the pot, she could hear the usual squabbles over whose turn it was in the bathroom, which made her wonder for the umpteenth time if she should dip into her savings and turn the small single bedroom currently used by Danuta into a second bathroom with a toilet. However, the thought was fleeting. The expense and upheaval it would cause would be wasted, for once all the girls had left and Anne was back in her cottage, one bathroom would suffice – and there was still the perfectly good outside lav if one got desperate.

Peggy looked up from the range as Rose and Emily came running into the kitchen, closely followed by their mother. She hugged the girls and cheerfully wished Anne a good morning. 'Did you sleep all right?'

Anne grinned. 'Like a log once I knew there were no nasty consequences of Grandad's daft carry-on with those ferrets. I was coming out of the bathroom when I overheard you giving Grandad earache and I asked Martin what it was about. He reluctantly confessed, and I thought we'd be in for a disturbed night, but the girls slept right through without out a murmur.'

'I'm glad to hear it,' said Peggy. 'Perhaps it would be a good idea to take them to the Anchor on Sunday so they can see the ferrets in their cage and get to understand them a bit more. It would be a shame if they stayed frightened of them. They're quite sweet really.'

Anne tucked her shining dark hair back from her face. 'I've never been that fond of them myself, but as Grandad seems intent upon carrying them about wherever he goes, I suppose they should get used to them.'

Anne settled the girls at the table and tied bibs around their necks. 'I'll wait until the last minute to dress them,' she said. 'They're bound to get dirty otherwise, and white is so unforgiving.' She glanced at the cleared table. 'Has everyone already eaten – and where's Daisy?'

'She's still asleep after all the excitement last night. I've left her to it so I can get on and clear up before Sally comes to do any last-minute alterations.'

Peggy glanced at the clock and doled out bowls of porridge and glasses of the free orange juice provided by the government to all children under five. 'Cordelia and the girls have had theirs, so I'm surprised Martin hasn't come down yet with all the noise they're making up there.'

'He was up at the crack of dawn as usual,' said Anne. 'I suspect he grabbed some bread and jam before he left for the airfield.' She rolled her eyes. 'He and Roger are evidently conferring about the meeting that's planned with the town council next week.'

'Then I hope he doesn't lose track of the time. Rita's counting on him being one of the ushers.'

'He'll be there,' said Anne firmly.

Peggy raised an eyebrow, but Anne wasn't going to elaborate further, and changed the subject. 'I'm so glad Sally's got her home dressmaking business up and running again. I thought she was quite potty when she started buying all those old wedding dresses and tatty ballgowns from jumble sales and so on, but she's actually been very clever and forward-looking.'

'Sally's always had a sensible head on her shoulders,' said Peggy, sitting down with a cup of tea.

Anne nodded. 'It's a case of having to grow up quickly with a useless mother like that, but it's stood her in good stead. I popped in to see her the other day and that front room is positively crammed with all those second-hand cast-offs, but she's slowly using the material from each and every one of them to make something new and utterly gorgeous.'

'You didn't happen to spot Rita's dress by any chance?' Peggy asked hopefully.

Anne laughed. 'No such luck. Sally had it covered very thoroughly by a sheet. And before you ask, I didn't see Ivy's either. So you'll just have to rein in that awful curiosity of yours, Mum, and wait like the rest of us.'

Peggy drank her tea, and when the children had finished eating, Anne went with them into the garden to feed the chickens and then play in the makeshift sandpit Ron had made out of offcuts of wood and pilfered sand from the beach.

Standing in the doorway for a minute to watch them, Peggy lit a cigarette and then tackled the last of the washing-up before going to wake Daisy. If she left her any longer there would be tears before bedtime, and nothing was allowed to spoil today.

Daisy threw a bit of a tantrum because she wanted to wear her new white dress with its frothy petticoat. Eventually, Peggy got her into dungarees and a jumper, and coaxed her into eating her porridge and drinking her orange juice. Grimacing at the taste of her daily spoonful of cod liver oil, Daisy then hurried off quite happily to play with Rose and Emily in the garden.

While Anne kept an eye on the children, Peggy took the opportunity to hurry upstairs to use the bathroom now it was free, and some minutes later, returned to her bedroom to put on her make-up. She planned to wear the lovely blue silk skirt and jacket Sally had made her five years ago for Anne's wedding, and it hung on the wardrobe door, fresh from the dry cleaner's, with the matching shoes placed beneath it. She'd splashed out on a new and very fancy hat for Ruby's wedding, and had worn it at Ivy's. It would do sterling service today, and next weekend when Doris and Colonel White tied the knot at the Town Hall, so it hadn't been money wasted.

Pausing in the act of putting on her lipstick, Peggy wondered again what had kept her sister from the party the previous evening, and decided she'd telephone her once she was finished here. Hunting out the delicately worked gold earrings and matching necklace Jim had sent her from Burma, she put them on and admired the effect in the mirror. They were utterly gorgeous, even though they looked rather incongruous teamed with a wrap-round apron. But that didn't matter, for she just knew they'd be perfect with her outfit.

Anne and the children were still in the garden, so Peggy went into the hall and got through to the exchange. Doris answered on the second ring and sounded a bit flustered. 'Hello, Doris. Is everything all right? Only we missed seeing you last night.'

'I thought it was the doctor returning my call,' she replied. 'John has hurt his back and he's in absolute agony – barely able to move. I couldn't leave him on his own, poor man.'

'Oh, Doris, how awful. But how did he do it?'

'His foot caught in a rabbit hole on the golf links and he fell awkwardly, aggravating an old injury. I'm sorry, Peggy, but I'll have to ring off. The doctor's receptionist promised he'd telephone the minute he finished morning surgery.'

'Let me know if there's anything I can do,' said Peggy, and put down the receiver.

Doris was clearly in a terrible state, which was hardly surprising as their wedding was only a week away. Peggy could only pray that John's back healed in time, and they weren't forced to cancel.

Her thoughts fled as there was a knock on the front door. Opening it, she found Sally and her husband, John, on the doorstep, their arms laden with cloth clothes bags.

'Hello, Auntie Peggy,' she said, stepping into the hall and kissing her cheek. 'I'm not too early, am I? Only I thought it would be best to come now so that I'd have time to do any last-minute alterations to Ivy's dress.'

'Not at all,' said Peggy, her fingers itching to open the bags and see what was inside. 'Come in, come in, the pair of you.'

'Sally!' Rita came running down the stairs with an equally excited Ivy following more slowly. 'Here, let me help you with those,' Rita said, quickly taking charge of John's burden before he let it slip to the floor. 'And thanks for giving Sally a lift up, John,' she added, glancing past him to the fire station truck parked outside. 'She'd never have managed to carry this lot up the hill.'

'There's more to come,' he said, shooting her a grin before he quickly ran down the steps and reached into the truck for two shoe boxes.

'Oh, Sal,' Rita breathed. 'You did it. You really managed it when I honestly thought it would be impossible.'

Sally laughed. 'John, you'd better give those boxes to Aunt Peggy. As you can see, Rita and I have our hands full.'

'I'll take 'em.' Ivy snatched the boxes from John before Peggy could get her hands on them. 'Don't want to spoil the surprise,' she said with a naughty wink to Peggy. 'You'll see everything all in good time, Auntie Peg.'

John left and the three girls giggled as they carefully carried the precious clothes up the stairs and into the large front bedroom. Peggy stood at the bottom of the stairs as the bedroom door was firmly closed behind them, and gave a frustrated sigh. One peek wouldn't have hurt, surely?

'Come on, Mum,' said Anne with a smile in her voice. 'You'll be up there the minute Rita's ready for you, so savour the anticipation and watch the girls for a minute while I go and get changed. I doubt Rita would want me turning up in these old trousers and twinset.'

Peggy went out into the garden to mind the children, her ears pricked for a call from Rita to come and help her get dressed. But there was still no summons by the time Anne returned, so Peggy went and got dressed in her finery, feeling more than a little put out that Rita didn't seem to want her help.

The ceremony was to be held at noon, and by eleven everyone but the bride and Ivy were downstairs, ready and waiting to leave for the church. The three little girls looked utterly cherubic in their white dresses edged with pink ribbon, the delicate froth of netting petticoat just peeking below the hem. They wore white shoes and socks and coronets of pink flowers were pinned firmly on their heads. Each would carry a small basket of confetti, but for now they were in Anne's safekeeping.

Martin had returned and quickly changed into a suit before hurrying off to do his duties as an usher, and Jack had arrived freshly barbered and shaved with a rose in the lapel of his new tailored suit. The bridal flowers had been delivered by the local florist, and Stan, the stationmaster, had provided the blooms from his allotment to decorate the church, which his niece, April, was busily arranging.

Jack had really splashed out for his only child's wedding, for not only had he organised limousines for the bridal party, but he had also booked the fully catered reception at the Officers' Club. Peter had paid for all the dresses and booked a short honeymoon in a swanky London hotel, with theatre tickets and a boat trip on the Thames organised.

With all the arrangements out of her hands, Peggy had nothing to do but relax and enjoy the day. But that was impossible, for time was swiftly disappearing, and still there was no call from Rita.

Sarah, Jane and Danuta had looked fresh and pretty in their summer frocks and straw hats when they'd left Beach View with Charlie in plenty of time to walk to the church, and Cordelia's friend Bertie had arrived looking as dapper as always, to ferry her there in his car. Peggy, Anne, Ivy and the three children would travel together in one of the limousines while Jack rode with Rita in the second. The liveried chauffeurs were now waiting outside, their gleaming black cars fluttering with white ribbons which drew quite an audience from neighbours and passers-by.

Peggy was trying not to fidget as she sat with Jack at the kitchen table which was laden with the bouquets, and distractedly watched the clock while Anne kept the three children amused by reading them a story.

Jack looked nervous and kept straightening his tie, which was already perfectly knotted, and continued to mutter the words of his speech under his breath.

Peggy smiled at him fondly and stilled his hand. 'Don't worry, Jack, you'll be fine. It's a good speech, and everyone will love it.'

Jack was about to reply when Ivy yelled from upstairs. 'Auntie Peg! Are you still down there?'

Peggy shot to her feet and hurried into the hall. 'Of course I am. What's the matter?'

'Nothing. Only Rita wants to speak to you.'

Peggy ran up the stairs to find Ivy and Sally waiting for her on the landing. Ivy looked positively radiant in a blush-pink dress that draped from a close-fitting bodice to just below her knees, and on her feet were matching pink shoes decorated with tiny, sparkling butterflies on the heels and toes.

'D'ya like 'em, Auntie Peg?' Ivy asked, excitedly waving her foot about. 'Ain't Sal clever? She made 'em all 'erself.'

'They are gorgeous, and so are you, Ivy. That pink really suits you.' She gave Ivy a gentle hug before turning to Sally. 'My goodness, Sally, you've done the most marvellous job. You are such a clever girl.'

'It's always easy when the bride knows what she wants,' replied Sally cheerfully. 'I'll be off home now to get changed. See you at the church.'

As the two girls went downstairs, Peggy eagerly stepped into the bedroom and gasped at the sight of Rita standing there looking so very beautiful that she could have stepped straight out of a fairy-tale book.

58

The sheath of white lace skimmed over her slender figure to the toes of her butterfly-studded white shoes, and pooled behind her in a short train. The neckline scooped from shoulder to shoulder with a scalloped edge, and the sleeves ended in an elegant point over her wrists.

On closer inspection, Peggy discovered there were tiny silver butterflies embroidered on the sleeves and hem which shimmered in the light. The delicate cloud of veil was tethered into her dark curls by the diamanté tiara Peter's mother had sent from Australia, and Peter's wedding gift of diamond earrings and necklace sparked fire at every beat of her heart.

'Oh, Rita,' Peggy managed, desperately trying not to cry. 'You're the most beautiful and regal bride I've ever seen. Fairy Queen Titania in all her glory couldn't outshine you today.'

Rita shot her an impish grin. 'I scrub up all right, don't I? Do you think Peter will like it?'

'Of course he will,' breathed Peggy. 'And consider himself the luckiest man in the world to have such a stunning bride. I still can't believe that my little tomboy could be so elegant and feminine.'

Rita reached for Peggy's hand. 'I love you so much, and I can never repay you for everything you've done for me and Dad over the years. You don't think too badly of me for deserting everyone, do you?'

Peggy took her gently into her arms and breathed in her delicate scent. 'My darling girl, I could never think badly of you. You and Peter are on the brink of having the most marvellous future, and although I shall miss you dreadfully, I wish you all the happiness and success in the world.' She touched her cheek to Rita's for a moment and then drew back. 'Do you want to have a word with Jack before you come down?'

Rita's eyes were suspiciously bright, and her lower lip quivered as she nodded.

'Remember, Rita,' said Peggy softly. 'You're only allowed to shed happy tears today.'

She went downstairs to tell Jack he was needed and assure Ivy that she didn't look fat and ugly, but really rather wonderful in the pink dress which made her skin glow and her eyes shine. She then put on her hat and checked there were plenty of handkerchiefs in her handbag; she and Cordelia always enjoyed a good cry at weddings.

Peter had been saddened to discover that one of the Polish pilots he'd come to know and like during his time at RAF Cliffe had been badly injured during a dogfight over Holland and was now recuperating at the sanatorium on the Cliffe estate. When he'd gone to see him, the large Pole had bellowed a delighted welcome and struggled from his seat to stand on his prosthetic legs to give him one of his famous bear hugs and enthusiastically plant smacking kisses on his cheeks.

Wing Commander Baron Stanislaw Kowalcyzk – or Stan as everyone called him – was a larger-than-life character who possessed a soft heart and generous soul. He cried easily and got emotional about everything except his own plight, and endeared himself to everyone he met. When he'd been in action, he'd had to cram his great body and long legs into the cockpit of his Spitfire – which was made for someone half the size – and would often yell 'Chocks away,' and be roaring down the runway seconds later to a whoop of sheer joy.

On his return to base, it had always taken two men to unplug him from the cockpit, and four to carry him out of the bar at the end of titanic drinking sessions and deliver him to his hut.

It seemed the loss of both his legs hadn't dented his humour or tamed his rather gung-ho attitude to life in general. As far as he was concerned, he'd been blessed, for he was still alive to drink copiously and enjoy the company of beautiful women. He loved women – and they were drawn to him like bees to nectar.

They had talked for hours on that first visit, and Peter had made a point of going to see him every day to make sure he really was following doctor's orders and not drinking. It was a forlorn hope, for Stan enjoyed his vodka and would bribe the orderlies to bring some in. Peter had taken Rita to see him, and he'd completely charmed her, so on his next visit Peter had asked him to be his best man.

Stanislaw had burst into predictable tears and hugged him so hard Peter could have sworn he'd heard his ribs creaking under the strain. The bachelor night had been riotous, with Stan taking centre stage at the Crown and proceeding to drink everyone under the table, until he'd had to be poured into a taxi. It had taken three days for Peter to get over it, but Stan was as bright and cheerful the next day as he always was, and had returned to the Crown to continue his outrageous flirting with the most receptive Gloria.

They'd hired a taxi to get them to the church in plenty of time, and as it pulled into the large car park, Stan looked up at the red-brick Victorian building and grimaced. 'Why the English build such ugly things? In Poland we make our basilica beautiful with gold and icons and mosaics.'

'I don't know, mate. Perhaps the Victorians liked their churches plain,' Peter replied. 'We have wooden ones in the outback. They're easy to rebuild if a bush fire shoots through.'

He paid off the taxi but didn't offer to help Stan out of the taxi because his friend loathed being treated like a cripple and always refused. Peter waited and watched nervously while Stan struggled out, swearing under his breath as he dug the two walking sticks firmly on the ground and heaved himself to his feet. Peter knew he hated those walking sticks with a vengeance, but they were a necessary evil, for without them Stan would fall over, and suffer the indignity of having to ask for help to get back up again.

Peter felt quite amazingly calm as he smoothed the hem of his blue-grey RAAF jacket and tugged the sleeves until they were aligned with his shirt cuffs. He'd been to the barber's earlier for a haircut and close shave, and had pressed the trousers until the creases were knife-sharp before spending over half an hour polishing his shoes, belt buckle and medals.

Stan had made an effort too, for he'd had a haircut and shave, and his thick black moustache had been carefully trimmed and waxed at the ends so he could twirl them to his heart's content. He was also in his dress uniform, the Polish eagle insignia on his cap and jacket lapels; his medals in perfect alignment across his broad chest.

As it was still early and there didn't seem to be anyone about yet, they found a bench in the garden of remembrance and sat down. The memorial to the fallen of both wars stood sentinel in the middle of the garden, and through an archway, they could see the graveyard.

'We have plenty time. Perhaps we go for a drink?' asked Stan hopefully.

'No flaming way, mate. We both need to stay sober.' Peter lit cigarettes for them both and leaned back. 'I hope your speech isn't too long or too rude. There'll be ladies there today and they might take objection to your dubious sense of humour.'

Stan waved away this comment. 'My speech will be beautiful,' he said. 'All the ladies will love it.'

Peter sincerely hoped that would be the case, but Stan could be unpredictable, and if he took it into his head to go off at a tangent, then there was no telling what he'd say.

'I will not spoil this special day, Peter,' murmured Stan. 'You have honoured me by asking me to stand with you, and I will repay that with the finest speech you've ever heard.'

He was distracted by something beyond Peter's shoulder and his brown eyes lit up. 'Who is that goddess with the hair of fire?' he breathed.

Peter turned and grinned. 'That's Fran, and she's well and truly spoken for, so keep those great Polish paws to yourself.'

'There will be other girls like that today?' Stan asked, his gaze following Fran until she disappeared into the church.

Peter chuckled. 'You're an incorrigible old rogue, and I feel sorry for any Sheila you pounce on today. But you could have your work cut out. Not all of them will fall for your charm – they're far too sensible.'

Stan's brown eyes were full of hurt. 'But, Pete, all women like to be charmed.'

'Well, now's your chance to look them over and decide on your victim,' said Peter, watching the elderly Cordelia being handed out of the car by Bertie as the Beach View girls appeared from around the street corner.

'She is lovely lady,' murmured Stanislaw, 'and like my grandmother, so she will laugh at my teasing.' His gaze moved on to the five girls who were approaching the church steps. 'Beautiful,' he sighed. 'Tell me their names, Peter.'

'The two blondes are sisters, Sarah and Jane; the little one in the velvet hat is April, and I'm not sure about the dark-haired plump one, but from what Robert said last night, it could be Mary.'

'And the pretty little one in the frock dancing with flowers?' asked Stan.

'Ah, well, you'll be glad to hear she's from Poland. Her name is Danuta Chimelweski or some such – you lot have unpronounceable names – and she's far too serious about things for you, Stan. In fact, she'll be leaving soon to go back to nurse in Warsaw.'

'Do you mean Chmielewski?' asked Stan with a frown. 'I knew a flier with that name. He was with me in the Spanish conflict. Aleksy was a very brave man and good companion. Sadly, he was killed during the Battle of Britain.'

'That was her brother,' said Peter. 'Rita told me that Aleksy had been billeted with Peggy for a while and Danuta turned up at Beach View looking for him within days of his death. He's now buried at St Cuthbert's alongside her baby. The baby's father was murdered by the Gestapo.'

Stan nodded thoughtfully and stroked his moustache, his sad gaze fixed on Danuta as she stood chatting with the other girls by the church steps. 'She is planning to go back to Poland, you say?' At Peter's nod he struggled to his feet and leaned heavily on the walking sticks. 'You must introduce me,' he demanded.

Peter took a deep breath and wondered if it really had been a good idea to have Stan as his best man when he seemed so determined to conquer every woman there.

Peggy was sharing the limousine with Anne, the three excited little girls and Ivy. The car made its stately way along Camden Road and up the High Street, the ribbons fluttering on the bonnet and the children waving to everyone they passed.

'I feel like a princess,' squeaked a breathless Ivy who was clearly as excited as the children. 'Ain't never 'ad a chauffeur before or been in one of these posh cars. It's smashing, ain't it?'

Dear Ivy, thought Peggy with great affection. She had missed her since she'd gone back to London, but life had certainly been quieter and calmer.

The car drew silently to a halt by the church steps where the photographer was waiting. The chauffeur opened the doors and Peggy shepherded the children out, warning them to stay together, wait for the bride, and smile to the man with the camera.

Ivy tottered out on her high heels clutching her posy of pink roses and white gypsophila, then straightened her dress. 'You go in,' she said to Anne and Peggy. 'I'll watch this little lot.'

'Are you sure?' asked Peggy with a frown.

'It'll be good practice for when this one comes,' she said cheerfully, patting her stomach.

Peggy looked beyond her, saw the second limousine slowly nose its way into the car park, and realised there wouldn't be time for any mischief. She smiled her thanks to Ivy and followed Anne into the church to be greeted by the familiar scents of damp stone, dusty old books and burnt candlewicks. Today there were the added perfumes of Stan's flowers which April had arranged in glorious profusion on the altar, by the choir stalls and lectern, and in small bunches at the end of the front rows of pews,

Despite the beautiful organ music that Mary was playing, their footsteps echoed up into the high, vaulted roof as they walked down the broad aisle of stone slabs and past the many empty back pews. St Andrew's was a vast, cold edifice even on the warmest summer day, but its saving grace was the stained-glass windows which had been revealed again now war was over, and the warmth of the colours drenched the entire chilly space in a soft, warm glow.

Peggy smiled a welcome to Gloria who was in bright pink, and to Rosie in her pale blue dress and coat. Ron looked very smart for once in a suit and tie, and Sally had changed into a floaty dress of rose-printed chiffon with a large-brimmed cream hat. Her husband and the rest of the fire station crew were all in uniform; Sally's brother, Ernie, was in his new school uniform, and little Harry, who'd refused point-blank to be a page boy, was in a smart jacket and short trousers.

Peggy's youngest son, Charlie, grinned back at her, resplendent in his first grown-up suit, and looking more like her Jim than ever, which made her heart twist. There was no sign of Doris or the Colonel, and Frank seemed to be without his wife Pauline. His son, Brendon, sat with Betty and their baby, and there was a smattering of patients from Cliffe who'd come to know Peter during his recuperation there.

As Anne went to sit next to Martin in the front pew, Peggy noted that Fran was now standing by the organ to accompany Mary on the violin, their music soft and unobtrusive as it mingled with the quiet murmurs of the wedding guests. Fran looked stunning as always in a crêpe de Chine dress of tawny ochre which set off her lightly tanned skin and autumnal hair to perfection.

Peter was standing rather nervously at the foot of the steps leading to the choir stalls and altar, the vicar murmuring quiet words of encouragement. The enormous and moustachioed best man seemed quite calm and sober, and Peggy breathed a sigh of relief. She'd yet to meet this Polish baron, but had heard enough about him to know he enjoyed a drink and could be the life and soul of the party, but it seemed he was on his best behaviour today.

She went to give Peter a peck on the cheek, assured him that his bride was on her way, and was introduced to Stanislaw, who bowed over her hand and kissed it.

'It is always a great pleasure to meet a beautiful woman, Mrs Reilly,' he murmured, his mesmerising gaze making her go weak at the knees. 'I hope you will do me the honour of talking with me later.'

Peggy nodded, then snapped out of her trance and retrieved her hand before quickly sitting down next to Cordelia. 'Whew,' she breathed, reaching for the order of service card to fan her hot face.

'He's quite the charmer, isn't he?' giggled Cordelia. 'My goodness, if I was three decades younger, I'd certainly give him a run for his money.'

'I have no doubt of it,' replied Peggy distractedly. 'No woman's safe with him around.'

'Stanislaw and I have a lot in common, so we do,' rumbled Ron, wriggling his eyebrows. 'To be sure I know how hard it is to be so attractive to women.'

Cordelia snorted. 'Only in your dreams, you deluded old rogue,' she retorted, swiping his arm with a gloved hand.

Their exchange was halted by the sound of the church door creaking open, and as the vicar nodded to Mary and Fran, the music soared to the rafters to welcome the bride.

There were soft gasps of delight, surprise and admiration as Rita slowly walked down the aisle on her father's arm. The silver embroidery on the hem of her dress and the tiny butterflies on her shoes shimmered with every step. Her veil couldn't quite dim the sparkle of the tiara, and her necklace and earrings caught the light from the windows and shot reflected fire around her like a halo, until it was as if she'd come from another world entirely and was being carried to Peter on a sunbeam.

Peggy could hear Cordelia sniffling beside her and she had to blink back her own tears as she shot a quick glance at Peter. The young Australian was clearly stunned, his gaze fixed in awe on this ethereal beauty approaching him.

Peggy lost her battle with her tears as the three little girls held hands and followed Rita and Jack towards the altar. They looked so endearingly sweet that she wanted to snatch them up and kiss them. But she managed to restrain herself, and mopped up her tears as Ivy brought up the rear and shot her a wink.

Rita had reached the steps and, having squeezed her father's arm in love and thanks, took Peter's hand and gazed up at him. He bent to whisper something in her ear and she giggled before turning her attention to what the vicar was muttering to them.

As the service was about to begin, Ivy took charge of Rita's bouquet, herded the children into the front pew where Anne and Martin were waiting for them, and then sat down next to Andy.

Peggy's tears soaked her handkerchief. She did so love weddings, and none could possibly be as beautiful or moving as this one.

Peter had always known that Rita was beautiful, but today she was so utterly stunning that he found he could barely breathe, let alone speak. He stumbled through the hymns and over the vows, making a complete hash of them and getting hot under the collar until Rita reached up to touch his face and whisper that she loved him.

He relaxed and smiled down at her and suddenly felt calmer than ever before. He promised to love, honour and cherish her until death parted them, and then carefully eased the gold band onto her finger.

'I now pronounce you man and wife,' said the vicar, his voice ringing out in the hush. 'You may kiss your bride.'

Peter lifted the veil from her beautiful face, saw the light of love in her eyes and with aching tenderness kissed her lips, his heart swelling with such emotion he thought he might weep at the power of it.

3

Danuta had watched Stanislaw work his charm on all the other women, and had coolly resisted his overtures. She knew that most Polish men of the noble class were just as chivalrous and over-attentive, and as it was as natural to them as breathing, she'd made little of it.

She'd managed to avoid him while the photographer fussed about outside the church, and had quickly climbed into the taxi with the other girls as he was busily shepherding the guests to their cars and ensuring no one got left behind. Just because they were both Poles, it didn't mean she had to get stuck with him.

'That Stanislaw's definitely got all the women in a fluster,' said Sarah on a giggle as the taxi headed for the Officers' Club. 'You want to watch out, Danuta, he's clearly got his eye on you.'

'He has eyes on all women,' she replied with a shrug. 'Polish men always think they are irresistible.'

'But you must admit, Danuta, he is handsome,' said Jane. 'And a baron too.'

'Maybe. But I am not interested.'

This flat statement was met with an awkward silence until Mary broke it. 'I would have thought you'd be delighted to meet someone from home,' she said quietly. 'After all, Danuta, he told me he knew your brother.'

Danuta felt a stab of surprise and eyed her sharply. 'He did not say this to me.'

'Well, I'm sure he's just waiting for the right moment,' Mary replied. 'He told me they'd trained together in Poland

and flown together in Spain and over here. He said he would have liked to talk to you about him, but you seemed a little frosty towards him.'

'Hmph. I was polite, is all. Because I not fall for his smooth talk, does not make me frosty.'

The three other girls giggled. 'I don't know about that,' said Jane. 'The look you gave the poor man when he kissed your hand should have felled him right there and then. It's no wonder he's been avoiding you ever since.'

'*I* avoid him,' she said firmly. 'Not other way round.'

She breathed a short sigh of relief as the taxi turned into the club car park, for this conversation was becoming too awkward. She didn't miss the silent exchange of knowing looks from the others, but said nothing as she climbed out and, with as much dignity as she could muster, made her way up the steps to the entrance.

Rita and Peter were standing with Jack, Ivy and Peggy in the doorway to the large reception room to greet their guests. Danuta was all too aware of Stanislaw watching her and knew she could avoid him no longer.

He bent over her hand, refraining from kissing it but keeping it firmly within his own. '*Spotykamy znowu, piekna siostra Aleksy,*' he murmured in Polish. '*Będę zaszczycony jak będziemy rozmawiać o twoim bracie?*'

'I prefer if we speak English,' she replied, not at all flattered by being called beautiful. 'Is polite in such company. But yes, I would like to hear about your friendship with my brother.'

'Later then,' he said, his dark, soulful gaze steady on her face.

Danuta felt pinned to the spot by his penetrating gaze, but managed to nod before swiftly retrieving her hand and moving away from the line-up. Gratefully, she accepted a glass of chilled wine from the waiter. She understood perfectly well how easy it would be for most women to be enraptured by his charm, and wasn't impervious to it, but she had more important plans to fulfil than falling for a large Pole with an even larger ego.

Peggy had witnessed that short exchange, and although Danuta had been stiffly polite, she'd seen the flush on the girl's cheeks as she'd turned away from Stanislaw, and had wondered if that brief moment might lead to something. Romances often started at weddings, and surely their meeting here was a sign that it was meant to be? She quickly pulled herself together. She was getting ahead of herself with all these wistful, romantic thoughts, and should concentrate on the delicious luncheon the club had provided.

Minestrone soup was followed by roasted local lamb with mint sauce and all the trimmings and a tinned peach Pavlova smothered in thick cream. The white wine was chilled to perfection, the red was dark and fruity, and according to the men, the beer was excellent.

Cigars and cigarettes were lit and buttons and belts discreetly loosened after this feast, and as the staff quietly went round to fill glasses with champagne for the toasts, they waited for the speeches.

Stanislaw struggled to his feet. 'It has been my honour to stand by my friend on this very special day,' he began. 'He is brave and clever, and I could tell many stories about him – but I have promised to keep them to myself today, for he is too modest, and I will not embarrass him.' He beamed a smile at his laughing audience. 'But of course, after today I can share some of our adventures with you.'

He raised his chin, his moustache twitching as he battled to hold back his emotions. 'He is very lucky man to have found such a beautiful woman in Rita, and I hope that one day I shall be as lucky.'

His gaze trawled the room and settled momentarily on Danuta, who dipped her chin, furious to be picked out like that, and even more furious at herself for blushing like a stupid schoolgirl.

'I know Peter will soon take Rita home with him to Australia, and our hearts will be sad. But they have so much love between them they will have a wonderful life there.' He blinked away his tears and turned to Ivy who was sitting next to him at the top table.

'Ivy, you have been best and most loving friend of Rita for long time, and she loves you very much. Today you are most beautiful bridesmaid, and your baby will be just as lovely I am sure.'

He gazed down to the three little girls sitting so obediently with Anne and Martin. 'Rose, Emily and Daisy, you are so pretty and sweet – and one day it will be your turn to be a bride. I hope you remember this day for all the love and happiness that surrounds you.'

He picked up his champagne glass. 'I ask you to raise your glasses to Ivy and our sweet little bridesmaids, and to wish them a long life and much happiness.'

Everyone got to their feet and enthusiastically responded, and Peggy noticed that Stanislaw's face was streaked with tears. *My goodness*, she thought. *I never realised how emotional he was* – but then Aleksy had been the same, the tears of joy and sorrow never far away.

Jack Smith got to his feet. 'Thank you, Stan,' he said, handing him a clean handkerchief, to everyone's amusement. He went on to thank everyone for coming and to offer his congratulations to the chef and staff for the excellent meal, and to the club chairman for allowing them to celebrate today in their magnificent function room.

'I always knew this day would come,' he went on more soberly. 'And have secretly dreaded it, for Rita's always been my little girl, and I rather selfishly wanted to keep her to myself. But now the day is here, and I see my daughter looking so radiant, and clearly deeply in love, I could wish no more for her.'

He reached for his glass, and his voice was unsteady as he continued. 'Peter, I have entrusted my most precious girl to your care, and I know you will love and cherish her as I have done. I wish you both joy and great success in your new life, and may all your tears be happy ones.'

There was barely a dry eye in the room as they toasted the bride and groom, and Peggy rather suspected she'd managed to cry away most of her make-up.

Peter responded to Jack's short speech, thanking him for his support, and once again offering him the chance to go with them to Australia – which Jack cheerfully refused. Then he raised his glass to toast his bride, and promised once again to love and cherish her to the very end of his days.

Stanislaw read out the many telegrams that had come in from Australia, the cake was cut, and then the five-piece band struck up with 'Moonlight Becomes You'. Peter led Rita onto the small dance floor for their first waltz as a married couple and minutes later were joined by Ivy and Andy, Sally and John, and Peggy with Frank – who turned out to be a surprisingly good dancer.

'Why didn't Pauline come?' she asked. 'Isn't she well again?'

'She's got one of her heads,' Frank said gruffly. 'The doctor's given her some pills, but they don't seem to help much.' He gave a deep sigh. 'She didn't want me to come today, but Rita's been so much a part of the family that I felt I should be here to wish her well. Do you think that was wrong of me?'

'Not at all,' she replied firmly. 'You have absolutely no reason to feel guilty, and I want you to enjoy yourself today, Frank. God knows you deserve to after all she's put you through lately.'

'She is trying to make amends with Brendon and Betty,' he replied. 'But Brendon's very protective of Betty, and Pauline's rejection of her bit deep. She's accused me of taking sides, but what else could I do, Peggy? He's my only surviving son, and I refuse to let her cause a rift between us.'

Peggy watched the young couple making their way slowly around the dance floor, and thought how tragic it was that Pauline couldn't accept their marriage because it had come some months after their son had been born. But she'd said her piece to Pauline and made it clear what she thought of her; now it was up to Pauline to make amends – to swallow her stupid, all-consuming pride and enjoy her family. Yet it seemed she was unwilling to make the effort, and poor Frank was shouldering the huge burden of trying to please everyone and still hold the family together.

Danuta knew it would happen, and that there was no point in trying to avoid it if she was to discover more about her brother's exploits after he'd left Poland. As expected, Stanislaw made a beeline for her the minute the band started playing, and as he plumped down in the chair beside her, she gave him a wary smile.

'Sadly, I cannot dance,' he said, tapping his prosthetic legs with a walking stick. 'But if I had my legs, I would have liked to dance with you all evening.'

'I'm not much good at dancing, so it really doesn't matter,' she replied. 'May I ask what happened to your legs?'

'I was in dogfight over the Netherlands at very end of war. My plane was shot up and I crash-landed into trees,' he said with little emotion. 'But I still live and love life, and one day I will learn to walk again without these,' he added, jamming the sticks between his knees. 'You are nurse. You know of these things.'

Danuta couldn't help but admire his stoicism in the light of such a life-changing injury. 'My brother was not so lucky,' she murmured. 'Where did you meet him?'

He poured them both a glass of wine, and after taking a sip, he leaned back in his chair and regarded her thoughtfully. 'Aleksy was with me at flying academy in Poland. We trained together and got our wings on the same day. I stay in

Poland, but Aleksy want to fight the Communists, so he went to Spain.'

He took a deep swallow of wine. 'I follow him, but we return to Warsaw just as Russians occupy the east, and Germans invade the west. He find his home destroyed, but no sign of you or rest of his family. Everyone in neighbourhood was scattered, he could get no information and feared you were lost – as my own family had been lost.'

Danuta felt a chill of remembrance and looked at him questioningly.

'My father was shot for leading the local resistance, and our home and estates in Kresy were stolen by Russians. I manage to get my mother and sister out and onto a ship, but it was sunk by a German U-boat.'

He wiped his eyes with a large handkerchief, took another swig of wine and then continued, his voice rough with emotion as he slipped into his mother tongue.

'At that time many thousands of military, naval and air force personnel fell into Soviet hands and were sent to Gulags in Siberia. The Russians didn't want to risk the educated classes rising against them, so Aleksy and I knew we had to escape before we too were captured. Like many before us, we managed to cross Romania and find our way into France where we joined the *Armée de l'Air*. It was vital to block the German invasion through northern Europe, and they were glad to have us Poles fill their ranks.'

'But why France?' she asked in Polish.

'A Polish government in exile had been set up there after the German invasion into Poland. But then France surrendered to Germany in 1940, and we were advised to get to Britain where the government had agreed to establish an independent Polish Air Force under British control.'

'That couldn't have been easy,' murmured Danuta, who'd experienced her own perilous escape through France. 'France was overrun by then and every port was heavily guarded.'

Stanislaw smiled and twirled his moustache. 'Aleksy and I managed to come to England on a fishing boat. Some came from Gibraltar, and there is a story about three who flew their Bloch MB fighters from France to Tangmere.'

'They were lucky not to be shot down,' said Danuta.

'War is all about luck,' he replied with a shrug.

Danuta took a sip of wine. 'When Aleksy came to England, he was billeted with Peggy at Beach View before he joined Bomber Command. Where were you?'

'I was sent to Blackpool to learn how to fly British fighter planes.' He chuckled and twirled his moustache. 'They were very modern compared to what we had in Poland and France, with retractable undercarriages we kept forgetting about.' He grinned. 'We had many belly-flop landings, which didn't do our reputation or our planes any good.'

Danuta smiled back. 'I can imagine.'

'It was difficult for all of us. None of us spoke much English, and we Poles found RAF procedures and formalities very strange. The British are very cool and formal, but we Poles have fire in our hearts and bellies and are not afraid to show it. The British commanders did not approve of our aggressive skills and tactics during the fighting, but we were here to kill the hateful Germans. It was not a time for good manners.'

Danuta nodded. 'I can see how the differences must have made things frustrating on both sides,' she said. 'Did you and Aleksy meet again before he was killed?'

'For a few hours before the Germans began to blitz London. We were both on leave and met in a pub outside the town of Croydon. We drank the place dry, I remember, but that was the last time I saw him.'

'The last time I saw him was in Warsaw shortly before he left for Spain. I came to Beach View too late, so I never had the chance to tell him what had happened to our family.'

Stanislaw gently placed his large hand over Danuta's. 'This is not the day for sad memories, little one,' he said softly. 'I can guess what happened to them. But how did you get here? Did you come alone all that way?'

Danuta nodded, unwilling to go into any detail of her hair-raising escape across Europe. 'It wasn't easy,' she said, 'and discovering I was too late to ever see Aleksy again, I counted myself lucky to have found a safe and loving home with Peggy.'

Stanislaw glanced across at Peggy who was now being whirled round the floor by Ron. 'She has a very beautiful soul,' he murmured. 'Her heart is on her sleeve as the English say. I am glad Aleksy found a good home with her before he went into battle.'

He knocked back the remains of his wine and poured more. 'Peter tells me you are planning to return to Poland soon '

'At the end of the month.'

His expression was suddenly very solemn. 'It would be most foolish to go back, Danuta. The Russians have been given control over most of Poland, and Stalin is determined to rid the country of all who may resist him. He does not believe in democracy, and already he is enforcing Communist rule.'

'But Poland's my home,' she protested, oblivious now that they were still speaking Polish. 'I've waited many years to return, and there is much need for my skills as a nurse now the hospitals are so overwhelmed with all the returning prisoners from the camps.'

'I share your desire to return to our fatherland, Danuta, but it is no longer free, democratic or independent. Our people fought for freedom from the Germans, but now are crushed once more beneath the Russian boot. No one is safe, Danuta, and I beg you to think again.'

'But the plans have already been made,' she replied. 'And I won't be travelling alone. Besides,' she added. 'I pose no threat to the Russians. I merely wish to do my nursing.'

He leaned towards her, his tone urgent. 'You would have to explain where you have been all this time, and that will make them suspicious. If they think you have returned to work with the resistance, then you will be sent to Siberia and simply disappear like so many thousands of others.'

'I'm sure that won't happen,' she said, quelling the sudden nervous flutter inside her.

He pressed her hand between both of his. 'It will, Danuta. Everyone is questioned, and if they don't like your answers … Please don't go. You're young and lovely, and I'm sure most brave – but you cannot fight these people. They do not listen.'

Danuta watched the swirl of dancers, but her thoughts were far from this room and the happiness of the celebrations. She was remembering the years she'd worked covertly behind enemy lines for the SOE and with the underground resistance fighters; the times she'd escaped capture by the skin of her teeth when someone had betrayed her; the horror of seeing her lover being shot; the nights and days of hiding in barns and under bridges from the Gestapo who were so determined to find and punish her – and finally the terrifying days she'd spent being interrogated and tortured by them.

She'd been saved by an Allied air raid which had destroyed her prison and offered escape, and had been so close to death that she was barely aware of anything as the resistance fighter had carried her to safety, and managed to get her on a British hospital ship to England. She'd survived, but at a terrible cost, for the internal injuries inflicted by the Gestapo meant she could never have children.

Could she really risk going through all that again? Did she have the strength and courage to face such a formidable enemy for the sake of doing her nursing? And did this longing to see her homeland warrant putting her life and Solly's in mortal danger? Her entire family was gone, so there was nothing left for her there, and if Stanislaw was right, it wouldn't be the Poland she remembered. For the first time in many years, her resolve began to waver.

'I am very sorry, little one,' Stanislaw murmured, putting his arm about her shoulders. 'I have said too much and have made you think of things which have made you sad.'

'I have dreamed of returning home for very long time,' she replied in English, easing from his embrace. 'Do you not wish to go back, Stanislaw?'

'Every moment of every day,' he replied. 'But I will not return until Poland is free again. And I cannot see that happening for a very long time.'

'But our people are foreigners here,' said Danuta. 'What if the British order you to go home?'

'Then we must resist with all our might. We helped the British to win this war, and have earned the right to stay.'

'Right-oh, you two, enough of that,' interrupted Peter. 'I'm taking Danuta for a dance.' With that, he drew Danuta to her feet and whirled her out onto the floor in a fast foxtrot.

'Sorry about that, Danuta. But you looked as if you needed rescuing. Old Stan's inclined to get too serious about things, and this is supposed to be a happy day.'

Danuta looked beyond him to Stanislaw who was now sitting alone at the table and making his way purposefully through a second bottle of wine as he watched her dance. He looked so sad, and despite all her previous misgivings, she realised he was as lonely as she in this exile, and her heart went out to him.

Peter thanked her for the dance and Danuta returned to the table and would have remained there if Stanislaw hadn't insisted upon her joining in the dancing. 'I like to watch you enjoying yourself,' he said. 'It's good to see you smile. You are too serious, I think, for one so young.'

She laughed at that, for she was well into her twenties, but accepted the offer to dance from Brendon, and then returned to Stanislaw's side to catch her breath and have another drink. She wasn't really in the habit of drinking much, and it was beginning to go to her head by the time

Rita and Peter were ready to leave for their London honeymoon.

Everyone trooped outside to where a taxi – suitably adorned with strings of tin cans and ribbons – was waiting to take them to the station. Rita had changed into a cream linen dress and jacket and a neat little hat. She hugged and kissed them all, and when it was Danuta's turn she held her for a moment longer.

'Have fun with Stan, Danuta,' she whispered. 'He's such a lovely man under all that bluff and moustache twirling.'

Danuta reddened. 'I keep him company, is all,' she stuttered.

Rita laughed. 'If you say so.'

And then the taxi was pulling away, the tin cans rattling as a shower of confetti rained down on it and everyone shouted their cheerful goodbyes.

Peggy and Cordelia were happily mopping their tears as they turned to go back into the reception room, and Peggy caught Danuta's hand on the way past. 'Such a happy day,' she breathed. 'I so love weddings, don't you?'

'Of course,' Danuta replied, smiling back with great affection.

'It'll be your wedding one day, Danuta, and I promise it will be just as wonderful.'

Danuta nodded and let her carry on into the clubhouse with Cordelia, while she stayed outside to let the fresh air clear her head. Peggy was a romantic, and weddings always made her over-emotional, and although Danuta knew she meant well and yearned to give her a beautiful wedding day, it was unlikely she would ever marry. Her body was scarred and ugly, and not something she'd ever wish to reveal – and what was the point of getting married when she couldn't have children?

Danuta made her way up the steps and found Stanislaw waiting for her with a fresh bottle of wine. 'I'm sorry,' she said, 'but I've had more than enough to drink. I'm on duty early tomorrow morning, so I think I will go home now.'

His welcoming smile faded into disappointment. 'Oh. Then of course I must not keep you any longer.' He began to struggle to his feet.

'Please, don't get up. I can see myself out,' she said hastily.

'I will stand to say goodbye,' he said stubbornly, jamming the sticks into the carpet to gain steady purchase before hauling himself to his feet. 'I am sorry if my talk of Poland has upset you, Danuta, but please, I beg you, think about what I have said – and don't just take my word for it – ask others. They will tell you the same. Poland is not safe.'

'Thank you. I will certainly give it much thought.' She reached out to shake his hand. 'It has been a pleasure to meet you and to talk of Aleksy.'

He balanced precariously on one walking stick, took her hand and softly kissed it. 'I am hoping you will do me the honour of having dinner with me tomorrow night,' he murmured. 'And I promise to talk only of happy things.'

The invitation was unexpected and not particularly welcome, because she didn't want him getting any wrong ideas. 'I'm not sure,' she hedged. 'My district round is long and sometimes I am not home until very late.'

'I will book table at the Grove for seven o'clock. I will wait for you, no matter how long.'

'Oh dear, you are persistent, aren't you?' she chuckled.

'It's what's kept me alive, Danuta, and you, I think, are worth waiting for.'

Danuta felt the heat rising in her face and withdrew her hand from his clasp. 'You really don't know anything about me, Stanislaw.'

'Then permit me to learn more.'

Danuta held his gaze, thinking that her life story really wasn't the most palatable subject to be discussed over dinner, but as hard as she'd tried to resist this man, he'd managed to charm her, and make her curious to know more about him. 'I'll see you tomorrow, then,' she murmured before quickly leaving.

The long walk home cooled the flush in her cheeks, but did nothing to quell the rather disconcerting flutter of excitement at the thought of seeing him again.

4

Peggy had very little time that Sunday to mull over the delightful thought that something might be going on between Danuta and Stanislaw. She'd planned to quiz her over breakfast, but the girl had shot out of the house very early this morning on her district nursing round before Peggy was even out of bed. It was all very frustrating.

However, she had rather more pressing things to occupy her today. Mary was coming with Rosie for a short visit before she had to catch her train back to Sussex, and Fran was due to pop in with Robert. Ivy had stayed at Gloria's last night, but would also be dropping by before she and Andy went back to Walthamstow. Frank was still snoring fit to bust on one of the hastily cleared bunk beds in the basement, and young Charlie was sleeping off the copious amounts of beer he'd consumed last night in an effort to keep up with his grandfather and uncle. Never a wise move, for they could drink anyone under a table.

She left Daisy to eat her toast and went down to the basement to knock on Charlie's door. 'Get up, son. You've got rugby practice in an hour.'

There was a grunt and an indecipherable mutter before everything went silent again, so Peggy opened the door. 'Get up, Charlie,' she ordered the lump beneath the mound of tangled bedclothes.

He looked blearily over his shoulder and grunted. 'I don't feel well,' he groaned.

'That's hardly surprising,' she replied mildly, regarding the discarded shoes and clothes strewn about the floor.

'A good breakfast will see to that hangover. Now stir your stumps and get out of that bed while I sort your uncle out.'

She left him to it and went to the second room which had become the repository for unwanted things that might one day be useful, and briskly rapped on the door. 'Frank. Frank. Wake up.'

'Go away,' he groaned.

'I'm not going anywhere,' she said flatly. 'And if you don't get out of that bed soon, you'll have Pauline coming down here to find out what's happened to you – and believe me, Frank, you don't want that.'

Another groan was followed by the squeaking of bed-springs, and then a hefty clunk, which elicited a soft oath. Peggy gave a wry smile, for he'd obviously hit his head on the upper bunk – but at least it might bring him to his senses.

Satisfied they were both on the move, she returned to the kitchen to find Anne giving breakfast to her girls while Martin drooped over a cup of tea, and Cordelia chattered nineteen to the dozen about the wedding.

'I was just saying how lovely our little Rita looked yester-day,' chirped Cordelia, 'and how lucky she is to have such a fine husband in Peter.'

'Yes, Grandma Cordy, we know all that,' sighed Anne. 'But do you have to be quite so cheerful at this time of the morning?'

Cordelia sniffed. 'You young things have got no stamina. I bet Ron's already up, bright-eyed and bushy-tailed, walk-ing the dogs.'

'I expect he is,' said Martin, rubbing at the still-livid scar on his temple. 'Though how he does it after the amount of drink he got through last night is a complete mystery to me.'

Cordelia tutted and concentrated on eating her bowl of cereal while Peggy finished browning more toast on the hob and spreading margarine on another slice for Daisy.

'You're not alone, Martin,' said Peggy, sitting down and patting his hand. 'Frank and Charlie are worse for wear too, and I've had to take a couple of aspirin to get me going this morning.' She glanced up at the clock. 'But if Frank doesn't get a move on, we'll have Pauline storming in looking for him.'

'Not a delightful prospect,' muttered Cordelia. 'But I doubt she'll darken this door again after that fierce ticking-off you gave her.'

'I heard it was a lot more than a ticking-off,' rumbled Frank as he came into the room. He helped himself to a cup of tea and sat down. 'Pauline told me Peggy had attacked her.'

Peggy folded her arms and glared at him. 'I gave her a slap and a good shake for treating her son and his family in that appalling manner. I can't say I'm proud of losing my temper like that, but she deserved it, Frank – as you very well know.'

'Yeah, I do,' he conceded, slumping in his kitchen chair. 'But the trouble she caused won't go away, Peg, and it will take more effort than she's willing to give to put it right.'

He gave a deep sigh and rested his chin in his large hand. 'I'd walk out tomorrow if she was well, but she's still being troubled by terrible headaches, and I can't just abandon her.'

Peggy smiled at him. 'I doubt you'll ever leave her, Frank, no matter how many times you threaten to, or how much she winds you up. But what does the doctor have to say about these headaches? Are they real or yet another ruse to keep you on your toes?'

Frank looked a bit sheepish, as if well aware of how easily his wife controlled him. 'He says it's probably stress and the onset of the menopause.'

'Would that account for such severe headaches?' Peggy asked.

Frank shrugged. 'I wouldn't know. But he's taken blood tests and so on, and is now talking about sending her to see a specialist in London.'

'What sort of specialist?' Peggy asked sharply.

'A neurologist, I think he said.' Frank grimaced. 'Someone who deals with people's heads, anyway.'

'That does sound serious.' Peggy experienced a pang of guilt, for she'd slapped Pauline's face very hard and given her a rough shaking during that altercation, and she was suddenly frightened that she might have done her some real damage.

Frank seemed to read her thoughts and reached for her hand. 'It was nothing you did that day to make her the way she is, Peg. She's been damned difficult for years.'

'That she has,' murmured Peggy. 'But these headaches are a new thing.'

Frank slurped from his cup of tea. 'It's always been hard to know what's ailing her, Peg. There's always something wrong, and she's back and forth to that doctor's almost every week. It's a good thing they're looking at making health services free. I dread to think how much money her hypochondria has cost me over the years.'

Charlie came into the kitchen looking like death warmed up just as Sarah and Jane took their places at the table. Peggy bit down on a smile as Charlie blushed to the roots of his black hair and ducked his head to concentrate on the bowl of cereal she put in front of him. At fifteen, her son was maturing fast, and clearly appreciated the sight of two pretty young women despite being hung-over.

Managing to resist stroking back his hair from his eyes, she sat back down and smiled at the two girls. 'You're looking very lovely today,' she said, regarding the flowery dresses, neat hair and immaculate make-up. 'Are you off to somewhere nice?'

'We're going to London for a couple of days,' said Jane. 'Jeremy has booked us into a small hotel close to Oxford Street so we can go shopping for our trip to Singapore.'

'Gosh. I didn't realise your plans were that advanced. But what about your job at the council offices, Sarah?'

'I telephoned my office manager yesterday morning and asked for the day off, and she was very good about it. She now knows I'm going back to Singapore and the reason for it, and has been most supportive.'

'Oh, that's good. But I do wish Jeremy was going with you. The thought of you young things travelling all that way unescorted is very worrying.'

Both girls chuckled. 'We managed very well on the journey here,' said Sarah, 'so I'm sure we'll be quite safe.'

'But you were on a ship with lots of other women and children. Not flying halfway round the world in a flimsy seaplane,' protested Peggy.

'They're really not that flimsy, Peggy,' said Martin. 'In fact, they're a highly efficient and safe mode of transport. The navy used them right through the war.'

'Well, if you say so,' said Peggy, not at all convinced.

Daisy, Rose and Emily had finished their breakfast, so Martin went out into the garden with them while Peggy and Anne tackled the washing-up. Charlie left a few minutes later for the rugby club, and Frank soon climbed into his ramshackle old truck to drive home to Pauline and face the music.

Sarah and Jane dealt with their crockery and then went upstairs to fetch their overnight cases. The table was finally cleared and the faded oilcloth wiped down as Cordelia went to fetch the Sunday papers from the wire basket beneath the letter box. She returned and settled down in her favourite chair, her half-moon glasses perched on her nose as she skimmed the headlines.

'We'll be off then,' said Sarah on her return to the kitchen. 'Say our goodbyes to Fran, Mary and Ivy, will you, Auntie Peg? We would have stayed, but we wanted to get the early train as Jeremy has promised to take us out to lunch at the Savoy.'

'Goodness me,' said Peggy. 'How very posh.' She smiled and hugged her before turning to Jane with a teasing glint in her eye. 'You and Jeremy seem to be seeing rather a lot of each other, and it was very generous of him to help with the flying boat tickets. Should I be planning for another wedding?'

Jane laughed. 'Not for a long while yet, Aunt Peg. I have the trip to Singapore first, and depending how things go, it could be some time before I can get back here. As for Jeremy, he's been offered a terrific job in Washington.'

'Washington?' Peggy gasped. 'But will that mean you'll go and live there too?'

Jane grinned and hugged her. 'I didn't say he'd taken up the offer,' she said. 'And who knows what the future will bring?' She kissed Peggy's cheek. 'Must dash, or we'll miss the train.'

Peggy was left none the wiser as she stood in the doorway to watch them hurry down the garden path. She returned their brief wave before they disappeared down the twitten then, with a deep sigh, went to tidy up the basement rooms.

Mary arrived with Rosie just as Peggy was bringing a tray of squash down into the garden for the children, so she quickly got Martin to fetch more deckchairs from beneath the tarpaulin that had once covered Rita's motorbike. Making sure everyone was settled, she went back upstairs to the kitchen to make a pot of tea and to hunt out some of the lovely biscuits Cordelia's family had sent from Canada.

The girls began to squabble over the toys in the sandpit, so Martin decided to take them down to the beach to let off steam. There was a bit of a kerfuffle to find their swimsuits and towels, and he finally left armed with all the paraphernalia needed for a trip to the beach with three small girls.

'It's lovely to see him looking so much better, Anne,' said Rosie. 'You must be delighted to have him back to his old self.'

'He's not quite there yet, Rosie,' she replied, 'but he's certainly come on in leaps and bounds since he's been here. He still has quiet days and troubled nights, but they aren't as frequent.'

'He's clearly learned to enjoy the company of his children again,' said Peggy. 'A few short weeks ago, he'd have sloped off with Roger to the airfield for the day, and not given you or them a thought.'

'Ron was telling me about this new air-freight service that Martin and the others are setting up,' said Rosie. 'That must surely have boosted his confidence and given him a new and exciting challenge?'

'Oh, it has,' said Anne. 'He never stops talking about it, and spends hours with Kitty, Charlotte and Roger poring over all the documents involved, and going to meetings with the authorities. They've finally gained permission from the RAF to use Cliffe aerodrome, and are up there most days with a team of men to get the runway cleared and repaired before they take delivery of their first plane.' She grinned. 'It's all terribly exciting.

'What plane have they bought?' asked Mary.

'It's a Douglas C-47 the Americans no longer want, and according to Martin, it's in good shape considering it was a real workhorse throughout the last two years of the war. I'm just so thrilled they want to fly again after all they've been through.'

'Will Kitty and Charlotte be flying too?' asked Mary.

'Definitely; but not until they have two planes and more orders under their belt – which shouldn't be too long now with all the emergency supplies being air-lifted into Europe.'

'It all sounds very exciting, Anne. I'm so pleased. But it does make my life seem utterly dull in comparison,' said Mary on a sigh.

'I'm sure it isn't dull at all,' said Anne. 'Not with your little boy to care for and your teaching at the local school.'

Mary giggled. 'John is a live wire, that's for certain, but he goes to nursery school in the village now, which gets rid of most of his enormous energy, and when I'm doing my private music lessons, he's looked after by my lovely in-laws, Joseph and Barbara. I'm very lucky really. Things would have been hugely different for us without having such wonderful support.'

'Do you have any more photographs?' asked Peggy. 'Only the last ones you sent were ages ago, and he was still very tiny.'

Mary dug in her handbag and passed Peggy an envelope. 'I took these before I came down here. You may keep them if you wish.'

'Oh, thank you, dear. How lovely of you.' Peggy eagerly looked at the small black-and-white images of a sturdy, laughing little boy of two, with a mop of curly dark hair. In one of them he was shown dressed in dungarees, shirt and wellington boots, sitting on his grandfather's knee and pretending to drive the tractor. 'My goodness, he's grown,' she breathed.

'He certainly has,' said Mary, 'and is the image of his father.' She blinked rapidly, touching the locket he'd given her on her eighteenth birthday. 'It's rather lovely, really,' she carried on, 'because it's as if Jack is still with us, and I know it brings a lot of comfort to his parents.'

The moment was broken by Ivy slamming through the gate and running down the path. 'I can't stay, Auntie Peggy,' she announced breathlessly, 'but I just had to come and say goodbye.' She threw herself at Peggy and swamped her in a hug as Andy rolled his eyes and looked at his watch.

'You shouldn't be rushing about in your condition,' Peggy softly chided.

'Yeah, I know, but I got up late and Andy 'as to get back for 'is evening shift at the fire station. And he promised 'is mum 'e'd drop in on 'er before we went home. So I ain't got much choice, 'ave I?'

'I suppose not,' laughed Peggy. She turned to Andy and gave him a hug. 'Try not to let her charge about so much,' she said.

'Chance'd be a fine thing,' he replied without rancour. 'My Ivy's a proper whirlwind, and nothing can stop 'er once she gets going.' He took Ivy's hand and smiled down at her. 'Come on, love, or we'll be chasing our tails all day at this rate.'

Ivy kissed Cordelia and Peggy, and waved to the others on her way back through the gate. Slamming it behind her, she blew more kisses before Andy propelled her down the twitten at a fast pace.

'I'd better go too,' said Mary, collecting her overnight case and large shopping bag from next to her deckchair. 'My train leaves in half an hour, and I'm in no condition to run up that awful hill.' She handed over the shopping bag to Peggy. 'I brought a few jars of jams and pickles from home, and there's also a pot of honey from the hives we keep on the farm.'

'Oh, Mary, how very generous,' gasped Peggy.

'It's the least I could bring after all you did for me,' she said, kissing and hugging Peggy and then Cordelia. 'Let me know when Jim gets back,' she said. 'And please keep writing, Peggy. I really love getting all your news.'

'I'll walk up to the station with you,' said Rosie. 'Ron should be back from exercising the dogs now, so he can organise our lunch.'

Peggy walked with them to the gate and waved goodbye to Mary before they turned up the hill to take the back roads to the station. She looked at her watch and wondered where Fran had got to, but decided she was probably having a lie-in after all the excitement of the previous day.

She sat down and explored the large shopping bag of goodies and exclaimed over the jars of delicious-looking jam. There was blackberry and apple, gooseberry, rhubarb and apple and quince jelly. The honey was clear and golden; the jars of piccalilli and different chutneys positively stuffed with vegetables straight from the farm's kitchen garden. And at the very bottom was a cooked ham wrapped in muslin.

'Good lord, will you look at that?' breathed Peggy. 'What a wonderful surprise, and so generous.' She quickly stuffed it all back in the bag. 'I'd better put everything away in the larder before it spoils in the sun.'

She dashed upstairs and reverently placed the ham on a dish at the very top of her larder, and then quickly put away the jars of jam and pickles with those she'd made herself. The smell of that ham made her mouth water, but she firmly closed the larder door and went back down to the garden, already planning to serve it for tonight's tea with some of the new potatoes Ron had brought round.

'Mary's a lovely girl, isn't she?' said Anne. 'I was already down in Somerset when she came here to live, and so only got to know her through your letters. I seem to remember there was some to-do which involved Rosie, her awful brother, Tommy, and that Eileen who used to live in the flats that got bombed. But you never really explained what it was all about.'

Peggy firmly blocked the dark and painful memories of that time. 'It's a complicated story, Anne, and I don't have the right to tell it. Let's just be thankful that Mary and Rosie have forged a lovely friendship through what was an extremely difficult time for everyone. Tommy's out of the picture and Eileen is dead, so that's an end to it.'

'Poor Rosie,' said Cordelia. 'Tommy was always a ne'er-do-well, and caused no end of upset.'

Anne nodded in agreement. 'I wouldn't put it past him to turn up again like the bad penny he's always been.'

'Well, he'd have great difficulty in doing that, Anne,' said Peggy. 'He was killed on the Normandy beaches. At least Rosie could take some comfort in the knowledge he'd been involved in something worthwhile before he died.'

Anne looked startled. 'Oh, I didn't know. I thought he was in prison.'

'He was for a short time, but because of his age and general fitness, he was drafted into the army. For all his conniving and slyness, he ended up giving his life for his country.'

Peggy tried hard to think of Tommy as a hero, but simply couldn't. He'd always been a rat, and she suspected that prison, war and the army hadn't changed him. She sipped the tea, which was now stone cold, and grimaced. 'I'll go and freshen the pot,' she muttered.

'I'm sorry if I stirred up painful memories, Mum,' said Anne.

'It's all right, dear, you weren't to know.'

She took the tea tray up the steps into the kitchen and dumped it on the table, the memories of Tommy, Mary and Eileen flooding back in all their painful clarity. Tommy had betrayed everyone by lying to Rosie and Eileen and taking baby Mary far away to be adopted. If Mary hadn't come looking for the truth, she would never have discovered how Eileen had been fooled into giving up her baby – and how Rosie had been cruelly denied the chance to adopt her.

Peggy gave a deep sigh, thankful that at least Rosie and Mary had mended things between them. Now that Eileen and Tommy were dead, there was little point in raking up the past. She filled the large kettle and placed it on the hob, and was about to wash up the cups when the telephone rang. Glad to have something else to think about, she hurried to answer it.

'Hello, Aunt Peg, this is Robert.'

'Robert! What's happened? Is Fran all right?'

'She's just exhausted and needs to rest,' he assured her. 'I shall be driving her back to London the moment she wakes, and I doubt she'll be fit enough to play at Doris's wedding. I've telephoned Doris to warn her that might be the case, and I'll get Fran to call you when she's feeling more herself.'

'Oh, dear, I knew it was all too much for her in her condition,' fretted Peggy. 'Are you sure it wouldn't be better to keep her at Gloria's and have her see the doctor in the morning?'

'I managed to catch Danuta while she was cycling past the pub, and she gave Fran the once-over. As long as she rests, she'll be fine. I'm sorry she couldn't come over, but I'm sure you understand.'

'Of course I do,' said Peggy. 'Give her our love, and tell her I'll look forward to her call once she's settled back at home.' She took a steadying breath. 'Are you all right, Robert?'

'I'm absolutely fine, but for a mild headache first thing, and one of Gloria's huge fried breakfasts cured that.'

'Well, you take care driving all that way. Goodbye, Robert, and thank you for letting me know.'

Peggy replaced the receiver and dug in her overall pocket for her cigarettes and lighter. Blowing smoke, she slowly returned to the kitchen to wash the cups and make the tea. However, the raking up of old stories and the worry over both pregnant girls made her careless and she broke the milk jug – just watched it slip from her fingers, hit the towel rail on the range and fall onto the floor.

Peggy wasn't normally superstitious, but after the emotional whirlwind of the past two days, the sight of those broken shards of china seemed to augur impending doom. She looked down at them through welling tears, and bent to gather them together.

'Ow! Damn and blast it,' she hissed as a sharp splinter sliced into her finger.

'Mum? Whatever's the matter?' asked Anne.

'I broke the milk jug and cut myself,' she replied, her voice choked with tears as she watched a bead of blood blossom on her finger. 'So stupid of me to be so careless.'

Anne reached for the dustpan and brush which were kept under the sink. 'It's just a small jug, Mum,' she said, calmly sweeping up the pieces. 'And there was no milk in it, so there's no reason to cry over it.'

'I know, but that's not the point,' she sobbed. 'I've had the blasted thing for years.'

Anne put down the dustpan and brush and took her mother's hand. 'You'll need a plaster on that,' she said.

'It's nothing, really,' she replied, desperately trying to stem her tears but failing miserably.

'Then what is it, Mum?' Anne asked softly, her brown eyes concerned. 'Why are you so upset over some silly old jug?'

'It's not the jug,' she sobbed. 'I'm just upset that Fran's feeling unwell and Ivy seems determined to rush about like a mad thing with no thought for the baby she's carrying.'

Anne frowned and gave her a handkerchief. 'Is that really all it is, Mum? Only I've had the sense that something's been troubling you these past two days.'

Peggy could no longer hold back the great tide of sorrow and disappointment, and she all but collapsed against Anne. 'It's your father,' she howled. 'He won't be home for Christmas.'

Anne held her close. 'Oh, Mum,' she sighed. 'Why didn't you say something earlier instead of bottling it all up like this?'

Now the dam had burst, Peggy felt slightly better and was able to check the tears and get her emotions back under control. She gently drew back from her daughter's arms and mopped her face with the handkerchief.

Taking a deep breath, she released it on a long sigh. 'The telegram came the evening of Rita's party. Then there was the wedding, and all the comings and goings this morning. I couldn't spoil things for everyone, could I?'

'It was certainly bad timing,' Anne murmured. 'Did he say why he couldn't come home?'

Peggy shook her head. 'He promised to write and explain, so I'm hoping to get a letter very soon.' Needing something to do, she took the dustpan from the table and emptied the broken crockery into the small rubbish bin she kept under

95

the sink. 'The bloody army better have a damned good reason for keeping him, that's all I can say,' she said fiercely.

Anne smiled and kissed her mother's damp cheek. 'Come on, Mum, let me find a plaster to put on that cut, and then I'll make the tea. Will you be all right telling Grandma Cordy about Dad, or do you want me to do it?'

Peggy dredged up a smile and used all the inner resources she'd come to rely upon over these past years to pull herself together. 'I'm perfectly capable of doing it myself, darling. Just ignore those silly tears – I'm quite, quite over them now.'

5

The day had been a busy one, for which Danuta had been quite thankful. It had meant she'd had little time to worry about Stanislaw's dire warnings over her return to Poland, and her meeting with him this evening. However, now and again she'd become distracted, and when she'd had to go back to the clinic for a third time to fetch something she'd forgotten, Sister Higgins, the senior district nurse, had not been best pleased.

Danuta had managed to get through the day without mishap and she was now back at the clinic to clean her instruments and restock her medical bag. Glancing up at the clock, she noted it was almost time for her to go home, and began to fret about how to get changed and back out of Beach View without Peggy wanting to know where she was going, and with whom. Her reluctance to say anything wasn't because her meeting with Stanislaw was a secret – nothing stayed secret for long in this town – but she didn't want Peggy to get the wrong idea about things. After all, she reasoned, there was no harm in being friendly with Stanislaw, he was good company, and it was lovely to speak Polish again. Romance had absolutely nothing to do with it.

Danuta briskly polished the leather bag with a soft cloth and then washed her hands thoroughly before taking off her cap and unpinning her hair. It had been brutally hacked off by the Gestapo, but now fell in thick black waves to just beneath her jaw.

She ran a brush through it and wondered if she should leave it down for this evening or pin it up again. The Grove

97

was a very smart restaurant that had opened just off the High Street during the VE Day celebrations and was rapidly becoming very popular with those who could afford to pay the prices they charged. Which posed a set of problems she hadn't thought about when she'd rather foolishly accepted Stanislaw's invitation. She didn't think it would be right to expect him to pay for her dinner, but she couldn't really afford to 'go Dutch' as the others called it – and then there was the fact she didn't own anything halfway smart enough to wear.

She put her hairbrush back in her shoulder bag and decided the whole thing had become far too complicated and worrisome. There was plenty of time to telephone the sanatorium at Cliffe and tell Stanislaw she couldn't make it. She eyed the telephone, torn between wanting to see him and not wanting to see him, but before she could do anything, it began to ring.

'Sister Danuta.'

There was a pause as money was slotted into the public call box. 'I know it's the end of your shift, but I need you to get to Mrs Wilson at number seven, Exchange Lane,' said Sister Florence Higgins. 'She's gone into labour, and I'm held up here with Mrs Frost.'

'Mrs Wilson,' murmured Danuta, swiftly writing down the address and checking the long list of expectant mothers pinned on the board. 'This is her third baby, I see.'

'Yes, and if it's like her other deliveries, she'll probably be making a lot of fuss and have it quite quickly, so you'd better get round there sharpish before that husband of hers passes out. I gave her the delivery pack last week, so she's well prepared. I'm sorry to dump this on you, Danuta, but Mrs Frost is taking her time, and I daren't leave her as this is her first and the poor little thing is scared witless. If you need me, I'll be here.'

Florence disconnected the call and Danuta quickly noted down Mrs Frost's address in case someone had to fetch help.

She then pinned up her hair again, settled her cap back on and picked up her bag, along with a small canister of gas and air, and a blanket. With a quick glance at the clock, she hurried outside, stowed everything in her bicycle basket and set off for Exchange Lane. She wouldn't have time to phone Stanislaw now, but if Mrs Wilson had a quick delivery, then she might be able to get to the Grove before it closed.

The two-up, two-down terraced house was close to the telephone exchange which was situated in the lane that ran parallel to the High Street. Danuta leaned her bike against the wall and grabbed her things out of the basket. She knocked on the shabby front door, noting the peeling paint on the window frame, and the snow-white lace curtains that hung behind the gleaming glass. The step had been recently scrubbed, and a small tub of petunias stood beside it. Mrs Wilson was clearly house-proud.

'Thank goodness you've come.' The harassed man who opened the door had a squalling toddler clinging to one leg and another squirming and hollering on his hip. 'The wife's upstairs screaming blue murder – which is upsetting the kids.'

'Thank you, Mr Wilson. I will go straight up while you see to the children.'

Mr Wilson disappeared with them into the back of the house and Danuta hurried up the uncarpeted stairs. She followed the sound of the yells coming from the front bedroom and pushed open the door.

'Now, now, Mrs Wilson,' she soothed the red-faced woman in the bed. 'What is all this noise?'

'It bloody well hurts,' she snapped. 'You'd yell too if you felt you were trying to push out a flaming wrecking-ball. None of the others were like this. Something's wrong, I just know it, and Fred's worse than bloody useless.'

'Your husband can't really do much in the circumstances,' Danuta said, putting her bag down on the bedside table. 'But I'm here now, so we'll get through this together.'

'Yeah, this is flaming women's work,' Mrs Wilson growled. 'We always get the rough end of the stick, don't we?'

Danuta reached into her bag for her stethoscope and slung it round her neck. 'Let me examine you, Mrs Wilson, and then I will make you more comfortable.'

'I don't see how,' she complained with a grimace. 'This baby seems determined to stay where it is, and has been giving me gyp all bloody day.'

Danuta gently felt the woman's hard, swollen belly to determine how the baby was lying and to give her some idea of how big it was and if the head was engaged. Satisfied that all seemed well, she listened to the baby's heartbeat and then examined her internally.

'Baby is well on the way,' she said cheerfully. 'And you're almost fully dilated, so it shouldn't be long now.' She grinned at Mrs Wilson. 'It feels as if you've got a real whopper in there.'

'Tell me about it,' the woman groaned. 'It's been like lugging a bag of coal about these past weeks.' She tensed as she felt the onset of another labour pain. 'Oh, Gawd, here we go again.'

Danuta took her hand and timed the contraction. 'Do try and relax and breathe through the pain as you were taught at the clinic. It will help enormously, believe me.'

The woman eyed her belligerently, but calmed down and began to puff and blow as the pain swelled and finally ebbed.

'When did the pains begin?' asked Danuta. 'And how far apart are they?'

'My back's been niggling all day, but it really started when I was scrubbing the front step and my waters broke. Bloody embarrassing it was, I tell you. The neighbours must have thought I'd wet myself.' She gave a sigh and squirmed around in the tangled bed trying to get comfortable against the pillows. 'They're about five minutes apart at my reckoning, and getting more painful.'

Danuta thought it was probably closer to two minutes, but said nothing as she plumped the pillows and pulled off the blanket and eiderdown, leaving just a sheet to cover her as it was warm in the neat little room. She saw that the bottom sheet had already been replaced by a rubber one, the cot was ready, and a small, clean white sheet had been prepared to wrap the baby in. But there was no jug of water, or bowl to wash in.

'You look very hot,' she said. 'Would you like me to sponge you down?'

'Yeah, that would be nice,' Mrs Wilson replied, pushing back her hair from her sweating face.

Danuta went to the door and called down for the husband to bring up a bowl and jug of warm water, and reached into her bag for a flannel, bar of soap and a small clean towel.

Minutes later, Mr Wilson duly arrived carrying the water. 'Has she had it yet? Only I don't know what to do about the kids' tea.'

'No, I bloody well haven't had it yet,' snapped his wife. 'Go and get fish and bloody chips.'

'It's Sunday,' he said with a hapless droop to his shoulders. 'The chippy's shut.'

Mrs Wilson glared at him and then began to groan as she was gripped by another contraction. 'Sort him out, Sister. He's driving me up the wall.'

'I cannot leave you,' said Danuta, giving up on trying to wash her. She turned to Mr Wilson who'd gone quite green and looked about to faint. 'There will be things in the cupboard,' she said, firmly pushing him out of the room. 'Fish fingers, beans on toast, bread and jam, perhaps?'

'I dunno,' he mumbled.

'Then you must find out, Mr Wilson. Your children are hungry.' She shut the door on him and went back to check on Mrs Wilson who was now straining hard to push the baby out.

101

'Don't push, but pant,' she ordered. 'That's it. Like a dog. If you push too hard too soon, you will tear and I will have to stitch you, and that will be most uncomfortable.'

She quickly checked on the baby's progress down the birth canal. 'The baby has crowned. Gently now, gently does it. Now you may push – but not too hard.'

Mrs Wilson didn't need telling twice and she strained and groaned and panted, and with a mighty roar she delivered the baby's head which was swiftly supported in Danuta's hands.

Danuta checked that the cord was free and not around the baby's neck, and then encouraged Mrs Wilson to push again as hard as she liked when the urge came.

Mrs Wilson gripped the sides of the bed and bore down with great determination, and Danuta caught the slippery little body, quickly cleaned the mucus from its nose and mouth and was rewarded with a lusty cry.

'You have beautiful very big boy,' she said, clamping the cord and tying it off before cutting it free.

'Oh, bloody hell,' Mrs Wilson sighed. 'I might have known after all that. I was hoping for a girl this time.'

Danuta wrapped the bawling baby in the clean sheet. 'He is very beautiful,' she said, hoping this would encourage the mother to take interest in him.

Mrs Wilson grinned. 'He's certainly got a good pair of lungs on him. Give him here, Sister, and let me see who he takes after.'

Danuta carefully transferred the squalling infant into his mother's arms, then went to wash her hands in the rapidly cooling water.

'Gawd help me, he's the image of Fred's dad,' chuckled Mrs Wilson. 'Poor little soul; what a way to start out in life, eh? No wonder he's making such a racket.' Despite her complaining, she crooned over him and soothed his cries by letting him suckle.

As Mrs Wilson seemed to have got over her initial disappointment, and was now happily feeding her baby, Danuta went to the door. 'I will ask your husband for more hot water,' she said.

She opened the door to find him and the small boys on the landing. 'It is another boy,' she said delightedly. 'Please get me more water – lots of it this time.'

'Can we come in?' asked Mr Wilson.

'Not yet. I will tell you when she is ready for visitors,' Danuta replied, closing the door firmly.

'Oh, my Gawd,' yelled Mrs Wilson, almost dropping the baby as she grabbed her stomach. 'It's started again. What's happening, Sister?'

Danuta quickly took the furiously protesting baby from her, laid him in the cot and hurriedly examined her. 'Mrs Wilson, I am thinking there is another baby.'

'No! There can't be!' she yelled. 'No one said nothing about two of them and—' Her protests were cut short by a piercing shriek as she was assailed by a strong labour pain. 'Oh, Gawd,' she sobbed. 'I don't flaming believe this.'

Mr Wilson chose that moment to knock on the door and open it a crack. 'I've got the water. What's happening? Is Kate all right?'

'Oh, I'm just fine and dandy,' yelled Mrs Wilson. 'What you flaming think's going on?'

'I don't know. How can I if you won't let me in?' he shouted back.

Danuta saw a grey, worried face staring wide-eyed round the door. 'Leave the bowl on the floor,' she ordered, 'and then leave. I cannot have you fainting.'

The bowl was placed on the floor by the bed, and with one terrified glance at his wife, Mr Wilson shot back out of the room and shut the door.

Danuta eyed the bowl, noting there was no steam rising from it. She quickly dipped her finger in and gave a cluck of annoyance. Mr Wilson had clearly needed to be told it should be warm water, for it was stone cold, and of no use at all.

She returned her attention to Mrs Wilson. 'Now, you know the drill, Mrs Wilson,' she said above the sound of the bawling baby in the cot. 'Relax, relax and pant, don't push. This one isn't going to wait.'

With much yelling, swearing and groaning from Mrs Wilson, and to the accompaniment of the first baby's demanding wails, the second baby's head was crowned.

'Stop pushing,' ordered Danuta sharply. 'The cord is round the neck.'

'But it'll be all right, won't it?'

Danuta didn't reply for she was concentrating on getting her fingers between the fragile neck and the pulsating cord. 'Do *not* push,' she said firmly. 'You must just keep panting no matter how strong the urge is to push this baby out.'

Mrs Wilson sobbed and panted, the baby boy roared his displeasure from the cot, and Danuta fought to get purchase on the slippery cord which kept eluding her grip. Her pulse was racing and sweat was stinging her eyes as she finally managed to hook the cord over the baby's head and away from danger. She searched for a pulse in the baby's neck and felt nothing – it was in trouble.

'Push now, Mrs Wilson. Push as hard as you like,' she said quietly and with far more calm than she actually felt.

The underweight baby girl slid from her mother into Danuta's hands and lay there as limp and waxen as a rag doll.

Danuta swiftly cleared the baby's nose and mouth and tied off the cord, then began to rub the inert little body with a towel.

'What's the matter?' screamed Mrs Wilson. 'Why isn't it crying?'

Danuta massaged the tiny chest, her heart thudding with dread as it remained lifeless. She held the baby up by the feet and slapped its bottom, but still there was no response.

With Mr Wilson yelling from the hall, the baby boy howling in the cot, and Mrs Wilson in hysterics it was hard to concentrate. But Danuta shut out everything as she determinedly tried to bring life to the little one she'd just delivered.

However, long moments passed, and the massage clearly wasn't working. There had been no response to the second slap – and even several puffs of oxygen into that tiny mouth had done no good. And then her gaze fell on the bowl of cold water and she realised there was one other thing she could try. It was unorthodox, but she'd seen it work before, and this tiny scrap deserved her very best efforts.

She picked up the baby and knelt on the floor to immerse her frail body in the cold water. There was no reaction, so she lifted her out, rubbed her roughly dry, and tried again. 'Come on, little one. Come on, breathe,' she whispered urgently.

'What you doing?' screamed Mrs Wilson who was now leaning over the side of the bed and watching in horror. 'Are you trying to drown my baby?'

'No. I am trying to get her to breathe,' said Danuta, once more plunging the tiny girl into the icy water and praying she was doing the right thing.

This time, baby's chest heaved at the shock and her frail arms and legs stiffened as she took her first breath and weakly began to cry. On the brink of tears, Danuta swiftly wrapped her in a clean towel, and got to her feet.

'I make shock to help her breathe,' she said, her legs trembling with relief as she laid the baby in Mrs Wilson's arms. 'You have your daughter, Mrs Wilson, but now your husband must telephone for ambulance.'

Mrs Wilson burst into noisy tears as she cradled her tiny baby. 'She's so small. Will she pull through all right?' she asked fearfully.

'We must get her to hospital,' said Danuta, unwilling to promise anything in the circumstances. She opened the door to once again find an ashen-faced Mr Wilson standing there.

'You must telephone for ambulance immediately,' she ordered, cutting off his questions.

He shot off down the stairs and Danuta turned back to Mrs Wilson. 'She is very small, which is why no one realised she was there behind her big brother,' she explained calmly to the distraught mother. 'But she is now breathing, and that is good. The hospital will look after you all.'

Leaving the newborn in her mother's arms, Danuta quickly cleaned up the baby boy with the tepid water in the bowl on the bedside table, and dressed him in the hand-knitted layette that had been stacked in the cot. Then she delivered Mrs Wilson's afterbirth, gave her a good wash, changed her into a clean nightdress and brushed her hair. She'd just finished cleaning the tiny girl when she heard the urgent clanging of the ambulance bell.

Mrs Wilson pointed her in the direction of the drawer holding more baby clothes, and Danuta dressed the under-weight baby which was now mewling to be fed, and wrapped her snugly into a blanket.

'There we are,' she crooned. 'All lovely and cosy.' Handing her to Mrs Wilson, who immediately put her to her breast, she smiled. 'Well done, Mrs Wilson. It's been a bit of an ordeal, I know, but they'll look after you and the babies in the hospital.'

'What about Fred and the kids?' she fretted as the heavy footsteps of the ambulancemen approached up the stairs. 'He won't be able to cope on his own.'

'He will manage because he will have to,' soothed Danuta. 'I will see that the boys have eaten and explain everything to your husband, so please don't worry about anything.'

Tears shone in Mrs Wilson's eyes as she reached for Danuta's hand. 'Thanks ever so,' she breathed. 'I dunno what we'd have done without you.'

The ambulance took Mrs Wilson and her two babies off to hospital, leaving Mr Wilson dithering anxiously on the doorstep.

'Come along,' said Danuta, rounding up the two children and steering them towards what she guessed would be the kitchen. 'Mummy will be back in a couple of days, so Daddy and I will write list for shopping and then get you ready for bed.'

Having done the list and organised Mr Wilson into clearing up the tea things and preparing the boys for bed, Danuta went back upstairs to clean and tidy the bedroom. She put clean sheets on the bed, changed the damp pillowcases and remade the cot. Then she packed her bag, wrapped the afterbirth in newspaper and carried the dirty laundry downstairs.

Placing the newspaper parcel in the dustbin outside, and the laundry beside the sink in the outhouse, she returned to find Mr Wilson settling into a kitchen fireside chair with a picture book and both little boys on his lap in their pyjamas.

'As you will see, I have put the dirty bed linen in the sink outside, and have tidied your bedroom. Mrs Wilson has done you proud today, giving you another son and a little daughter, so it is now time for me to go home.'

He looked up from the book and smiled shyly. 'Thanks for all you done,' he said. 'I'll get the shopping first thing and see to these two.' His worried gaze settled on her. 'Kate and the babies will be all right, won't they?'

'I do believe they will,' she said firmly. 'Mrs Wilson and your new son are most robust. But your little girl is very small and weak, so it could be some time before she is able to come home.'

'Will you stay for a cuppa? It's the least I can offer after all you've done tonight.'

Danuta caught sight of herself in the mirror above the hearth and noted that it was now almost ten o'clock. She couldn't possibly turn up at the Grove looking like this, even if Stanislaw had waited for her as he'd promised – and even if she went home to change, the place would have closed by the time she got back there.

'Thank you. A cup of tea would be most welcome,' she sighed, sinking gratefully into a chair.

The cup of tea had revived her somewhat, and out of curiosity she'd cycled past the Grove on the way back to the clinic. It was all in darkness and the street was deserted. Stanislaw had clearly not waited, but then she could hardly have expected him to hang about in his condition.

Danuta sorted out her instruments, restocked her bag and stuffed her dirty apron in the laundry basket. She took off her cap, brushed out her hair and headed back outside to her bicycle. Smothering a vast yawn, she slowly pedalled home, still a little shaken by the traumatic events of the evening.

Parking her bicycle alongside the deckchairs beneath the sheet of tarpaulin, she trudged into the basement of Beach View and up the steps to the kitchen.

'There you are at last,' said Peggy brightly. 'We were wondering where you'd got to.'

'I say to Peggy she not worry. You working and something important must have happened to keep you so late.' Stanislaw struggled to his feet from the fireside chair.

Shocked to see him in Peggy's kitchen, Danuta's fogged and weary mind couldn't form a reply and she just stared at him.

'I did wait for you as I promised,' he said. 'But they close early on Sundays, so I had to leave. I hope you are not angry that I come here?'

'No, not at all,' she stammered. 'Just a bit surprised.' She dumped her medical bag on the table and took off her coat. 'I'm sorry if I appear rude, but it's been a difficult night.'

'You haven't eaten either,' said Peggy. She quickly uncovered the plate on the table to reveal ham, potatoes and salad. 'Mary brought the ham and the pickles,' she explained, placing jars and a plate of bread and margarine on the table.

'Now sit down and enjoy all that while I make another pot of tea.'

Stanislaw seemed to sense she would feel awkward eating in front of him, and reached for his coat and hat. 'Now that you are home safely, I will leave you to relax and enjoy your supper,' he murmured.

Danuta instantly felt guilty. 'You don't have to go,' she said.

'But I must.' He smiled down at her and reached for her hand. 'You are tired and hungry, little one. I shall telephone tomorrow, if I may, and arrange another outing.'

'But how will you get back to Cliffe?'

'Ron has very kindly offered to take me. He will be waiting outside now, I think, as he said he would be here at this time.'

Danuta smiled up at him. 'I'm sorry all your plans were spoiled, but babies come when they are ready regardless of how inconvenient it might be.'

He kissed her hand. 'To see you smile is worth the wait.' He turned to Peggy and kissed her cheeks. 'We will meet again, beautiful lady,' he murmured before turning away and slowly walking into the hall with Peggy fluttering nervously behind him in case he should trip or fall.

Danuta watched as Ron leapt out of Rosie's car to help him down the steps, and once he was settled in the passenger seat, Stanislaw waved to her and Peggy, and Ron drove away.

Peggy closed the front door and grinned. 'Well, well, Danuta. You are a dark horse, aren't you?'

Danuta blushed. 'I don't know what this dark horse means,' she muttered.

'It means you kept your date with Stanislaw a secret, you naughty girl.'

'Was not a date,' she said. 'It was just for dinner.'

'You can call it what you like,' said Peggy on a chuckle. 'But that man is smitten with you, and I get the feeling you're not exactly immune to him.'

'You are too romantic, Mama Peggy,' she replied, heading for the kitchen. 'You see things that are not there.' She sat down at the table and tucked into the ham salad. 'Thank you for keeping this for me. I am very hungry.'

Peggy refreshed the teapot and put a cosy over it. 'So what happened tonight to keep you so late?' she asked.

As she ate, Danuta explained about the twins and the heart-stopping moment when she'd thought the little girl wouldn't survive. 'All is well now, I think. She should thrive in the hospital incubator, and Mr Wilson will find he can cope with the boys if he doesn't panic like he did earlier.'

'They're a lovely couple,' said Peggy. 'Kate wears the trousers, though, because Fred can be a bit dithery and needs a strong woman to guide him in the right direction. He'll be lost without her. Perhaps I should pop in tomorrow evening with a bit of that ham and some pickle, and make sure he's coping.'

'I'm sure he will be most grateful,' said Danuta. She smiled fondly at Peggy. 'You are very kind to everyone, Mama Peggy, and thank you for looking after Stanislaw this evening.'

'It was a pleasure,' she replied, lighting a cigarette. 'He's a really intelligent, interesting man when he's not trying to charm the pants off everyone.' She took a puff of her cigarette and then her expression became solemn. 'He told me how dangerous it would be for you and Solly to try to go back to Poland, and begged me to dissuade you both.'

'I have listened and will try to find out more before I decide,' Danuta told her.

'Solly isn't a well man, Danuta, and no matter how urgently he needs to find the surviving members of his family, it's not wise to risk his life – or yours, for that matter. Have you discussed the dangers with him?'

'I have been very busy all day and not had the chance, but I will see him tomorrow to talk it over.' Danuta finished the cup of tea and went to the sink to wash her supper dishes.

'We all want to go back, Mama Peggy. Poland is in our hearts, no matter how happy we have found it here.'

'Of course I understand the pull of one's country. I'm sure I'd feel the same if I was forced to live in exile. But you've been through enough, Danuta, and the thought of you endangering your life again fills me with dread.'

Danuta dried her hands and put her arms gently round Peggy's neck to kiss her cheek. 'I will of course think very long and hard before I decide what is best,' she murmured. 'Now, I must go to bed. I am tired.'

Despite the bone-aching weariness that consumed her, Danuta lay awake long after the house had settled for the night, the heartbreaking images of the people and places she'd left behind etched in her mind. Her home had been bombed, the pleasant, wealthy neighbourhood she'd grown up in utterly destroyed, the residents scattered.

She and the remnants of her family had been forced to rent a cold-water flat in Warsaw where they were subjected to frequent searches by the Gestapo, and had to witness many of their neighbours being rounded up and loaded into trucks, never to be seen again. The bitter winter combined with starvation and disease had taken its toll, and Danuta had buried her loved ones in the iron-hard ground before leaving to fight with the resistance. She'd continued to work with them, learning skills that would prove useful much later.

And then she'd helplessly witnessed the Germans slaughter her comrades and her lover, Jean-Luc. She'd escaped the same fate merely by chance, and knowing she was carrying Jean-Luc's baby, she'd taken the long, perilous journey through Europe to find sanctuary with her brother in England.

It had been to no avail, for her baby and her brother now lay at rest in St Cuthbert's churchyard.

She reached for the gold medallion Aleksy had given her and, clutching it to her heart, she rolled onto her side to look at the faded photographs that had survived her escape from Poland. Her family had been destroyed by this war and she was the only one left to remember them. If she went home and fell into Russian hands, they would soon discover that she'd been sought by the Germans for her work with the resistance, and death would follow – if she was lucky. Once she was gone, their family with its long history would be obliterated from memory.

Danuta gave a soft, tremulous sigh. She'd fought hard all through the war for the right to be free, and knew better than most how precious that freedom was, and how tenuous life could be. To disregard those precious gifts and endanger everything she'd striven for since leaving home would be an insult to those who'd perished. Her war was over, her fighting done.

Danuta turned out the light and closed her eyes. She would live the life she'd been granted, and fulfil the hopes and dreams of those who'd loved her, and whose spirits still walked beside her. It was the only gift she could give them.

6

Peggy had spent a troubled night worrying about what Stanislaw had told her, and as Danuta didn't seem to be heeding his warning too seriously, she decided she would take matters into her own hands. She left Beach View earlier than usual that Monday morning, and after dropping Daisy off at the factory crèche, she climbed the stairs up to Solly's office.

'Good morning, Madge,' she said brightly. 'How are you today?'

Madge looked up from her typing. 'I'm fine, thanks, Peggy, but I'd tread carefully, if I were you; Solly's like a bear with a sore head this morning.'

This didn't bode well, for she'd known Solly since their schooldays and his volcanic rages were not something she wished to provoke. 'Oh dear. What's upset him now?'

Madge shrugged. 'I have no idea, but Rachel's with him, and from what I've overheard, it's something to do with this hare-brained scheme of his to go to Poland.'

'Thanks for the warning, Madge.' She listened to the raised voices in Solly's office, took a deep breath and tapped on the door.

'What do you want?' roared Solly.

'It's me, Peggy. I need to have a word with you.'

'Then get in here and say your piece,' he shouted.

Peggy had faced Solly's rages before and knew they soon blew out like a summer storm, but they were still quite frightening, and so she steeled herself for the coming confrontation.

Solly was pacing the room, his cigar smoke forming a thick layer below the ceiling, while his wife, Rachel, opened the window. 'I'm sorry to butt in like this,' said Peggy. 'But what I have to say is important.'

'Then spit it out, woman,' he snarled.

Rachel turned from the window and gave an exasperated shrug of her elegant shoulders. 'I'm sorry, Peggy, but I don't know what to do with him today,' she said. 'He won't listen to a word I say, and if he goes on like this he'll have a heart attack.'

'Is this about the trip to Poland?' Peggy asked.

'Yes. And I hope you've come to try and persuade him out of it. It's sheer madness, Peggy, but he refuses to see it. Perhaps he'll listen to you.'

Peggy very much doubted it, for when Solly was in one of these moods he'd listen to no one.

'I am here, you know,' he rumbled. 'And I'm quite capable of making my own damned decisions.' He flung himself into his chair, making the springs groan beneath his weight. 'Danuta and I have it all planned, and we're going,' he said, forcefully stubbing out the cigar in the ashtray.

'Your doctor told you it would be madness to travel far in your condition,' said Rachel with tightly held calm.

'What does that *meshugana* know?' he retorted.

'He knows you've got high blood pressure which is putting a strain on your heart,' Rachel retorted. 'You pay him enough for his advice. It's a shame you don't take it.'

'If I might just say something,' interjected Peggy.

Solly raised his chin, his beady gaze warning her he was on the point of exploding. 'If it's more of the same, then you can keep quiet, Peggy. I have heard enough from Rachel.'

'Then clearly you haven't been listening, Solly,' she dared reply. 'Danuta has a friend – a Polish pilot who's kept up with the news back in Poland. He told me that now the Russians are in charge over there, it would be extremely dangerous for either of you to go, even though you both have British passports.'

Solly's face reddened further and his eyes became flinty. 'Rumours,' he said dismissively. 'Just rumours.'

'Stanislaw has first-hand experience of what the Russians are capable of and is in touch with people still living there who've warned him very strongly against going back.'

'Who is this man? What people? There's nothing in the newspapers about any sort of crisis in Poland,' said Solly belligerently.

'But you were warned you might not be safe there,' said Rachel. She turned to Peggy, her face lined with anxiety. 'I wrote to the Foreign Office as soon as he and Danuta started planning this trip, and was told it would be most unwise for any British citizen to travel into Poland until things are properly settled. And if he ignores the warning and goes, then the British government would not be able to assist him or Danuta should they run into trouble, as East Germany and Poland are now out of their jurisdiction.'

Shocked, Peggy sat down with a thump. 'Does Danuta know this?'

Rachel shook her head. 'The letter only came on Saturday morning, and although I tried to telephone, no one seemed to be at home.'

'I told her it was a lot of fuss about nothing,' said Solly. 'It's just the British diplomats protecting their own rear ends. Danuta and I are free citizens of this country with valid British passports, and should be allowed to travel where we wish.'

'Not if it's going to put your lives at risk,' retorted Peggy, her tone sharper than she'd intended. 'Have you given a moment's thought to how Danuta will fare if you got ill – or God forbid – got arrested?'

'Why should I be arrested?'

'I don't know,' she admitted. 'But you've got a hot temper, and if you're thwarted in any way, you're inclined to lose it and speak without thinking – and that could lead to all sorts of trouble, for you and for Danuta.'

'I would never endanger Danuta,' he rasped.

'Not knowingly,' said Peggy. 'But she had a life before coming here – a secret life – and if the Russians get an inkling of what that was, she could very well be killed – or sent to some labour camp in Siberia.'

'We know something of her other life, but not all,' he mumbled. 'But she is going back as a British citizen to nurse the poor souls who survived those awful camps. The Russians will have no reason to question her.'

'According to Stanislaw they don't need a reason to interrogate anyone,' she snapped. 'And that girl has been through enough, Solly. I will not allow it. Do you hear?'

'I hear, I hear you,' he barked. 'Oy vay, Peggy; the whole town can probably hear you.'

Peggy held his angry gaze and softened her tone. 'Then damned well listen to me, Solly. What about your heart? Do you really want to risk falling ill over there? Are you expecting Danuta to nurse you as well as everything else?'

Solly heaved an enormous sigh and threw his hands up in the air. 'My heart, my heart,' he stormed. 'There's nothing wrong with the damned thing. Why do you women keep on and on about it?'

'Because we both know you're likely to drop down dead one day if you keep this up,' shouted Rachel, banging her fists on the desk. She burst into tears. 'Solly, Solly. Please listen for once. I don't want to lose you, and yet you seem determined to kill yourself. And for what? They're all gone, Solly. Every last one of them murdered in the camps.'

Solly looked stricken. 'We don't know that for certain,' he breathed.

'If they'd survived they would have found a way to let us know,' she sobbed. 'Please, Solly, don't go. I beg you.'

He reached across the wide desk to take her hand, his face drawn with concern. 'Rachel, please don't cry. You know I hate seeing you like this.'

Rachel lifted her tear-streaked face to him. 'Then stop being such a stubborn old fool and listen to what we're telling you. You can't ignore your health, Solly, and if you go on like this ...'

As Solly hurried round his desk to comfort his wife, Peggy quietly left the room and softly closed the door behind her.

In answer to Madge's enquiring look, she managed a smile. 'Rachel's got him where she wants him,' she murmured. 'Her tears always work, and he'll listen to her now. I'd leave them to it for a while until things have calmed down.'

'He's changed his mind about going to Poland, then?'

Peggy nodded.

Madge gave a long sigh. 'Thank goodness for that. It was a fool's errand, wasn't it?'

'The lure of home and family is very strong, Madge. You can't really blame either of them for wanting to go back.'

Peggy left the factory and hurried along Camden Road, and then on up the High Street and the hill to the factory estate. Seeing Jack working in his motor repair shop, she gave him a wave before entering the small clothing factory unit and switching on all the lights. She still had time to spare before the workforce arrived, so she went into her office and telephoned Beach View.

'I'm glad I caught you, Anne,' she said. 'Could you leave a note for Danuta? Tell her not to go and see Solly until at least this afternoon. He and Rachel have a lot to talk over.'

'They're always falling out,' Anne said lightly. 'What is it this time?'

'The trip to Poland. And add to the note that Rachel had confirmation from the Foreign Office that it isn't safe to travel there at the moment. That should make her change her mind, if nothing else.'

'All right,' Anne said hesitantly. 'But you know how stubborn she can be. She might decide the risk is worth it.'

'I sincerely hope not,' said Peggy with a shudder. 'If she wants to speak to me, I'll be here all day.' She looked through the glass partition and saw the first few workers clocking in. 'What are your plans, Anne?'

'I meant to tell you earlier, that I got a letter the other morning from the people who've been renting our cottage. They're moving out two weeks earlier than planned, so I need to go up there and check that everything is as it should be. Martin's taking care of the girls until I get back, and then he's off to oversee the work on the airfield. I'm meeting Betty this afternoon at the new school. The headmaster has called for a staff meeting before the start of term, to show us around.'

'It sounds as if you have a busy day ahead of you,' said Peggy. 'But with your tenants leaving, will that mean you'll be moving out soon?'

'It will all depend on the state of the cottage,' said Anne. 'But with Auntie Doreen and her three about to descend this weekend, it will probably be better for everyone if we moved out. Three small girls make enough racket – I dread to think what it will be like with six little ones in the house.'

Peggy was rather looking forward to the chaos of a full house and the sound of lively children, but she did accept it might become intolerably noisy – and really, it would be good for Anne and Martin to be in their own home again.

Once she had disconnected the call she sat for a while, lost in her thoughts, and then decided there wasn't much she could do about anything. Things would sort themselves out one way or another, and she had work to do. But first she would telephone Doris and find out how John's back was doing.

Doris replaced the receiver and hurried into her bedroom to finish dressing. She was running very late, but then it had been a busy morning what with taking breakfast round to John and seeing to it that he was as comfortable as he could be lying on that board on the floor. Life would be very much easier if they lived in the same bungalow, but as it was, she was going back and forth like a pendulum.

She brushed her hair and grabbed her handbag, her mind already on all the things she had to do today – not only in the office, but in the town. With her wedding to John only days away, she was due for a final fitting at the dressmaker's, and still hadn't found the right hat to go with her outfit. She also had to book an appointment at Julie's to get her hair and nails done on the Saturday morning, and then go and see Rosie to discuss the idea she and John had had about the tenancy on her bungalow. It would be the ideal solution really, but it all hinged on what Rosie had to say about it.

A glance at her watch told her she was wasting time, so she quickly closed the front door behind her and rushed next door. 'It's only me,' she called from the hall. 'I hope you're decent.'

'I'm in the kitchen and very respectable, thank you.'

'You shouldn't be in here, let alone doing the washing-up. You know what the doctor said,' she fussed.

He carefully turned from the sink and dried his hands on a towel, his smile making his blue eyes sparkle. 'I'm fine, really, my dear. Please don't worry about me.'

'Oh, but I do,' she breathed, stroking back his thick silver hair from his temple. 'You've been in such pain and the doctor was most insistent that you lie flat on the floor – not be dashing about doing things.'

He kissed her softly on the brow and then grinned. 'I'm hardly dashing anywhere, dear heart, but I can't bear lying about doing nothing, and I really think that moving around is better for my back. It already feels so much easier.'

'That's probably due to those strong pills the doctor gave you,' she said worriedly. 'Leave all that and I'll make you a nice cup of tea before I go to work. If you're feeling well enough, then why not sit in the garden? It's a lovely day.'

'I'm afraid you're doing too much,' he said with a frown.

'Silly man,' she replied lightly. 'I've got enough energy for both of us at the moment, and besides, I enjoy looking after you.'

He smiled down at her and then slowly made his way out of the back door and into the neat vegetable garden where he sat rather gingerly on the bench.

Doris saw him wince and quickly took him out a cushion before returning minutes later with the tray of tea things. 'I'll pop in at lunchtime to make you a sandwich,' she promised with a loving smile. 'So you can stay here and enjoy planning what you're going to plant for the winter. Peggy telephoned to ask how you were doing. She missed us at Rita's wedding, and hopes you'll soon be better.'

'Of course I will,' he said stoutly. 'Nothing's going to make me miss our wedding.' He took her hand and raised it to his lips. 'I love you, Doris. See you at lunchtime.'

'I might be a little late back, so don't worry. It's just that I have things to do in town which really can't be put off any longer.' She kissed him softly on the lips and left the bungalow to walk to the factory estate.

It was a beautiful summer's day, the birds were singing, the sky was blue and her heart was light with love and happiness. She had so much to look forward to, and still couldn't quite believe how fortunate she was after the disastrous events that had led her to Ladysmith Close and her office work on the factory estate. She might have lost her home in a V-1 attack, and suffered the heartache of losing her estranged husband only to discover he'd left her almost penniless, but she'd found a home here, had reconciled with her sister, Peggy, and met the love of her life in Colonel John White.

It was an enormous disappointment that Fran probably wouldn't be playing at their wedding, but it was important the girl took care of herself. The only real cloud on her horizon was the worry over John, whose back was still being troublesome despite all his protestations to the contrary. She could only hope that the pills the doctor had given him would lessen the pain, but not encourage him to do too much which could aggravate things. She had little doubt that he would go through with their wedding come hell or high water, but she wanted him to be well enough to enjoy it and partake fully in the celebrations, and the week's honeymoon they'd planned in the Lake District.

She was still blushing at the thought as she arrived at the office. There was a stack of mail waiting for her, and various memos regarding the leases and rents on the small factory units. It seemed John had been right when he'd said the place would soon be buzzing again, for all the units had been rented out, and the conversion of the armament factory was in full swing, with applications already pouring in to rent one of the large spaces.

Doris opened the letters one by one and placed them in order of urgency on her desk. She could answer most of them, but a couple would need some advice from John before she replied.

The last letter was addressed to her in an unfamiliar hand, and she sliced through the envelope with the opener, wondering who would write to her here. Unfolding the single sheet of paper, she saw the signature at the bottom and her heart missed a beat. It was from John's son Michael.

Mrs Williams,

> *I received the invitation to your wedding with some surprise, as I'm sure you and Father are fully aware of my feelings on the matter. If this invitation is Father's way of trying to persuade me to accept the situation, then he's sorely mistaken, and I must decline the offer.*
> *Major M. White*

Doris's hand was shaking with fury as she folded the sheet of paper back into the envelope. She was tempted to tear it into a hundred pieces and commit it to the bin, for if John read it, he'd be deeply hurt. But she realised he'd have to know what his son had written if their new life wasn't to begin with her keeping things from him, no matter how good her intentions. She'd already witnessed his reaction to her having fibbed over something, and never wanted to see such disappointment in his eyes again.

'You're a nasty piece of work, Michael,' she muttered. 'And you should be ashamed of yourself.' She shoved the letter in her handbag, deciding she'd wait for the right moment to show it to John – if there ever could be such a thing.

Danuta had read Peggy's message with some exasperation. Peggy had clearly been unable to resist meddling, and although she'd undoubtedly meant well by going to see Solly, Danuta did wish she'd left things alone.

The revelation that the Home Office was advising British passport holders not to travel to Poland had come as a surprise, but it seemed to underline the dangers Stanislaw had warned her about, and went some way to easing her guilt at changing her mind about going. However, the tone of the message suggested that Peggy's visit to the factory had caused some disagreement between Solly and his wife, so she decided she would do her rounds before going to see them.

The morning flashed past as she dressed ulcerated legs and bathed the elderly patients who couldn't do it for themselves. She attended the ante-natal clinic straight after a lunch of Spam sandwiches, and once it was over, approached Sister Higgins.

'I am sorry to make things difficult for you, Florence,' she began hesitantly. 'But would it be all right if I took back my notice and stayed on?'

Florence's broad face broke into a beaming smile. 'Oh, my dear. You don't have to apologise. Of course you can stay.

I'm just so relieved you aren't going back to Poland. Dr Sayers and I were very worried about you.' She regarded Danuta fondly. 'What changed your mind?'

'I realised that this is my home now. I have Peggy and Ron, and work that I love. It seemed to me to be very foolish to leave when I have so many things here to be grateful for.'

Florence threw her arms about her and held her to her generous bosom. 'Dear Danuta, I'm so very happy you're staying – and I know Peggy and all your patients will be too. You've become an important part of our lives, and we really didn't want to lose you.'

Danuta enjoyed being cuddled by Florence, for it was like being embraced within layers of soft cushions, but still shy of such strong emotions, she gently disentangled herself. 'Did you read my report on Mrs Wilson?' she asked, straightening her cap.

'Yes, and you did very well, Danuta. It was a tricky one, and not always resulting in a happy ending. I've seen the trick with the cold water done once before, although I doubt the powers that be would approve. Still, if it works when nothing else has, it's definitely worth a try – as you proved.'

'I am hoping to visit Mrs Wilson later to see how she and the babies are doing.'

'There's no need, dear. I went in early this morning. Mrs Wilson is blooming, as is baby Daniel, and little Evie is safe in an incubator and expected to pull through as long as she doesn't get an infection.'

'Peggy will go to see Mr Wilson tonight to make sure he's managing,' said Danuta, packing away her instruments. 'But I think he knows he must cope and will do his best.'

Florence sighed. 'Yes, the poor man isn't capable of much and was turned down for enlistment on medical grounds. His nerves, I believe. But by all accounts he's a wizard when it comes to Cliffehaven's gardens, and the council know they're jolly lucky to have him. He planted the carpet gardens, you know – the ones on the bomb site of the Grand

Hotel. Lovely, they are. You should take time to go and see them while they're still at their best.'

Promising that she would, Danuta finished helping to clear away everything before setting off on her bicycle for her final two house calls. She felt lighter in spirit now she'd decided to stay, and the sun seemed to bring out the colours more vividly in the window boxes and small gardens. *Yes*, she thought. *I've made the right decision – but I still have to tell Rachel and Solly.*

Rachel and Solly Goldman lived at Starlings, a large house set back from the main road which led out of Cliffehaven and over the hill towards the next town. It wasn't as far away as the Memorial Hospital, but it was far enough, and the hill steep enough to leave Danuta fighting for breath that early evening as she reached the imposing gateway set into a high rhododendron hedge.

She waited to catch her breath before opening the gate and wheeling her bicycle along the neat brick path lined with pretty red flowers that led to the front porch which was smothered in roses and clematis. She loved this house, and never tired of drinking in its tranquil atmosphere.

Starlings had given temporary shelter to numerous Jewish refugee children who'd been sent to England when it became clear they wouldn't be safe in Europe, and both Solly and Rachel still kept in touch with them. The house was old and rambling, with whitewashed walls and dark beams beneath a thatched roof. The diamond-paned windows glinted in the late afternoon sun, and the heady scent of roses and clambering honeysuckle filled the still, warm air. Lawns as smooth and green as billiard tables stretched to the hedged boundaries on three sides, and the flower bed borders were positively bursting with colour.

Danuta could hear the busy humming of the bees as they flitted in and out of the flowers, and she stopped to watch some goldfinches swoop down to eat from the bird table, or splash in the ornate basin held in the hands of a stone nymph. She gave a deep sigh of pleasure. It was truly a paradise, and she could have sat in this garden for hours, dreaming away the day in these peaceful surroundings.

She reluctantly pulled the black metal rod by the door which rang a bell in the hall, and breathed in the fragrance of the cascade of pink roses which rambled over the porch.

'Hello, Danuta,' said Rachel, looking cool and svelte in a cream linen dress and strappy sandals. 'We were expecting to see you after Peggy visited this morning. Come in, my dear. We're in the back garden as it's such a lovely evening. Have you eaten? Would you like a drink?'

Danuta smiled, for Rachel was the consummate hostess, always worrying that her guests didn't have enough food or drink. 'I will eat at Beach View later,' she replied. 'But a drink would be welcome after tackling that hill.'

'Of course, of course. Everything is waiting outside.' Rachel touched Danuta's arm and drew her to a standstill in the large, galleried hall. 'Solly has been in a terrible mood all day, but I think I have persuaded him against going. The letter from the Foreign Office was the clincher, really. But it will do no harm for you to dissuade him.'

She regarded Danuta sharply. 'You *have* decided not to go, haven't you?'

Danuta nodded. 'Reluctantly, it seems wise.'

'Thank goodness for that.' Rachel put her arm around Danuta's shoulder and steered her gently through the hall into the elegant drawing room which had French doors leading out to a terrace overlooking the sweep of the back garden. 'Just tell him straight, Danuta,' she murmured. 'Then he can't argue.'

Danuta smiled at that, for Solly could argue black was white if he put his mind to it.

'Look who's here, Solly,' said Rachel cheerfully.

He turned his great head and eyed Danuta with all the welcome of a bad-tempered bulldog before he got to his feet. 'I suppose you've come to bully me too,' he stated.

'Not at all,' she replied. 'I've come to tell you I've changed my mind and will be staying here.'

'I see,' he muttered. 'So Peggy got to you too, did she?'

'It was entirely my decision,' she said firmly. 'And after hearing about that letter from the Foreign Office, I have concluded it was the correct one.' She sat down in one of the wicker chairs and Rachel handed her a tall glass tinkling with ice.

'A gin and tonic,' said Rachel, shooting a glance at her husband. 'Works wonders on tired bodies and bad tempers.' She raised her glass. 'L'chaim.'

Solly joined in the toast to life, then plumped down into the cushions of the sturdy wicker chair and glowered at the beautiful garden. 'Who is this man Peggy talks about? The Pole who put these ideas in your head, Danuta?'

'He's just someone I met at Rita's wedding,' she replied lightly. 'And it seems he was right to warn me if that letter from the Foreign Office is anything to go by.'

'Hmph.' He took a long draught of his drink, and then placed the empty glass on the table for Rachel to replenish. 'We will all go back one day, Danuta. That's a promise.'

'Yes,' she murmured. 'But until then we must give thanks for the beauty of this home we have here, and for the people who love us.' She smiled at him. 'Is it not said by the Jewish people that when we are no longer able to change the situation, we are challenged to change ourselves?'

Solly nodded. 'Everything can be taken from a man but one thing – the last of the human freedoms – to choose one's own way.' He smiled, bringing warmth to his dark brown eyes. 'You are wise for one so young,' he said softly.

She smiled back at him with great affection. 'I have a very old soul.'

7

Doris had had a rather splendid day, and if it hadn't been for Michael's nasty letter burning a hole in her handbag, it would have been perfect.

She returned to her bungalow in Ladysmith Close, and decided to try her new hat on once more before going next door to check on John. He'd been resting when she'd popped in at lunchtime, and seemed quite cheerful as he'd told her to enjoy her shopping trip and not rush back, so she was taking him at his word.

Doris lifted the hat from its box and carefully placed it just so on her head. Turning this way and that she gave a little sigh of satisfaction. The hat was navy with a broad cream ribbon tied in a bow at the side of the crown, and edging the wide brim, and as her cream dress and coat were piped with navy, it was just perfect. She had hoped Sally would make her wedding outfit, but she'd been so busy, Doris had been forced to find someone else, but the woman had proved to be most proficient, and Doris had been delighted with the result when she'd gone for her final fitting.

She returned the hat to its box and placed it on top of her wardrobe, eager now to see John and tell him all about her successful day – although she wasn't looking forward to showing him Michael's letter. Changing into more comfortable shoes and slipping on a cardigan, she went into her kitchen and collected the bowl of raspberries and the Woolton pie she'd made this morning for their supper and carried it next door.

John was in the sitting room, a sulky fire smouldering in the hearth, his face ashen and lined with pain. 'Hello, my love,' he said. 'I'm so sorry, but I can't get up. The pills seem to have worn off.'

Doris quickly put the pie in the oven and hunted out the pills. Fetching a glass of water, she went back to him. 'I really do think I should call the doctor again,' she said fretfully. 'There must be something he can do to get you right.'

John swallowed the pills and gave a sigh. 'There isn't really,' he replied. 'I damaged my back in the trenches shortly before the end of the First War. The medic got the shrapnel out, but the muscles around the spine were never quite the same, and when they go into spasm, I'm as helpless as a kitten.'

'Oh, John. I so wish there was something I could do to help.'

'A cup of tea would go down a treat, if you wouldn't mind, my dear, and once these pills kick in, I'm sure I'll be right as rain.' He caught her hand and smiled. 'Have you had a good day, my darling?'

'I'll get that tea and then tell you all about it,' she said, kissing his brow before hurrying into the kitchen.

She hated seeing him brought so low with the pain, for John was a vibrant, energetic man when he was well, and the knowledge that the letter she had to show him would do nothing to raise his spirits made her hesitate. She eyed the gas ring on the cooker, wondering if she should just burn the damned thing and pretend it had never arrived – and then was forced to accept she wouldn't be able to live with the guilt, so made the tea and carried it on a tray into the sitting room.

'Here we are,' she said brightly, setting the tray down on a low table between the fireside chairs. 'I've put a Woolton pie in the oven for our supper, and there are fresh raspberries from the garden with evaporated milk for dessert.'

He regarded her lovingly, his blue eyes brighter now the pain was being alleviated. 'I could get used to being spoilt,' he teased. 'So, tell me about your day. Was there much to do in the office? And how did you get on at the shops and with Rosie?'

'I brought a couple of letters I need you to look through before I reply to them,' she said, opening her handbag and handing them over. 'And there was a private letter addressed to me,' she added hesitantly as she drew it out.

'To you?' he asked with a frown.

Doris nodded. 'It wasn't a very pleasant letter, but I don't want you getting upset, John, because I've had the day to think about it, and have accepted there's really no point in worrying over something I can't resolve.'

His frown deepened. 'Who's been writing you unpleasant letters, Doris? Let me see.'

'It's from Michael,' she replied, still holding back from giving it to him. 'He's turned down our invitation to the wedding.'

'I rather expected he would,' said John. 'But there's no call for unpleasantness. Let me see that.'

Doris reluctantly handed it over and waited with bated breath as he scanned the hostile short note.

'I see,' he murmured, folding it back into the envelope. 'I apologise profusely for my son's lack of good manners, Doris, and I'm extremely sorry you had to read that.' He slowly and deliberately tore the letter to shreds and threw the pieces onto the fire. 'I think that's the best place for it, don't you?'

Doris bit her lip as she nodded. She could tell that despite his brave words he was deeply hurt by his son's rejection, and that although the letter was now burning to ashes, the message would remain with him for a long time. 'I'm so sorry I had to show you that,' she said quietly. 'But I knew I couldn't hide it from you.'

'Perhaps that was what he'd been hoping for when he sent it to you personally,' said John bitterly. 'He knows I hate secrets, and it would have driven a wedge between us if you hadn't been honest about it.'

'I know.' She poured the tea and lit them both cigarettes, deeply thankful she'd followed her instincts and not destroyed that letter. 'Apart from that, I've had a very productive day,' she said, changing the subject.

He smiled. 'You found a hat?'

'I did indeed,' she replied, glad to see him smile again. 'And you'll see it on Saturday – not before. My outfit is almost ready and looks very smart, and I managed to book an appointment at Julie's to get my hair and nails done on Saturday morning.'

'Clever girl,' he said fondly, the smile almost banishing the lines of pain and weariness from his handsome face. 'And how did you get on at the bank and with Rosie?'

'Rather well, as it happens,' she replied with a touch of smugness. 'I spoke to the man at the estate agency to get some idea of how much the bungalow is worth and, armed with this information, I was able to talk to the bank manager about a mortgage. He was quite agreeable to me taking out a loan as you own your bungalow outright, and I'm working full-time, and as it isn't for a large amount, he suggested a short-term mortgage with repayments that I can easily manage.'

'Goodness, you have been busy,' he said. 'How much will you be borrowing, Doris? I don't want you getting into debt.'

'The bungalow is worth about two hundred and fifty pounds on the open market, but I'm borrowing three hundred so we can have the work done to turn the two places into one.'

'And how did Rosie react to this idea?'

'She thought it was very sensible in the circumstances, and agreed to the offer of two hundred and twenty-five pounds.' Doris grinned. 'Oh, John, I know it will mean a lot of mess and turning things upside down, but when it's finished, we'll have the finest house in the road.'

'We will indeed,' he replied on a chuckle. 'Now, you're not to worry about the mortgage repayments, I'll help with those, and any extra work that might need doing to turn the two bungalows into a proper house. Why, we might even think about converting the attic into a large double bedroom, bathroom and dressing room. What would you think to that?'

Doris was aglow with happiness as she softly kissed his lips. 'It will all be wonderful as long as we're together, John.'

'Indeed it will, dear heart,' he murmured, 'and I can hardly wait for Saturday.'

Sarah returned alone to Beach View late that Monday night to find Peggy and Cordelia alone in the kitchen listening to the wireless. 'Gosh, you're up late,' she said, dumping her numerous shopping bags on the table.

'We've been celebrating Danuta's decision not to go to Poland,' said Cordelia. 'She's exhausted, poor lamb, so has gone to bed.' She regarded her great-niece over her half-moon glasses. 'Where's your sister?'

'Jane's staying on in London to spend time with Jeremy before we leave for Singapore,' said Sarah, taking off her hat and jacket. 'He's off to Washington soon, so they won't have much chance of being together for a long while.'

'It comes to something when you young girls gad about without the benefit of a wedding ring on your finger,' huffed Cordelia. 'I don't know what the world's coming to.'

'You look tired, Sarah,' said Peggy, who rather agreed with Cordelia, but kept her own counsel. 'Come and sit down and have a sherry. There's still a drop in the bottle.'

Sarah kicked off her shoes, sat down and gratefully accepted the glass of sherry. 'I feel as if I've walked the entire length and breadth of London,' she said after taking a sip. 'My poor feet are killing me.'

Peggy smiled as she glanced at the shopping bags. 'But it seems you've bought up half of London, too, so it must have been worth it.'

'None of it is very exciting,' Sarah said. 'It's not as if we're going on a pleasure cruise.' She wriggled her stockinged feet and gave a sigh. 'The temperature in Singapore will be in the mid-eighties and probably quite humid, so I've stocked up on cotton underwear and night things, a couple of light-weight day dresses, a linen skirt and two cotton blouses. I found a very nice pair of sunglasses and managed to get some make-up in Harrods. Anything else I need can be bought there.'

'So you're all set then,' said Cordelia.

'I suppose I am,' she replied, 'but to be honest, I'm not really looking forward to it.'

'That's hardly surprising,' said Peggy. 'Neither of you know what you'll be faced with, and the place is bound to have been changed beyond all recognition after the Japs took it over.'

Sarah nodded sadly. 'It's not the homecoming either of us dreamed about, and I dread to think how Mother will cope if neither of them have survived.'

'Jock is a Fuller,' said Cordelia firmly. 'The men in my family are as tough as old boots. I'm sure he'll come through.' She drained her glass and set it down. 'Let's not dwell on things we have no control over, it's too depressing. Where will you all stay out there?'

'Pops owned a bungalow we used for holidays on the Raffles Road, but it was flattened by the Japanese during their first attack on the island. I'm hoping that the Bristows' bungalow is still standing – we used it after Elsa had left for Sydney with her girls and the Brigadier moved into army quarters. It became a haven of sorts while Pops was trying desperately to get us passage on a ship.'

'And what if it isn't available?' asked Cordelia. 'The Bristows might need it for themselves.'

'That's certainly a possibility, so to be on the safe side, I went into Thomas Cook's this morning to see if they could book us into Raffles. It was no go, unfortunately, as the hotel has been requisitioned by the British Forces to accommodate their administrators. It seems they've taken over most of the hotels in readiness for the release of the Allied prisoners, so if the bungalow isn't available, we'll probably be camping out somewhere.'

She sipped the sherry. 'But there's one piece of good news. The flying boat will be leaving from Southampton instead of Poole, which will mean a much shorter train journey. Evidently, it was decided that the bigger harbour in Southampton was better placed, and a whole new pier and customs house are in the course of being constructed.'

'Well, that's a blessing,' said Peggy. 'Poole's miles away down in Dorset, and it would have taken you an entire day to get there.'

Cordelia's mind was clearly still on their accommodation, for she changed the subject back. 'I don't like the sound of you camping out, Sarah. What about your home on the plantation? Surely you could go there?'

'It's right up in the Malayan jungle and too far from Singapore, Aunt Cordelia. We need to be at the centre of things for when the prisoners are released, so we have little choice but to stay in Singapore. Perhaps, later when we know ...'

She saw that her hand trembled as she held the glass and quickly put it down. 'I can't begin to imagine how we'll find two men among the thousands that will be coming in, and can only pray that the Japs kept some sort of record of those they held.'

'With the British in charge again, things will soon be brought into order,' said Cordelia with all the certainty of someone steeped in British pride. 'I'm sure that if you tell them who you're looking for, they'll do their utmost to find them.'

Sarah found it hard to have faith in that, for with the chaos of so many prisoners pouring into Singapore, it would be like searching for a needle in a haystack. However, she didn't want to upset Cordelia by voicing this doubt, for none of them really knew anything, and why destroy the hope she'd clung to for so long?

'It seems everything is up in the air at the moment,' said Peggy. 'I got a telegram from Jim the other day, warning me he wouldn't be home for Christmas. I have no idea why, and as there was no letter from him in the post today, I'll just have to wait to find out.'

'Oh, Peggy, I'm so sorry to hear that,' sighed Sarah. 'I know how much you were looking forward to having him home. But perhaps he's being sent to Singapore as part of this new British takeover?'

Peggy sniffed and got to her feet. 'Yes, well, we can't all have what we want, Sarah, and, Singapore or not, it seems the army has more need of him than I, so I'll just have to lump it.' She filled the kettle and placed it firmly on the hob. 'Tea anyone?'

Sarah shook her head. 'Thanks, but not for me, I'm off to bed. I have work in the morning.' She kissed both women goodnight, gathered up her purchases and slowly went up the stairs to her bedroom.

Closing the door behind her, she leaned against it for a moment, dropping her shopping to the floor, and then sank onto the single bed. Contemplating the photographs of her family, she gave a deep sigh. She was dreading the journey, and what she might find in Singapore. But the die had been cast and only fate would determine the outcome.

Peggy poured the boiling water over the tea leaves, knowing the weak brew wouldn't really revive her, but she needed the comfort of a cup of tea, no matter how tasteless, to soothe her troubled spirits before she went to bed.

134

'I wonder if she's heard from Delaney again,' she said, waiting for the tea to steep.

'Not since he wrote saying he was in one piece and back in America,' said Cordelia, taking off her glasses and rubbing her eyes. 'And I doubt she will again as she told me she was quite firm about breaking things off with him.'

'She might have said she was,' said Peggy, 'but in her heart it was the last thing she wanted to do.'

Cordelia gave a deep sigh. 'It's all terribly sad, isn't it? Sarah's holding fast to her promise to Philip despite loving another man – and poor Sybil is determined to believe he and my nephew are alive. This journey to Singapore is fraught with disaster. I can feel it in my bones.'

Peggy thought about the broken shards of china scattering across her kitchen floor, and an icy chill feathered her spine. She chose to ignore it as she poured out the tea. 'There's nothing we can do about any of it, Cordy,' she said, handing her the cup. 'Especially not with this horrid tea. I must try and remember to buy some tomorrow.'

'You don't fool me, Peggy Reilly,' said Cordelia softly. 'I know you're worried sick about the girls, and still deeply upset by the news that Jim won't be home any time soon. But for all your strength and determination to put on a brave face, there are times when you must talk and let all those feelings out. I'm always ready to listen, Peggy.'

Peggy took her hand. 'I know, Cordy, and believe me I have cried and stormed and let it all out – and I've realised I just have to accept that I can't solve everyone's problems or change things.'

Cordelia smiled with deep affection. 'Well, that's a start, I suppose.'

Peggy came down from the bathroom the next morning with Daisy to find everyone but Martin and Danuta already at the breakfast table. She'd slept pretty well, for she was convinced a letter would come from Jim today, and was feeling quite sprightly. Sitting Daisy at the table with a bowl of cereal, she poured herself a cup of tea and put an egg on to boil.

'Martin's gone to see Jack about buying a good second-hand car,' said Anne. 'And Danuta dashed off early to get her rounds started so she could meet her Polish chap for afternoon tea.' She smiled. 'It seems she isn't quite so impervious to his charms as she's made out.'

'It's hardly surprising,' replied Peggy, setting the timer for the egg. 'He could charm the birds out of the trees, that one – and being Polish is an added bonus for Danuta, I'm sure. She must feel quite homesick at times, and I think she enjoys speaking her mother tongue again.'

'I'm sorry we didn't have much chance to catch up yesterday, Mum, but time just flew and once the girls were in bed, Martin and I soon followed. Both of us were worn out.'

'I'm not surprised. You both had a very busy day. So, what sort of state is your cottage in?'

'In pretty good shape considering we haven't been near it for years,' Anne replied, cutting the toast into soldiers for Rose and Emily to dip into their boiled eggs. 'Mr and Mrs Smethurst have looked after it very well – given it a coat of paint and done repairs as and when needed, and he's got a flourishing vegetable garden going at the back. I think they're rather sad to be leaving.'

Peggy felt guilty that she hadn't been over there to meet the Smethursts and keep an eye on the place, but what with one thing and another, there just hadn't been time. 'Where do they come from originally?'

'Sheffield,' said Anne. 'Their son wrote and told them he was home from the army and that the house was still standing – but empty – so they decided they needed to get back there before someone took advantage of it and moved in. Evidently the housing shortage is as bad up there as everywhere else, and people are camping out wherever they can.'

'So I suppose that means you'll be moving out at the weekend, then,' Peggy said sadly.

'We've decided to do it bit by bit, if that's all right with you, Mum,' said Anne. 'I'd like to freshen the place up a bit with new curtains and carpet and so on, and the kitchen and bathroom could certainly do with being modernised. But it shouldn't take long, and I'm hoping we'll be out of your hair by the weekend.'

Peggy felt a twist to her heart but plastered on a smile. 'You know I've loved having you here,' she said, 'and you're welcome to stay as long as you wish. But it's right that you and Martin have your own home again.'

Anne smiled. 'We know you've enjoyed having us, Mum, and we've loved being here. But it's time we went home, and we're both looking forward to it tremendously. Grandad promised to help with Frank and one of his plumber pals to update the kitchen and bathroom, and once they're done, we'll be all set to move in.'

'If your grandfather's in charge then be prepared for delays,' warned Peggy. 'He's very good at promising things, but he takes his time about actually doing anything.'

'I've promised to lend a hand,' said Charlie. 'We're going over there after breakfast to make a start on ripping out the kitchen.'

'Goodness me,' breathed Peggy. 'But what about the Smethursts?'

'They left yesterday afternoon,' said Anne. 'So the house is empty.'

'Oh, I see,' said Peggy and quickly left the table to see to Daisy's boiled egg. 'I'm sorry I can't do much to help, Anne, but what with work and everything ...'

Anne rose from the table and put her arm about her mother's slim waist. 'It's not as if we'll be far away,' she said quietly. 'And with the school just down in Camden Road, I shall probably see you every day.'

'I know,' she managed, scooping the egg from the boiling water. 'It's just that I've only got used to you being home and now you're leaving again.' She blinked back her tears. 'Ignore me, Anne, I'm being soppy.'

'I know you're finding it difficult, what with all the comings and goings,' murmured Anne. 'But if you get your car back from Chalky's barn and have Jack look over it, you'll be able to drive over and see us whenever you want.'

Peggy nodded, put the egg in the egg cup and placed it in front of Daisy. Tapping the top and peeling back the shell, she didn't need to urge Daisy to tuck in, for this was her favourite breakfast.

'That's a good idea, Anne,' she said, sitting back down to drink her tea. 'I might very well do that. Cycling all that way over the hills is beyond me, and I don't trust that seat on the back for Daisy. It's far too flimsy, and she wriggles about quite alarmingly.'

'I'll ask Uncle Frank to drive up to Chalky's and arrange to bring the car back,' said Charlie. 'I'll have a look at the engine if you like, Mum.'

'Thank you, dear,' she said on a smile, resisting the urge to brush his dark hair off his forehead. 'That would be kind, but I think Jack better give it the once-over as well. It's been up on bricks for years in that old barn, and I suspect the rats and mice have been having a field day in it.'

Charlie shrugged as if this would pose him no problem and helped himself to more toast. There was a commotion at the back door, then Ron arrived with the dogs, which burst into the kitchen with great enthusiasm to greet everyone and beg for any scraps that might be going.

'Come on, wee boy,' Ron said jovially. 'The sun's been up for hours and we've got work to do. You can eat that on the way.'

Charlie regarded him with a frown. 'Are we walking?'

'And how else d'ye think we'll get there?' asked Ron, his bushy eyebrows wriggling.

'Well, I thought you might bring Rosie's car,' the boy replied, pushing back from the table. 'It's a long way, and we'll have tools and things to carry.'

'Ach, so it's the life of leisure you'll be wanting, is it? To be sure, you have two fine legs to be walking, ye wee scamp,' he said, ruffling the boy's hair and grinning. ''Tis a grand day, so it is, and the walk will do you good.'

Charlie stuffed the last of his toast into his mouth and chewed on it as he grabbed the flat cap he'd taken to wearing lately. Shoving it over his thick mop of dark hair, he pulled on an old jacket over his dungarees and swallowed the toast. 'See you all tonight then,' he said gloomily.

'To be sure, 'tis a grand thing Frank has the utility outside,' said Ron on a sigh. 'So get a move on, boy. The day is wasting.'

Charlie looked at him askance at being so easily fooled. 'Grandad!'

Ron winked at him then headed back down the steps to the basement, the two dogs chasing at his heels.

Peggy couldn't help but smile as her son hurried after him. 'Ron certainly fooled him there. But he'll learn.'

'I'd better get off too,' said Sarah, pulling a cardigan over her light summer dress. 'It wouldn't be right to turn up late after having yesterday off.'

Peggy kissed her goodbye and as the girl hurried down the steps, she cleaned the egg from Daisy's face and helped her down from the table so she could play with Rose and Emily in the hall.

'How did it go at the staff meeting yesterday?'

'It's going to be a big school when it's finished,' Anne replied. 'As you know, they've built on the old school site as well as where the two blocks of flats used to be. The junior classrooms, main hall, staff room and gym are finished, but the seniors will have to use the prefabs until the rest is done – but that won't be for much longer, because the work's proceeding at quite a pace. The headmaster, Mr Rowney, was deputy head when I taught there before the war, so I know we're in good hands.'

'What are you going to do about Rose and Emily while you're at school? Martin won't be around much once the air-freight business is up and running.'

'I was rather hoping you could help with that,' said Anne.

'Oh, Anne, you know I don't have the time to babysit, however much I might want to,' Peggy replied on a sigh.

'And I don't expect you to, Mum. But the factory crèche would be ideal, and as I understand it, the numbers are right down at the moment with so many workers going back to their homes. I wondered if you could persuade Solly to let the girls go there. I would pay the going rate, obviously,' she added quickly.

'It's certainly a very good idea,' agreed Peggy, 'and Nanny Pringle is simply marvellous with them all. I'll pop in on my way to work and see how the land lies. But I warn you, Anne, he might not agree to it.'

'I know, but it's worth a try.'

'What's Betty doing about childcare for Joseph?'

'Now Brendon's back on the trawlers with Uncle Frank, he was hoping Pauline would lend a hand, but it seems she's far too busy with her office job at the Red Cross – and actually they don't really trust her to look after him properly. So they've found a nice, respectable little woman who lives nearby who is only too pleased to look after Joseph along with her own baby for a couple of pounds a week during term-time.'

'It's a great shame Pauline can't help. But I suppose I shouldn't be surprised.' Peggy was about to get on with the washing-up when she was alerted to the sound of the post being dropped into the wire box.

Rushing into the hall, she quickly sifted through the letters and, with a sigh of thankfulness, plucked out the one from Jim. 'It's from your father,' she said gleefully, placing the rest of the post on the kitchen table.

'Sit and read it, then, while I clear up,' said Anne.

Peggy's hand was trembling as she tore open the envelope and drew out the two pages.

Darling Peggy,

I know how upset you must have been to receive that telegram, but I wanted to tell you what was going on here before you heard something on the wireless that set you off into a panic. Believe me, sweetheart, I was truly shattered by the news as I know you must have been, and I'm still finding it hard to believe that it could be several months before I'll be allowed to come home.

I don't know what the papers have been saying, but I expect you've heard that now the Japanese are on the point of signing the unconditional surrender, the British government is determined to take back Malaya and Singapore as swiftly as possible. There will be a British Administration put in place to govern Singapore until there can be a proper general election – and in fact there is already quite a British contingent out there to keep order, mop up any resistance and begin the process of trying to find and repatriate our POWs.

We have just been informed that we're to be shipped over there as part of a vast land, sea and air force to take control, and assist the administration in dealing with those thousands of British POWS who will soon be pouring in. I understand that some of those imprisoned on the island and in Changi have already been released, but there's no way of knowing yet if Sarah's father or fiancé are among them.

I can promise you I will <u>not</u> be involved in any fighting, Peggy. We will be there simply to bring order, help rebuild, supply much-needed medicines and food and see to it that the poor souls who survived those camps of horror are given the very best care.

I've been unfortunate enough to witness the aftermath of the Japanese brutality, and the sight of once sturdy fighting men reduced to barely living skeletons is something that will haunt me until the day I die. I hope to God Sarah and Jane never have to

141

witness such a thing, and would advise them strongly to stay in England. The authorities will contact them with any news, and once I'm there, I'll do my very best to find out what has happened to Jock and Philip.

This is necessarily a short letter, for I have to pack and prepare for the sea crossing – which I'm dreading – but which probably won't be as awful as some of the rough flights I've experienced during my time here. Sea-sickness won't be half as bad as what it feels like to be bounced about in a small plane in the middle of a tropical storm with the thunder crashing and the lightning hammering against the fuselage until you can barely think for the terror of it all.

I love you, Peg, and I'm so very glad Anne, Charlie and the girls are back home with you to keep you company after what must have been long, lonely years without us all. I know you've had Cordelia and Dad and your chicks for company – but the comfort of being surrounded by your family cannot be beaten. Give my love to everyone, and I'll write again from Singapore.

Loving you always and for ever,
Jimxxx

Peggy handed the letter to Anne. 'Sarah was right to guess your father was being sent to Singapore,' she said. 'I'd better have a word with the girl this evening,' she added fretfully. 'God knows what she and Jane are heading into.'

8

The next few days went by in a flash, and so much had happened, Peggy was finding it hard to keep up with it all. Frank had towed her Ford down to Jack's garage, where Rita and Peter, fresh from their weekend honeymoon, set to work to replace the chewed wiring and hoses and give the engine a thorough service. The Ford had been old and temperamental before she'd stored it for the duration of the war, and now the leather upholstery had dried and cracked, and there were signs of a mouse nest in the corner of the back seat. The large headlamps were fogged and cobwebbed by damp; the chrome trim was going rusty; the windscreen wipers shrivelled to nothing, and it needed four new tyres as well.

As the cost of all the work began to spiral, Peggy hoped she'd actually be able to afford to run it, for petrol was still rationed and expensive, and the insurance premiums were high. But she consoled herself with the thought it would mean she could visit Anne, and not have to walk home from the town in all weathers lugging her shopping.

She'd taken a day off today to make all the arrangements, and now she was now putting the finishing touches to the large top-floor bedroom where her younger sister, Doreen, and her baby, Archie, would sleep. They were due to arrive tomorrow evening in good time for the wedding on Saturday. Evelyn was now almost eleven and her sister Joyce was eight, so they were too old to be sharing with their mother. Peggy had cleared out the second basement bedroom for them and brought a cot up for little Archie, who was barely over a year old. It had meant a lot of cleaning, sorting and chucking out, but it was worth it, for she knew Doreen would love being up here with the view of the sea, and the girls would be quite safe downstairs next to Charlie.

She tweaked the freshly washed and ironed curtains so they hung straight and stared out of the window, her thoughts still occupied with all that had occurred these last few days.

Doris had also retrieved her car from Chalky's, but it was in slightly better condition and hadn't needed as much work doing to it, so Charlie had been in his element giving it a service during the evenings. The news that Doris was buying the bungalow from Rosie was a bit of a surprise, but Rosie seemed quite happy to be shot of it as she was now seriously planning to sell the Anchor, and the money would come in handy for when she bought a house.

Peggy thought Doris and John were being very adventurous to convert the two bungalows into one, but she didn't envy them the expense and upheaval it would cause and it worried her a bit. Doris had already lost everything when her house in Havelock Road was bombed and she discovered her estranged husband had used it as collateral to pay off his debts to the bank, and therefore she wasn't entitled to any compensation. Now she was borrowing money to buy the bungalow and set up home with John.

Peggy knew John was a trustworthy, honest man who would never cheat Doris, but she did hope he'd have the foresight to ensure she would not be left homeless if anything – God forbid – happened to him. His son had proved to be a complete rotter, and Peggy wouldn't trust him to tell her the time of day – let alone honour his father's commitment to Doris.

Wiping a speck of dust from the windowsill, she turned her thoughts to lighter things. With Rachel's help and a good deal of coaxing, they'd persuaded Solly to allow Anne's children to attend the factory's crèche at a very reasonable rate. This had certainly relieved Anne of a good deal of worry, for the autumn term would begin next week.

Jack had managed to find a lovely little Ford with very low mileage for Martin which helped enormously now he and Anne were back and forth to their cottage on the other side of the Cliffe estate. Much to Peggy's surprise and relief, work was going well on refurbishing the bathroom and kitchen, for it seemed that having Charlie and Frank to chivvy him along meant Ron was actually getting things done and not merely talking about doing it.

She turned from the window and headed downstairs to check on the evening meal that Cordelia had prepared and put in the oven earlier. She didn't really have time to worry over everyone, although John's back was still giving him trouble, and his wedding to Doris was in two days' time, and Sarah seemed determined to keep her arrangements about leaving for Singapore – which was now less than two weeks away. It was Anne and Martin's last night at Beach View, and thanks to Frank supplying the fish, there was a lovely pie simmering in a white sauce beneath a thick potato crust in the oven, and she'd managed to put together a trifle, which would be a real treat.

She checked on the fish pie and moved the large baking dish into the cooler oven so it didn't dry out, and then placed the saucepans of sliced beans and garden peas on the hot-plates to simmer. Someone had already laid the table, she noted, so there wasn't much to do until it was time to dish up. She glanced up at the clock which was surrounded by all the photographs the girls had sent her, and smiled with great pride and affection.

There was Suzy looking radiant in her pregnancy with her little boy Teddy; Mary with her small son; Andy and Ivy on their wedding day; Ruby and Mike on theirs; and another of Rita and Peter taken on the church steps with Bertie's Box Brownie. Doreen had sent a snapshot of herself with her girls and baby Archie looking very happy on a rug in the gardens of the private school where she worked as a secretary to the headmaster.

There were photographs of Fran and Robert; Cissy in her taxi company livery; Anne with her two girls; and one of Jim, looking rakishly handsome in his tropical uniform and slouch hat; and last but never least was one of Sally with Ernie and her little Harry.

Another array of photographs graced the mantel in the dining room – all lovely reminders of the girls who'd come to stay for a while during the war. They'd been happy days despite the terrors of the air raids and the dubious protection of the Anderson shelter. And once some of them had moved away from Cliffehaven, they'd written to thank her and tell her how they were getting on, often sending little handmade gifts for her and Daisy to remember them by.

Peggy was still smiling as she went down the cellar steps to join Cordelia, Daisy and Sarah in the garden. She'd heard from quite a few of her chicks recently and it was a delight to know they were making new lives for themselves, but it was a worry that she'd had nothing from Ruby, but then she suspected she was taken up with finding her feet in Canada and had little time to spare. The fact that she hadn't heard from Jim since his last letter didn't worry her, for he was probably already at sea, making his way towards Singapore.

'Tea will be ready in about half an hour,' she said, sitting in a deckchair to watch Daisy playing in the sandpit with her bucket and spade. 'I hope everyone gets back in time, or that fish pie will ruin.'

'I've never known Charlie to be late for a meal yet,' said Cordelia wryly. 'My goodness, that boy can eat.'

'There's a lot of him to feed,' giggled Peggy. 'I'm sure he's grown at least another inch since he came home, and it's going to be the devil's own job to find a school blazer to fit him.'

'I get the impression that he's not too happy to be going back to school,' said Cordelia.

'He's had too much freedom and fun all summer, that's the problem,' Peggy said. 'But he's only got another year to go to get his school certificate, and then he can look forward to the engineering course at the tech. He'll soon make friends and settle in, I'm sure.'

Once everyone was home, the atmosphere in Peggy's kitchen was light and happy as they tucked into the delicious fish pie and Peggy questioned Danuta closely about her afternoon tea with Stanislaw.

'We had very nice tea, thank you,' said Danuta with a twinkle in her eyes. 'And tomorrow we will have morning coffee at Cliffe so I can meet some of his Polish friends.'

'I expect he's very relieved you've decided not to go to Warsaw,' said Peggy over the noise of Rose playing up and Emily grizzling.

'Of course,' she replied, the corners of her mouth twitching with a suppressed smile. 'Not that it is really any of his concern.' She finished her fish pie and pushed back from the table. 'I have some calls to catch up on as I was off for the afternoon. So if you would all excuse me?' She put on her cap, picked up her medical bag and left the house.

Peggy rolled her eyes. 'I give up trying to find out what's going on there,' she said to no one in particular. 'And it's most frustrating.'

Anne and Sarah laughed. 'You'll find out soon enough if she wants to tell you,' said Sarah. 'Honestly, Aunt Peggy, you're the most incorrigible romantic.'

'Mum sees romance everywhere,' said Anne fondly before turning sharply to her girls. 'Rose, sit still and stop banging that fork on the plate,' she ordered crossly. 'And, Emily, that's enough grizzling. If you both go on like this there will be no trifle for pudding.'

This blackmail worked for a while, but as soon as they'd eaten the trifle it became clear that both children would put up a fight when it came to bedtime.

'I don't know about you, Mum,' said Anne wearily. 'But I'm in no mood for a tussle tonight. How about we take a drive out to the cottage so you can see all the wonderful work that's been done?'

Peggy grinned and quickly cleared the table. 'I think that's a splendid idea, but how will we all fit into that small car?'

'I'm off to the rugby club,' said Charlie, scooping the last of the trifle from the bowl and licking his spoon. 'The fixture list for the coming season is due out, and I want to see who we're up against – and then I've got to finish Aunt Doris's car. She'll need it for Saturday.'

'I've got letters to write,' said Sarah. 'But I'd love to visit sometime in the next two weeks.'

'Well, I've got nothing to do,' said Cordelia huffily. 'Can I come?'

'Of course you can,' said Anne with an affectionate smile. 'We wouldn't dream of leaving you behind, Grandma Cordy.'

Martin pushed back from the table. 'Why don't you drive them up there while I go to have a chat with Roger and the others? I shall see enough of the cottage after tomorrow, and it won't be such a squash in the car.'

'Well, if you're sure,' murmured Anne.

He smiled down at her and softly kissed the top of her head. 'You enjoy showing the place off, Anne. I'll see you later.'

Once the dishes had been dealt with and the kitchen tidied, jackets and cardigans were fetched, outdoor shoes slipped on and they trooped outside to the Ford which was parked by the front steps. The sun was low in the sky, but it would probably still be light on their return as the summer days were long.

Peggy helped Cordelia into the front with Daisy on her lap, and then climbed into the back with Rose and Emily who promptly settled into her side and plugged in her thumb.

'I can't remember the last time I went out for a drive in the evening,' Peggy said. 'It feels as if I'm on holiday.' She giggled. 'Silly of me, I know, but it will be lovely to have my own car again and be free to come and go as I please. I have missed it.'

Anne merely smiled as she started the car and set off.

Peggy cuddled Emily and Rose as they sped up the hill and turned onto the road that would take them past Solly and Rachel's lovely house, the Memorial Hospital and out into the countryside beyond the Cliffe estate and towards the airfield. The smell of newly mown hay and cow parsley drifted in through the window on the warm, still air, and it was a pleasure to look out at the scenery. However, the weight of the small girls leaning against her was a sad reminder that she would miss not having her grandchildren to cuddle and spoil every day, but at least she would get to see them often once her car was roadworthy.

Rose Cottage was in a hamlet that nestled in the valley between Cliffe estate and the aerodrome. Warren Cross consisted of four cottages, an ancient church, an equally ancient pub, and a farm which belonged to Cliffe estate. The fields spread as far as the eye could see, and as they drove along, they watched a farmer and his labourers hard at work bringing in the wheat harvest.

'I suppose Bob's doing the same down in Somerset,' said Peggy wistfully.

'He's bound to be. And once that's done, he'll be ploughing and planting for the winter crops.' Anne slowed the car and turned down a narrow, rutted lane overarched by trees which threw dappled shadows over it. 'Now Vi's got extra hands on the farm, Bob will find things much easier, so don't worry, Mum. He'll be home for a visit very soon.'

Peggy nodded. 'Yes, he promised to come home for Christmas in his last letter. It will be wonderful to have you all there again after so many Christmases of being apart.'

She gave a tremulous sigh. 'If only your father could be with us it would be perfect.'

'He'll be with us in spirit, you can be sure of that,' Anne replied, bringing the car to a halt in front of a five-bar gate. She leapt out and unlatched the gate, pushing it as far as it would go into the hedge, and then climbed back into the car.

'You'll be amazed at what Grandad and the others have achieved,' she said, her voice light with suppressed excitement. 'And now we've got all our best furniture out of storage it really feels like home again.'

The little car ran smoothly over the newly gravelled driveway, and as it came round a gentle bend, they had their first sighting of the early Victorian two-storey house, which to Peggy's mind was really too big to be called a cottage since it had been added onto over the years and was fairly substantial.

Set in a garden ablaze with cottage garden flowers, the honey-coloured stone seemed to have soaked up the warmth of the day's sun. Harlequin roses of red and yellow tumbled over the porch, and the fresh white paint on the doors and window frames gleamed. It was an attractive, neat house, with four large windows and a central door beneath a shingled roof with a pie-crust trim. Today, it looked utterly enchanting.

'Oh, Anne,' Peggy breathed in delight. 'It is as pretty as a picture.'

'You wait until you've seen inside,' she giggled. 'You'll hardly recognise it.'

Peggy could only vaguely remember two rather shabby reception rooms, an old-fashioned kitchen and a poky bathroom downstairs, with four big bedrooms above them. When Anne and Martin had first moved in it had been empty for some time, so they'd done what they could to refresh it before Anne had had to evacuate to Somerset with Rose, and Martin moved into officers' quarters at the aerodrome.

Rose scrambled out as Peggy helped Cordelia and, with Emily on her hip, took Daisy's hand and followed Anne and Rose through the porch and into the narrow hallway which smelled of new paint.

Anne was grinning like a Cheshire cat as she took charge of the children. 'Have a wander round and tell me what you think while I put the kettle on for a cuppa, and give the girls some squash.'

Peggy could see that the hall floor had been sanded and waxed, and there was fresh sprigged paper on the walls above the newly painted white panelling. It looked much lighter than she remembered, and as she and Cordelia went through into the sitting room, she could see a similar transformation. The floors were again sanded and waxed, and the walls had been painted a pale yellow that made it feel as if the sun was always shining. There was a lovely original fireplace surrounded by beautiful tiles, and Anne had cleverly picked out the same colours in the curtains, cushions and floor rugs. It all looked lovely and cosy and she could just imagine the little family sitting around that hearth in the winter.

The room on the other side of the hall was painted white, and at its centre was a large dining table with bulbous legs and a shine you could see your face in. The eight chairs were upholstered in a rich, deep red which matched the velvet curtains that hung right to the floor and were tied back with tasselled ropes of thick gold cord. There was another original fireplace in here too, but for now Anne had filled it with an arrangement of flowers in a pretty vase.

Peggy admired it all, but thought that so much dark wood and deep red made the room rather sombre, but she supposed they would only use it in the evenings when it would actually look very luxurious and intimate – a far cry from her rather battered dining room which had become a dumping ground for unwanted furniture.

'This reminds me of my old house,' said Cordelia. 'I must dig out my silver candlesticks. They'd look lovely on that table with my rose bowl.'

'You've given Anne enough,' said Peggy softly. 'That diamond and emerald brooch was worth a fortune.'

'That was her wedding present,' she replied firmly. 'The candlesticks and rose bowl will be a house-warming gift to both of them, and I'll discuss it no further.'

Peggy realised no amount of argument would budge her, so followed her out of the room and down towards the kitchen where they both came to an abrupt halt. The room had been transformed beyond recognition, for it was now twice the size and there was no sign of the dilapidated cupboards, worn wooden draining board or faded lino.

The butler's sink now stood proudly at the centre of a smooth wooden work surface under which was an array of cupboards and shelves along with a very smart washing machine. The old range had been ripped out and replaced by a modern gas cooker, and there was a huge fridge standing in one corner.

The floor had once again been sanded, but instead of being waxed, it had been painted white to go with the walls, the cupboard doors, the fridge and washing machine. A large window took up most of one wall and overlooked the back garden where the previous tenants had planted a flourishing vegetable patch and a couple of fruit trees.

'It's a bit different, isn't it?' Anne was grinning with delight. 'Charlie had great fun knocking out the old bathroom and helping Frank and Ron put in an RSJ, so we could have a larger kitchen. What do you think of the fridge? It's American, and I bought it at auction when the Yanks were selling off their kitchenware. Super, isn't it?'

Peggy ran her fingers over the washing machine and enormous American fridge with awe and some undeniable envy. 'My goodness, Anne. You're very well set up, aren't you?'

'I know I'm lucky, Mum, but you're earning the money now, so why don't you do something similar at Beach View once you have the house to yourself again?'

'I wouldn't know where to start,' she confessed, opening the fridge to inspect the inside, and marvel at the way the light came on to shine on the shelves and special nooks and crannies for eggs and milk, and how the bottom compartment was to freeze things.

She closed the door and gazed around in awe, for the simple act of combining the bathroom with the kitchen had given Anne a large but homely space with enough room for a scrubbed pine table and four chairs. She couldn't begin to think how she'd achieve such a thing at Beach View – not with her bedroom, the chimney breast and the hall in the way and no room to extend back or front.

'But where's the bathroom now?' she asked, leaning over the pristine stone sink with its lovely brass taps to look out of the window.

'We turned one of the bedrooms into a bathroom, like you did at home all those years ago. Why don't you go up and have a look while the tea mashes?'

Peggy followed Cordelia slowly up the stairs which had a runner of dark red carpet that was held in place by shining brass rods. The bannisters had been painted white, she noticed, like the panelling, and the same pretty sprigged paper lined the landing walls. It all smelled so lovely and clean, without a hint of damp and not a cobweb to be seen.

The three bedrooms were all big enough for double beds, and Anne and Martin had taken the one at the back of the house which overlooked the lovely garden. The girls had a room each with matching counterpanes and curtains, their white-painted single beds giving them plenty of room for cupboards, shelves and toy boxes. Colourful rugs had been laid on the waxed floors, and framed prints from Beatrix Potter's enchanting books were on the walls.

Peggy sighed inwardly, wishing wholeheartedly that her little Daisy could have such a wonderful room instead of having to share with her. She turned away and headed for the bathroom.

'Oh my goodness,' she breathed as she opened the door. 'It's a positive palace, Cordelia.'

They stood in the doorway to admire the white tiles and new bathtub on clawed feet; the bright blue linoleum on the floor which matched the towels on the rail and the curtains at the frosted window. There was a sink with brass taps and a very posh lavatory, both bearing the gold insignia of the Grand Hotel.

'I see Ron's been up to his old tricks again,' tutted Cordelia. 'He must have been keeping those in his shed ever since the place was reduced to rubble by that bomb.'

'Oh well, at least it's saved them a bit of money,' sighed Peggy. 'All this work must have cost a fortune.' She wistfully closed the bathroom door and helped Cordelia back down the stairs, her imagination now on fire.

Beach View was looking decidedly shabby, and if Ron, Charlie and Frank were capable of doing such a fine job on Anne's place, then they could jolly well set to and bring it up to date. She'd pay them, of course, and get the experts in for things like electrics and plumbing, but seeing Anne's lovely home, and hearing Doris's plans for the two bungalows, she knew it was time to stop dithering and get on with it.

Returning home an hour later, she put Daisy to bed and plucked her bank book out from the bottom of her underwear drawer. Taking it into the kitchen, she lit a cigarette and then leafed through the pages. The sum she'd accumulated was quite impressive, and far more than she'd expected – but then most of her wages had gone in there, and a fair amount of Jim's money was regularly deposited straight from the Army Pay Corps.

'You're up to something, Peggy Reilly,' chuckled Cordelia. 'I've seen that expression before.'

Peggy closed the little book and grinned. 'Things are going to change around here, Cordy, and although it will mean a lot of upheaval and noise, it will be so worth it in the end.'

'Jim might have a word or two to say about that if there are too many changes,' Cordelia warned softly.

'I'll write and tell him my plans once I've got them clearly in my mind,' she replied. 'And when he comes home he'll be as pleased as punch. You wait and see.'

Cordelia pursed her lips, clearly not convinced.

Peggy put her arm about her narrow shoulders and gently hugged her. 'Just think, Cordy. We could have a new kitchen and bathroom – a freshly painted and papered hall with a new stair carpet – and a really smart dining room. Daisy and Charlie will have their own rooms upstairs, and I shall have the washing machine I've always dreamed of as well as a smart new fridge.'

She clapped her hands in delight. 'Oh, the bliss of never having to use that blessed mangle again,' she sighed. 'And won't it be absolute heaven not to have the milk and meat go off on a hot day – and be able to put the washing in the machine and just leave it while I'm doing something else? I shall have so much spare time I won't know what to do with myself.'

'I doubt you'll ever be idle, my dear,' the elderly woman replied. 'But please don't rush into things. I know you're excited now, and want what Anne and Doris have, but you need to think long and hard before you make too many changes.'

'Well, of course I will, Cordy. The whole enterprise will cost a lot of money, even with Ron, Frank and Charlie doing their bit, and I've never been one to rush into anything, as you know. Besides, nothing can be done until we have the house to ourselves again, so please don't fret.'

Cordelia smiled, but her eyes were troubled as she thought about Jim, who would have fond and lasting memories of his home, and expect it to be exactly the same on his return. What he would make of all Peggy's ideas was a mystery, but she had an uneasy feeling he'd be hugely disappointed to find it had changed beyond recognition.

9

Doris had been on tenterhooks all Friday, for although John's back seemed much better, she was terrified he'd overdo things and not be right for Saturday. She'd forbidden him to come into the office today as it involved a bit of a walk and a steep climb up wooden stairs to get to it, and had ordered him firmly not to do any gardening or heavy lifting.

Yet try as she might, she was finding it hard to concentrate on her work, for not only was she preoccupied with John, the purchase of her bungalow, her wedding and the delightful thought of having her son Anthony at home for a while, but she was also facing the imminent arrival of her younger sister, Doreen.

Doris wasn't really looking forward to seeing her again, for they'd never really got on, and the last time they'd met, Doreen had been insufferably rude and insensitive, which had properly put Doris's back up. But two years had passed and they were both more settled in their personal lives than before, so maybe it was time to mend fences.

However, she certainly wouldn't put up with any nonsense from Doreen, who to her mind wasn't leading an altogether respectable life. She might have a good secretarial job down in Wales, and be a loving mother to her children, but she was divorced; the baby she was raising was the illegitimate offspring of some seaman she'd been having an affair with; and now, by all accounts, Doreen was carrying on with one of the schoolmasters. Archie Blake's death had been unfortunate, and Doreen had been very cut up about it, but that was no excuse, really, for getting pregnant without a wedding ring on her finger, and behaving like a trollop.

Feeling a bit better after her inner rant, Doris had managed to get through the most pressing issues that had crossed her desk, then she shot home at lunchtime to make sure John was behaving himself, and to take charge of her wedding outfit which the seamstress delivered to her door at one o'clock. On her return to the office she'd instructed the temporary secretary on how things should be done during their absence, and as the woman seemed very capable, she left the factory estate at four o'clock feeling content that the office would be in good hands.

Doris walked home slowly, enjoying the warmth of this late summer day and the smell of newly cut grass. The sky was clear blue, the horizon shimmering where the sky met the sparkling sea, and the gulls hovered almost lazily over the hills and the town. It was a perfect day, and if it was like this tomorrow, then she and John would be blessed.

She came to a halt outside John's bungalow and gave an exasperated sigh. The pocket handkerchief lawns in front of both bungalows had been mowed despite all she'd said, and if John's back had suffered, then he'd really get the sharp edge of her tongue. She marched up the path and let herself into his bungalow.

'I told you not to exert yourself,' she said crossly.

He came out of the kitchen grinning. 'It wasn't me, Doris. I promise.'

'Then who ...?'

'Hello, Mother,' said Anthony, coming from the sitting room and swamping her in a hug. 'We thought we'd come a bit earlier than planned, and as I had nothing better to do, I cut the grass.'

Doris hugged him tightly. 'Oh, Anthony, dear boy, how kind.' She pulled back from him as she heard childish laughter coming from the sitting room. 'Is that my Teddy?'

Without waiting for an answer, she dashed in to find Suzy in an armchair with little Teddy at her feet playing with a wooden truck on the hearthrug.

'Hello, Susan,' she said distractedly as she bent to scoop the small boy into her arms and smother his face in kisses. 'Oh, Teddy, darling,' she murmured, holding him close and breathing in the deliciousness of his thick fair hair and baby skin. 'What a big, beautiful boy you are for your grandma.'

Teddy squirmed and pushed away from her, his little face scrunching up as if he was about to wail in protest. Doris quickly put him down, her heart aching that her only grandchild didn't know her.

'He'll be all right once he's settled in,' said Suzy, rising from her chair to coolly kiss Doris's cheek before picking up her son to soothe him. 'It's been a long journey down from Cambridge and everything's a bit new and daunting.'

Doris bit down on a sharp reply, for reminding them that she'd hardly seen any of them since they'd moved away would only make the situation more awkward. She forced a smile. 'Well, it's lovely to see you all,' she managed. 'You're looking well, Susan.'

Suzy smiled and put Teddy back down on the floor with his truck. 'I'm feeling very much better, thank you, Doris, and really looking forward to catching up with everyone tonight. It's such a shame Fran's not well enough to come, but she telephoned this morning and asked me to give you her love and best wishes.'

'That was very kind of her,' Doris muttered. Actually, she was bitterly disappointed that Fran couldn't play the violin at her wedding. 'Tonight will be a very quiet affair. We're just meeting for a few drinks at the Officers' Club,' she continued stiffly. 'My sister Doreen is due to arrive from Swansea very soon, and Rosie has kindly offered to babysit for a couple of hours while Ron takes charge at the Anchor.'

159

She gave a little sniff of disapproval. 'Ron blotted his copybook the last time he was left to look after the children, so he won't be asked again.'

'Oh dear,' said Suzy with laughter in her blue eyes. 'Poor Ron will never learn, will he?'

'It seems not,' Doris replied, unwilling to discuss Ron's unedifying behaviour with her daughter-in-law. She glanced at her watch, and then headed out to the kitchen where Anthony and John were in deep discussion about the Japanese surrender.

'I wouldn't put it past the Japs to renege on the whole thing,' said Anthony. 'It's highly suspicious that they're taking so long to sign the surrender, and I suspect they're plotting something.'

'Surely not?' said John. 'They've been thoroughly beaten throughout the Pacific, and after those atomic bombs – which must have killed hundreds of thousands of their people – surely they won't want to risk another being dropped.'

Anthony shrugged and turned to his mother. 'Sorry about being so gloomy on the eve of your wedding, Mother, but we got talking and ...' He kissed her and put his arm round her waist. 'John and I will spend a quiet evening at your place with Teddy while you girls paint the town red. I brought some fillet steak and a good bottle of wine, so we'll be quite content.'

Doris giggled girlishly. 'We won't be painting the town red – but perhaps with a tinge of pink. I'll need my wits about me tomorrow.'

'John told me about your plans to turn the two bungalows into one. It's a splendid idea, Mother.'

'Yes, isn't it? We're both very excited about it. Work won't start until we get back from our honeymoon, but we hope to have it all finished by Christmas.'

'It'll be our best Christmas ever,' murmured John, kissing Doris's hand.

Feeling slightly embarrassed, Doris blushed. 'I've made up my spare room for you, Anthony, and borrowed a cot for Teddy. So here's a spare key. Come and go as you please.'

'Thank you, Mother. Now I propose we have a cup of tea and a slice of Suzy's lovely Victoria sponge before you girls get all dolled up for your evening out.'

Doris had to reluctantly admit that Suzy's baking skills were as good as her own, and when it was time to return to her bungalow to put Teddy to bed, the girl had asked her if she'd like to bath him and read him a story. Doris was beginning to warm to Suzy, but to her chagrin, there was still a tiny nub of jealousy that niggled away at her, for her son was committed wholeheartedly to the girl and would never really be her boy again.

Doreen climbed down from the train with Archie junior on her hip, the girls leaping out before her onto the platform. It was lovely to be home again, even if her last memories of Cliffehaven and Beach View had been overshadowed by Archie's father's tragic death in that London tube station.

She took a deep breath of the warm, salty air to banish the awful memories of that day. 'Stay together and don't wander off,' she ordered the girls. 'I have to get the pram and suitcase out of the guard's van.'

'I'll do that, Doreen,' said Stan jovially.

'Uncle Stan!' she exclaimed in delight, giving the stationmaster a hug. 'How lovely that you're still here. I thought you must have retired by now.'

He hugged her back and then looked down at her with sad eyes. 'I'm afraid I won't have much choice in the matter soon,' he said. 'But I'll tell you more once we've got your things out of the van.'

Doreen watched him lumber down the length of the train and frowned. She'd known Stan all her life, and he was so much a part of this station that she couldn't imagine him anywhere else, so why was he retiring?

Stan carried the suitcase and wheeled the large pram down the platform. He took charge of nine-month-old Archie, who grinned and made a grab for his peaked hat. 'Goodness me,' he chuckled. 'He's a lovely big chap, isn't he?'

'As handsome and sweet-tempered as his father,' said Doreen proudly. 'Heavy too,' she added with a grunt as she took him from Stan to plonk him into the pram and strap him in. 'You were saying about maybe having to retire,' she prompted.

'There's talk they'll be closing this branch line,' he said sadly. 'Now the troop trains and special services are no longer running, the railway company deems it unprofitable.'

'But what about your lovely cottage?' she asked in horror. 'Surely they aren't just going to pension you off and leave you homeless?'

He smiled down at her. 'I'll get a good pension, and they've promised they'll only charge me a peppercorn rent for the cottage until I turn up my toes. Then it will either be sold off or pulled down to make way for new housing.'

He gave a deep sigh. 'Which means my niece, April, and her little Paula will have to find their own place to live. I had hoped she could just carry on renting it, but the rail company won't hear of it.'

'Oh, Stan, I'm so sorry,' Doreen commiserated. 'It's been your family home ever since your father was stationmaster.'

'Aye, well, at least I can live out my last days there, and I've got a bit of money put by, so I can help April out when it comes to getting her own place.'

Doreen caught sight of her girls wandering off in boredom to inspect Stan's large tubs of flowers. 'I'd better get on, Stan. Peggy's expecting me, and I don't want to be late for Doris's drinks tonight.'

Stan's eyes twinkled. 'I bet you never thought you'd see the day your sister got wed again,' he said. 'A lot of things have changed around here during the past few years, but none so much as Doris. I think you'll be pleasantly surprised.'

'I'm sure I will,' said Doreen, now eager to be on her way. 'I'm here for a few days, Stan, so I'll pop up and see you for a chat and one of your lovely rock buns. You are still making them, aren't you?'

'Not as many as before, because I have to watch my weight. But for you, Doreen, I'll bake a special batch.' He patted her shoulder, tweaked Archie under the chin and winked. 'It's good to have you home, lass, even if it is only for a short while.'

Doreen grinned back at him, then called the girls to her. Balancing the suitcase across the end of the large, coach-built pram, she hurried out of the station.

As they walked down the High Street, Doreen was shocked by the number of bomb craters and empty spaces that had once been shops, the cinema and the old Mermaid pub. She noted that the Crown was still standing but looking a bit worse for wear, and that a new restaurant had opened up since she'd last been home. It looked very smart, and a quick glance at the menu board in the window told her it catered only for those with deep pockets.

'Why can't we go on the beach, Mum?' asked Evelyn.

'Because there isn't time today,' she said, wheeling the pram into Camden Road.

'But I wanna go to the beach,' whined Joyce, scuffing the toes of her shoes on the pavement.

'Well you can't,' said Doreen firmly. 'And stop damaging those new and very expensive shoes.'

She ignored their moans and groans as Archie clapped his hands and beamed at everyone they passed. As she approached the Anchor, she saw Ron and Rosie standing in the doorway with welcoming smiles.

'To be sure, it's grand to see you, wee Doreen,' said Ron, giving her a bear hug.

Doreen had always loved Ron and she hugged him back before kissing Rosie's cheek. 'How's married life, you two? I have to say, you both look well on it.'

'We're doing fine, Doreen,' said Ron. 'Are ye looking forward to seeing your sisters again?' he asked with a naughty twinkle in his eyes.

'Peggy definitely, but I'm not so sure about Doris. We parted on bad terms back in '43, so it could be a bit awkward.'

'Ach, she'll have forgotten all about that by now,' he said airily.

Doreen wasn't so sure, but she made no comment. 'I'd better get on. I promised Peggy I'd get to her by five, and it's almost half past now. Will I see you tonight, Rosie?'

'Only for a few minutes. I'm babysitting at Beach View so you and Peggy can go out and have some fun. Doris is holding her drinks party at the Officers' Club, so you should have a good time.'

Doreen rolled her eyes. 'Typical. I suppose the Anchor isn't good enough for her?'

Rosie didn't look at all put out. 'I think she wanted a quiet evening. This place gets quite rowdy on a Friday night now we've got a new piano.'

Doreen set off again, pointing out the new school that was almost finished in the footprint of the old one which she and her sisters had attended, and then the shops that had been there for as long as she could remember. She waved to Fred the Fish and Alf the butcher and hurried on across the main road leading up from the seafront and into the twitten behind Beach View.

'What's this place?' asked Evelyn, her nose wrinkling as she turned to look at the bomb site and then regarded Beach View's vegetable plot, the outside lav and the chicken coop.

Doreen realised her daughter had become accustomed to the manicured playing fields and formal grounds of the boarding school, and used to living in part of a gracious old manor house, so wasn't really surprised by her shock at seeing poor old battered Beach View.

'This is the house I was born in.' Doreen opened the gate and pushed the pram onto the path. 'And it's where we'll be staying with my sister Peggy, so I don't want you turning up your nose like that, young lady. It's rude and hurtful.'

Evelyn had the grace to look ashamed and ducked her chin as Doreen opened the back door and called out to Peggy.

Peggy had been restless with anticipation as the time had ticked away, but at the sound of her sister's voice, she leapt to her feet and ran down the cellar steps to greet her.

Doreen was looking stunning with a bright blue hat on her wavy brown hair, a matching jacket and a sprigged cotton dress. She threw her arms about her.

'It's so lovely to see you again,' she said breathlessly after they'd hugged and kissed. Turning to the girls, her eyes widened as she took in their neat plaits and pretty appearance and the coltish limbs of Evelyn who was looking more like her mother than ever. 'My goodness, haven't you both grown? The last time I saw you, you were tiny tots.'

Evelyn and Joyce withstood Peggy's effusive greeting with awkward grace.

'And this must be Archie,' sighed Peggy, drinking in the sight of the smiling, chubby little boy. She quickly unstrapped him and took him in her arms. 'Oh, my, he's quite a weight, isn't he?' she giggled as Daisy came out to see what all the noise was about.

'This is Daisy,' Peggy said proudly. 'Daisy, these are your cousins, Evelyn and Joyce, and they'll be staying with us for a while.'

As the girls eyed each other warily, Peggy turned to Doreen. 'I do hope you'll be staying for more than just the weekend,' she murmured. 'It'll be so lovely to have you home again. I've missed you and we have so much to catch up on.'

'I know, and I've missed you too. But let's get indoors,' said Doreen, lifting the case from the pram. 'I hope you've got the kettle on, Peggy, because I'm gagging for a proper cuppa after that awful stewed offering at Euston Station.'

The pram proved to be too big to wheel into the scullery, so once they'd had a cup of tea and been shown their rooms, Peggy helped Doreen lug it up the front steps and into the hall.

'Whew,' breathed Doreen. 'I don't fancy doing that too often – especially once Archie's in it.'

'I could lend you Daisy's pushchair,' said Peggy. 'She's happy to walk everywhere now as long as it's not too far.'

Doreen grinned with delight and headed back into the kitchen, where Daisy and Joyce were helping Cordelia find her glasses so she could read them a story.

Evelyn clearly thought she was a bit old for such things, and had gone off to find something to read on her own. She returned from the basement with Charlie's copy of *Black Beauty* and settled down quite happily.

'I don't know what he'll say about her borrowing that,' murmured Peggy. 'He's very protective of his books.'

'She'll be careful with it,' Doreen assured her. 'She's an avid reader and has great respect for books.' She lit a cigarette and then grinned. 'So, tell me about Doris and this chap she's marrying tomorrow. Has she really changed that much?'

'Indeed she has, and she's much happier for it,' said Peggy. 'John's a lovely man – a true gentleman, handsome, too, with a bit of money behind him by all accounts.' She went on to tell Doreen about their plans for the bungalows, and her worries over John's son.

'If you're that worried about it, you should have a quiet word with her, Peg. After all she's been through, she'd be very silly to jump in feet first without giving it a great deal of thought.'

'I thought I might broach the subject this evening, but it's hardly a happy topic on the eve of her wedding, is it?'

'I could have a word if you'd prefer,' said Doreen.

'Oh, I don't think that would be wise,' said Peggy hastily. 'You didn't exactly part on friendly terms, and she might still hold a bit of a grudge.'

'So she hasn't changed that much then,' said Doreen waspishly. 'It's all water under the bridge as far as I'm concerned, and if she's willing to make up, then so am I. But I'm not putting up with any of her snooty nonsense, Peg. I've had more than enough of that over the years.'

Peggy heaved a sigh. 'Oh, Doreen, do try not to wind her up.'

Doreen giggled. 'Me? Wind my dearest older sister up? As if I would.'

Peggy chuckled. 'You know damned well you would. Honestly, Doreen, you haven't changed in thirty-seven years.'

'Who else is coming tonight, Peg? Please tell me that awful Pauline hasn't been invited, because I'd rather stay at home if she has.'

Peggy shook her head, still smiling. 'She and Doris don't get on, so she hasn't been invited even though she's family. Anne will meet us there. She'll be driving in with Brendon's wife, Betty, and then there's you, me, Suzy, Cordelia, Sarah, Danuta – and of course Doris.'

'A good number, then. I'm looking forward to meeting Betty after all you've said in your letters – and to seeing Anne again. It's been years since we've been in the same place. I feel as if I already know Danuta and Sarah from your letters, so it will be lovely to see them in the flesh as it were.'

She picked up a grizzling Archie. 'This one needs his nappy changed and a feed. I'll be back down in a minute.'

During a supper of fish cakes, salad and new potatoes fresh from the garden, Doreen tried to come to terms with how much Charlie had grown since she'd last seen him, how old and frail Cordelia had become despite her lively spirit – and how very little had changed at Beach View since Peggy had taken over from their parents. But hearing all of Peggy's plans to refurbish and renovate, she offered enthusiastic encouragement and urged her to do it before all her ideas went off the boil.

As Charlie had delivered her car earlier, Doris had driven Suzy up to the Officers' Club, and they were already settled in the members' lounge with drinks when the others arrived. She was rather surprised that Peggy had come by taxi, but then she supposed Cordelia would never have managed the hill otherwise.

'Hello, Doris,' said Doreen with a bright smile, but making no attempt to kiss or hug her. 'What a lovely venue. Are you having your reception here as well?'

'We're having it in the private reception room at the golf club, actually. John is up for the captaincy next year, and they think most highly of him there.'

Doris didn't see Doreen's expression harden as she turned to wave rather imperiously at a waiter who came to take their drink orders, then settled back in the comfortable chair, curious to discover more about Doreen's life in Swansea and the lover Peggy had hinted at.

'I'm just the headmaster's secretary,' Doreen replied, aware that Peggy had tensed beside her. 'But the job comes with a lovely ground-floor flat in the school grounds, and there's a generous discount on the girls' fees, so I'm extremely lucky.'

'Indeed you are,' said Doris. 'Your girls are the first in our family to have the privilege of going to a private school. I hope they are taking full advantage of it – seeing as how intimate you seem to have become with a particular member of staff.'

Doreen ignored the sly jibe, having absolutely no intention of talking about her new man to Doris. 'They're both bright, and Evelyn is at the top of her year, so they'll do all right, Doris.' She changed the subject by raising her glass. 'I'd like to propose a toast to Doris and wish her all the very best for her new life with John.'

The toast was drunk, Peggy relaxed, and as Doris chatted to Anne, she turned to Suzy for a lovely long catch-up.

'Ladies! How wonderful to find so many beautiful ladies all in one place!'

Doris twisted round and glared at the enormous man with the waxed moustache who was making his way slowly into the room on two walking sticks. 'This is a private party,' she said frostily.

He ignored her admonishment completely, took her hand and kissed it, his brown eyes regarding her with great amusement. 'Baron Stanislaw Kowalcyzk at your humble service, dear lady.'

There were stifled giggles from the others and Doris went scarlet. 'I doubt you were ever humble, Baron,' she stuttered, retrieving her hand and not daring to look him in the eye. She'd heard rumours about this man, and it was clear he was an absolute terror with women.

'That is probably so,' he agreed and smiled. 'But I have come to wish the bride the very best of happiness for tomorrow and all her life – and to buy you all champagne.'

Doris cleared her throat. 'That's very kind of you, Baron, but it's really not necessary.'

His dark eyes widened and he clasped her hand again. 'Oh but it is, and for such a beautiful bride only the very best champagne will do.'

He nodded to the hovering waiter who popped the cork expertly and began to pour the champagne into glasses.

Once everyone had a glass, he took one for himself. 'To the future Mrs White. Long life and much happiness,' he bellowed before downing it in one, and only just resisting the time-honoured ritual of smashing the glass onto the floor.

Danuta tutted and rolled her eyes, Doris blushed an even deeper scarlet and the others just about managed to stifle their giggles enough to return the toast and sip the delicious champagne.

'I will leave you now,' he said grandly, before winking at Danuta. 'But I shall see you again.'

'Good heavens,' breathed a flustered Doris once he was out of earshot. 'Who on earth *was* that? Is he really a baron?'

'He is Polish baron,' said Danuta, her eyes twinkling with mirth. 'He is very loud, I think, but has good heart and the manners of all Polish gentlemen.'

'Gosh,' said Doris, hugely impressed. 'A real baron living in Cliffehaven. Who would have thought it?' She eyed Danuta sharply. 'How did you get to meet him?'

'At Rita's wedding,' said Danuta rather coolly. 'He is my friend.'

'Well, I never,' sighed Doris before taking another sip of champagne to steady her racing pulse. She'd never met a baron before, and to think that he was Danuta's friend was quite extraordinary, for the girl didn't have much going for her. She would invite him to dinner once they'd returned from their honeymoon, she decided. But what on earth did one feed Polish royalty? She'd have to go to the library and do some research.

The mood lightened and once the bottle of champagne was empty, they were presented with another, compliments of the baron, who they could hear talking and laughing in the bar.

Consequently, Doris was a bit squiffy by the time they had to go home, so Suzy drove the car back and then went to bed leaving poor Anthony to listen to his mother's excited chatter about the baron. It seemed that Doris could still have her head turned by a title, so not that much had changed, after all.

*

Jack had delivered Peggy's car earlier that morning, before hurrying back to make inroads on the number of vehicles still waiting to be serviced and repaired. Even with Rita and Peter doing their bit, they were inundated with work. He'd told Peggy that when Jim came back there was a job waiting for him, as he couldn't manage on his own once Rita and Peter had left for Australia.

Peggy was delighted to think that Jim could walk straight into a good job on his return home, and her spirits were high as she carefully drove her lovely, shining car up to the Town Hall with Doreen and the children in the back and Cordelia in the front.

Martin had left earlier with Anne and their two children because he was John's best man and needed to be there to keep him steady should he need steadying. Peggy smiled at this thought as she helped Cordelia out and up the Town Hall steps, for it was probably Doris who would need steadying after her run-in with Stanislaw last night.

It was almost midday, the sun was shining, and although there were a couple of clouds in the sky they didn't look too threatening, so it was very possible they could hold the start of the reception in the golf club garden. She made sure Cordelia was safely in the lift with Evelyn, who'd clearly decided she needed to look after her, and then they trooped up the stairs to the familiar wedding room.

John and Martin were in their best suits and John looked remarkably calm as he chatted to Bertie Double-Barrelled and gave everyone a welcoming smile. Brendon and Betty came in with baby Joseph, followed by Frank and a rather sour-faced Pauline who glared at Doreen and then blatantly snubbed her by turning her back to talk to the registrar.

All the little girls looked very sweet in their best dresses, and Archie was utterly adorable in his blue romper suit and matching sunhat – although that didn't stay on for long as he preferred to chew it rather than wear it.

Peggy doubted she'd cry at this particular wedding, but she'd brought several handkerchiefs just in case. There were lollipops in her handbag should the children start to fidget, and Doreen had brought a bottle and several clean nappies for Archie. Peggy sat down next to Cordelia and smiled at Danuta and Sarah as they quickly took their places in the row behind them.

Ron turned up without Harvey for once, but with a very glamorous Rosie on his arm. 'We've left the dogs at home,' he told Peggy, who'd been worried that something might have happened to them. 'They've had their walk, and the mayor made it very plain that Harvey was no longer welcome. To be sure, I'll be having a word with that man, so I will.'

Rosie tugged his arm and pulled him down to sit beside her. 'Don't keep on, Ron,' she sighed. 'Honestly, Peggy, anyone would think his dog was royalty the way he pampers that animal.'

'Well, it looks as if everyone's here,' said Peggy as Suzy came in with little Teddy, and sat next to Sarah and Danuta. 'All we need now is the bride. I hope she isn't going to be late like Ivy was.'

'She'll be waiting to make a grand entrance, so she will,' muttered Ron.

'Well, it is her wedding day, and all brides want to make an entrance,' defended Peggy.

Ron waggled his brows. 'Aye, and none more so than your sister,' he said with a grin.

The registrar switched on the piped music as the doors opened and Doris appeared on her son's arm. She held him back for a long moment to make sure everyone had realised they'd arrived, and then they slowly made their way down towards John and Martin.

Peggy didn't think she'd ever seen her sister look as lovely or as radiantly happy as she did today. The beautiful cream linen coat and jacket were discreetly piped with the same navy blue as her broad-brimmed hat, and her slender, well-shaped legs were enhanced by the navy peep-toed high heels. She carried a small bouquet of cream roses that were nestled into dark green ferns, and there were pearls in her ears and round her neck.

John's gaze never left her as she walked slowly towards him, and it was clear to all that he simply adored her.

Peggy felt the prick of happy tears, for her sister deserved to be well loved after all she'd been through with duplicitous Ted, and she had the feeling that John would cherish her until his last breath – and that they would have a long and very happy life together.

Much later that night when Peggy had finally fallen into bed ready for sleep, she sighed with pleasure at the feel of lovely clean sheets and pillowcases. Doris's wedding had gone off without a hitch. The reception had been very grand even though it had started to rain this afternoon – and a ruckus had been avoided between Doreen and Pauline when Pauline complained of having one of her headaches and ordered poor Frank to drive her home. Doreen had resisted teasing Doris and managed to avoid the subject of the schoolmaster she was walking out with, which she'd known would be an irritant to her nosy elder sister, and cause unpleasantness between them.

Peggy snuggled down beneath the blanket, thinking of John and Doris who were already on their way to the Lake District, and realising yet again that she hadn't had a proper talk with her sister about her finances. She nestled her head into the pillow and after blowing a kiss to Jim's photograph, turned out the bedside light. She would have to leave it now until Doris came back from her honeymoon.

PART TWO

10

A week had passed since Doris's wedding, and Doreen would be leaving Cliffehaven on the noon train. Danuta was out on her district nursing rounds and Sarah was upstairs doing her packing, but the kitchen was far from quiet as the three girls chattered away at the breakfast table, Archie banged a spoon against the high chair, and Charlie teased Cordelia who wasn't in the best of moods this Saturday morning, and had switched off her hearing aid.

Peggy rushed to retrieve the morning post, and amongst the letters for Sarah and Jane, she found a lovely postcard of Lake Windermere, and an airmail from Ruby which she would read once the house was quiet again and she could fully concentrate on it. She handed Doreen the postcard across the breakfast table.

'It sounds as if Doris and John are having a lovely time now his back has improved,' she said with a smile in her voice. 'I'm so glad things are going well. She was terribly worried about him, you know.'

Doreen flicked over the card and read the neat handwritten message. 'Let's hope they carry on that way. Doris is still a terrible snob despite having mellowed because of John, and I dread to think what her plans are for poor Stanislaw.' She grinned. 'He's a nice chap, isn't he? And he's clearly very smitten with Danuta.'

Peggy nodded and then sipped her tea. 'It's such a shame about his legs, though. His future prospects don't look bright when it comes to finding work, and although he appears to have money, I doubt it will last very long the way he spends it.'

She eyed her sister over the rim of her teacup. 'Talking of nice chaps. What's this new fellow of yours like?'

Doreen chuckled. 'I knew you couldn't resist asking, Peg, and I'm amazed you've left it this long. But walls have ears,' she added, shooting a glance at her girls who were just finishing their cereal. 'I'll tell you later.'

'That means Mum doesn't want to talk about Mr Kent,' muttered Evelyn to her sister, who giggled. 'Mr Kent has a beard,' she informed Peggy with a grimace and a flick of her plaits. 'Yuck.'

Peggy raised a brow and tried very hard not to laugh. 'You don't like beards then, Evelyn?'

The girl's neat plaits swung as she shook her head. 'But Mummy does. I saw her kissing him. Yuck and double yuck.'

Joyce tried unsuccessfully to smother her giggles.

Doreen went red and busied herself with Archie, who had most of his breakfast down his front. 'Now you've finished you can get down from the table and go outside to play,' she said, sounding flustered. 'That's not the sort of thing we talk about at breakfast.'

Evelyn gave a world-weary sigh and rolled her eyes at Charlie, who was grinning. 'Don't you just hate being treated like a kid? We never get to hear the really interesting stuff.'

'It's not really the sort of nonsense I'm interested in, Evie,' he replied before draining his teacup and pushing back from the table. 'Come on, I'll take you all down to the beach for a bit so our mums can have a good gossip.'

Doreen and Peggy found all the necessary paraphernalia for a trip to the beach, and once Archie was strapped into Daisy's pushchair, Charlie set off cheerfully with the three girls in tow.

Sure in the knowledge that Cordelia couldn't hear a thing as she'd turned off her hearing aid and was engrossed in her newspaper, Peggy lit them both cigarettes. 'So, your Mr Kent has a beard, does he?' she asked with a twinkle in her eyes.

Doreen nodded. 'Beard, moustache, long, floppy dark hair and eyes as brown as molasses,' she replied. 'Bill teaches art and drama, and has dreams of writing the definitive best-selling novel one day – though I've yet to see him start anything.'

'Is it serious between you?'

'Not really,' she replied on a sigh. 'He's a nice man, great fun to be with, and suits my needs at the moment – but he's not my Archie. No one could ever take his place, Peggy.'

Peggy reached for her hand. 'It's still fairly early days, Doreen. Of course you feel that way.'

'It's been nearly two years, Peg, and I thought I'd be over him now. But he's still here in my heart, and I see him every day in little Archie.'

'Does this new chap remind you of him? Is that why you're involved?'

Doreen's smile was wistful. 'Not in the least – apart from the beard. Bill's slender, softly spoken and has probably never done a day's hard labour in his life. Whereas Archie was a great bear of a man with a working man's hands, loud voice and huge personality. A bit like Stanislaw in a way.' She blinked back the sudden tears and began to clear away the dirty dishes.

'It's neither here nor there, really,' she continued, 'because Bill applied for a teaching post in Scotland, and he might not even be there when I get back.'

'Oh, Doreen, I am sorry.'

Doreen patted her shoulder. 'Don't be. I'm actually happier on my own with the children, and life is less complicated.'

Peggy collected the rest of the dishes and filled the sink with hot water. 'I shall miss you, Doreen. It's been so lovely having you home again.'

'I've loved coming back, too, but my home's in Swansea now. The children are settled, I've made some good friends and I enjoy my work.' She started to dry the clean dishes. 'You could always come to visit, Peg, once you've renovated this place and time is your own again.'

'I'd love to, but Solly relies on me to keep his new factory going smoothly, and of course I'll always have Cordelia to look after.'

She glanced over her shoulder at the elderly lady who was studiously going through the death notices in the local paper to see who she'd outlived. 'Not that she's any bother,' she added quickly.

Charlie came back with the children an hour later, Ron and Harvey following closely behind them. Harvey greeted Doreen and Peggy and then rushed to Cordelia and put his cold nose up her skirt which made her jump.

'Harvey!' she exclaimed, pushing him away. 'Naughty boy. You don't do that.'

Harvey slunk off, but soon decided to hinder rather than help Ron bring down Doreen's large suitcase. Dashing round his feet, he almost got trampled on and earned a sharp admonishment from Ron. 'Gerroff, ye heathen beast,' he rumbled, dumping the case in the hall. 'To be sure, you're a ruddy nuisance at times.'

'It takes one to know one,' said Cordelia, twiddling with her hearing aid. 'That animal takes after its master, if you ask me.'

'To be sure no one did,' Ron muttered before going back into the hall to lift the large pram down the front steps to the pavement.

With the sand washed from the children's hands and clothes, and a fresh nappy on Archie, Doreen was ready to leave. She embraced Charlie, thanking him for being so lovely with her children. 'And for goodness' sake, stop growing,' she teased. 'You'll be taller than your father at this rate.'

She turned to Sarah who'd come downstairs to say goodbye. 'Take care over there,' she murmured. 'I do hope things go well for you and your sister – and when you see Jim, which you're bound to, tell him to write to me. I haven't had a letter in ages.'

Then she hugged Cordelia. 'Goodbye, Cordy,' she said affectionately. 'It's been lovely seeing you again.'

Peggy hated saying goodbye to the people she loved, for she'd seemed to be doing it too many times over the past six years. She pulled on her jacket, strapped a protesting Daisy into her pushchair and followed Doreen and the children down the steps to where Ron was keeping an eye on the pram and the case.

With the older girls skipping along in front of them, and Harvey watering every lamppost he came across, they slowly walked up the High Street towards the station where Stan was on the platform waiting for them.

'Here's a little something to enjoy on your journey,' he said, handing over a paper bag. 'I made them this morning.'

Doreen smiled in delight at the sight of the eight lovely rock buns that glistened with brown sugar. 'Thank you, Stan,' she sighed, giving him a hug. 'That was very generous of you. I hope things pan out all right for you and your niece, and that you have a wonderful retirement. I expect your allotment will benefit from it.'

The train pulled in, and Stan returned her hug then hurried down the platform with Ron to unload Archie and put the pram and suitcase in the guard's van.

Ron returned with Archie in his arms, their smiles equally wide. 'He's a grand wee wain, so he is, Doreen,' he enthused, giving the baby a smacking kiss on the cheek which made him gurgle in delight. 'I'm thinking he'll be Charlie's size before you know it.'

'Not for a while yet, I hope,' laughed Doreen, taking charge of the boy and hugging Ron. 'Try and behave yourself, Ron.

And I'm keeping you to your promise to come and visit me. Rosie will love Swansea. There are a lot of shops.'

'Ach, you women and your shopping,' he replied with an exaggerated roll of his eyes. 'To be sure, a man's wallet is not his own once Rosie spies a shop window. We'll be down once my Jim's home and settled in, never you mind.'

Doreen and Peggy embraced as steam and smoke billowed around them. 'Look after yourself, Peggy,' Doreen murmured. 'And don't worry about me. I'm fine.'

'Will you come home again?'

'Perhaps next summer during the long holidays, but who knows where we'll all be in a year's time?'

She gave her another swift hug, kissed Daisy, patted the dog and climbed onto the train with her girls. Pulling down the carriage window, she leaned out. 'Let me know how the work's going on Beach View, Peggy,' she called down. 'And send me lots of photographs when it's finished.'

Ron raised his eyebrows and looked at Peggy sharply. 'What work?'

'We'll talk about it later,' she said as the train began to draw away.

Doreen waved out of the window until the train had rounded the bend and slowly disappeared from view, leaving only a column of smoke in its trail.

Peggy turned away and slowly wheeled the pushchair back down the platform. She had no idea when she might see Doreen again, and as it was unlikely she would ever manage to get to Swansea for a visit, it would probably mean more years of separation.

'What work, Peggy?' Ron was walking alongside her as they left the station and headed back down the High Street.

'Renovations,' she replied, her mind still on her very dear sister. 'The place needs a facelift, Ron, and seeing what you, Charlie and Frank have done for Anne, I'd like you to start on it as soon as Sarah and Jane leave for Singapore.'

'Well now,' he hedged. 'I have other things to be doing and Frank is out on the trawlers a good deal of the time now he has Brendon working with him.' He shoved his pipe in his mouth and dug his hand into his poacher's coat pocket for his roll of tobacco. 'Besides, Charlie starts back at grammar school next week.'

'I'm willing to pay you,' said Peggy, 'so you can stop making excuses. And I shall need the name of the plasterer, plumber and electrician you used, so I can get estimates of how much it will all cost.'

He came to an abrupt halt, took the pipe from his mouth and stared at her. 'What exactly are you planning to do with the place, Peggy?'

As she told him her ideas his eyes widened and when she'd fallen silent, he shook his head. 'To be sure, wee girl, Jim will not be liking all that change.'

'I've written to tell him what I want done, but as it's me who has to live there with all its inconveniences, and me who has the money to pay for it all, there's no reason for him to complain.'

'Reason or not, he won't like it.'

Peggy felt a dart of uncertainty and chose to ignore it. 'Well, I mean to have it done one way or another, and if you and Frank won't help, then I'll find someone who will. There are plenty of men about who need the work.'

'Aye, and most of them don't know one end of a screwdriver from another,' he rumbled, setting off again.

She almost had to run to keep up with him. 'So, Ron, will you help? I'll pay the going rate.'

He stopped again and regarded her from beneath his brows. 'There's no need for that. I'll do it for the price of as many cups of tea as you can make if you stop nagging me. But I can't speak for Frank.'

Peggy hugged his arm and stood on tiptoe to kiss his cheek. 'Thanks, Ron, I knew you wouldn't let me down.'

'Humph.' He shrugged his shoulders and reddened. 'Enough of that, Peggy. I've to be running the bar, so I do, and I'll have Rosie nagging me if I'm too late.'

'Could you start at the end of next week, then?' she asked.

'Aye, all right, But it won't be an easy task, wee girl. I doubt it will all be done by Christmas.'

'Oh, but I—'

He held up a grubby finger. 'It'll take as long as it takes, Peggy, and that's an end to it.'

Peggy was smiling as she watched him stomp down the hill, his dog at his heels. After her Jim, Ron was her most favourite and beloved person in the world, and now her dreams were about to be realised, she felt the sadness of Doreen's departure begin to lift. They would see each other again, she was sure of it – and when she next came home, Beach View would be a positive palace.

Returning home an hour later, Peggy found Cordelia sitting in the sunlit garden with a book, Sarah beside her in a deckchair doing some sewing. She unstrapped Daisy from the push-chair and once she was happily messing about in the sandpit with her doll, she rushed upstairs with her grocery shopping and quickly retrieved Ruby's letter from her apron pocket.

With the kettle on the hob, she sat down at the kitchen table, lit a cigarette and carefully unfolded the thin blue paper, rather surprised by how neat Ruby's writing was.

Lot 23, Jonquiere, Quebec, Canada
Dearest Peggy,

I'm sorry it's taken so long to write, but the journey here seemed to take for ever, and everything is so different, I'm finding it difficult to take it all in and find me feet. The crossing on the SS Lady Nelson *was quite rough, and despite the pills the doctor give me, I were sick for the first two days which weren't much fun for poor Mike, cos it were supposed to be our honeymoon.*

When we arrived in Nova Scotia it were lovely and warm and sunny, and the scenery was like nothing I ever see before, so we stayed for a couple of days and Mike bought a car so we could do a bit of sight-seeing before we went on to Quebec and then his family home up in the mountains. Everything is so big and empty here, Peggy, even in the towns, and within minutes of landing, I realised that nearly everyone spoke French – which come as a nasty shock, I can tell you. I have enough problems with English, let alone trying to speak foreign!

But although they speak French or the local patois, as Mike calls it, it were really strange to see places called Liverpool, Truro, Yarmouth, Dartmouth and Glasgow. Mike explained it was because the first white settlers came from them places and wanted to be reminded of home, and I'm beginning to understand why. Tell Rita, there's even a place called Sydney!

We drove up through New Brunswick which has a huge mountain range, a massive rocky coastline and nothing much else but lakes, rivers and trees – lots and lots of trees – which smell lovely, but make it ever so dark and gloomy when the sun's low. Quebec City is ever so old, with a castle and everything, and the streets are all narrow and cobbled, but there's lots of paper mills and pulping plants, as well as mining, so it's quite a busy town with docks for the big container ships that come in. It reminds me a bit of Tilbury.

Mike's parents' place is about two hundred miles north of Quebec City, and another three miles outside a really small settlement which is part of Jonquiere. It doesn't have a proper name, and probably hasn't changed since the year dot. Mike reckons there are about thirty people living in and around it all the time, but the numbers are increased when the mill and logging workers come back in the autumn for the logging season. He says it's easier to chop the timber in winter when the sap ain't rising, and transporting it over snow is quicker than hauling it by horses and chains. When the thaw comes, the rivers run real fast, and they send all the logs down on them to the port – which is something I find hard to believe. I mean, who ever thought of such a thing?

185

Everything is made out of wood here – cos of the trees, I suppose – there's enough of them. The main street is hard-packed earth, with one long veranda and walkway that runs past a bar and caff, a barber, a feed store and a general store that seems to sell nothing but old-fashioned dresses, work clothes, tools, canned food and dried stuff in huge sacks. I even seen men coming in on horses which they tie to the railings just like real cowboys! Oxford Street it ain't and even Brick Lane Market is better stocked.

The houses don't have names here, and Lot 23 is stuck outside this so-called town in the middle of the massive forest which Mike tells me runs right down to the St Lawrence River which is on the other side of the mountain. The house is made of huge logs, with a deep porch – or stoop as Mike calls it – and is very large with one big room for eating, living and sitting, five bedrooms and a bathroom which I don't really trust cos of spiders and things coming in from all them trees what surround the place. There's a generator for electricity, but all the cooking and heating comes from a range that's got to be three times bigger than the one in your kitchen, Peggy, and is a swine to rake out every morning.

Mike's parents, Claudine and Gerard, are ever so nice and made me feel welcome with an enormous meal of steak and potatoes. I think they must be quite rich, because Mike's dad owns a logging company and paper and pulping mills, and although it feels as if I've walked into one of them Hollywood westerns, the stuff they have here is good quality and there's always plenty of food.

I'm not really sure what I'm supposed to do all day while Mike's off with his father setting up the logging camp, but Claudine is nice company and there's always housework or gardening in the vegetable plot to get on with. So nothing much has changed. I had hoped to get a job so I'd have me own money, and was going to ask them at the bar in town if they would take me on as they needed a barmaid. But Claudine said the women in her family don't go out to work – and certainly didn't frequent

*rough places like that bar – so I suppose I'll just have to get used
to being a stay-at-home wife and take up knitting or something.*

*Reading this back I've made it sound as if I'm unhappy, but
I'm all right, Peggy, really I am. It's lovely to be Mike's wife, and
the people are ever so nice and welcoming. As long as we're
together I'll find a way to get used to not having lots of people
around me and the miles of nothing but trees. I suppose I'd better
try and learn French, because Claudine and Gerard speak it all the
time and when Mike joins in, I feel a bit left out.*

*I hope all is well with you, and that Rita and Ivy's weddings
went off all right. I'm still waiting to hear from them, but of
course they will only just have got my address.*

With lots of love,

Ruby xxx

Peggy folded the letter and sat quietly for a moment to
think about what Ruby had revealed. She might have pro-
fessed to being all right, but it sounded as if she was lonely
and homesick, and feeling very much out of place – and
what a place, stuck in the middle of nowhere with only her
mother-in-law for company.

'Oh, Ruby,' she sighed. 'I do hope you come to settle there
more happily. I hate the thought of you feeling so isolated.'

'Talking to yourself again, Peggy?'

She looked up, startled, and smiled at Jack. 'At least I can
have a sensible conversation that way.' Her smile faded as
she realised Jack wasn't smiling back. In fact, his face was
quite ashen, and his eyes were troubled. 'Whatever's the
matter? Has something happened?'

He sat down heavily at the kitchen table. 'You could say
that, Peg. Peter got notice this morning that he and Rita will
be leaving on the fifth of September.'

Peggy closed her eyes momentarily, sharing his anguish,
and then gripped his arm. 'You knew this day would come,
Jack – we both did.'

'It doesn't make it any easier, Peg,' he said, his voice breaking with emotion.

'Sit there and I'll get us both a drop of gin. There's some left over from the other night, and I reckon we both need a pick-me-up.'

She went to the larder for the gin and a bottle of tonic water and then hunted out a couple of tumblers. Her hand wasn't quite steady as she sloshed the gin into the glasses, and she realised that she was as cut up as Jack about Rita leaving them.

'Cheers,' she said, tapping her glass against his. 'Here's to making sure Rita and Peter have the very best six days with us.'

Jack swallowed his drink straight down and helped himself to another. 'I'm going to miss her, Peg,' he managed, his eyes bright with unshed tears. 'She's been my little girl for over twenty years. How am I going to get along without her?'

'We're all going to miss her, Jack,' soothed Peggy softly. 'But she's no longer a little girl – she's a woman and a wife, and we have to let her go no matter how painful it is.'

Jack nodded and once again drained his glass. 'I know all that, Peg, but the thought of her going so far away ...' He topped up his glass again and added just a splash of tonic water.

'Drowning your sorrows won't help,' said Peggy, removing the bottle. 'And if you're planning on going back to work this afternoon, you'll need to have your wits about you. The last thing Rita needs is for you to have an accident.'

Jack took a deep breath, stretched his neck and eased his shoulders before he concentrated on rolling a smoke. 'I'm sorry to make a fuss, Peg,' he said gruffly. 'You have your own worries, and it wasn't fair of me to come crying to you.'

She regarded him with deep affection. 'You and I go a long way back, Jack, and you can come to me any time you like. Goodness knows we've put the world to rights ever since we were at school together, and seen each other through good times and bad. As for my worries, they're very few really. Jim might not be here, but at least he's not in the thick of fighting, or stuck out in some jungle somewhere.'

She reached for his hand. 'We'll get through this together, Jack, just as we did all those years ago when you lost Maria.'

He lit his cigarette, blew smoke and then sipped his drink. 'Thanks, Peg. I knew it was right to come to you because you always say the right things.' He looked around the shabby kitchen and smiled. 'I've always loved sitting in here, you know. It's the heart of the home and like nowhere else.'

Peggy just managed not to blurt out that she was planning to rip the place to pieces and change the entire downstairs, and instead sipped her own drink. 'Come whenever you want, Jack, and I insist you spend Christmas with us. I'm not having you sitting up there on your own in that bungalow with a plate of Spam and a beer.'

'You're looking a long way ahead,' he replied with a smile.

'Someone has to,' she said, knocking back the last of her gin and tonic. 'Christmas takes a lot of organising.'

11

Singapore

It was the second day of September, and Jim and Jumbo stood with seven hundred other men in the glaring sun on the deck of the escort carrier, HMS *Hunter*. The massive convoy of ninety ships sailed majestically down the Strait of Malacca, passing the Raffles Lighthouse, and into Singapore Harbour with their flags fluttering and all the hooters and water cannons going. They knew they were making history and were a spectacular sight for the swarms of people watching and waving excitedly from the shore, and Jim felt his heart swell with pride. This joyous freedom was what they'd fought so long and hard for – this was their reward for being away from home and loved ones for years.

It was an exciting moment, made even more so by the arrival of nine Royal Australian Air Force Catalinas coming in low over their heads to land on the water and slowly make their way up the beach. These were the seaplanes that carried medical supplies and personnel documents in preparation for the Japanese surrender and the liberation of thousands of POWs. The Australian ship HMAS *Hawkesbury* blasted its hooters in welcome, and the crew on the repatriation transport *Duntroon* whistled and waved.

According to the debriefing that morning, the smaller British naval force which had sailed from Trincomalee in Ceylon had liberated Penang with very little opposition, despite the fact the Japanese surrender had come as a surprise to Itagaki, the Japanese Commander in Singapore.

General Itagaki had evidently ordered the remnants of his army defending Singapore to resist the Allies and fight to the death – indeed, there had been rumours of orders to massacre all Allied POWs on the island – but his commanding officer had overruled him by following his Emperor's orders and sending the signal of surrender to Mountbatten. It was rumoured that hundreds of Japanese officers had committed ritual suicide rather than lose face by surrendering and being taken prisoner.

Jim, Jumbo and the others watched the show and took numerous photographs of the badly damaged Japanese destroyer and two cruisers which had been used as floating anti-aircraft batteries, and the two German U-boats that were now being held in the naval base. Cameras clicked and rolls of film were used up as a sour-faced General Itagaki, his Vice Admiral and aides were brought aboard HMS *Sussex* to discuss the details of the surrender, and by six that evening the British flag was raised to signal that the Japanese had surrendered their forces on the island.

The formal and final surrender of the war throughout the Pacific would take place on the twelfth of September at Singapore City Hall, in the presence of Lord Louis Mountbatten.

Jim had become inured to the heat and humidity of Burma's jungles, so he was feeling quite comfortable as he disembarked early the following morning and strode along the wharf with the others to their billets. Arriving at the small hotel which had been requisitioned by the army, he dumped his bags on the bed and set off to explore the town. Taking one of the many rickshaws, he told the bare-footed Malay boy to take him to Raffles, and then sat back to enjoy the ride, marvelling at the skinny youth's ability to haul him and the sturdy rickshaw at a run through the crowded, noisy streets.

The evidence of war was everywhere in the dilapidated buildings, the untended gardens and rough roads, but there was an atmosphere of excitement and relief amongst the traders and those who trawled the markets for food, vegetables, trinkets and cheap second-hand clothing and furniture – and a real sense of purpose in the many army personnel already helping the new administration.

Jim grimaced at the sight of Japanese prisoners wearing little more than loose trousers as they dug ditches and repaired the roads. *They don't look so full of themselves now*, he thought, *but it's the very least they deserve after the cruelty they meted out to their own prisoners.*

As the youth ran along Beach Road, Jim was able to admire the façade of one of the world's most famous hotels. Raffles rose two storeys high and filled an entire block behind a row of swaying palm trees. As the boy paused to let a large, official-looking car sweep out of the driveway, Jim realised that the old building had survived the years of the Japanese occupation rather well. The gardens were lush and well tended; the imposing edifice carefully maintained – no doubt because the Japanese officers wanted to experience the high life, and had turned the place into their headquarters.

He paid the boy what seemed to be a pittance and added a bit more before tucking in his shirt and straightening his hat. The tropical uniform of shirt and shorts had been crisp and fresh when he'd put it on this morning, but it was already feeling a bit limp and sweat-stained. Thinking he might not be allowed entry to such a posh place, he hesitated, but was greeted by a smart salute from the smiling Malay concierge who opened the door for him with a white-gloved hand.

Jim stepped into the large reception area that was cooled somewhat by many ceiling fans, and realised that everyone else looked as hot and uncomfortable as he felt, and that the place seemed to be heaving with army officials, and rather harassed women who were dashing about with clipboards and armfuls of brown cardboard folders. As no one took any notice of him, he decided to have a wander about and see for himself why this place had made such a name for itself.

Having strolled through the crowded bar, the dining room which could seat five hundred people, the magnificent ballroom and elegantly appointed and hushed billiard room, he then made his way into the Palm Court. Looking at the lush palms, the silent-footed, bowing servants, the comfortable rattan furniture and fancy lighting, he could just imagine the rich and famous lolling about here, and got a glimpse of how it must have been for the wealthy ex-pats who'd come to socialise and be seen in these grand and luxurious surroundings. This was a world far removed from Beach View and Cliffehaven, and he finally understood how difficult Sarah and Jane must have found it to settle in after experiencing all this.

With that thought, he headed back to the reception area and asked the smiling Malay behind the desk where he could find the person in charge of repatriating the British POWs.

He followed the man's directions and eventually found his way to the small back office and tapped on the door. Receiving a brisk response, he stepped inside and was met by a scene of utter chaos.

Files and folders were piled up on every flat surface and stood teetering on the floor. A ceiling fan distributed the muggy heat in a desultory fashion, and although there was a bamboo blind pulled down over the single open window, the sun's glare easily penetrated the thin, damaged strips, sending shards of brilliant light across the mess.

The dark-haired woman behind the overloaded desk looked up at him over her glasses and gave an impatient tut. 'I don't know what you want, but I probably don't have it,' she said abruptly. 'I hope you're the assistant I've been promised, because if I don't get help soon, I shall be buried beneath this lot, never to be found again.'

Jim took off his hat and smiled down at her, thinking that if she hadn't looked so tired and fraught, she would have reminded him of Peggy. 'I'm sorry, but I'm here for personal reasons,' he said. 'I've just come to ask about two British POWs.'

She sat back in the creaking chair and gave a sigh as she took off her glasses and rubbed her temples. 'You and everyone else,' she said sadly. 'Look around you, Lieutenant. Every file here holds at least a dozen names, and unless the people you're looking for were imprisoned here on the island or in Changi, I'm very much afraid I can't help you.'

Jim saw the shadows beneath her tired eyes and the lines of stress around her mouth. It was clear she was barely coping and probably hadn't slept or eaten properly in days. 'The name's Jim Reilly,' he said. 'Pleased to meet you.'

'Elsa Bristow,' she replied, shaking his hand. 'I'm sorry, Jim, but as you can see, I'm snowed under – and it will probably get even worse once they start bringing in the POWs from the camps.'

'But surely you're not handling this all on your own?' he gasped.

She shot him a weary smile. 'Not entirely – although it does feel like it at times. I have several secretaries, but unfortunately those really in charge find paperwork irksome and prefer to deal with other, more interesting things.'

She cocked her head and regarded him thoughtfully. 'Who were you looking for?'

'John Angus Charles Fuller – who was known as Jock and was a plantation manager in Malaya, and Philip Tarrant, the owner of the plantation.'

'I remember them both very well,' she murmured and gave a weary sigh. 'I'm sorry to hear they didn't get out in time – but my husband did write and tell me they'd managed to get Jock's wife and daughters on ships before Singapore fell.'

Jim nodded. 'Sarah and Jane came to live with me and my wife in England, and with so little news coming out of this part of the world, they're frantic to learn what happened to their father and Sarah's fiancé.'

'And their mother, Sybil?'

'She and the baby got passage to Australia and she's living with her parents in Cairns. But my wife tells me they're all planning to come here to look for Jock and Philip.'

She sat straighter in the creaking chair. 'Then you should send a telegram immediately to stop them,' she said firmly. 'This place is overrun as it is, and will soon be even worse. The last thing any of us needs is distraught relatives clogging up the place.'

'I can understand that,' he replied, surveying the chaotic filing system.

Elsa put her glasses back on. 'I'm sorry if I come across as blunt, but you can see how it is, Jim. This is no place for Sybil or her girls, but I will certainly do my best to track Jock and Philip down, even if it means the worst news possible. Send that telegram today, Jim. It would be best for all concerned.'

Realising he would get no further for the moment, he smiled. 'I'll leave you to it, then.'

He strode out of the office and made his way to the dining room where he collared a waiter and ordered a pot of tea, a plate of sandwiches and a bowl of fruit – it seemed fruit grew in abundance here and the selection was positively mouth-watering. While he waited, he drank a Singapore Sling from a tall, frosted glass, and then ordered another on the waiter's return before following the man back to Elsa's office.

She looked up at him in astonishment.

'I thought this might perk you up a bit,' he said, clearing a space on the desk for the waiter to unload the tray. 'All work and no play isn't good for anyone.'

Elsa's eyes were suspiciously bright as she surveyed the simple meal. 'How very kind you are,' she murmured.

Jim paid the waiter, and once he'd closed the door behind him, he shifted the toppling stack of files off a chair and sat down. 'Please, eat and enjoy it, and try to relax. You're as bad as my Peggy, getting all wound up like a clock and forgetting to take care of yourself.'

Elsa's broad smile made her look instantly younger and rather attractive, and she tucked hungrily into the delicate chicken sandwiches which had been cut into triangles, the crusts carefully removed.

'Tell me about your Peggy, Jim,' she said once the initial pangs of hunger were satisfied. 'How long is it since you've been home?'

'Too long,' he replied. Sipping the refreshing Singapore Sling, he told her about his family, his home, the evacuees they'd taken in, and the town of Cliffehaven. He glossed over the part he'd played during the Burma Campaign and the medals he'd been awarded, and once she'd eaten her fill and shared the fruit with him, he lit cigarettes for them both and asked about her war.

'It was all a bit boring really,' she confessed. 'My husband was in the army and sensed things were about to go horribly wrong, so managed to get me and our daughters on a boat to Australia before the trouble really started. We ended up in Sydney where we lived with his maiden aunt, who rather grudgingly took us in and complained constantly about the inconvenience we were causing.'

She gave him a wan smile. 'The poor old duck was very set in her ways and extremely Victorian in her outlook on things, so one could hardly blame her for feeling put out. I eventually managed to find a place to rent in the city and spent most of the war ferrying the girls about and doing the admin for various charities. The only bit of excitement we had was when a Jap submarine was spotted in Sydney Harbour – but that was soon dealt with.'

'So your husband didn't make it out of Singapore, then?'

She shook her head. 'Reginald was a brigadier and of course had to stay on here to defend the island. Unfortunately, he was taken prisoner shortly after the fall of Singapore, so the minute the surrender was declared I came back to try and find him.'

Her hazel eyes dimmed with sadness. 'He died in Changi within weeks of being captured – but at least I know what happened to him. I can't imagine what it must be like for Sybil and her girls not knowing if their loved ones are alive or not.'

'So you knew them well before the war, then?'

She nodded. 'The ex-pat community is quite small, and Sybil was a shining light on the social scene. She and her girls were very popular, and they became close family friends. In fact, Reginald made sure they had somewhere to stay while they waited to catch a ship, and even managed to round up a few of their house boys to make their stay more comfortable.'

She blew smoke and then stubbed out her cigarette. 'I don't know what happened to the house boys, as they'd run off at the first sign of trouble, but I've heard since that their *amah* stayed on after they left and got kitchen work at Changi so she could be near Jock.'

She gave a deep sigh. 'Singapore was a very different place back then, and I don't think any of us realised just how pampered and spoilt we all were. The Japanese invasion came as a nasty shock to the system, I can tell you. We thought the place was impregnable.'

'Is there really no chance of tracking them down?' Jim edged forward in the chair. 'They were both held in Changi for a while, and then sent to camps.'

'I'll go through the Changi prison records again and see if the administrators kept a list of where the prisoners were sent from there. But even if there are lists, they could have been sent unrecorded from one camp to another, right across

197

Asia to the shores of Japan itself. It's a rat's nest of disinformation, and because the Japs destroyed most of their records the moment peace was declared, it's like hunting for a needle in a haystack.'

'I see.' Jim dipped his chin, realising it was a hopeless task.

'If they're alive, they'll be picked up,' said Elsa, setting aside the dishes and reaching for a file. 'There are teams already out there searching for the camps and liberating them. It's a vast operation, Jim, and one that can't be hurried if we're to find everyone. You'll just have to be patient and hope they've survived.'

'Is it likely?'

She brushed her slender fingers over the cardboard folder and gave a sigh. 'The odds aren't good,' she said softly.

He nodded and got to his feet. 'I'm billeted at the Palm Hotel. Should you get any news of either of them, you can reach me there.'

'Are you sure you wouldn't like to come and help with all this admin, Jim? I really do need someone to lighten the load.'

Jim realised he had to say something, although the thought of being stuck in this poky office day after day filled him with horror. 'I'll talk to my CO and see what he has to say – but I suspect he might send me elsewhere.' He reached out his hand. 'It's been nice meeting you, Elsa.'

Her warm smile made her look a decade younger than the tired, overwrought woman he'd first met. 'It's been a pleasure to meet you, Jim Reilly,' she said, shaking his hand. 'Thanks for the lunch.'

Jim left the office and wandered through the bar which he found had been taken over by a herd of braying military officers who'd become red-faced and loud through the amount of alcohol they were consuming. He found sanctuary back in the Palm Court, thinking of how Elsa was struggling while her senior officer was no doubt getting plastered, and decided he would have a word with his CO and see if he could round up someone to help her.

Returning to the heat and humidity of the streets, he hailed another rickshaw to take him to the hospital, and after enquiring fruitlessly about Jock and Philip, left his name and address with the woman in charge, before going back to his billet.

His first day on the island had certainly been an eye-opener, but at least he'd made a friend – and if things went according to plan, he could very well have eyes and ears in that office and be at the heart of things when the prisoners were brought in.

12

Cliffehaven

Peggy, Danuta and Cordelia had prepared the special supper for Sarah and Jane's last night at Beach View, and had then sat down with Charlie to listen to the wireless as the scenes in Singapore were described on the early evening news.

They could hear the sounds of hooters and horns in the background, and of people cheering as the Catalinas roared over the vast fleet and into the harbour, so it all felt very real. Peggy was thrilled to think that her Jim was actually there on this historic occasion, and could only hope that he remembered to take lots of photographs. And yet the Japs seemed to be dragging their feet about the whole thing, as this appeared to be just the start of the peace process and it wouldn't be finalised for another nine days.

She turned to Jane and patted her cheek before once again admiring the gorgeous diamond engagement ring the girl had shown off so excitedly on her arrival home from London. 'The British will sort things out by the time you reach Singapore,' she said. 'And now Jim's over there, I'm sure he'll do everything he can to help you.'

'It'll be nice to see him again,' said Jane. 'Is there anything you'd like us to take to him? It would have to be light and small, I'm afraid. We've been restricted in the amount of luggage we can take.'

'I have, as it happens,' Peggy replied, reaching for the large brown envelope she'd tucked behind the photographs on the mantelpiece. 'I've written him a long letter and Daisy has drawn him a picture. I've enclosed a number of photographs from the past few weeks of weddings and so on as Jim loves seeing pictures of us all – and he'll adore the ones of Daisy, Rose and Emily all togged up for Rita's wedding. I've added a couple of Doris and John as well, just to prove to him how well Doris looks and how happy she's become. There's also letters from Anne, Doreen and Charlie, and I suspect Ron might have something too.'

'I'll keep them all in here so they stay safe,' said Jane, taking charge of the envelope and tucking it away in her handbag. 'Jeremy sends his regards, by the way, and I already have a letter from him to Mother asking formally for my hand in case ... Well, you know,' she tailed off.

'Indeed I do,' murmured Peggy as she caught sight of Sarah looking wistfully at Jane's beautiful ring which had caused such surprise and delight. She wished she could do something to ease the girl's pain of knowing she'd burnt her boats as far as Delaney was concerned.

Unwilling to linger on such sad thoughts, Peggy went to check on the evening meal. Jack had brought a chicken over earlier this morning and it was now roasting in the oven with stuffing and potatoes; the vegetables had been freshly picked from the garden and they'd have the last of the bottled plums for pudding, so there would be quite a feast.

Soon after, Jack arrived with Rita and Peter, who would be leaving for Australia in a matter of days, but despite the air of sadness that lay beneath the jollity of the evening, it seemed everyone was determined to make this last night for Sarah and Jane special.

Peggy sat back in her chair and lit a cigarette once the meal was over and listened to the excited chatter going round the table, all too aware of the impending loss in Jack's eyes and the ache in Sarah's heart. She wished she could console and comfort them, but it was impossible, for she too was beleaguered by the knowledge that soon these young ones would stretch their wings and fly the nest – perhaps never to return – and she was finding that very hard to deal with.

She glanced across at Cordelia, and as their eyes met, she realised she was not alone in her sadness. Reaching out to take the elderly woman's hand, she gave it a gentle squeeze to let her know she understood how difficult she was finding all this upheaval and loss.

'Whatever happens out there, our girls will be all right,' said Cordelia quietly beneath the chatter. 'And they'll come home again, I'm sure of it.' She glanced across at Rita and Peter and gave a shallow sigh. 'But we must make the most of those two while we can, Peggy. For once they're gone, I doubt we'll see them again.'

Nodding her agreement, Peggy caught the look on Jack's face as he watched his daughter with such tenderness, and knew his heart was breaking. 'We'll have to take very good care of him once they've left, Cordy.'

'Of course we will,' she murmured. 'He's family.'

The quiet moment between them was broken by the arrival of Ron and Rosie with Harvey and Monty. After greeting everyone with great enthusiasm, both dogs flopped down on the old hearth rug to promptly fall asleep.

'We thought you might enjoy a wee dram of the good stuff,' said Ron, pulling a bottle of Jameson's Irish whiskey from his coat pocket.

'Where did you get hold of that?' asked Peggy suspiciously.

Ron tapped the side of his nose. 'To be sure, if you ask me no questions, I'll tell ye no lies, wee girl. Just enjoy it.'

'That stuff's as rare as hen's teeth,' muttered Cordelia, holding out her glass. 'I wouldn't say no to a drop or two.'

'And 'tis only a drop you'll be getting, old girl,' he rumbled with a twinkle in his eyes. 'For this is not to be downed the same way you polish off the sherry.'

'Are you suggesting I drink too much?' she asked with a glare that didn't quite match the smile tweaking her lips.

'If the cap fits, wear it,' he replied, splashing a tot into the glass. 'Get that down you, woman. It'll put hairs on your chest, so it will.'

'I sincerely hope it won't,' she retorted before taking a pleasurable sip.

Ron poured the drinks – making sure Charlie had only a snifter – and then raised his glass. 'Here's to the four of you. May you travel safely and keep us always in your hearts as you shall be in ours. *Sláinte*.'

They drank in silence, each lost in their own thoughts until Sarah stood and called for attention. 'I'd like to say something to Peggy and Ron and Aunt Cordelia,' she said. 'You have given me and Jane a loving home, wise counsel and support, making our transition to a new country so much easier than we ever could have expected. I know I speak for Jane when I say we love you all, and we will never forget the warmth and kindness you have shown us.' She raised her glass. 'To Peggy, Cordelia and Ron.'

The toast was echoed by the others, and then their glasses were replenished by Ron who was looking decidedly tearful. 'If we go on like this the bottle will soon be empty,' he grumbled.

'Drinking the evidence is the best way to hide your nefarious dealings, you old rogue,' said Cordelia before knocking back her tot and offering her glass up for more. Satisfied Ron had poured enough in, she stood. 'Now I'd like to say something, if I may.'

Ron rolled his eyes and groaned theatrically. 'Do you have to?'

'Indeed I do, Ronan Reilly, so keep quiet.' She sent him a glare which had little effect on him and then looked at those gathered around the table.

'I've lived a long and very comfortable retirement in this home Peggy has made for us all, and I want to thank her for taking me in and making me feel a part of this wonderful family.'

Her gaze swept over Rita, Danuta, Jane and Sarah. 'As for you girls, I want you to know how privileged I feel to be regarded as your grandmother, and how I've appreciated the way you've made me feel useful and wanted – even if I do drive you all potty at times.'

Ron grunted and her amused gaze fell on him. 'For all your shenanigans, you've been a rock to both me and Peggy during the war years, Ron, and I will always love you for that.'

Ron went scarlet. 'Do get on with it, woman,' he rumbled, not able to meet her gaze. 'The whiskey's evaporating in the glass while you're rambling on.'

Cordelia smiled beatifically at him and raised her glass. 'To you, my family, I wish you long life and the joy of knowing how very much you are loved. Cheers.'

'Cheers!'

The sound of so many raised voices woke the dogs momentarily and they looked up to see what was going on – but as it didn't involve food, they went back to sleep.

The evening continued in the quiet chatter of fond memories – and the not so pleasant ones of enemy raids, queuing at the shops, rationing and factory closures. And then the clock struck eleven, reminding them that they had an early start in the morning.

Rita was the first to make a reluctant move. Rising from her chair, she hugged Sarah and Jane, wishing them both good luck and a safe journey. 'Me and Pete will be off in three days, and I've barely started on my packing, so it's an early start for me too tomorrow.'

She handed Sarah a slip of paper. 'This is the address where we'll be staying in Cairns until we buy a place. Promise you'll write and tell me how you get on in Singapore.'

'Of course I will,' said Sarah, 'though it might take a while before we find out anything.' She hugged Rita again, and kissed her cheek. 'Stay safe, Rita, and have a wonderful life in Australia.'

Rita was unable to hide her pent-up excitement. 'Oh, we will, Sarah,' she breathed. 'Pete and I have so many plans, we can hardly wait to get there and make a start on them.'

Sarah caught the flash of pain in Jack's eyes, and unable to bear such stark misery, quickly turned to hug Peter. 'You never know, Peter, we might come and look you up if we have to go to Cairns with Mother.'

'Fair go, Sarah, you know you'd both be very welcome.'

Everyone trooped out to see them off, and Ron rounded up the dogs. 'We'll be off too,' he said, giving both girls a hug. 'Would you be after giving this to my Jim when you see him? It's just a wee letter and a few snaps of our wedding.'

'Of course I will,' Sarah replied before giving Rosie a hug. 'Goodbye, Rosie. Thanks for all the marvellous nights we've spent at the Anchor. We'll always remember them.'

Ron embraced both girls swiftly and then stomped down the garden path with Rosie and the dogs following him. He clearly hated saying goodbye as much as Peggy did.

Much later that night when everyone else was asleep, Sarah lay awake and thought about the journey they were about to make within the next few short hours. There was a modicum of excitement at the thought of returning to Singapore and seeing her mother, but it was overshadowed by the knowledge that the homecoming would not be an easy one however things might turn out.

She turned and snuggled beneath the blanket, praying for sleep to come, but every time she closed her eyes she saw Delaney. How she longed to see him just once more – to hear his voice and feel his arms around her. Yet she knew that all the wanting in the world wouldn't change things, and she had no choice but to carry on without him.

13

It was barely light when Sarah and Jane came downstairs with their cases to find Peggy and Cordelia waiting for them in the kitchen. 'Oh,' breathed Jane. 'You didn't have to get up so early.'

'Of course we did,' said Cordelia rather brusquely. 'We weren't about to let you leave without saying goodbye.'

'Sit down and eat something. You're going to need it for that long journey,' said Peggy, hurrying to pour cups of tea and put cereal in the bowls.

Jane and Sarah were too keyed up to eat much, but they managed a cup of tea, their eyes constantly darting towards the clock. Their train left at six-thirty and they couldn't afford to miss it.

'I'm driving you to the station, so there's no need to fret,' said Peggy. 'Please try and eat something.'

They nibbled a piece of toast with little enthusiasm, and Peggy realised it was too early and they were too tense to enjoy anything at the moment. She left the table and set about making a pile of tomato sandwiches which she wrapped in newspaper and tucked into a string bag.

'You can take these with you and enjoy them later,' she said, handing the bag to Sarah.

'Thanks, Aunt Peggy,' she said softly before pushing back from the table to embrace a tearful Cordelia.

'I do wish you didn't have to go,' whimpered Cordelia. 'I'm going to miss you both so much, and I hate the thought of you being so far away.'

'We'll come back, Cordy,' Sarah soothed. 'I promise. And I'll send you a telegram as soon as I know anything about Pops and Philip.'

Jane joined in the embrace. 'We love you very much, Cordy, so you make sure you stay fit and well for when we see you again.'

'I'll do my best,' sniffed Cordelia, gently easing from their embrace. 'Now, I want you girls to take care out there and look out for one another. The place will no doubt be swarming with soldiers and sailors, and two pretty young things like you need to stay alert.'

Jane bit down on a smile. 'I'm sure we'll be fine, and don't forget, we'll have Mother to chaperone us.'

Cordelia tutted and dug in her apron pocket for two envelopes. 'Take these. As you can see, one is addressed to your mother, the other is for you. Wait until you're on the plane before opening it, please.'

Peggy saw Jane frown before she exchanged a glance with her sister and then tucked the envelopes in her handbag.

'I feel as if I'm working for the Post Office with all the letters I'm carrying,' Jane joked. 'But I'll see she gets it, Cordy.'

'When is she due to arrive in Singapore?' asked Peggy, stripping off her wrap-round apron and reaching for her jacket.

'The same day as us,' said Sarah. 'We'll meet at the docks if all goes well – if there's a delay we've arranged to meet in the Palm Court at Raffles.'

Peggy glanced at the clock. 'We'd better get going,' she said tightly, determined not to let her emotions run away with her. 'I'm sorry Charlie isn't awake to see you off, and I can't imagine where Danuta has got to.'

'We said our goodbyes to both of them last night,' said Jane, 'so don't fret, Aunt Peg.'

Peggy watched the flurry of hugs and kisses between Cordelia and her great-nieces, then, unable to bear the sight of Cordelia's tears, hurried outside to where the car was parked in the cul-de-sac.

Cordelia came out onto the front steps to wave them off, her little face drawn and tear-streaked as the girls loaded their cases and climbed into the car. One last blown kiss, and promises to write, and Peggy drove away from Beach View, heading for the station, her sight blurred by her own tears. Poor Cordelia was obviously feeling bereft; she would have to keep a close eye on her from now on.

The town was deserted at this time of the morning but for the milkman's dray which was being pulled by an enormous shire horse as it made its slow way up the empty streets. A glance in the rear-view mirror told Peggy that Jane was remembering the time she'd steered that lovely big horse through these streets on the milk round, and was glad she'd found time yesterday to go up to the dairy to say goodbye.

Turning the car into the station courtyard, she parked and switched off the engine. She'd known this day would come, but how had it arrived so quickly? Tamping down on her emotions, she climbed out and followed the girls onto the platform where the train was already drawing in.

She nodded to Stan and then drew the girls to her, kissing their cheeks and holding them close. 'Good luck, my darlings,' she murmured. 'Have a safe journey, and please let me know when you've arrived. I'll be on tenterhooks until I know you've got there all right.'

The girls hugged and kissed her one last time and then quickly boarded the train as Stan prepared to blow his whistle. Leaning out of the window, they reached for Peggy's outstretched hands until the very last minute, and then waved just before the train rounded the curve and she lost sight of them.

Peggy burst into tears, and when she felt Stan's sturdy arms around her, she sobbed against his broad chest.

'There, there, Peggy, lass,' he murmured. 'They'll soon be back, you'll see.'

Feeling utterly ashamed at the way she'd let herself go, and knowing she must look ridiculous standing here in Stan's arms, she eased herself from his embrace and mopped up her tears with some vigour. 'I'm sick and tired of saying goodbye,' she managed. 'And I'll have to do it all again in three days' time when Rita and Peter leave.'

'I know, lass. It's hard for everyone, but we have to let the young ones go. It's why we fought this war, so they could be free to get on with their lives.' He held her arms and beamed down at her. 'Just remember all the good times, Peg, and look forward to having your Jim home again.'

Peggy shot him a brave, tearful smile. 'Bless you, Stan. Of course I will. Now I'd better get home. Poor Cordelia's really cut up about the girls leaving, and Daisy will be waking up and wondering where I've got to.'

Sarah took Jane's hand and held it tightly as the train huffed and puffed its way along the coast towards Southampton. Leaving Peggy, Cordelia and Beach View hadn't been as hard or painful as leaving their parents and Philip in Singapore, but it was a close-run thing, and neither girl felt much like talking.

They'd sat with their own thoughts while the train carried them further and further away from the only home they'd known since coming to England, and as they drew nearer to the flying boat terminal, their focus became fixed on the long journey ahead of them.

'I don't know about you, Sarah, but I've got butterflies in my stomach,' said Jane as they got their first sight of the flying boat waiting by the dock.

'I feel the same, but I'm not sure if it's fear or excitement. At least the plane looks nice and sturdy, so that's quite comforting.'

The train drew to a halt at the newly built terminal, and the girls stepped down onto the platform with their cases.

They looked at one another and linked hands. 'This is it,' breathed Sarah. 'Are you ready?'

'As ready as I'll ever be,' replied Jane. 'Let's get on with it.'

Almost an hour later they joined the other twelve passengers in the comfortably furnished cabin to wait nervously for the plane to take off. Within minutes, the engines spluttered into life and began to roar as the propellers turned faster and faster until they were just a blur.

Jane and Sarah clutched each other's hands in fear and excitement as the flying boat began to glide across the water, so swiftly that great jets of water rose on both sides from beneath the broad floats. And then they were lifting into the air and soaring above the Solent and the Isle of Wight.

The girls looked at each other and breathed a sigh of relief. They were finally on their way home.

Despite her hurried departure from the station, Peggy took her time going home, not yet ready to face Cordelia or Daisy and the busy day she would have at the factory. She drove down to the seafront and parked the car, then climbed out and went to sit on one of the newly repaired benches.

Lighting a cigarette, she tried to relax and prepare herself for Cordelia's tears, Daisy's chattering, and the long list of things she had to do. She gazed out to the horizon where the last vestiges of the sunrise streaked the pearly sky with slashes of pink and orange which were reflected in the Channel waters. Yet despite the beauty of this early morning, the pink sky heralded rain, and as she sat there, she could smell the tang of it in the strengthening breeze that was now tugging at her hair.

It was so quiet and peaceful down here with only the gulls for company and the soft hiss of the waves breaking on the shingle, that it was tempting just to stay here and enjoy it. The enemy fighter plane had finally been removed from the rusting ribs of the pier ballroom; the bandstand gleamed with fresh paint, and the refurbished Victorian shelters along the promenade looked as good as new. Soon the council workers would come to put out the deckchairs, the café at the end of the promenade would open and the tourists would appear from their hotels and boarding houses to take their chances with the weather to sit or take a stroll.

Peggy turned to admire the beautiful carpet garden that Fred Wilson had laid as a memorial to all those who'd died when the Grand Hotel and its neighbouring boarding house had taken a direct hit. Ron and Harvey had rescued a young woman and her baby from the depths of the rubble, she remembered, but they'd been the lucky ones, for many had died on that awful night.

She finished her cigarette and stubbed it out beneath her shoe before dumping it in a nearby bin. She'd kept an eye on Fred Wilson while his wife was in hospital, and he'd coped admirably well once she'd pointed him in the right direction. Now Kate was at home and baby Evie growing stronger every day, things had settled down and they were getting on with life, so they didn't need her popping in every day.

But because they had so many little mouths to feed, Kate would soon go back to work on a part-time basis at Solly's Camden Road factory while the children were looked after in the crèche. Fred had been promoted to head gardener by the council, which had given him a huge confidence boost, so they wouldn't be struggling too much over money.

Peggy glanced at her watch and was surprised to find she'd been away from home for almost an hour and a half. She reluctantly pulled on her headscarf and hurried back to the car. The wind was quite brisk now, and she thought she'd felt a few spots of rain. It seemed that summer was drawing to a close and the breath of autumn was already in the air. The circle of life kept on turning like the seasons, and as one phase ended another began – just as she must begin again.

Arriving back at Beach View, she ran up the front steps, took a deep breath, slotted in the key and stepped into the hall, her apology for being so late dying on her lips as she saw Cordelia sitting on the chair by the telephone.

One look at her face told Peggy she was agitated and very upset. 'Whatever's the matter?' she asked, hurrying to her.

'Where on earth have you been, Peggy?' she asked tremulously. 'I've been waiting and waiting for you.'

'I'm so sorry, Cordy. I just needed a bit of time to myself before I came back. What's happened to get you so upset?'

'This arrived for Sarah and Jane minutes after you left,' she said, handing her the telegram. 'It's from Jim.'

Peggy's pulse was hammering as she took it from her and swiftly read the abrupt message.

*Chaos here * Vital stay England * Will inform when have news **
*Jim **

Peggy carefully folded the slip of paper back into the brown envelope, the guilt of having left Cordelia to worry over the telegram weighing heavy. She gently helped Cordelia to her feet and gave her a hug before steering her into the kitchen.

'It's too late to do anything about it now,' she said softly. 'But the girls are intelligent enough to realise that it's bound to be chaotic over there.'

She settled Cordelia in her favourite armchair and briefly cupped her sweet face in her hands. 'They know their way around Singapore, and will have Jim and their mother to look after them, so please try not to worry, Cordy.'

'Easier said than done,' Cordelia replied, dabbing her nose with a handkerchief. 'I know our Jim will look after them if he can, but he's there to do a job and simply might not be able to. From what I've learnt about Sybil, she'll be as useful as a chocolate teapot, and if the Bristows' bungalow isn't available, heaven only knows where they'll end up.' She grasped Peggy's hand. 'We must do something, Peggy. They can't go.'

'I don't really see how I can stop them,' said Peggy. She glanced up at the clock. 'They'll be in Southampton by now, I should think, and about to board the plane.'

'Then telephone the airport or whatever it is and try to get a message to them,' Cordelia persisted.

Peggy couldn't see what good that would do, but to appease Cordelia, she went back into the hall and lifted the telephone receiver.

'Hello, April, dear. I wonder if you could help. I'm trying to get hold of the flying boat station at Southampton.'

'Oh. I don't know if I have the number for that,' the girl replied. 'I'll have to put you through to directory enquiries.'

Peggy silently blessed her for not wasting time by asking questions, and stood fidgeting for what felt like ages until the operator on directory enquiries put her through. It seemed to ring for hours, but when it was finally answered, she was informed that the plane had already taken off.

'They've gone, Cordy, I'm sorry,' she said, returning to the kitchen. 'The chap in the office said they could have relayed a message to the pilot, but only in a dire emergency situation – and as I didn't want to cause the girls any further worry, I decided to leave things as they are.'

Cordelia gave a tremulous sigh. 'We'll just have to wait to hear from them, then. I'll make a fresh pot of tea while you wake Daisy. Charlie's up and about already, but Danuta left for work shortly after you went to the station.'

Danuta hadn't really needed to leave so early this morning, but she wanted to get through her rounds as quickly as possible so she had time to cycle up to the Cliffe estate to see what was happening with Stanislaw. She hadn't seen him for almost a week and he hadn't telephoned either, so she was worried about him. He'd clearly been overdoing things, and she could only hope he hadn't made himself ill.

She read through the list of calls she would have to make that day and then took her time to polish her bag and pack it with clean instruments and all the paraphernalia she would need, her thoughts turning to Sarah and Jane. She would miss both girls, but especially Jane, who she'd come to know very well during her time at Bletchley Park.

Jane had worked in the decoding room alongside Alan Turing, and for a time had been Danuta's only contact with England, deciphering the messages she'd sent and passing on information and the new coded passwords that had been so vital to her survival behind enemy lines.

Of course they hadn't been able to acknowledge one another as they would have liked – they'd both signed the Secrets Act which forbade them ever to mention the roles they'd played during the war – but they'd managed to get together in private for a few minutes at a time to reminisce about the men and women they'd worked alongside. They'd both agreed that if it hadn't been for the genius of Turing who'd broken the Germans' Enigma code, the world would have suffered many more years of warfare.

Jane had been introduced to that covert world through Doris's son Anthony, who'd spotted her keen ability to solve complex mathematical problems, whereas Danuta had become involved through Ron's contacts in the SOE. They'd both been mentored by the glamorous Dolly Cardew who'd gladly come out of retirement to pass on her expertise gained during her undercover work in the First War. Dolly had been a stalwart supporter throughout, and it had come as a shock to Danuta to discover she was Pauline Reilly's mother, for no two women could have been more different.

Danuta finished packing her bag and carried it out to the bike shed. She grimaced as she felt the first few drops of rain splash on her face, and knew she was in for a miserable day. Perhaps she should think about asking Jack if he could get hold of a little second-hand car. With winter just around the corner, it would make life so much easier – and it wasn't as if she couldn't afford it. Dolly had given her fifty pounds before she'd left for America, with a note ordering her to spend it on something nice for herself.

Dumping her bag in the bicycle basket, she shrugged on her raincoat, tied a scarf over her bright red beret and set off for her first call of the day, the thought of owning a car giving her added energy as she tackled the steep hill up to Mafeking Terrace.

With ulcers bathed, newborns weighed and checked and postnatal mothers put at ease over their worries, Danuta cycled through the teeming rain to Jack's workshop. She stepped inside and shook the rain off her coat and scarf. 'Hello, Jack. On your own today?'

He looked up from servicing a car engine. 'It seems that way,' he replied. 'You look as if you need a cuppa. Come in and sit by the heater while I put the kettle on.'

'I am very wet,' she agreed. 'And a cup of tea would be most welcome.' She dragged off her sodden scarf and beret and ruffled her fingers through her damp hair. Taking off the raincoat, she shook it vigorously and hung it up above the heater to dry out before perching on an upturned crate.

Jack handed her a mug of tea. 'Get that down you before you catch your death of cold,' he said, sitting on a nearby oil-drum with his own grubby mug. 'So, Danuta, what can I do for you today?'

'I have come to ask about buying a small car. It will not be new, of course, but it must be reliable because I have to use it for my work.'

'I might have something coming in at the end of next week,' he replied, eyeing her over the lip of his mug of tea. 'How much were you thinking of paying?'

Danuta smiled at him. 'That depends on how much you are asking, and if the car is worth it.'

Jack chuckled. 'There's no flies on you, are there, girl?'

Danuta frowned in confusion. 'I have no flies. They do not come out in the rain.'

215

Jack tipped back his head and laughed. 'You're right,' he spluttered eventually. 'It's too cold and wet for flies.' He looked at her fondly. 'I'll see what I can do about a car,' he said. 'Can't have you out in all weathers. But they're pricey, Danuta, and then there's the running cost and insurance.'

'How much is new car?' she asked solemnly.

'Over three hundred quid,' he replied, 'but I can probably find a little second-hand one under the hundred.'

'Oh, I see.' Her spirits plummeted. 'And what could I get for fifty pounds?'

She saw Jack bite back a quick answer, and, crestfallen, had to accept she was nowhere near being able to afford such a luxurious thing as a car.

He must have seen her disappointment, for he patted her shoulder and shot her an encouraging smile. 'I'll see what I can do, but I can't promise anything, love. Fifty quid doesn't go very far these days when it comes to motors – but we could get lucky.'

She nodded gratefully and drank the last of her tea. 'I will keep my fingers crossed, Jack. Now I must go to Memorial Hospital to see Stanislaw. He is not well, I think, and I worry for him.'

Jack eyed the rain that was pelting down, and tossed the remains of his tea out into the nearby drain. 'I'll take you up there in the truck,' he said. 'Can't have you pedalling all that way in this.' Without waiting for a reply, he handed her the medical bag and hoisted her bike into the flatbed.

Danuta dragged on her coat, beret and scarf, and once Jack had locked the workshop door, quickly hopped into the cab, so grateful she could have hugged him – but of course she didn't, for it would have embarrassed both of them.

The journey took no time at all, and soon he was pulling up at the bottom of the front steps. She jumped out and ran for cover beneath the portico as he unloaded the bike and brought it to her. 'If you want a lift back, give me a ring,' he said, handing her a business card. 'I'm in the workshop all day.'

'You are very kind, Jack. Thank you so much.'

He shot her a wink and ran back through the rain to the truck and within minutes he'd gone.

Danuta stowed her bike in the shelter of the portico and carried her medical bag into the mansion which had been turned into a respite hospital for those who were not yet well enough to be released to their homes. Stanislaw's room was at the back of the building on the ground floor, and as she made her way there she exchanged greetings with many of the patients and nursing staff she'd come to know over the years since her return to England.

She saw Sister Brown in the corridor, and knowing she was looking after Stanislaw, she stopped to talk to her.

'Hello, Danuta. How lovely to see you. You're looking very well, I must say.'

'Thank you, but I am worried about Stanislaw,' she replied. 'Is he not well?'

Sister Brown bit her lip, clearly reluctant to discuss her patient even though it was with another nurse. 'He's been better,' she hedged. 'The doctor has prescribed total bed rest.'

'He has done too much, I think.'

'Look, Danuta, I shouldn't really be telling you this, but as you're a nurse and he has no family to care about him, I should warn you he isn't in a good way.'

Danuta's pulse thudded and she felt the colour drain from her face. 'What has happened?'

'He's been overdoing everything – especially the drinking – and he's not been taking care of his stumps properly and doing too much walking; consequently, he has to go without his prosthetics until the stumps are healed. He also has a chest infection which we're monitoring closely in case it turns to pneumonia.'

She took a breath and let it out on a sigh. 'All in all, Danuta, he's a sick man and we're all worried about him.'

'I must see him. I can go now?'

'Don't be too hard on him, Danuta. He's had an earful from the doctors as well as me, and knows he's been a silly billy.'

Danuta had never heard that expression before, but could guess what it meant. She thanked Sister Brown and hurried down the corridor to Stanislaw's room. Knocking lightly on the door, she waited a moment and when there was no reply, she opened it a crack and peeked in.

Stanislaw was lying in bed on his back fast asleep and gently snoring. The bottom half of his body was hidden beneath sheets and blankets which had been tented over a metal frame to keep the weight off his stumps.

Danuta closed the door softly behind her and crept to the bedside chair. Sitting down, she noted how drawn and strangely vulnerable he looked. There was a series of drips attached to his arms, and there was a catheter tube and bag fixed to the base of the bed to monitor his urine output. It looked suspiciously cloudy, but she couldn't see any blood in it which was a huge relief.

She settled back in the chair and watched him sleeping, only just resisting the urge to stroke back the dark curl of hair which was flopping over his brows, and struggling not to keep looking at his naked, muscled chest which rose and fell above the bedding. He was a lovely, vibrant bear of a man with such a vast capacity for love and life that it tore at her heart to see him like this.

Shocked by her reaction and the strong emotions that washed over her, she reached for one of the many books piled on the bedside cabinet and tried to concentrate on something else. But although the book was in Polish and the story was a familiar and much-loved one, her concentration kept slipping and she found herself gazing at his chest, wondering what that golden skin would feel like beneath her fingers.

The warmth in the room and the gentle rhythm of his snoring must have sent her to sleep, for she jolted awake to find he was leaning on his side watching her with great interest, the sheet now barely covering his hips.

'Ah, so my sleeping beauty awakes,' he said and smiled.

'I didn't mean to go to sleep,' she protested, tearing her gaze from that flat belly and the line of hair tracing its way beneath the sheet. 'But it's warm and airless in here and it's been a long morning.'

'Of course, of course,' he replied, nodding his great head and pulling the sheet up to his chest. 'I will ask the nurse to bring us some tea.'

'Only if you want some,' she said, flustered.

His gaze captured her like a moth in a web, his eyes dark and so mesmeric she couldn't look away. 'We both have a thirst, little one,' he murmured in Polish. 'I have seen how you look at me when you think I am sleeping, and I wish very much to taste the nectar of your lips.'

She went scarlet and it took all her willpower to tear her gaze away. 'Don't talk such nonsense, Stanislaw,' she retorted briskly. 'You're in no fit state to kiss anyone, and I'm in no mood for your your shenanigans,' she blustered.

He chuckled and she was sorely tempted to slap him.

'It's no laughing matter,' she went on in rapid Polish. 'Look what you've done to yourself, you silly man. Why can't you behave yourself instead of causing so much worry and making yourself ill?'

'You are worried about me? That's nice,' he sighed.

'It's not nice,' she snapped. 'How dare you lie there and flirt with me when you could be at death's door? And all through your own stupidity. You've got to stop drinking so much, Stanislaw, and not push things so hard you damage your stumps to the point where you have to go without your prosthetics.' She could feel the tears coming and was unable to stop them. 'You're killing yourself, Stan,' she rasped. 'Please, please stop it.'

He reached for her hand, his face lined with deep concern. 'Please don't cry. I cannot bear to see your tears.'

219

She snatched away her hand and swiped at her shaming tears. 'Do you promise you'll stop drinking so much and take things slower?'

He sat up in the bed and reached for her hands again to gently draw her towards him, his expression solemn. 'I promise on the souls of my family that I will be sensible about my drinking and behave from this day on,' he said. 'But may I ask something of you, Danuta?'

She blinked away her tears. 'Of course,' she murmured.

'Could you love me?' he asked. 'Could you love this broken man with no legs who can only be a burden to you, but who loves you with all his heart, all his soul and every fibre of his being?'

The tears streamed down her face and she nodded wordlessly as her own heart and soul reached out to him. 'But only if you keep your promise to behave,' she managed.

'It is a promise to keep now I know we will be together someday.' He didn't attempt to kiss her, but drew her into his arms and held her so close she could feel his heart beating against her own.

In that moment Danuta knew she'd come home, and regardless of the trials ahead, she would love and treasure this man until her last breath.

Rita softly closed the door and looked up at Peter with a grin. 'I told you there was something going on between those two,' she whispered. 'But I think we should keep this to ourselves for now, or Peggy will be planning a wedding before you can blink.' She took his hand. 'Come on, let's get out of here and leave them to it. He doesn't need our daily visit now.'

'She'll have a hard time of it keeping him in order,' said Peter as they retraced their steps to the front door. 'Stan can get wild at times.'

'That's what put him back in bed,' said Rita. 'But Danuta's tough. She won't stand any nonsense.'

They stood beneath the portico and watched the rain teeming down to form puddles on the driveway and gurgle through the drainpipes. 'So, what are we going to do for the rest of the day, Pete?' she asked, pulling on her leather gloves. 'I don't fancy riding about in this, and I can't really face poor old Dad with his sad eyes and forced smiles.'

He put his arm round her shoulders and nuzzled her neck. 'Let's go back home to bed. Seeing Stan and Danuta like that has given me ideas.'

Rita giggled and dug him in the ribs with her elbow. 'You don't need them to give you ideas, you naughty man,' she teased. She pulled on her crash helmet and fastened the ancient flying jacket up to her neck. 'So what are you waiting for?'

They ran out into the rain and clambered onto the motor-bike. With Rita's arms around his waist and her body resting tightly against his back, Pete kick-started the engine and sped for home.

14

'Do stand still, Charlie, for goodness' sake,' hissed Peggy, tugging at his sleeve. 'How can I be expected to see if this blazer fits properly if you keep fidgeting?'

'I'm fed up, Mum. It fits all right. I don't know why you're fussing.'

'It fits now, but it won't in a year's time,' she retorted. 'Not with the way you're growing.' She pulled the blazer off and hurried out of the changing room in search of one that was a bigger size.

The new grammar school term would start tomorrow, and this was the first time she'd managed to pin Charlie down long enough to get him kitted out in his uniform. The price of it all was quite shocking, and because he was so big, she had to find suitable shirts, trousers and shoes in the men's department, which meant using up the precious clothing coupons Sarah and Jane had so generously donated for the cause.

She hurried back to the changing room, aware that her lunch hour was rapidly dwindling. 'Let's see if this one has some room to grow in it,' she ordered her grumpy son.

Charlie dragged the blazer on and stood in stoic silence as she buttoned it up and checked the length of the sleeves.

'That will have to do,' she said on a sigh. 'It's the biggest they've got. Is there anything else you'll need?'

'Football kit,' he said gloomily. 'And my rugby boots are pinching my toes.'

Peggy closed her eyes momentarily and took a breath. She'd known this expedition would be costly, but hadn't realised how quickly it would all mount up. 'Do you really need football kit? Won't they let you off as you're in the local rugby team?' she asked hopefully.

He eyed her patiently. 'The school plays football, and I don't want to be seen as different to the others. I might not like the game, but I can play it well enough to get by.'

Understanding how important it was for him to mix in with the others, Peggy took him down to the sportswear department. With everything wrapped up and the bill paid, she loaded it all into Charlie's arms. 'You'll have to carry that home. I've got to go back to work,' she said briskly. 'And don't just dump it on the floor, hang it up properly.'

Charlie rolled his eyes and gave a deep sigh before striding out of Plummers and down the High Street.

Peggy watched him go, thinking once again how very much like his father he was. They shared the same broad shoulders, narrow waist and long legs – the same dark hair and jaunty walk. Realising she was wasting time, she snapped out of her day-dreaming and headed up the hill to the factory estate.

Jack was standing in the doorway of his workshop, staring gloomily out at nothing in particular, his thoughts clearly on Rita's departure for Australia tomorrow.

Peggy didn't stop, for he didn't look as if he wanted company, and she would see him later anyway. They had all been invited to Jack's bungalow for supper, so they could ensure that Rita and Peter's last night in Cliffehaven went with a swing. Though she doubted Jack would enjoy it much, poor man.

With her thoughts focused on Jack, she almost missed seeing Pauline emerge from the Red Cross offices, laughing and chatting rather flirtatiously with a silver-haired, handsome man she could only assume was one of her bosses. About to dodge round a corner to avoid her, she realised it was too late. Pauline had spotted her and was now purposefully heading her way.

With very little enthusiasm, she went to meet her sister-in-law, already planning a speedy escape. 'Hello, Pauline. How are you?' she asked with a brittle smile.

'Extremely well,' she replied coolly. 'And you?'

'Muddling on as usual,' said Peggy, noting the other woman's carefully applied make-up and smart suit. 'Sorry, Pauline, but I can't stop to chat. I'm already late getting back to work.'

Pauline's smile was frosty. 'Always busy, aren't you? Rushing here and there without much thought for others.'

Peggy bridled. 'What do you mean by that?'

Pauline pursed her scarlet lips and patted her tightly permed hair. 'I was expecting you to call in and see how I was after I had to leave Doris's reception so hurriedly,' she said.

'It never occurred to me that you'd appreciate a visit after the last time we crossed swords,' said Peggy with equal coolness. 'Besides, Frank told me you'd been to see that headache specialist and he'd passed you fit.'

'That's no thanks to you,' snapped Pauline. 'You should think twice before slapping people, Peggy. It could do a great deal of damage.'

'To your ego, maybe, but clearly not much else,' retorted Peggy, eyeing the tailored suit and high heels. 'How are Brendon and his little family?'

'They're very cosy in their new house – not that I go there often – I don't feel welcome. But I'm sure Frank's told you all about it.'

'Look, Pauline, if there's nothing in particular you needed to say to me, then I really must be going.'

'Well, I do have something to tell you, actually. I've been offered another very important promotion,' she announced with a glint in her eyes. 'Which is one in the eye for you and Mother, as neither of you thought I was good for anything. But I'll let Frank tell you all about it as you seem to prefer talking to him rather than me.' With that, she stalked off, head held high and handbag swinging.

Peggy turned to watch her in astonishment. 'What the hell was that all about?' she muttered before shaking her head and going into the factory.

Sitting behind her desk in her glassed-off cubicle, Peggy sat and watched the women who were busy at their machines. The workings of Pauline's mind had always been difficult to fathom, and frankly, Peggy had given up trying. She was an unpleasant, selfish woman who'd alienated her only surviving son, her mother and her sister, and made poor Frank's life a misery. It was no wonder he spent most nights at sea in the trawler.

Jack had taken his time to wash and shave and clean the dirt and grease from beneath his nails before getting dressed. He could hear Rita and Peter talking in the kitchen and could smell the turkey roasting in the oven, but the last thing he needed tonight was food – or company – and he was dreading having to smile and pretend that everything was all right.

He regarded his reflection in the bedroom mirror and plastered on a smile which was more of a grimace really, but that couldn't be helped. He didn't want to upset Rita and spoil her last night in England, so it was time to pull himself together, ignore his bruised heart and get on with it.

He emerged from the bedroom just as Rita opened the door to Peggy, Cordelia, Danuta, Daisy, Ron and Rosie. 'Glad to see you all,' he said with forced cheerfulness. 'It's going to be a bit of a squash, so we've put up a trestle table in the sitting room and borrowed chairs from the scout hut.'

They all trooped in as Rita picked up Daisy to give her a kiss and cuddle, and Peter rushed to make sure everyone had a drink.

'Here you go, Jack,' said Ron, handing over a crate of bottled beer. 'And there's a nip of the hard stuff to stiffen your spine,' he added quietly, slipping him a half-bottle of gin. 'Just don't let Cordelia catch sight of that or she'll have the lot.' He winked, patted his arm and followed the others into the sitting room.

Jack managed to survive the evening by letting Peter and Rita do the honours as hosts, and drinking his way through several bottles of beer. He laughed at the jokes, joined in with the reminiscences of Rita's childhood, and even supplied a story or two of his lighter moments and mishaps during his time in the army. However, he hadn't really tasted any of the meal Rita had cooked so beautifully, and was fully aware of the surreptitious looks of concern Peggy and Ron kept darting at him. They understood what he was going through, but thankfully had said nothing.

'By the way, Danuta,' he said during a lull in the conversation. 'I was up at the Cliffe estate yesterday to look over the cars Lord Cliffe took on in the deal he did with Chumley's receivers. And there's a nice little Austin 7 with low mileage on the clock and a good service history which I thought might suit you.'

'How much does Lord Cliffe want for it?' she asked, blushing at being the centre of attention.

'Fifty quid,' he replied, ignoring the fact it was worth three times that.

'You are sure of this?' she asked with a frown.

'Lord Cliffe wants shot of all of them quickly so I paid for a job lot,' he said airily.

'Is good car?' she asked, clearly still suspicious that he was asking too little for it.

'Chumley bought it for his housekeeper and she rarely used it. I'll give it a good tune-up, and you'll be all set.'

'I'd snap it up if I were you,' said Rita. 'Think how easy it will be to do your rounds and get up to Cliffe to see Stan without having to cycle about in all weathers.' She grinned naughtily at Danuta. 'How is he, by the way?'

Danuta went a deep scarlet and couldn't meet her gaze. 'He is not very well.. The doctor says he needs to take things very quietly for a while.'

'You'd better warn him that Doris will be back from her honeymoon next week and is planning to ask him round for dinner,' said Peggy.

'Stanislaw is not well enough for that,' said Danuta firmly. 'He has much to do before he is fully recovered.'

She looked across at Jack. 'May I take a drive in the car before I buy it?' she asked. 'Only I have not driven since I was in Poland and will find it strange to be on wrong side of road.'

'I'll take you out early Sunday morning for a test drive while there's not much traffic about,' said Jack. 'You'll soon get the hang of it again.'

'Perhaps you could take Stan out for a run in the country,' said Rita with a teasing light in her eyes. 'He'd enjoy getting away from the hospital for a while.'

Danuta met her gaze, knowing that she somehow knew things had progressed with Stanislaw but determined to give nothing away. 'I'm sure that he would. But only if the doctor gives his approval.'

The evening broke up shortly after that exchange, and once all the dishes had been washed and put away, and cardigans and jackets collected, Jack stood rather unsteadily by as Rita and Peter were kissed and hugged and wished the very best of luck for the future.

Peggy and Cordelia were close to tears, and Jack wished he could give in to his own – but there would be plenty of time to cry once his beloved girl was gone. For now he would hold back the emotions that churned inside him and see that she left with no regrets.

He closed the door as the two cars were driven away. 'That went well,' he said. 'Everyone seemed to enjoy themselves, and that was a lovely bit of turkey, Rita.'

She put her arms round him. 'You don't fool me, Dad,' she murmured against his chest. 'I know you hardly tasted a thing. But thanks for being so brave and supportive when I know how hard tonight must have been.'

He held her close and rested his chin on her head, unable to speak.

She eventually drew back from the embrace and looked up at him with a smile. 'Fifty quid for a good Austin 7? Have you lost your marbles, Dad?'

'She's a lovely, hard-working girl, and I don't like the thought of her on that bicycle in all weathers. It's no skin off my nose, Rita. I'll make a handsome profit from the other cars, never you mind.'

'You're just an old softie really, aren't you?'

'I suppose I am,' he said on a sigh. He kissed her brow and gave her a swift hug. 'Now I'm off to my bed. We've a very early start in the morning.'

He shook Peter's hand, then closed the bedroom door behind him to sink onto the bed and stare out into the darkness beyond the windows. This time tomorrow his little girl would be boarding a train that would take her far from home, and by the end of the week she'd be on a ship heading towards her new life. But Peter would love her and look after her, he was certain of that – and if he kept on making good money at the workshop, he'd soon save enough to take a trip out there to see them.

With that pleasant thought, he prepared for bed and, with help from the gin, quickly fell asleep.

Rita hadn't slept well knowing that her father was still troubled by her imminent departure. She dressed quickly in comfortable trousers, lightweight jumper and cotton blouse, and slipped her feet into her low-heeled shoes before tiptoeing out of the bedroom to use the bathroom. She'd leave Peter sleeping for a while longer as there was plenty of time for them to have breakfast before they caught the train.

With her hair brushed to a gleam and a light application of make-up, she eyed her reflection in the bathroom mirror and was pleased with the effect. Marriage had certainly brought light and colour to her face, and there was no doubting that the excitement for the coming adventure also had something to do with it.

She went into the kitchen and found her father leaning in the back doorway, smoking a roll-up and sipping from a mug of tea as he stared out at the unkempt garden. 'You'll have to ask Ron to help you with the garden,' she said, slipping an arm about his waist. 'It's probably time to put in some winter vegetables.'

He looked down at her and grinned. 'I was thinking of concreting the whole thing over. Much less trouble.'

'That's just being lazy,' she replied, digging him in the ribs. She went to pour out a cup of tea and then hunted through the cupboards for the makings of breakfast.

The bacon was sizzling in the pan and the table was laid by the time Peter emerged from the bathroom, freshly shaved and looking very bright considering the amount of beer he'd had last night. The three of them sat down to eat and drink their way through a second pot of tea, the silence growing ever more tense as the minutes ticked away and the time of their departure drew nearer.

Rita got up to wash the dishes as Peter went to fetch the cases. 'Leave that,' said Jack. 'I'll do it later. Come and give me a hug instead.'

She stepped into his embrace and held him close. 'It won't be for ever, Dad. You'll come and visit, and who knows, we might come back at some point to see you all.'

'I'll hold you to that,' he murmured, not really believing she would. He squeezed her tight and then let her go. 'I won't be coming to the station to see you off, if you don't mind,' he said gruffly. 'It's better if you and Peter start your adventure together just as you mean to go on. Easier for me too.'

'Oh, Dad, I do wish you could be happy for us.'

He looked at her in astonishment. 'But of course I'm happy for you,' he gasped. 'You couldn't have a better husband than Peter, and I rather envy the adventure you're setting out on.' He caressed her cheek. 'I'm just feeling sorry for myself, that's all. You must take this chance with both hands and make the very best of all the opportunities there are out there – and not worry about me. I've got more work than I can handle, and if I need company, there's always the Anchor or Beach View.'

He looked over her head to Peter who was standing in the doorway with the suitcases at his feet. 'Get out of here, the pair of you,' he said with a forced smile. 'You don't want to miss that train.'

Peter grasped his hand. 'It's been good getting to know you, mate,' he said. 'Thanks for everything, and no worries – I'll look after her.'

'I know you will,' he replied gruffly.

He followed them into the hall and Rita kissed his cheek before hurrying to join Peter who was waiting by the motorbikes. The cases had been strapped to the back and he was holding out her crash helmet.

Jack watched them ride away – two vibrant, ambitious young people who looked so fine together that surely they could conquer anything. He returned Rita's wave as she paused briefly at the corner of the street, and once she'd ridden out of sight he closed the front door and leaned against it for a while to take control of the emotions that were ripping through him.

The bungalow already felt empty and the silence was heavy as he wandered from room to room and then stood in the kitchen eyeing the dirty dishes. He lit a cigarette and went into the back garden hoping the fresh air would clear his head, but the emptiness was there too – almost mocking him.

Unable to stand the solitude any longer, he fetched his clean overalls from the bedroom, picked up his lunchbox from the kitchen and slammed the front door behind him.

Work would be his saviour, and thankfully there was enough of it to keep his mind occupied for weeks.

They'd stowed the motorbikes in the guard's van, and Rita went to hug Stan the stationmaster and take charge of the paper bag filled with freshly baked rock buns. Turning to gaze for the last time down Cliffehaven's High Street, she broke into a smile.

'I knew you'd come,' she said as Peggy rushed from the car park and enfolded her in her arms.

'I couldn't let you go without saying one last goodbye,' Peggy murmured, holding her tightly. 'I know you'll be absolutely fine and will make a huge success of things out there, so I don't want you worrying about Jack. Ron and I will look after him.'

'Thanks, Auntie Peg. And I promise to write often and let you know how we're getting on.'

'You make sure you do.' Peggy turned to Peter and hugged him. 'I know you'll look after our girl, so I have no worries there. I hope your homecoming is all you wish it to be, Peter. It's been lovely to get to know you.'

Stan was fidgeting with his flag and whistle. 'Sorry, lass, but if I don't blow the whistle soon, the train will be late leaving.'

Rita swiftly hugged Peggy again and followed Peter onto the train. She tugged the leather strap on the window and leaned out as Stan blew his whistle and waved his flag. 'Bye, Aunt Peggy, bye, Stan. I love you,' she shouted above the deep grind of the train wheels as they began to turn.

The train gathered speed and rounded the bend, taking her away from Cliffehaven and everything she knew. She sank down beside Peter and nestled against his side as she fought back her tears and tried very hard to be brave.

'It's all right, love. You've got me,' murmured Peter. 'And I love you enough to make up for everyone you're leaving behind.'

Rita closed her eyes on the tears and held him close, sure in the knowledge that as long as they were together, all would be well.

Peggy hadn't really planned to go to the station to see them off, but she hadn't been able to resist, for no matter how hard it was to say goodbye to her chicks, each and every one of them deserved a proper send-off.

She hurried back to the car, her eyes blurred with tears. Beach View already felt deserted, but how much worse it must be for Jack. He'd clearly been unable to face seeing them off at the station this morning, and she could only imagine how bereft he must be feeling now he was alone in that bungalow.

She drove carefully back home, aware that she wasn't really in any fit state to be driving while in tears. Parking outside the front of Beach View, she sat for a moment to gain some control over her emotions and then climbed out purposefully. She had a busy day ahead of her, and she didn't have the time to sit here moping and feeling sorry for herself. Rita and Peter would be perfectly all right, she just knew they would.

Charlie was dressed and ready for his first day at his new grammar school. Ron had taken him to the barber's yesterday for a proper haircut, and she suspected it wouldn't be long before he started shaving, for there was a definite dark shadow on his top lip and jaw.

'Charlie's going to school,' announced Daisy. 'I go to school too. He come with me?'

'No, darling. He's going to big people's school,' said Cordelia. 'But when you're five, you'll be going to school down the road.'

Daisy gave a dramatic sigh. 'That's a long time,' she said. 'Why can't I go now?'

Peggy closed her ears to Daisy's endless questions and left Cordelia to answer them as she turned to Charlie. 'Now, have you got everything?' she asked as he picked up the over-stuffed satchel.

'Bar the kitchen sink,' he replied with a grin.

'Do you want me to walk with you to the bus stop?'

'Mum,' he protested. 'I'm fifteen. I don't need walking anywhere.'

She smiled lovingly at this man-child who'd come home in place of the small, eight-year-old boy she'd sent away all those years ago. 'No, I don't suppose you do.' She handed him the cap and gave his perfectly knotted tie a tweak. 'Have a good day, son, and I'll see you at teatime,' she murmured, longing to kiss his cheek but knowing it wouldn't really be appreciated now he was so grown-up.

'Yeah, bye, Mum. See you all later.'

Peggy gave a sigh as he slammed the back door behind him. The guilt of having sent him and his brother away would always be with her. Had they any inkling of how very hard it had been for her to let them go – or understood that she'd done it to keep them safe?

She turned her thoughts to more pleasant things. 'Has the post come yet?' she asked Cordelia who was now cleaning Daisy's face of jam.

'It has, but there was only a paper bill and a letter for me from Canada.' She eyed Peggy over her half-moon glasses as Daisy ran off to play with her toys. 'How did it go at the station?'

'They got off on time, and of course I couldn't help crying as usual,' she replied, pouring out a cup of tea. 'I'll pop in and see Jack on my way to work and ask him to come to supper tonight. He'll find it very hard being on his own.'

'It was kind of him to find a car for Danuta,' Cordelia commented, clearing away the dirty plates. 'And at such a good price too.'

'Yes. I wondered about that,' murmured Peggy. 'Where is she, by the way?'

'Sleeping in. It's her day off, remember?'

Peggy lit a cigarette. 'I have so many things on my mind at the moment that I barely know what day it is, let alone remember Danuta's duty roster,' she said on a sigh.

'I suppose you've noticed there's something going on between her and that baron,' said Cordelia with a twinkle in her eye.

Peggy smiled. 'Oh yes, but like Rita, I'm keeping that to myself until the girl's ready to tell us.'

Cordelia raised an eyebrow. 'That's most unlike you, Peggy Reilly. I'd have thought you'd be making wedding plans by now.'

'I never said I wasn't,' she replied with a wink.

15

The past few days had flown by and Peggy was relieved that Saturday had come round. She could lie in for a while longer and look ahead to a lovely quiet day with nothing much to do other than watch Charlie play his first rugby match, and think about the new curtains she'd ordered for the big room upstairs that would soon be hers if things went according to plan.

The factory was busy with new orders flooding in, and she'd been kept on her toes making sure they were fulfilled and delivered on time. Solly was like a dog with two tails in his delight at how well everything was going, and had given Peggy a generous pay rise – which turned out to be very useful indeed now that Ron had started decorating the bedrooms. Wallpaper and paint were costly, and soon she'd have tradesmen to pay as well.

She'd met with the plumber, electrician and plasterer and they would start next week on the basement, so Charlie would have to move upstairs into Jane and Sarah's old room now Ron had finished in there. There was still a lot of clearing up to be done in the basement, but she'd made a good start on it during the evenings, and Charlie had built a bonfire in the garden to get rid of all the accumulated rubbish.

She stretched and yawned before slowly getting out of bed, and, still in her nightclothes, went in search of a nice cup of tea. Daisy was still asleep, so she'd leave her for a while and have a few minutes to herself.

Cordelia was already at the breakfast table with Charlie who was stuffing down toast and baked beans as if his life depended upon it. 'For goodness' sake, Charlie, stop gobbling your food. You'll get indigestion,' Cordelia admonished mildly.

'I'll be late for the team meeting if I don't get a move on,' he said through a mouthful. 'We've got a match this afternoon and the coach wants us to have a good warm-up session.'

'What time are you playing?' asked Peggy, sitting down with her cup of tea. 'We'd love to come and watch, wouldn't we, Cordy?'

'Three o'clock,' he said, pushing back from the table. 'Grandad and Uncle Frank are coming, and as it's the first game of the season the club's laying on tea for everyone, so don't be late, or you'll miss out. They're a bunch of gannets down there.'

'We'll be there,' said Peggy, a smile twitching her lips at his audacity for calling others gannets when he could put away enough food to feed a family for a week. 'Will you be back for lunch?'

He shook his head. 'I'm eating at the Anchor.'

With a depressing sense that she still didn't really know him, Peggy watched her youngest son gather up his things and leave the kitchen without saying goodbye. There had been a time before the war when she could gauge his moods and almost read his thoughts, but five years of being apart meant that although she loved him deeply, they were virtual strangers. They'd never really broached the subject of his evacuation, or how he'd felt about being sent away. It seemed to be something neither of them were willing to discuss – perhaps because the reality of how it had affected them might be too painful.

Peggy wondered fleetingly if he was happy to be home again, or if he was missing Aunt Vi and life on the Somerset farm. It wouldn't have surprised her, for he'd spent his formative years there and had grown extremely fond of Vi, who'd taken on the role of surrogate mother in her absence.

This was something that had made Peggy profoundly jealous, but her innate good sense had soon made her realise how selfish that was. The main thing was that Charlie had been given a loving, stable home. Of course he'd been lucky to have his sister, brother and nieces with him – and they'd all managed a very short visit home to see Jim before he was sent to India – unlike so many evacuees who'd had no contact with their families for years.

She listened to him clattering about in the basement, and then heard the slam of the back door. He seemed to be more settled now he was back on the rugby field, but he didn't confide in her as he'd once done, and clearly found any sort of intimacy very awkward. She could only hope that he used the time he spent with his grandfather and uncle to open up and talk about the things that worried him.

Her thoughts were broken by Cordelia. 'There's post for you this morning,' she said, pushing the letters and cards towards her. 'I read the postcards as they were addressed to no one in particular. They all seem to be having a high old time,' she added before returning to her perusal of the newspaper headlines.

Peggy felt a thrill of pleasure as she saw there was a letter from Jim and another from Ruby, as well as the four postcards. The one from Rita showed a view of Portsmouth docks, the note on the back clearly written in haste and excitement, for they were about to board the ship and she wanted them all to know she was thinking of them.

The picture postcards from Jane were more exotic, showing the port of Tripoli basking in the Mediterranean light, the pyramids of Cairo, and an ornate domed mosque in Bahrain. She turned them over one by one to read the messages.

It seemed Tripoli, Cairo and Bahrain were scorching hot and dusty and the food highly suspect even though they'd been staying in first-class hotels. They were expecting more of the same as they left for Karachi and Calcutta.

The flight had been surprisingly smooth and comfortable, but as they went further east they were hoping not to get caught up in the summer storms that had been forecast, for it would make the flight most unpleasant. They were on schedule to arrive in Singapore by Sunday, and promised to send a telegram the minute they arrived.

'My goodness,' Peggy breathed. 'They must be almost there by now. What an adventure they're having.'

But she found she was talking to herself, for Cordelia had turned off her hearing aid and was fully immersed in a newspaper article about the British Administration in Singapore. She tore open Jim's letter, disappointed to find it was short and clearly hurried.

My darling girl,

I received your telegram saying the girls were on their way, and I will watch out for them on Sunday, although this is the worst possible place for them to be. I can only hope there is good news regarding Jock and Philip, but going by what I've learned already, it's highly unlikely.

I write this in haste because there is so little time between my duties, and when I return to my billet, I'm so drained – physically and mentally – that all I want to do is sleep. The heat is the same as in the jungles of Burma, the monsoon clouds are gathering and the humidity is unbearably high – but that isn't what is so exhausting, Peggy. It's the sight of the prisoners arriving from the outlying camps that drain the soul from me.

They are all nationalities, with different horror stories to tell, and amongst them are women, old, young and in between, all of them covered in tropical sores and weakened by starvation and a long list of fevers and diseases. It's a miracle they've survived. But hearing them talk, and seeing how close they've become through their ordeal, I've realised these women are strong in mind and spirit and have refused to be broken. Though God knows how it will affect them during the rest of their lives.

However, it's the children that break my heart, Peggy. Very few have survived – the babies and little ones that were too weak to withstand the brutal regime were buried in the camps spread right across the islands and into Thailand itself. These older children who've come through what sounds like hell on earth don't know how to play and they look at you with eyes that hold the horrors of all they've seen and experienced – they're practically feral and mistrustful of everyone, and who can blame them? In those moments I think of little Daisy, of Cissy and Anne; the grandchildren, and Bob and Charlie, and thank God they never had to go through such a thing.

I've met Elsa Bristow who was a friend of the Fullers, and is now a widow. She's returned to Singapore as a tireless and rather forceful member of RAPWI, an organisation set up by Mountbatten for the recovery of Allied prisoners of war and internees. Although I fought long and hard against it, she persuaded the powers that be to assign me to help take witness statements from the returning prisoners so the Japanese commanders and guards can be justly punished for their heinous crimes.

I'm sick at heart, Peggy, for their stories will haunt me to my dying day, and I've never wished harder to be back at home with you, and to feel your arms about me, my children at my side. I don't really think I can believe that you're all truly safe until I can see you all again.

I will write again soon, but for now I must try and sleep. I love you with all my heart. Give my children and grandchildren a hug from me and hold them close. They are so very precious.

Jim xxx

Peggy fumbled with the thin paper as the tears rolled down her cheeks. She couldn't bear the thought of Jim having to go through such a horror – but neither could she heal his pain or his longing, and that was what hurt the most.

She mopped up her tears quickly before Cordelia noticed them and went into her bedroom to look down at their darling little girl who was just stirring. She couldn't begin to imagine how it must have been for the women who'd had to watch their babies die – to have to bury them in some jungle clearing and then, on liberation, be forced to leave them behind.

'Good morning, sleepyhead,' she murmured, gathering Daisy into her arms and holding her close. The weight of her was soothing, and she kissed the warm, soft cheek, breathing in the scent of her daughter, thanking God she was safe from harm.

Daisy began to wriggle and squirm, demanding breakfast, so Peggy released her reluctantly and followed her into the kitchen where the child ran straight to Cordelia for her morning cuddle.

Cordelia discarded her newspaper and let Daisy clamber onto her lap. Looking at Peggy sharply over the child's head, she raised a questioning brow.

'Jim's letter,' said Peggy quietly, pushing it towards her. 'I warn you, it doesn't make easy reading.'

While Daisy chattered away and ate her breakfast, the two women tried their best to respond, but Jim's letter had had a profound effect on them both, and they frequently drifted off into their own thoughts.

Peggy knew she couldn't just sit here and have Jim's words going round in her head, evoking terrible images – but then again she couldn't find the energy to read Ruby's letter, for she suspected it would be full of her woes, and she'd had enough sadness for one day.

Once Daisy had finished eating, she sent her out into the garden with Cordelia, got dressed, and tackled the week's washing. There wasn't so much of it now there was only the five of them in the house, and before long, it was all out on the line.

Peggy sat in the garden with Cordelia and played with Daisy in the sandpit, dreaming of the day when she'd have a proper washing machine and could commit the old mangle to the tip – but despite the sunny day, the darkness of what was happening in Singapore seemed to overshadow everything.

Charlie hadn't lied to his mother exactly – there was a practice session at the rugby ground though it was much later than he'd implied.

He swung the holdall containing his sports kit over his shoulder and walked down the twitten to the main road, where he paused. He had several choices, but with the mood he was in they held little appeal. He could go down to the seafront, or along Camden Road towards the playing fields, which would take him past the Anchor, and run the risk of being seen by Ron or Rosie. He didn't feel like talking, although there were so many thoughts and feelings swirling about inside him he thought he would explode with it all.

He looked over his shoulder and, after a momentary hesitation, turned back towards the silence and open spaces of the hills that reminded him of Somerset. Ducking quickly out of sight of his mother's kitchen window, he hurried up the steep incline until he'd reached the top. Pausing to catch his breath, he dumped his kit bag beneath a stand of bright yellow gorse and shoved it out of sight. He'd come back for it later, but for now he needed to think and clear his head.

He set off at a brisk pace across the tough, windswept grass, the salt-laden breeze ruffling his hair, the sun warm on his face. Gulls mewled and shrieked overhead as they swooped and hovered at the cliff edges, and he could see Frank's small fleet of fishing boats coming in after a night at sea.

He stopped to watch until they were lost to sight beneath the overhanging chalk cliff where they would be beached. He enjoyed spending time with Frank and Brendon on the trawlers with the sound of the water slapping at the side of the boats and the night sky filled with stars as they'd heaved in the nets filled with silvery, flapping fish. He didn't much like having to clean and gut them ready for market, but the money he'd earned during the summer had certainly been welcome.

Charlie accepted that his grandfather and uncle hoped he would follow in the footsteps of his family and join the long line of Reilly men who'd fished off these shores, but he already knew that wasn't the life for him. Fishing was a precarious and sometimes dangerous way of earning a living, and although it held little fear for him, his heart was already set on being an engineer.

He loved engines in all their shapes and sizes, was fascinated by their intricacies, their faults and how to mend them so they ran smoothly again. He hoped one day to work on aircraft, for they were the up-and-coming thing with new technologies being tested almost every day, and he really envied Jane and Sarah's journey on the seaplane. Air travel would soon be as normal as catching a train, and he couldn't wait to be a part of this new and exciting venture.

The money he'd saved had paid for a covert bus trip to the county town where he'd had a long, interesting talk to an RAF recruitment officer. It was a thrill to know that if he passed the fitness test and all his school exams, the RAF would take him on at eighteen and pay his university fees. Once he'd gained his degree he would become a fully-fledged engineer and valuable member of the RAF.

It was something to savour and work towards, but he'd kept it to himself for the time being, as his mother seemed set on him going to the technical college and then staying on in Cliffehaven to work for someone like Jack Smith.

He dug his hands in his pockets and resumed walking until he reached the abandoned ruins of the farmhouse, and then sat on a fallen, rotting beam to stare out at the fields and hills which spread before him. The summer crops had been harvested, the hay cut and stacked in ricks across the fallow fields. Soon the ploughing and planting would begin for the winter crops, and this made him think about his older brother down in Somerset.

Charlie missed Bob, even though he could be overbearing and bossy at times – missed the camaraderie of harvest and haymaking – missed the farmhouse and the evenings when they'd all gathered to discuss future plans for the farm. But most of all he missed Auntie Vi. Lovely plump, motherly Vi who'd cuddled him out of his tears and soothed his homesickness with so much love and understanding.

Tears gathered and he blinked them away as he reached into his pocket for the packet of cigarettes he'd bought from one of the older boys at school. Having lit one, he dug in his pocket again for the quarter bottle of whisky he'd filched from his mother's larder.

There wasn't much left in it, and he doubted she'd notice it was gone, but all the same, he felt rather guilty as he sipped at it and felt the familiar warmth burn his throat. He didn't really like the taste of the whisky or the cigarette, but they'd become a small defiance against the sense of disorientation he'd been subject to since his homecoming.

'To be sure, I hope ye've saved a drop for me,' said Ron, settling on the beam beside him.

Charlie had been so deep in his misery that he hadn't heard him approach, and he started guiltily, quickly stamping out the cigarette. 'I was just …'

'Aye, I know, wee boy,' said Ron, taking the bottle from him and draining the last of it. He dropped the bottle into his pocket and eyed the trampled cigarette before taking his time to fill his pipe.

'I saw you coming up here, so left the dogs with Rosie,' he muttered. 'It looked as if you had the weight of the world on your shoulders and needed someone to talk to.'

'I'm sorry, Grandad,' stuttered Charlie. 'I didn't mean for you to …'

'It's grand that you're sorry, lad, but I'm thinking 'tis only because you've been caught. What your mother would say, I dread to think.'

'You won't tell her, will you?' he gasped in horror.

Ron shook his head and puffed contentedly on his pipe for a while. 'I found it very difficult on my return home from the trenches,' he said eventually. 'Things and people were changed, and it took me a long while to repair relationships, find my feet and settle down.'

Charlie realised this was a cue to talk about his feelings, and although he wanted to, he didn't know how without sounding pathetic. 'I've found it's best to just keep my head down and do what's expected of me,' he said finally. 'School's okay, and I'm enjoying being back in a rugby team again, but ...'

He plucked a dandelion from the grass and proceeded to shred it. 'I miss Auntie Vi and the farm, my friends, and all the old engines I was working on,' he said in a rush.

'That's only natural,' said Ron calmly. 'It was your home for five years, and it must have been a wrench to be brought back here where everything is so different.'

Charlie felt the weight of anxiety slowly lift. His grandfather understood. 'I want to fit in, really I do,' he said. 'But I was just a little kid when Mum sent me away, and nothing's how I remember it.'

He was unable to keep the resentment of that banishment from his voice. 'I don't know her or Cordelia, and yet I'm expected to feel the same for them as I did when I was eight – and it's really odd having Daisy about the place even though I knew she'd be here.'

'Your mother still loves you,' said Ron. 'She's always loved you, and sending you away was the hardest thing she's ever had to do, believe me, wee boy.'

He took a breath and let it out on a sigh. 'I know how you must resent being sent away, Charlie, but what you have to understand is that your mother had little choice in the matter. The government at the time was badgering every mother in the land to do the right thing by sending their children away from danger. Peggy was of an age when she could remember how it had been during the First World War, and although she resisted for as long as she dared, the knowledge that this war – like the one in Spain – would be fought from the air, made it more terrifying.'

Charlie absorbed this in silence as he gazed out at the quiet valley that shimmered in the morning's heat.

'This might seem peaceful now, but we were living in what became known as "Bomb Alley" during the war,' Ron continued. 'You can see for yourself how hard Cliffehaven was hit, and when your school was bombed, Peggy knew she had to protect you. It broke her heart, Charlie, and she's had to bear the terrible guilt of sending you and Bob away ever since.'

'I never thought of it that way,' murmured Charlie, feeling sick at heart for his mother's pain. 'But why did she stay here and keep Daisy with her? Lots of mums with very small children came with them to our village. We could all have been together then.'

'She knew she was taking a terrible risk, Charlie, but she had responsibilities here with Cordelia and all the evacuees she'd taken in.' He chewed his pipe stem. 'I think she needed to keep Daisy by her, especially after your father was sent abroad. Peggy had lost all the rest of her family once you'd gone to Somerset, and Daisy was her only consolation and tie to you all.'

Charlie remained silent, envying his baby sister's closeness to their mother, and wishing he didn't, for it seemed churlish and unfair after what his grandfather had told him. Yet he could remember so clearly how he'd cried and cried once he'd realised the journey was not a new and exciting adventure, but that he was expected to stay there, not knowing when and if he would ever go home again. Through Vi's love and tenderness he'd knuckled down to getting on with things, and slowly, inevitably, the attachment to his mother and home had dwindled until it was lost.

'It's been hard for you,' said Ron into the silence. 'I can understand how confusing and hurtful it must have been as a small boy to be sent away, but there is another side to it, Charlie.'

He paused to relight his pipe. 'Your mother wouldn't thank me for telling you,' he went on. 'But she keeps her grief to herself. This war might have been difficult for you, but for her it was a terrible trial. Not only did it take her sons, daughter and grandchildren away, it took your father to the other side of the world, leaving her to battle on during the numerous air raids, the ever-increasing terror of the V-1s and V-2s and the news that your father had been wounded. And yet through it all she's remained steadfast in her faith that you'd all come home one day, and be a family again.'

'I do love her, really,' mumbled Charlie. 'Of course I do – deep down. But she's different to what I remember, and I don't know how to be with her. She's all hustle and bustle and sharp angles and isn't at all the same as Auntie Vi. I feel shy around her, especially when she tries to hug and kiss me – and I can't talk to her about Somerset and Auntie Vi because I can see how upset she gets, and it makes me feel guilty for loving Vi so much. So I keep my thoughts and feelings to myself. But there are times when I think I could burst with it all.'

Ron clamped a heavy hand on Charlie's shoulder and gave it a squeeze. 'I'm guessing that today is one of those times, wee lad,' he murmured. 'But you don't have to bear this on your own, Charlie. Why don't you talk to me, so I can understand and maybe do something about it?'

Charlie heaved a ragged sigh and blinked rapidly against the gathering tears. 'I don't know that there's anything you can do,' he said helplessly. 'I'm stuck here now, and will just have to make the best of things.'

'Aye. But you're intelligent enough to know that whisky and cigarettes aren't the answer, son,' said Ron with a smile in his voice.

There was a long silence between them, and Charlie realised in horror that fat tears were rolling down his face as the great dam he'd built to hold back his emotions began to crumble.

Then he felt Ron's strong arms about him, holding him tightly against his broad chest. The dam burst and all the anguish and anxiety flooded out, enabling him to finally speak from the heart and ultimately begin to heal.

They'd just finished their lunch of home-made vegetable soup and toast, and Cordelia had returned to the garden with Daisy so Peggy could read Ruby's letter.

It was as she'd thought, for Ruby was clearly finding it very hard to settle in Canada. Peggy was initially delighted to read that there was a baby on the way, but Ruby was feeling sorry for herself in the misery of morning sickness. The logging season would soon begin and she was dreading the long weeks when Mike would be away from home and the small, isolated settlement was cut off from the world by snow so deep it would be impossible for the men to come home even for a short while.

She'd heard the timber wolves howling and seen a couple of black bears moving in the trees behind the house, and despite all her determination to fit in with this new and very different life, she couldn't help but yearn for Cliffehaven and Beach View. She confided that there had been times when, like the wolves, she just wanted to howl at the moon.

Peggy gave a deep sigh. There was nothing she could do to relieve Ruby's loneliness and fears for the future, and she could only pray that Mike's parents would do their best to console her. At least, once her baby was born, Ruby would have someone to love and cherish, which would take her mind off her homesickness.

She decided she would write to her tonight and send her some baby clothes she'd been keeping in tissue paper ever since Daisy had grown out of them, and was about to put the kettle on when Frank came up the cellar steps into the kitchen.

'Hello, Frank. I wasn't expecting to see you until the rugby match,' she said, dredging up a smile. 'What can I do you for?'

Her smile faded and she dropped the teasing tone as she noted his sour expression, and the fact that he seemed to have dressed in a hurry, with mismatched socks and the buttons of his shirt all askew. She'd heard from Brendon that Frank and Pauline had been arguing furiously all week and that the atmosphere at Tamarisk Bay had become quite poisonous. No doubt he was here for some respite and a bit of pleasant company – which was the last thing she was capable of giving today after those letters.

'You look like you could do with a cuppa,' she said lightly. 'Sit yourself down.'

He plumped into the chair and sat there in silence until she'd placed the cup in front of him. Taking a sip, he leaned back and began to roll a cigarette. 'You've no doubt heard that me and Pauline haven't seen eye to eye lately,' he muttered.

They hadn't agreed on anything for years, but Peggy let it pass. 'Did this latest falling-out have something to do with her new promotion at work?' she asked.

He looked at her sharply. 'So you know about that?'

Peggy nodded. 'She mentioned it in passing the other day when I bumped into her at the factory estate.'

He finished rolling the cigarette and, having lit it, reached into his coat pocket and drew out an envelope. 'I came home from last night's fishing to find this,' he said, tossing it onto the table.

Peggy eyed the envelope with Frank's name scrawled on it, and a feeling of dread washed over her. She really didn't know if she could cope with any more bad news today.

'Go on, Peg. Read it,' he urged. 'Dad and Brendon already know what's in it, so it's hardly private.'

She reluctantly took the letter and opened it to find a single sheet of writing paper covered in Pauline's neat handwriting.

Frank,

It has become clear to me that we cannot go on like this, and I'm exhausted from all the unpleasantness my exciting news has caused. You've refused to accept that I need to do something more than keep house for a man who seems to prefer his fishing and the company of others rather than spend time with me. You have shown little interest in my job, have consistently taken the side of those who've been against me and caused me hurt – and the time has come for me to follow my dreams and ambitions and make a new life for myself where I will be truly appreciated.

The new promotion means I have the chance to leave Tamarisk Bay and the house which has become a prison to me ever since the loss of my boys, and to prove to myself that I'm worth much more than people expect of me.

I will write once I'm settled in the flat the Red Cross is providing, but I have no wish to see you again, which I'm sure will come as a great relief to you. I ask for nothing from you except your agreement to the divorce proceedings which I will begin as soon as possible so we can both be free.

Should Brendon want to see me, then of course he'd be welcome, but only if he's alone. Peggy and Ron will no doubt rally round and make a fuss, but that's only to be expected as they never were able to resist meddling in things that don't concern them. As for my mother and sister – they've never shown the slightest interest in what happens to me, so I'll leave you to tell them. Personally, I'm glad to see the back of all of them, and am delighted to be shaking off the dust of Cliffehaven and heading for pastures new.
   Pauline

Peggy dropped the letter as if the barbed words had stung her. She reached for Frank's hand. 'I'm so sorry, Frank,' she murmured. 'It was a nasty thing for you and Brendon to come home to.'

'Aye. It wasn't pleasant,' he said on a sigh. He picked up the letter and shoved it back in the envelope. 'But neither was it a real surprise,' he added. 'Things had come to a head over this promotion, and although I did my best to dissuade her, I can't say that my heart was fully in it, and she must have realised that.'

Peggy regarded the big man sitting opposite her, and wished she had the words to comfort him. He'd tried so hard to keep his marriage going over the years – had been faithful and caring even when Pauline had been at her worst. He must have been shocked by the letter, and seen her desertion as a betrayal.

'Don't feel sorry for me, Peg,' he said, shifting in the chair. 'It's Brendon who's been hurt by this. But even he realised things had gone too far this time, and although it might take a while, he'll accept his mother's reason for leaving and keep in touch with her.'

'Where's she going?' asked Peggy.

'The Red Cross London headquarters where she's been promoted to the chairman's office as his private secretary.' He shot her a wan smile. 'Despite what she said in that letter, I'm immensely proud of her and wish her well. She'll be nicely set up there with the flat, a good salary and the opportunity to travel with her boss to Geneva quite regularly.'

Peggy had a sudden memory of Pauline laughing and joking with the prosperous-looking man outside the distribution centre and wondered fleetingly if he'd had something to do with her promotion and the eagerness with which she'd left husband, home and family. She'd certainly smartened up these past few months, and there had been a glow about her Peggy had put down to her feeling pleased with herself – or had that been for a very different reason?

The idea of Pauline having an affair was quite shocking – but then her upping sticks and going off to London so abruptly was equally startling. It just went to show one never really knew the people who were so much a part of one's life.

'How do you really feel about all this, Frank?' she asked.

'I was stunned at first, but now I've had time to think about it, I just feel relieved that it's all over and I can come home without fear of having to face another row and more histrionics.' He regarded her rather sheepishly. 'I'm sorry if that sounds heartless, Peg. But I couldn't have taken much more of it, to be honest – and there's been little love between us for years.'

'Not heartless at all,' she replied, refilling his cup. 'What was Ron's reaction?'

'I went round there before coming here. He didn't say much after reading the letter, but I could tell he wasn't too bothered by her leaving. They'd never got on, as you know, and he was more concerned about how I was feeling.'

His smile was easier now and lit up his blue eyes. 'I think he had visions of me rushing off to London to bring her back – but that's never going to happen, Peggy. We'll be very much better apart.'

Peggy agreed with him, for he'd threatened to leave Pauline many times over the past years, and she suspected he'd soon find his feet and get on with his life without much of a backward glance.

He drained the remains of his tea and glanced at the clock. 'We'd better get a move on. The match will start in half an hour and we mustn't miss our young Charlie's ninety minutes of glory. I've got the truck outside, so I'll drive you all up there.'

Peggy knew that despite his smile and cheerful words Frank was hurting inside – not because he loved his wife still, but because she'd abandoned him with barely a thought after all the years he'd stayed with her out of loyalty to his marriage vows.

She gave him a hug, fastened his shirt buttons in the right order and then reached for her cardigan. She fervently hoped that Pauline achieved all she wished for in London, and never darkened their lives again.

16

Peggy had avoided going to the recreation ground ever since the family picnic two years ago which had ended in the terror of an enemy rocket heading straight for them. The V-1 had come down in Havelock Road and completely destroyed the end three houses. Peggy could still remember the shock and horror of that day, and the profound fear that she'd lost Doris in the inferno.

However, she'd discovered that time was a great healer. Her fear had been unfounded as Doris had not been in the house at the time, and was now due to return to her bungalow tomorrow, fresh from her honeymoon. Life had moved on, and in her sister's case, it had improved no end and brought harmony between them after many years of strife.

Peggy had been a bit put out that she hadn't been asked to help with the tea the club provided after the match, but she soon learned that for the first match tea was always provided by the club chairman and committee members, and that she'd definitely be roped in for future home matches. She recognised some of the other mothers and could see that there were several senior players watching from the club-house – one of whom was young Dr Michael Sayer, who'd now taken over the practice from his father.

Michael was with his snooty wife, Eunice, who was trying to keep their toddler amused and losing the battle. Peggy had never taken to Eunice, because she'd been perfectly horrid to Julie Harris when she'd come to Beach View as an evacuee and worked at the surgery. Eunice had pursued Michael quite vigorously and seen poor Julie as a rival, even going so far as to endanger Julie's position at the surgery with her spiteful talk. Peggy watched the lack of interaction between Eunice and her husband and wondered fleetingly if either of them was happy.

The match was finally won by the Cliffehaven side. Charlie had played well, even scoring a try, so he was very pleased with himself, and both Frank and Ron were so hoarse after shouting encouragement they'd had to down several cups of tea so they could speak.

Peggy left Cordelia with Frank, who would drive her home, and walked slowly back to Beach View with Daisy. The early clouds had melted away and as the afternoon had waned to evening, the air was soft and warm. Her thoughts turned to Frank, who seemed to be holding up well, despite the shock of Pauline leaving him so suddenly. She rather hoped he'd find a nice little woman who could love him as he deserved – but that was for the future.

Daisy ran on ahead to greet Rosie, who was sweeping the first of the autumn leaves from the pavement with much hindrance from Monty, and Peggy smiled at the sight. Rosie was dressed up to the nines, with high heels and a figure-hugging frock. 'You're a bit overdressed for that job, aren't you?' she teased.

Rosie grinned and her blue eyes sparkled. 'I suppose I am, but Ron's taking me out dancing tonight, and I just needed to clear this lot away so they don't get trampled into the bar.'

Peggy's smile hid her envy, for she couldn't remember the last time Jim had taken her dancing. 'Where's he taking you?'

'The Pier Hotel,' Rosie replied. 'They've opened up the basement and the dance floor is rumoured to be marvellous.' She lifted Daisy into her arms and perched her on her hip so the child could inspect her sparkling earrings. 'Why don't you ask Danuta to babysit and come along with us, Peg? I'm sure you could do with a night out.'

'I'd feel a bit of a gooseberry, Rosie.'

'You could always ask Frank to come with you,' said Rosie with a naughty grin. 'He's footloose and fancy free at last, and is quite the dancer.'

'It's a bit soon, don't you think?'

Rosie shrugged. 'Probably, but he should start getting out and about and enjoying life again. Living with Pauline can't have been much fun.'

'I don't expect it was,' agreed Peggy. 'But her leaving like that came as a nasty shock, and he'll need time to find his feet again.'

Rosie winced as Daisy tugged at her earring. 'Don't pull, darling,' she said. 'That hurt.' Daisy looked mutinous, so Rosie put her back on her feet so she could pat Monty.

'Changing the subject,' she said, rubbing her ear and clipping the earring back on, 'all the paperwork has gone through on Doris's purchase of the bungalow, so I expect they'll start the building work any day now. How are your renovations going, Peg? I hope Ron's getting on with it and not spending half his time drinking tea.'

'He's been very good, really. There's only Danuta and Cordelia's bedrooms to do now and upstairs will be finished but for the landings. The big upheaval will start on Monday when the men begin work on the basement.'

'It will all cost a pretty penny, Peggy. I hope you're not stretching things too far and leaving yourself short.'

'I have been a bit over-ambitious with all my plans,' Peggy admitted. 'The cost of everything is terrifying, and now there's only Danuta and Cordelia paying rent things are tight.' She gave a sigh. 'I might have to shelve some of my bigger ideas until next year.'

Rosie nodded. 'That's a shame, but understandable. The rationing is worse than ever and the cost of everything is rising almost daily. It's one of the things I plan to argue against once I'm on the council. We're in the heart of the countryside with fields and farms all around us, but even the most basic things like butter, eggs, potatoes and bread are rationed so we can send food to Europe. It's simply not right.'

Peggy grinned. 'There's no need to get on your soapbox for me, Rosie. I'm in full agreement. But what will you do with the Anchor if you get on the council?'

'Not if, Peggy, but when,' she chided softly. 'We shall have to sell it. Ron prefers to be out and about rather than standing behind a bar, and since his accident, his back really isn't up to lifting barrels and being on his feet all evening. Though he wouldn't thank me for telling you,' she added with a wink.

'I suppose the brewery would take it on like a shot. The Anchor's become a real little gold mine since you took it over.'

'That would be my last option, Peggy. I'd really prefer to keep it freehold so that whoever buys it can do what they want with it. Once a brewery takes over they make demands for changes and start charging high rent, and you're tied to buying all your beer from them.'

She gave a little sigh and caught Monty's collar to stop him jumping up at Daisy. 'I was hoping a young family might take it on, or a returning serviceman, but there's simply no money about, Peggy. So it looks as if we'll be here for a long while yet.'

'Well, I for one am glad. I really don't like the thought of you and Ron moving away from Cliffehaven.'

Rosie giggled. 'There's no chance of that. If we do sell, we'll find somewhere here to move into.' She gave Peggy a hug. 'You don't get rid of us that easily.'

Peggy hugged her back, then rounded up Daisy and headed for home, thinking how lucky she was to have such a good friend in Rosie.

Daisy was tired after her long walk, and once she'd had her bath and some cocoa, she was soon asleep.

Peggy stood and watched her for a while and then quietly opened the bottom drawer of her tallboy and drew out the baby clothes she'd kept wrapped in tissue paper. Most of Daisy's layette had been donated to charity, but she'd held back these few pieces because Daisy was the last baby she'd ever have. It had been through nostalgia and a sense of time slipping away that she'd needed to keep these mementos, but it felt criminal to hang on to them when they could be put to good use elsewhere.

She carried the matinee jackets, bootees and knitted bonnets into the kitchen and carefully put them on the table while she made a pot of tea, and hunted out a writing pad and pen from the dresser drawer. Once she'd taken a restorative sip of the rather weak tea, she parcelled up the baby clothes, thinking about how to answer Ruby's sad letter.

Peggy decided to keep it light-hearted and full of gossip, so she started by congratulating her on her terrific news and telling her there would be a parcel in the post for her very soon. She sympathised over the morning sickness but consoled her by saying it wouldn't last for long, and she'd soon be feeling fine. Then she told her about Charlie's first week at the grammar school, and his rugby match.

She wrote about the work she was having done on the house, and Rosie's plans to sell the pub once she was on the council. Making light of Pauline doing a flit, she went on to tell Ruby that Rita and Peter were now on their way to Australia, and that Sarah and Jane would arrive in Singapore very soon and finally discover what had happened to their father and Philip. There was the news that Danuta was courting a Polish baron of all things, and that although he'd lost both legs during a dogfight over Holland, it was clear the pair of them were over the moon with each other, and she was expecting an engagement to be announced any day now.

Peggy finished off by saying that once her baby was born, Ruby would feel much more settled as she'd have someone other than herself to care for during those lonely days when Mike was away, and not to be too downhearted in the meantime. Everything resolved itself in the end, and as long as she had Mike, she'd soon find her feet and start enjoying life in Canada.

Peggy read the letter through and couldn't think of anything else to say, so she signed it and added a few kisses in the hope Ruby would know she was loved and missed.

She had just finished a similar, newsy letter to Jim when the back door crashed open and Charlie came up the stone steps. 'What time do you call this?' she asked mildly.

Charlie squinted at the mantel clock. 'Five past seven,' he replied, giving her a cheeky grin before he sank into a kitchen chair.

'I'll have less sauce from you, you young rapscallion,' she said affectionately. 'What's happened to Frank and Cordelia?'

'They stopped off at the Anchor for a drink with Grandad before he takes Rosie out dancing. I think Uncle Frank's a bit reluctant to go home to an empty house, so he's chatting to Brenda.'

Peggy felt a dart of hope which she quickly quelled.

'Have you got anything to eat, Mum? Only I'm starving.'

Peggy rolled her eyes. 'But you had an enormous tea at the club.'

'That was hours ago, and I've only had a bag of chips since then.' He got up to rummage about in the larder.

Alarmed, Peggy quickly pulled him out and firmly shut the door. 'There's soup in the pot on the stove, and bread in the crock. Everything else is for tomorrow.'

He grinned down at her just as his father used to do when he wanted his own way over something. 'Are you sure I can't have a bit of that tinned ham?' he wheedled.

'Positive,' she replied, trying not to laugh.

'Oh, Mum,' he sighed, putting his arm round her shoulders. 'I do love you, you know. And I'm sorry I've been such a pain.'

Peggy's heart melted, for this was the first time her son had said anything close to an endearment, and it was the most precious of moments. 'I love you too,' she managed.

He drew her into his embrace and held her close for a moment and then softly kissed her cheek. 'Sorry I haven't done this before,' he murmured. 'But I've been all of a muddle.'

'I know you have,' she replied, fighting back her happy tears. 'And I do understand why, Charlie.' She smiled back at him. 'But if you think this has softened me up into letting you have some ham, you've got another think coming.'

He tipped back his head and roared with laughter before hugging her again. 'I'm happy with soup,' he said finally.

Much later that night Peggy was warmed by the memory of that embrace and the joy of the moment when her son had finally accepted he was home. She didn't know what had brought it about, and didn't care, but she'd sneak him an extra slice of ham for lunch tomorrow – not just for his cheek, but because she was so happy to have her son back to his old self again.

Danuta had spent the previous Sunday getting the hang of driving on the left side of the road, doing hand signals and working out the gears. Jack Smith had been really patient with her, never raising his voice or giving exasperated sighs when she stalled the engine or crunched the gears.

The little car ran beautifully, and Danuta was absolutely thrilled with it. However, she was still suspicious that Jack was charging her far less than it was worth, and she'd queried the amount again. He fended her off and then quickly changed the subject, warning that she'd need to take a test before she was allowed to drive it on her own. Over the following week, he'd taken her out each evening, teaching her the Highway Code and making sure she knew what to expect from the examiner.

Danuta had passed the test yesterday, and had gone straight to Jack to proudly show him her licence, and they'd celebrated with a cup of tea and a bath bun from the bakery. Now it was Sunday morning, the weather was fine and Danuta planned to take Stanislaw out for a drive to cheer him up. Physically, he was very much better after resting quietly in bed and completely cutting out alcohol, but he'd been feeling very down these past few days. However, Danuta had a plan, and if things went as she hoped, then he would have something to work for and aim at.

She kept her plans to herself as she kissed Peggy and Cordelia goodbye and ran down the front steps to where her little car was parked at the kerb. She stood and admired it for a moment, then climbed in and gave a sigh of pleasure as she ran her fingers over the leather seat and mahogany dashboard. She still couldn't quite believe she owned such a wonderful thing, but she'd decided it was definitely female and she would therefore call her Bessie – which echoed the registration plate D3I 4489.

Danuta drove carefully out of Cliffehaven towards the Cliffe estate, revelling in the sheer joy of making the journey so effortlessly after going everywhere by bicycle. She passed between the grand pillars and up the driveway and parked by the ramp which had been placed over the front steps to give the less mobile patients easier access to the grounds. Grabbing her handbag, she softly closed the car door and then ran up the steps, eager to see Stanislaw and show him her car.

She found him sitting in his room staring gloomily out of the window, clearly deep in thought. 'Hello, there. My goodness, you've got a long face for such a lovely day,' she said cheerfully.

He looked up at her sorrowfully, and held out his arms. 'I have missed you,' he said, gathering her on to his lap and kissing her. 'Why you not come to see me yesterday?'

259

She perched there within his embrace. 'I did tell you, Stanislaw. I was working all day and then taking my driving test – and I passed. So come on, let's go for a lovely drive in the country.'

'You are clever girl,' he said, giving her another kiss and then regarding her thoughtfully. 'You are beautiful and have good life, Danuta, with so many things to still achieve. Perhaps it is not wise for you to tie yourself to a man who will only be a burden.'

Danuta moved from his lap and looked down at him. 'That's defeatist talk,' she said in Polish. 'And I won't have it. You are perfectly capable of doing many things if only you put some effort into it.'

He shrugged and couldn't meet her gaze. 'I have tried. But is no use. I cannot walk, and without legs, I am only half a man and cannot provide for you.'

Danuta realised he was in one of his darker moods, so instead of arguing with him, she fetched his prosthetic legs and held them out to him. 'Are you going to sit and sulk here all day, Stanislaw? I have plans for us, and you will spoil my surprise if you don't put these on and come with me.'

He heaved a great sigh, and then muttered a litany of moans under his breath as he slowly began to strap the legs on.

Danuta ignored the comments about bossy women and how a man couldn't be left in peace, and handed him the walking sticks. 'I know the stumps haven't fully healed yet,' she said, 'so you can't walk too far. Therefore, I shall put the wheelchair in the boot of my car.'

'I'm not using that,' he grumbled.

'We'll see,' she murmured, steadying him as he struggled to his feet and balanced himself with the walking sticks.

She collected the wheelchair and followed him closely as he began the long walk down the corridor, ready to push the chair beneath him should he falter. They eventually reached the front door. 'There,' she said. 'That wasn't so difficult, was it?'

He scowled and grunted, and then eyed the little car. 'Is very small,' he grumbled. 'I not fit in that.'

'Bessie is big enough to take you and the wheelchair,' she retorted.

He eyed her quizzically. 'Bessie? You give the car a name?'

'Yes,' she said firmly.

He broke into a chuckle. 'I will never understand you women,' he said. 'But if I can fit into that, it will be a miracle.'

Danuta was actually having second thoughts herself, but was determined not to let him see that. She wheeled the chair down to the car, and then came back to steady him as he slowly negotiated the ramp.

Opening the car door, she waited for him to position himself and then lower his rump onto the seat – which he did with an alarming thud that rocked the little car and made the springs complain.

Trying not to think about the damage he might be doing to her precious Bessie, she took the sticks from him, then lifted up his legs and tucked them into the well beneath the dashboard. It was a tight fit, for his head touched the roof, he took up one and a half seats, and his prosthetic knee-joints had to stay bent even with the seat ramped back as far as it would go.

'I feel as if I am ship in bottle,' he grumbled. 'I hope we not go too far.'

Danuta closed the door on his grumbling and quickly folded up the wheelchair to put into the boot. It wouldn't fit, no matter which way she tried, and she was almost at the point of giving up when a helpful porter came along with some rope and lashed the boot handle to the back bumper.

Thanking him profusely, she climbed into the car, found she was squashed between the door and Stanislaw and had to wriggle about to get comfortable behind the steering wheel. The handbrake was digging into Stanislaw's bottom, and when she released it, he sighed gratefully.

'I hope we are not going far,' said Stanislaw. 'We are like beans in a can, and it is very hot in here.'

'Then we must open the windows,' she said, winding hers down. They were indeed like beans in a can, she realised as she drove away from the recuperation centre, but it was just something they'd have to get used to if he wasn't to be stuck at Cliffe every day.

'Where are we going?' he asked as she turned out of the driveway onto the country road.

'You'll find out any minute now,' she replied, the excitement bubbling up inside her.

Stanislaw folded his arms. 'We will have lunch there?' he asked hopefully.

'Probably not,' she admitted. 'But then you must have only just had breakfast.' She drove past the fields where a farmer was ploughing to the accompaniment of a flock of seagulls, and then slowed to turn off through the open gates leading to the airfield.

'Why we come here?' he demanded, shifting in his seat and making the springs twang.

'Because today is the inaugural flight of the new freight service,' she replied, bringing the car to a standstill. 'Kitty, Charlotte, Roger and Martin will be here with Anne, the children and everyone from Beach View to celebrate.'

'You should have told me, Danuta,' he gasped. 'I would have brought champagne.'

Danuta didn't reply as she drove down the newly laid track past the Nissen huts which had been developed into weather-proofed, comfortable homes for the men and their families who would work for this new venture. She knew that many of them had been out of work and virtually homeless before Roger and Martin had started recruiting, and they'd worked hard to turn the derelict Nissen huts into decent dwellings and bring the airfield back into a service-able state.

'There has been much work here,' murmured Stanislaw as they passed the reconstructed control tower and drove parallel to the smooth, weed-free runway. 'Oh, look,' he said excitedly, 'a pair of DC-47s.'

Danuta smiled inwardly and continued down the track to the far end of the field where a large gathering clustered around a sturdy wooden hut bedecked with bunting. She'd known Stanislaw's interest would be piqued by the sight of the planes, and she just hoped that the excitement of the day would chase away his depression and give him something new to think about.

She parked the car a little distance away from the office hut and it was instantly surrounded; the door was thrust open and Stanislaw almost unceremoniously hauled out to be embraced by his fellow flying officers, and introduced to the ground crew.

Danuta smiled as she saw the light return to his eyes. Stan hadn't flown with Roger or Martin, but the brotherhood of airman was tight-knit, and soon he was laughing and jok-ing, and making his way towards the planes.

Danuta realised she'd been forgotten in the joy of this meeting, but that was all part of the plan, and as Kitty helped her to free the wheelchair, they shared a knowing smile.

'That'll be the last we'll see of any of them for a while,' said Kitty cheerfully. 'Once they get talking planes, we might as well not be here. Come and have a cup of tea, Danuta. Charlotte baked a lovely Victoria sponge, I made some sandwiches, and the other wives brought all sorts of goodies, so no one will go hungry.'

'I did not expect so many people to come,' said Danuta, eyeing the large crowd.

'We felt we had to celebrate properly and involve every-one who put so much time and effort into this venture. We couldn't have done it without them, and this is a very special day for all of us.'

'How is Charlotte feeling about it all?' Danuta asked quietly.

'A mixture of sadness that Freddy can't be here and a sense of pride that we've seen all our plans come to fruition.' Her smile wavered. 'It's how we both feel, really, but this isn't a day for looking back. Freddy wouldn't have wanted us to.'

She linked arms with Danuta and they walked over the uneven grass towards the gathering. 'So, do you think your plan will work on Stanislaw?'

'With some help from you, yes, I think it is very possible,' Danuta replied, glancing across at the men who were inspecting every inch of the cargo planes with their bright new logo of a phoenix emblazoned on their tails. 'I like the phoenix,' she said.

'We decided on it because it represents new beginnings from the ashes of the war, and Phoenix Air Freight is much more memorable than what we first thought up.'

She stopped and turned to Danuta. 'I will do my very best to encourage him, Danuta, and have coached Roger and Martin to do the same. But you do realise he has a very long way to go?'

Danuta nodded. 'Of course I do, and I will be with him every step of the way.'

Kitty grinned. 'I hope he realises how very lucky he is to have you by his side.'

Danuta giggled. 'Every day I tell him this, so he knows.'

The morning sped past as she was introduced to the wives and families of the ground crew, drank tea, chatted to Peggy, Anne and Cordelia, and kept a watchful eye on Stanislaw who was in danger of getting worn out from all the walking and standing.

Ron and Frank turned up with the dogs, shortly followed by Brendon, Betty and baby Joseph. It became a real family gathering with children and dogs racing about as the women gossiped and the men went into huddles to talk engines and flight paths and the vagaries of the weather.

As midday approached the men dispersed and Roger and Martin returned with their co-pilots, dressed in their flying gear. An expectant hush fell over them all and even the children stopped playing to watch the men kiss their loved ones and then stride across to the planes. Climbing up the steps, each man waved before the door was shut.

A breathless silence fell to be broken by the splutter and roar of the powerful engines. Chocks were hauled away, another brief wave from the cockpit window, and the first DC-47 raced down the runway and lifted up into the sky, shortly followed by the second.

A huge cheer went up and everyone waved, but the two cargo planes were now almost beyond the edges of the cliffs and lifting higher and higher above the English Channel, the sound of their engines fading.

'I wish I was with them,' sighed Kitty, holding Charlotte's hand. 'Still, our turn will come soon enough with so many orders to fulfil.'

Stanislaw had chosen to ignore the wheelchair and was jammed into a deckchair. He shaded his eyes against the sun until the two planes were mere specks in the distance. 'Roger tells me you were both ATA girls,' he said. 'I met many such beautiful girls in the war. They were all very brave.'

'There was nothing brave about it,' said Charlotte. 'We were merely doing a job. But we both miss it, don't we, Kitty?'

'Indeed we do, but now I'm expecting again, I shall soon be grounded by Roger, who seems to think being pregnant will make me extra delicate and unable to think straight.'

Stanislaw smiled, but his thoughts were clearly elsewhere. 'You lost a leg, and yet you are flying again.'

'It wasn't easy,' admitted Kitty. 'I had a lot of very hard work to do before I could be passed fit enough.' She grinned and sat next to him, deliberately letting her prosthetic lower leg show from beneath the cuff of her linen trousers.

'But flying gets into the blood, doesn't it?' Kitty went on. 'I just knew I couldn't give it up, so I did everything I could to climb back into a plane and feel that adrenaline rush of taking off and soaring through the skies.' She grinned. 'There's nothing quite like it, is there? Did Roger tell you that I flew us both away from our wedding reception?'

Stanislaw nodded thoughtfully, his gaze fixed on her leg. 'How long did it take you to be passed fit?'

'Almost a year, I think. It felt much longer, and I had some very bad days as well as good ones. But I never gave up, Stan, and it was all worth it in the end.'

Danuta watched as Stanislaw digested this in silence. Kitty was doing a brilliant job of jolting him out of feeling sorry for himself and opening up a whole world of possibilities.

'Would it be difficult for a man like me with no legs to fly again?' he asked quietly.

'Douglas Bader managed it through the war until he had to bail out over Germany, and was taken prisoner,' said Kitty. 'I hear he still flies for pleasure, even now.'

'But will someone employ such a man now the war is over?'

'I'm sure that if he's competent and has passed all the medical requirements, he'd be snapped up,' said Kitty.

'It is something to think about,' he murmured. 'Thank you, Kitty. You are an inspiration.'

He struggled to lever himself up from the chair and gave up with a roar of laughter. 'Perhaps it is wise for me to learn to get out of chair before I climb into cockpit,' he said, his eyes dancing with humour. 'May I ask someone to be so kind as to unplug me?'

There was a great deal of laughter and joking as Stanislaw was hauled out of the chair and onto his feet, but he took it all with great humour. 'I think now I must return

to Cliffe. Thank you all for a most pleasant and informative morning.'

Danuta's plan to spur Stanislaw out of his misery and
give him something exciting to think about had worked. She
was to discover over the following months that he was now
determined to fly again, and she watched with admiration
and heart-stopping concern as he used all that stubbornness
and strength to push himself to the very limit of his
endurance.

Doris felt she must be positively glowing she was so happy.
The honeymoon had been a triumph in every way, with the
first-class hotels, the meals, the lovemaking, and of course
the wonderful views and walks in the Lake District.

John drew the car up to the kerb and switched off the
engine. 'Here we are, my darling,' he said. 'Home safe and
sound.' He climbed out of the car and went round to open
the door and help her out. 'Do you want me to carry you
over the threshold?' he asked with a naughty twinkle in his
eye.

'You'd better not,' she giggled. 'We don't want your back
going again, and I have plans for you tonight.'

He squeezed her hand. 'Well, in that case, we'll forget the
threshold and just go straight to bed.'

Doris blushed furiously as he collected their cases from
the boot and then hesitated between the two front gates.
'But which bed do we choose?' he asked. 'Mine or yours?'

'Mine,' she said. 'It's bigger and I made it up with clean
sheets before we left.'

He led the way up the short path and she slotted in the
key. Pushing the door open they found a pile of mail waiting
on the mat. Doris quickly gathered it all up and shuffled
through it, then gasped in delight. 'There's one from our
solicitor and another from the planning department.'

He put down the cases and looked over her shoulder as
she opened each letter. The purchase of the bungalow had

gone through; her first mortgage payment would be due at the end of September, and planning permission had been given to turn the two properties into one.

'Oh, John,' she breathed, turning into his embrace. 'Our dreams really are about to come true.'

He kissed her softly on the lips. 'Mine already came true when you agreed to marry me, darling girl,' he murmured, gently divesting her of her coat, hat and scarf. 'Let's celebrate all this good news in the best way we know how.'

It was quite a while later before they could think about anything else but each other, and it was only the need for the bathroom, a cup of tea and something to eat that stirred them from the bed. Having washed and dressed in their night things, they sat in the kitchen over a pot of tea and went through the rest of the post.

'There are a lot of bills,' sighed Doris. 'I hope all the work we're having done won't prove too expensive.'

'You let me worry about those,' said John firmly. 'My pension and the salary I get is more than enough to cover everything, and I do have some savings should we need anything extra.'

Doris bit her lip, reluctant to speak of what had been worrying her ever since they'd decided to do the building work and take out the mortgage.

Seeming to sense her unease, John took her hand and lifted it to his lips. 'You're not to worry about anything, do you hear me? I know you lost everything because your first husband didn't take proper care of you, but if anything happens to me, you'll be absolutely secure – I promise.'

'I know I can trust you, John,' she replied. 'It's just seeing all these bills and estimates has worried me a bit. The amount we're spending didn't seem so vast until I saw it all written down in black and white.'

John pulled her gently onto his lap. 'You can't have omelettes without breaking eggs, and although it all looks frightening now, think how marvellous it will be when the work's finished.'

'Do you think it will be done in time for Christmas?'

'I'm not sure, but I'm hoping so. It would be perfect to spend our first Christmas together in our new and very smart house, don't you think? Perhaps Anthony and his little family could visit. Suzy will have had the baby by then, and you'll be able to enjoy your grandchildren.'

Doris snuggled up to him, happier than she'd ever been, her worries disappearing in the glow of being loved and cherished by this wonderful man.

PART THREE

17

Karachi to Calcutta

They'd left Karachi earlier that morning despite the fact that dark clouds had been gathering and the heat had intensified. There was electricity in the air, and Sarah could taste the copper of the gathering tropical storm as the plane jolted and dipped alarmingly through the clouds.

'This doesn't look good,' she managed. 'I hope the pilot knows what he's doing.'

The plane suddenly seemed to drop out of the sky, making her feel weightless, only tethered to her seat by the safety belt, her stomach suspended somewhere beneath her ribs. She clung to the armrests, her heart in her mouth as the lunch trays went flying and suitcases began to topple from the overhead lockers. She closed her eyes and held on as the plane began to rise again and level out, then carry on juddering and thudding towards Calcutta.

'Sorry about that, ladies and gentlemen,' said the Australian pilot rather tersely over the intercom. 'I'm afraid we're in for a bumpy ride until we get to Calcutta. Keep your seatbelts fastened, and your fingers crossed that this storm doesn't break. I'm going to try and get beneath the turbulence, so don't be alarmed.'

Sarah and Jane exchanged horrified looks. 'Why did he take off if the weather's about to break?' asked Jane, who'd gone quite ashen. 'I don't like this, Sarah. Really I don't.'

Sarah didn't either and wasn't too impressed by the pilot, who seemed to have taken a very gung-ho attitude to the approaching storm. Yet they had to keep faith in him, for he must have experienced these sorts of conditions before and would know how to get them safely to Calcutta.

The plane dipped and rose with heart-stopping regularity as the hostesses quickly cleared away the uneaten lunches and fastened the scattered luggage firmly back into the lockers. They handed out paper bags, checked the seatbelts were correctly locked, their smiles fixed and never quite reaching their eyes. As the thunder began to roll and grumble around them, they hurried to their seats at the back of the plane, clearly as unnerved as their ashen-faced passengers.

The thunder crashed and boomed, drowning out the sound of the engines and the sharp cries of fear from the passengers. And then the cabin was lit up by the flash of lightning – so bright it hurt their eyes. Jagged bolts of electricity crackled and fizzed as they speared the roiling black clouds as if in search of the plane. Never had Sarah felt so small, insignificant and vulnerable in this metal box being tossed about by the elements thousands of feet above ground.

Her pulse was racing and she gripped the armrest as the plane bucked and juddered, then dipped and rose with alarming and stomach-churning frequency. And then it began to slowly descend, the pilot guiding it below the storm clouds and into clearer skies.

But the respite was short-lived and soon they were plunged back into darkness, with momentary flashes of lightning as the thunder growled and boomed. It felt to Sarah as if Thor himself was beating the fuselage with his war hammer, and the awful noise filled her head, reverberating right through every part of her body until nothing else existed.

She began to tremble, and the fear she'd been holding back threatened to overwhelm her. She and Jane were about to die. They'd never see their mother again. Never know what had happened to their father and Philip.

'I'm sorry,' shouted Jane over the noise, reaching for her sister's hand to grasp it tightly. 'I should never have risked this. If we die today, I want you to know that I love you, Sarah.'

Sarah squeezed her fingers and gave her a strained smile. 'We're not going to die,' she said, despite her belief to the contrary. 'The pilot will get us through this.'

'You've got more faith in him than I have,' said Jane, grimly clinging on as the plane suddenly plunged and rocked in the maelstrom. 'I promise you one thing, Sarah. If we get out of this alive, I will kiss that pilot and I don't care who sees me.'

Despite her terror, Sarah couldn't help but smile at her younger sister's defiant declaration. This was the Jane she remembered from Malaya, who acted on impulse, was childlike in her eagerness to make everything all right, and who dared to speak her mind. Not the self-assured young woman who'd returned from her secret wartime posting with aplomb and a steely determination to live her life as she pleased.

The plane was flying more evenly now, and although Sarah could see the rolling, storm-filled clouds above them, there was land beneath – a barren red land with ribbons of silver glinting amidst the scudding shadows of the overcast sky, and huddles of settlements formed from ochre-stained adobe within the soft folds and jagged promontories of a harsh and unforgiving landscape.

Flashes of sheet lightning and rolls of thunder continued to accompany the plane as it slowly approached the urban sprawl of Calcutta. Flying low over the city, Sarah and Jane could now see the sights that had been described in the guidebook they'd bought in London.

There was the wide Hooghly River which divided the city on the east bank from vast stretches of wetlands on the western side, and fed into the mouth of the Ganges. They looked down at dilapidated buildings, grand mogul palaces, overcrowded slums, and narrow streets jammed with kiosks, wandering cattle, scavenging dogs, thieving monkeys and people – so many people they were like an ever-shifting tide of colour and confusion.

As the pilot took the plane into a wide arc over the mouth of the Ganges into the Bay of Bengal, they saw exotic temples, street markets, hovels and towering pillars of buildings jammed close together and leaning like weary soldiers on parade. These clearly housed many families within their ochre walls, for they could see lines of washing hanging out and people moving in and out of it. Women in gloriously coloured saris were doing their laundry on the banks of the river where children splashed and others bathed, perhaps following the timeless rituals of their Hindu religion in this holiest of waterways.

The plane began to descend as the heavens opened and rain thundered on the fuselage to streak over the windows and blot out the view. With a roar of its engines it hovered for a moment above the choppy water and then landed with a soft bump to a smattering of relieved applause from the passengers.

The floats churned across the water as the seaplane turned and slowly headed for the series of docks they could see at the foot of the busy wharf. There were three other planes lying idle, and Sarah wondered if they'd been grounded because of the weather. Certainly, it would have been madness to set out in this.

As the hostesses bustled about and everyone hastened to get out of their seats, the pilot came into the cabin with a broad smile. 'Welcome to Calcutta,' he drawled. 'I reckon we might have to stay here for a while until this weather passes over, but we'll be on our way to Singapore as soon as we can. No worries.'

Jane leapt from her seat and threw her arms around him, dealing him a resounding kiss on both cheeks. He looked shocked and went red, and the others in the cabin tittered, unsure of what was going on.

Jane ignored them all. 'Thank you so much,' she breathed. 'I really thought we'd bought it – but you got us through.'

He went an even deeper scarlet. 'Fair go, miss. I didn't spend the flaming war fighting the Luftwaffe for nothing, you know. When the going gets rough, a bloke's gotta get tough. Otherwise where would we all be, eh?'

He earned himself another round of hearty applause and suddenly everyone wanted to shake his hand and thank him.

Sarah rolled her eyes at her sister and fetched their bags. 'Honestly, Jane. The poor man didn't know where to put himself. Do try and behave.'

Jane just laughed, took charge of her bag and headed for the door. 'In my book, he's a hero – and that deserved some recognition. Now which hotel are we in tonight? I could murder a gin and tonic before dinner.'

Sarah wasn't at all sure they had such a thing in Calcutta, but said nothing as she followed her sister down the steps and hurried through the teeming rain into the terminal building.

The first thing to hit them was the all-pervading smell of mixed spices with the tang of onions, garlic and curry powder which seemed to hang in the humid air like a thick pall. The second was one of too many people crammed together in the reception hall, their sing-song voices clamouring to be heard in the confusion of noise and colour. The third, and most uncomfortable, was the overtly hostile stares.

As they stood there amid the babble of noise and confusion, an obsequious and rather plump Indian man in a crumpled linen suit pushed his way through the melee and introduced himself. He was their guide and spoke excellent English, assuring the bewildered flying-boat passengers that he'd soon have them at the very finest hotel in Calcutta.

He clearly knew his way through the red tape of the chaotic customs system, for they were soon following him outside to a covered walkway where he pointed out with great pride the ramshackle bus that was coughing exhaust fumes by the steps.

Sarah watched as their luggage was packed on top of the bus and firmly tied down by the porters. The bus was positively ancient, with bald tyres and rusting bodywork, but every inch of it was decorated with lurid designs of every colour imaginable, with the added flourish of scarlet and yellow swags and tassels, flags, tinsel and streamers and even tiny bells strung from ribbons. In fact, there were so many things dangling over the windscreen, Sarah was sure the driver couldn't see much of where he was going.

A swarm of ragged, barefoot urchins suddenly came from nowhere, their hands out, or tugging at their clothes as they begged and yelled and chattered for money. Their guide shouted at them to little avail, then chivvied everyone on board.

The inside of the bus was stifling even with the windows down as far as they would go and the leather seats were cracked and spewing horsehair stuffing. The door was shut and the driver set the bus off with a crunch of gears and a groan of reluctance, the swarm of begging children chasing after it, still yelling.

Their guide extolled the glories of the ancient city as they trundled along at an alarming pace, narrowly missing meandering, skinny cows, darting dogs and children. The rain was hammering down, filling the potholes and filthy gutters to wash a flood of debris beneath people's feet and into the doorways of shops and homes.

Sarah could see by her sister's expression that she too was reminded of the poorer areas in Malaya and Singapore, but the poverty and sheer volume of people here was quite overwhelming.

It was with great relief that they turned in through a set of elaborate gates and saw their hotel. It looked like a palace, with lush gardens of exotic flowers and cooling palm trees, raked driveway and marble steps leading to a marble-floored veranda where servants waited in their uniforms of scarlet and gold embroidered jackets, white trousers and leather sandals.

As the bus ground to a halt, the servants dashed from the veranda to collect the luggage or provide umbrellas. Everyone prepared to alight, but their guide held up his hands for silence, asking them to wait for a moment.

'Welcome to the Rajah Palace Hotel. It is the finest hotel in Calcutta and it is an honour for us that you will be staying here.' He eyed them all, his smile fading. 'But it is to my greatest sorrow that I must ask you not to leave the hotel grounds unaccompanied – especially you ladies.'

He quelled the uneasy murmurs by raising his hand again. 'There is much trouble in our beautiful country,' he said. 'There are those who are becoming vociferous in their demands for an independent India, and these trouble-makers are also stirring up unrest amongst the Muslims and Sikhs. The British Rule is under great pressure, with many attacks upon their homes and offices. If you do leave the confines of the Rajah Palace, then I strongly advise you to hire a guide who will also act as a guard.'

He smiled and reached into the top pocket of his sweat-stained jacket. 'My company is proud to supply such people, so I will give each of you my business card as you leave the bus.'

'There's a surprise,' Jane muttered cynically. 'And here's me thinking he was actually concerned for our safety.'

'Hush. He'll hear you,' replied Sarah, joining the shuffling queue to leave the bus.

They took the card from the bowing man and, sheltered by the servants carrying umbrellas, made their way to the veranda. More servants quickly appeared as the luggage was placed in the enormous reception hall which was three floors high and topped by a cupola decorated in filigree gold and bright blue. The reception hall was furnished with deep couches, low tables, large ferns in brass pots, a tinkling water fountain, and numerous fans which cooled the torpid heat of the afternoon.

They were assigned their room and followed the porter up the highly polished teak staircase to the second floor. 'Goodness,' breathed Jane as she stepped into a room redolent with the heavenly scent of sandalwood and white lilies. 'This reminds me of Malaya.'

Sarah tipped the servant and waited for him to close the door before she took in the surroundings. The room was large and airy with plenty of ceiling fans to dispel the heat. There was heavy, dark furniture which had been intricately carved with animals and flowers; a decorative hand-painted screen hid twin bathtubs on clawed feet, and a tiny privy, and the two wide beds were covered with silk spreads and beautifully embroidered cushions. White mosquito nets of the finest mesh had been tied back to the barley-sugar bedposts, and delicate voile curtains gently swayed from the draught of the fans over the floor-to-ceiling shutters that covered the window.

Jane threw the shutters open and exclaimed in delight. 'Oh, do come and look, Sarah. We've got a balcony and the garden below is utterly divine.'

Sarah grinned and went to see what all the fuss was about, and although it was still raining which meant the garden was for now out of bounds, had to agree that they'd been fortunate to have a room at the back of the hotel. The cacophony of the road in front would have been awful.

'Let's get bathed and changed into something cooler and then go in search of a large gin and tonic. I'm fairly certain a place like this will have it.'

She turned from the window and opened the suitcase she'd been living out of for the past few days. Most of her clothes were crumpled now – especially her linen dress. She shook it out and hung it up by the window in the hope that the warm, damp air would get rid of the creases.

'Oh,' giggled Jane from behind the decorative screen. 'It looks as if we'll have to ring down and ask for hot water if we want a bath. There are no taps.'

'Just like Malaya, then,' said Sarah, coming to inspect the baths. 'It seems we're going to have to rely on servants again, Jane. Wouldn't Peggy have loved all this?' she added, feeling the softness of the stack of towels and admiring the luxury of it all.

'She certainly would,' agreed Jane before giving a deep sigh. 'Talking of servants, I wonder what happened to Amah after we left her behind.'

'Well, we know from Pop's note which she smuggled out that she got a job as a kitchen skivvy at Changi prison. Where she is now, is anyone's guess.'

'I hope she's all right,' said Jane. 'She was already old when we left Singapore, and working in a kitchen would likely have proved too much for her.'

Their conversation was interrupted by a discreet knock on the door, and Sarah went to answer it.

The servant bowed low and held out a silver tray. 'A telegram for you, Miss Fuller.'

'Thank you. Will you wait to see if I need to answer it?'

At his nod, she felt Jane look over her shoulder as she tore open the envelope.

Arrived Singapore * *Meet Raffles* * *Mother* *

'I will have to think how to reply,' Sarah said to the man, 'but in the meantime, could you arrange for us to have hot water for our baths, and a jug of gin and tonic with plenty of ice?'

She closed the door as he hurried off and then sank down onto the bed. 'What do I tell her, Jane? With the weather the way it is, we could be stuck here for some time.'

'I certainly doubt we'll be there on Sunday at this rate,' Jane agreed. She found a small writing pad and a pencil which had been placed by the telephone next to the bed. After a few minutes of indecision and crossings-out, they'd agreed on the wording.

In Calcutta * weather inclement * arrival date uncertain * Jane and Sarah *

When the servant returned with a tray of drinks, he was accompanied by several maids carrying buckets of hot and cold water. Sarah handed him their reply to be sent directly to Raffles Hotel in Singapore, tipped him a few rupees and waited for the maids to fill the baths.

Their creased clothing was whisked away to be ironed, and the silent-footed women left the room, their bright saris and scarves drifting elegantly around their slender figures.

It was amazing how quickly she'd fallen back into the easy life of servants, thought Sarah as she slid into warm water fragrant with rose petals and basked in the joy of feeling clean again, and the delights of icy gin and tonic.

Singapore

Sybil had gone to the ship's radio room before disembarking in order to send her girls the telegram. She had their itinerary written down, so was confident it would find them. She realised she was a few days earlier than planned, but the crossing from Australia had been quick and untroubled. Once she was satisfied that her girls knew she'd arrived safely, she hailed a couple of rickshaws to take her and her luggage to Raffles.

The sounds and smells of Singapore hadn't changed much, she realised as the rickshaw boy pulled her along the busy streets, but the sight of what war had done to this beloved island playground shocked and saddened her. Some of the old buildings were gone, or reduced to rubble in which ragged children foraged for anything they could use or sell. Other buildings were crumbling, and the once fine parade of stores, bars and cafés where she used to spend hours window-shopping or meeting friends for drinks had become nothing more than makeshift kiosks selling second-hand goods, fly-blown fruit and meat, or tawdry trinkets.

The people too had changed, for despite the end of hostilities, most of the natives looked half-starved and as downtrodden, weary and decrepit as their surroundings, and she noted a marked absence of the usual number of Chinese traders. There was a smattering of European faces amongst the milling crowds, but they seemed to be dressed in tropical service uniform, though Sybil noticed that some of the women looked far from healthy, and their skirts and shirts bore no regimental markings. It was all very strange, and didn't feel like coming home at all.

She stared in horrified fascination at a line of manacled Japanese prisoners, bare-footed and wearing loincloths, being herded along like cattle by a British army officer. None of them met her gaze, hanging their heads so the conical straw peasant hats hid their shame. Sybil had heard enough from the wireless and newspapers of their heinous crimes to regard this treatment as rather tame. In her opinion, the lot of them should have been shot.

She looked away and deliberately turned her thoughts to more pleasant things even though she knew she was being foolish to cling to her fantasies. However, those dreams had kept her going from the moment she'd fled Singapore with baby James, and she would hold tightly to them until it was proved to her absolutely that her faith in Jock and Philip's survival had been misplaced. But that was something she didn't dare contemplate.

Sybil let her mind wander through the visions of how it would be when Jock and Philip were released. She could see it all so clearly that it was impossible to think it might not happen. She would hire a car and they could all go back to the rubber plantation where they'd been so happy. There, the men would be able to rest and relax, get all the food and medicines they needed, find their bearings after what was bound to have been the most awful ordeal, and slowly pick up the threads of a normal life again. Her parents would bring little James over and stay for a while; Philip and Sarah would marry and move into the Tarrant house as they'd planned before the fall of Singapore, and everything would be perfect.

Except perhaps for Jane, who seemed to have grown a very uppity stubborn streak since living in England and constantly refused to have anything to do with all the meticulous plans Sybil had put together for their family reunion. But her father would soon sort her out. Jock had never stood for any nonsense from either girl, and she was sure that wouldn't have changed.

Sybil's parents hadn't approved of her almost desperate need to remain positive, and had warned her not to make too many plans, for none of them had any idea of what she might find in Singapore, and she could be heading for a terrible fall. The same caution had been repeated frequently in Sarah and Jane's letters, but she'd chosen to ignore them. Without hope there was little point in carrying on, and she was absolutely determined to keep that flame of hope alive. After all, she reasoned silently, Jock had probably done the same thing throughout his ordeal, and she wasn't about to let the side down now.

She was snapped from her thoughts by the boy coming to a sudden halt. They'd arrived at Raffles, and the joy of seeing it again stopped her from reprimanding him.

The building looked so wonderfully familiar, and it was clear that even under Japanese occupation it had been regarded with respect – and quite rightly. The gardens were lush, the palm trees were still there, and everything looked freshly painted.

With eager anticipation, she paid off the two rickshaw boys, adjusted her broad-brimmed hat and waited for the

Raffles servants to collect her luggage and carry it into the reception hall. Following them inside, she came to an abrupt halt.

The place looked the same, even smelled the same, but it was full of army officers and scurrying women who she guessed were aides or secretaries – and there was a group of rough-looking European women, some with equally ragged children, who were conducting a furious row involving a good deal of swearing, finger-pointing, pushing and shoving.

Sybil clutched her handbag to her chest, certain that a fight would break out at any minute and she might get caught up in it. What had Raffles become? Who were these ghastly people – where on earth had they come from – and why wasn't someone throwing them out?

As the argument grew louder and the shoving became more violent, Sybil heard the coarse vowels of the East End of London mixed with the plummy tones of Mayfair, the twang of Australia and the clipped accent of a Dutchwoman – or was it German? Astonished, she found she was rooted to the spot and could only stand and stare.

And then a tall, dark-haired, handsome man dressed in the uniform of a British lieutenant stepped into the fray. 'Now, ladies, please try and calm down,' he said reasonably. 'I know you're tired after your long journey, but there's no need for this.'

'There flaming well is,' retorted a short, skinny blonde with a strong Sydney accent and terrible sores on her face. She grabbed hold of one of the other women by the scruff of her neck and shoved her towards him. 'This bitch has no right to be here after what she got up to. She should be thrown into jail like the rest of the collaborators.'

A chorus of agreement went up, and the woman who'd been singled out drew her young son close to her side to protect him. 'I didn't do nothing wrong,' she protested in a Cockney whine. 'Me kid were starving, and any decent mother would have done the same.'

'You'd better come with me,' the officer said calmly. He looked at the others who were spitting venom and complaining about unfair treatment. 'I'm taking her and the boy to arrange for another billet,' he said, shooting them a smile that made him more handsome than ever. 'I suggest the rest of you go to the bar and cool off.'

He reached into his shirt pocket and pulled out a wad of paper. 'These chits can be exchanged for any drink you want,' he said, handing them over. 'Your rooms will be ready by six, and dinner's at eight.'

Sybil saw him walk away with the woman and her son and breathed a sigh of relief as the mob broke up, giggling, and rushed into the bar. Feeling slightly shaken by it all, she found she needed to sit down for a while.

Having restored her spirits with a Singapore Sling, she finally approached the reception desk.

'I'd like to book my two usual rooms,' she said. 'The name is Mrs Jock Fuller. I don't know how long my daughters and I will be staying, but it could be for some time.'

'I'm sorry, Madam, but the hotel is full,' said the Malay receptionist.

'Surely you must have something,' said Sybil, drawing some money from her purse in the hope that a bribe could still ease the way.

'I do apologise,' he said, ignoring the notes with a rather snooty air. 'But the hotel has been requisitioned by the British Administration, and all the rooms have been set aside for the women and children who have been released from the prison camps. In fact, all good hotels have also been requisitioned. There is hardly a room to be had anywhere in Singapore.'

Sybil felt a pang of guilt mixed with her annoyance, for now all was explained, and she shouldn't have jumped to conclusions about those women. 'Then what should I do? I've just come from Australia in search of my husband who was taken prisoner, and my daughters are expected to arrive tomorrow.'

'Perhaps I may be of service?'

Sybil turned sharply and looked up at the man who'd quelled the rowdy argument. 'I'm not sure how,' she replied. 'It seems every hotel in Singapore is filled to the rafters.'

He smiled down at her, his bright blue eyes quite startlingly attractive in his tanned face as he took in her elegant shantung silk suit and smart hat. 'Would I be right in guessing that you're Mrs Fuller?'

'Yes,' she replied, rather startled. 'But how on earth did you know that?'

'I overheard some of your conversation with the receptionist,' he said without a hint of bashfulness. He held out his hand. 'I'm Second Lieutenant Jim Reilly, and your daughters have been living with my wife in Cliffehaven.'

'Good Lord,' breathed Sybil as she found her slender hand being swamped in a dry, firm grip. 'What a very small world it is. You're the last person I expected to meet here.'

'It's the last place I really want to be,' he admitted with a twinkle in his eyes. 'But if you come with me, there's someone you know who'll be able to help you find accommodation.'

'Jock?' she gasped.

His smile disappeared and he looked mortified. 'I'm so sorry to have given you false hope,' he replied softly. 'There's no news of him or Philip yet, but we're doing our very best to find them.'

'Then who?' she asked in bewilderment. 'The girls aren't due in until Sunday.'

'Elsa Bristow,' he replied. 'But I must warn you, Mrs Fuller, the Brigadier didn't survive his imprisonment.'

'Oh no, poor Elsa,' she gasped. 'I must go to her. Where is she? What's she doing here?'

'Let me make sure your luggage is locked away first,' he said, eyeing the expensive matching suitcases. 'Things have a habit of disappearing round here.'

She looked at him, aghast. 'At Raffles? Surely not?'

He shot her a grin. 'The clientele has changed drastically since your last visit, and the women are like magpies after being deprived of everything over the years, and anything left lying about is fair game. It's a habit they picked up in the camps where things could be bartered for extra food, a pillow, a comb, a cigarette – or anything to make their ordeal a little easier.'

'I hadn't realised there were women and children in the camps,' she murmured. 'How on earth did any of them survive?'

'A great many of them didn't,' he said grimly. 'I'm sorry, Mrs Fuller, but it's best you know right from the start that the odds of finding your husband and Philip alive are remote.'

Sybil digested this advice and decided he had to be exaggerating the situation. If women and children had survived, then surely men like Jock and Philip – healthy, strong men in the prime of their lives – could too. Feeling more positive despite his warning, she watched him as he went to talk to one of the porters and helped stow her suitcases in a room behind the counter.

It was interesting to meet him in the flesh, for she'd heard a great deal about Jim Reilly and his wife Peggy from her girls' many letters, but she hadn't expected him to be quite so handsome or charming. Yet it was fortuitous that he was here, and placed in a position where he could be a huge help in tracking down the men. Sybil had always believed that who you knew was far more important than what you knew.

She saw how easily he conversed in Malay with the porter, how the young women flashed their eyes at him as they sashayed past and how he smiled back appreciatively. He was a charmer, all right, and she suspected that Peggy must have had many uneasy moments while he'd been away, for it was clear that he had an eye for the ladies and that they were drawn to him.

However, she kept her thoughts to herself as he returned to her side. 'You were going to tell me what Elsa's still doing here,' she prompted.

'Like you, she came in search of her husband.' he said softly before explaining her position with RAPWI and the overwhelming task that lay ahead of them.

Sybil frowned. 'But what about her girls? Are they here too?'

'They're both married now, so she left them in Sydney,' he replied, leading her through a labyrinth of corridors to Elsa's office. 'I'll leave you both to catch up,' he said, opening the door.

Sybil thanked him and stepped into the small, stifling room and tried not to show her shock at seeing Elsa looking so much older – in fact, she looked quite haggard, and her clothes were horribly rumpled. 'Elsa, my dear,' she said, approaching the cluttered desk. 'I'm so sorry to hear about Reggie.'

Elsa rose to greet her and after a brief hug, tried to smooth out the creases in her skirt and tidy her hair. 'I realise I must look a fright,' she said, eyeing Sybil's immaculate turn-out. 'But I've barely time to breathe let alone worry what I look like.' She gave Sybil a regretful smile. 'I do wish you hadn't come, my dear.'

'I had to,' said Sybil. 'And my girls will be here soon. They're coming over from England. Now I know you and Jim Reilly are in charge, I'm certain things will move on swiftly.'

Elsa shook her head. 'It's not that simple, I'm afraid.'

Sybil sat in the stiflingly hot little office and her spirits plummeted as Elsa told her in quite graphic terms what she could expect.

'Singapore is in chaos and far from what you and I remember,' said Elsa. 'The Chinese fled or were killed, the

Malays forced into slave labour. Without the ships bringing food and medicines, everyone would starve. The prisoners are only just beginning to be flown in from the jungle camps, and most of them are in dire straits and being sent straight to the hospital which is becoming quite overwhelmed. The Dutch, Australians and Americans are trying to repatriate their nationals as quickly as possible, but with more and more coming in every day, the task is painfully slow.'

Elsa paused and ran her fingers through her already untidy hair. 'All we know so far is that Jock and Philip were sent from Changi to work as slave labourers on Philip's rubber plantation. One of the Malay workers recognised them, but they were not amongst those who were liberated.'

'Slave labour? On their own plantation?' gasped Sybil in horror.

Elsa gave a weary sigh. 'They could have been sent anywhere after that, Sybil. The lack of documentation is our biggest problem in trying to find the thousands of men still out there, so you could have a very long wait ahead of you.'

'I've waited three years, Elsa. A few more weeks won't hurt.'

Elsa regarded her thoughtfully. 'To be brutally honest, Sybil, you and the girls will simply be in the way – but if you want to do something useful while you wait for news, I suggest you go to the hospital and help on the wards. They're desperate for more pairs of hands.'

Sybil didn't want to appear unhelpful, but she shuddered at the idea. 'I'll go there once I've found somewhere for us to stay,' she murmured.

'You and the girls can bunk in with me at the bungalow,' said Elsa as a girl rushed in with an armful of brown cardboard folders and fidgeted impatiently by the desk. 'It's a bit basic, I'm afraid, but better than nothing. Come back at seven and we can go together.'

Realising she was being dismissed, Sybil gathered up her handbag and wandered back through the maze of corridors to the Palm Court which had always been a favourite place of hers to socialise and while away a pleasant afternoon in idle chatter or games of bridge.

Ordering a long, cold drink, she lit a cigarette and watched the comings and goings of people she didn't know, over-hearing snatches of conversation that worried her deeply. She finally came to realise that all her plans and dreams added up to nothing in the light of what Elsa had told her, and that she'd been foolish in the extreme to think otherwise.

She shouldn't have come – and certainly shouldn't have insisted upon her girls making this long, hopeless journey. For the first time in her life, Sybil Fuller felt out of place, utterly useless and very much alone.

Much later that evening, Jim stood on the front steps of Raffles and gave a deep sigh as he watched Sybil climb into Elsa Bristow's car and be driven away. He felt very sorry for her and the situation she'd found herself in, but he was actually quite glad to see the back of her after a very long, difficult day. His life was fraught enough without the added burden of having Sybil to look after.

Very much against his advice, she'd insisted he take her to the hospital, but the scenes of so much suffering had hor-rified her, and she'd hurried away, unable to contemplate spending another minute there, or in the overcrowded clinic and makeshift camps that had been set up for the returning prisoners. When he'd suggested she might help Elsa in some way, she'd confessed she wouldn't know where to start as she'd never worked – let alone in an office.

Jim lit a cigarette, remembering how overwhelmed she'd become with it all, to the point where she'd been fighting back tears by the time he'd brought her back to Raffles. Sybil had clearly led a pampered, sheltered life, never having to lift a finger to anything or face anything more trying than what to wear for a party. Now she found herself adrift here, with few skills to be of any use to anyone, and carrying the very real fear that her husband might not have survived. She was most definitely a woman on edge, and he suspected she was only just beginning to realise what a mistake it had been to come.

He wished he could have given her some hope, but that was a dangerous thing to do in these circumstances, and he was dreading the moment she would be forced to face the inevitable outcome of Jock and Philip's imprisonment. In a way, he thought sadly, it would be better if they'd both died in captivity. At least then Sybil and her girls wouldn't have to witness the harsh reality of what three years of starvation and brutality could do to a once fit, healthy man.

He finished the cigarette, noted it had at last stopped raining and determinedly turned his thoughts to other things as he stepped down from the veranda. Hailing a rick-shaw to take him back to his billet, he sank back into the cushions and closed his eyes. He felt he could sleep for a week, but he very much doubted he'd be allowed to, for he was sharing a room with Jumbo.

Jumbo had discovered that his little Welsh nurse, Myfanwy, was now working at the main hospital, and if she was on duty, he would spend the evening extolling her beauty and rabbiting on about what a brilliant and caring nurse she was, and how she could sing like a lark and kiss like an angel.

Jim gave a wry smile as the man pulled him along through streets that were crowded even at this time of evening. Jumbo had got it bad, and now he'd found love, it seemed he was hell-bent on marrying the girl. What she would think of marrying a man who lived in a bothy on an isolated island was something that didn't bear thinking about – and Jim was bracing himself against the fallout should she turn him down.

18

Calcutta

Sarah and Jane had become restless and very anxious over the past four days. With only brief contact from their mother and no news of Jock or Philip, each day had seemed to drag interminably. Even the luxury of the hotel had begun to pall, and they'd grown weary of making polite conversation with the other passengers, and feeling like prisoners in this gaudy palace.

'I simply can't take another day of this,' said Jane, flinging a magazine to one side. 'To heck with our guide's advice. Let's go and see something of the city. These walls are closing in on me.'

'I feel the same way,' said Sarah. 'But I don't know if it would be wise to go out there on our own. The guide was adamant we should hire an escort.'

'That's only because he wants to make more money out of us,' said Jane, snatching up her handbag to riffle through it for a comb and lipstick.

Sarah realised her sister was determined to go out, so went to find sturdier shoes and a lightweight shawl. 'It's probably best if we leave all our valuables and passports in the safe behind reception,' she said. 'Just take enough money for a bit of shopping, and a scarf or something to cover our heads.'

'A headscarf in this heat?' gasped Jane.

'If there is ill-feeling out there, then we must be careful and show respect for their different culture by covering up a bit.'

Jane gave an exasperated sigh, snatched up a scarf and headed out of the room.

Sarah followed her and they went down into the lobby to have their valuables stowed away. Slipping the key to the security box into her handbag, Sarah draped the thin shawl over her head and shoulders and stepped outside onto the veranda.

It was raining again, so she took one of the umbrellas from the nearby stand and unfurled it before going down the steps and heading for the gate. She paused for Jane to catch up. 'Which way, do you think?'

Jane fumbled with the street map the hotel had provided and quickly made up her mind. 'That way,' she said. 'There's a market, an old palace and a couple of temples I'd like to visit. The guidebook said they'd be well worth it.'

They set off down the unpaved street, swerving to avoid the puddles in the deep potholes and watchful stray dogs, and trying not to notice the human waste floating in the stinking roadside ditch. Within seconds they were bombarded by a pack of demanding street urchins who pulled and tugged at their clothes and tried to snatch at their handbags.

The further they walked the more they were harassed as men in long, filthy thawbs pressed their wares on them, throwing scarves over their shoulders or thrusting carved ornaments against them, all the while jabbering and gesticulating in their faces.

Jane and Sarah knew better than to make eye contact, and tried to ignore them, tossing away the unwanted wares and clutching their handbags to their chests as they hurried along, desperate to escape.

Sarah saw a doorway into a shop and pulled Jane in after her. But there was to be no respite, for the owner loomed out at them from the dark interior and began to badger them with his sales talk.

They both sensed an underlying danger as they noticed the sly, dark glares from the knot of men at the back of the shop, and as they stood there not knowing what to do they were roughly jostled by two of them. A couple of scrawny dogs started to bark and snarl, and the men who'd jostled them were now barring the doorway.

Sarah was all too aware of the threat of the situation and tried to pull Jane out of the shop, but the owner grabbed her hand and yanked her back in, insisting she buy the set of copper bowls on display.

The dogs were now barking furiously, a crowd had gathered, and the men by the entrance were closing in.

Truly frightened now, Sarah wrenched her hand from his grip and reached for Jane. 'No,' she said firmly. 'We're not buying today. We want to leave.'

He'd roughly grabbed her arm when a man's voice boomed out. 'The lady said no. Let her go.'

Sarah's arm was quickly freed, and the advancing men melted into the shadows as the shopkeeper glared with naked hostility at the intruder. She spun round to see that their saviour was their Australian pilot, but she didn't have time to thank him, for now he was pulling them both past the surly men, and through the muttering, hostile crowd of watchers.

She and Jane found themselves being propelled along the street at a fast pace as the storekeeper yelled after them, the vicious-looking dogs ran beside them, and the horde of jeering and mud-slinging urchins followed.

They finally reached the shelter of the hotel veranda, and the pilot released his hold on their arms. 'Sorry about that, but I needed to get you out of there before things turned really nasty.'

'Thank you so much,' said Jane breathlessly. 'I really thought we were done for.'

'What the blue blazes were you doing there in the first place?' he roared. 'Weren't you warned never to go out alone?'

'Well, yes, we were,' Jane admitted, 'but we got so bored just sitting about in the hotel, we thought we'd explore.'

He expelled an exasperated breath. 'Strewth, lady, don't you realise how close you both came to being seriously molested? I'd stick to being bored if I were you. It's a flaming sight safer.'

'There's no need to be quite so rude,' said Sarah, dredging up the last of her dignity.

'Rude?' he barked. 'You've seen nothing yet, lady. Now get indoors and dry off.'

Jane giggled. 'Gosh, you are cross, aren't you? Would saying sorry for putting you to so much inconvenience make you feel better?'

He relaxed his shoulders and the furious expression softened into a rueful smile. 'I reckon I might have come on a bit strong,' he drawled. 'But the guide warned you for a reason, and you should have taken notice of it.'

'We realise that now,' said Sarah. 'And won't be leaving the hotel again, I promise.' She held out her hand. 'I'm Sarah Fuller and this is my sister, Jane.'

'Captain Joe Hamilton,' he replied, shaking their hands. He glanced across at the wide-eyed servants who were standing by the doors. 'Let's get inside before we draw any more attention to ourselves.'

Sarah caught sight of them all in one of the vast mirrors and realised why the servants had looked at them with such shock. She broke into a chuckle. 'Good heavens,' she managed. 'We all look like drowned rats.' It was then that she realised in horror they'd lost the umbrellas they'd borrowed from the hotel.

'No worries,' drawled Joe. 'They're ten a penny and probably won't be missed. Can I get you ladies a pot of tea or something stronger?'

'I think we'd better go upstairs to wash and change,' said Jane. 'But thank you anyway. Will we see you later?'

He shook his head. 'I'm not staying here. I only came to tell everyone that we'll be flying out tomorrow morning, eight sharp. The last of the storms have shot through and the forecast is good.'

'Oh, that is a relief,' sighed Sarah. 'Our poor mother must be wondering what's happened to us.'

They shook his hand again and hurried up to their room to discover that the mud the boys had thrown had stained their clothes, the sleeve of Jane's blouse had been torn, and that they looked as if they'd been dragged through a water-mill.

Stripping off, they rang down for hot water and a very large pot of tea, then slumped down onto one of the beds wrapped in dressing gowns. The reaction set in and both started to tremble at the thought of what might have happened if Joc hadn't stepped in. Linking hands, they huddled together, profoundly thankful that they would be leaving India in the morning.

Singapore

Sybil had now been in Singapore for almost a week and was getting very bored and on edge. She had become used to the long, dry days of summer heat in Australia, as well as the steady downpours during 'the wet', but she'd forgotten how much it rained in Singapore with its two seasons of monsoon and ninety per cent humidity. She stood at the window of Elsa's bungalow dabbing the perspiration from her brow and watched the downpour that filled the storm drains and sent the water rushing downhill. Would it never cease?

Turning from the window, she wandered aimlessly through the bungalow, wishing she had something useful to do. Elsa was all hustle and bustle and clearly in her element now she was involved with RAPWI, but Sybil just couldn't dredge up the energy to do anything. Raffles wasn't the same, all the people she'd known had been scattered to the four corners of the world, and there were no decent shops. As for the sights and sounds of the hospital, the clinics and those awful respite camps for the returned prisoners, she could no more go there again than fly to the moon. She was stuck here, with no one to talk to and no servants to do the housework or organise the evening meals and food shopping.

Elsa had told her where to go for the best produce, but everything had changed so much, she'd lost her way in the labyrinth of the back streets, and fled back to the bungalow empty-handed and in panic. This had infuriated Elsa and made things very awkward between them, to the point where Sybil wished she could find somewhere else to live. But there was nowhere to go except the house in the rubber plantation – and that was a day's drive away which would make her more isolated than ever.

It wasn't that she was ungrateful to have a roof over her head and somewhere for the girls to come when they finally arrived, but Elsa had been an army wife, and she still had the rather disconcerting habit of issuing orders and expecting them to be obeyed to the letter.

Sybil looked at the telephone, wondering if she could call Jim Reilly and ask him if there was any further news on when the girls might arrive. Then she realised she would just be a nuisance to the poor man, for he had quite enough on his plate already. No doubt if there was another telegram, Raffles would either tell Elsa or ring here.

She lit a cigarette and watched the birds preening their feathers in the trees as the rain dripped down on them. She wished she could feel cool, but the humidity was so high that the ceiling fans were really struggling, and Elsa had warned her against taking too many cold baths because despite the rain, clean water was at a premium now the island was so highly populated.

Reaching for a magazine she'd already read from cover to cover, she contemplated having a long gin and tonic – but it wasn't yet eleven, and she knew how easy it would be to get into the habit of drowning her sorrows. She gave a deep sigh and discarded the magazine. If only there was news of Jock, or Philip. This waiting was agonising.

The tapping on the door was so light she almost missed it. Getting to her feet, she hurried to answer it hoping it was Jim Reilly – or anyone who could relieve this stifling boredom.

She opened the door and was met by the sight of a large black umbrella shielding a tiny, barefoot figure in a mud-stained sari. Thinking it must be some child coming to beg, she was about to send her away when the umbrella was tilted back to reveal a pair of intelligent brown eyes in a face lined with age and painful experience.

'Oh, *Mem*, I'm so very glad to see you,' the old woman said tremulously.

'Amah?' Sybil gasped, taking in the withered arms and the thinning grey hair that had once been so abundant and silky.

She put her hands together and bowed her head. 'Yes, *Mem*. It is your Amah come to find you.'

Sybil tenderly drew her in out of the rain and, wary of brittle bones and a body so frail a strong wind might blow it away, embraced her. 'Oh, Amah,' she breathed. 'It's so very good to see you. The girls will be thrilled to know that you're all right.'

'Are they here?' the elderly woman asked eagerly.

'Not yet. They've been held up in Calcutta for several days because of the tropical storms. But I'm hoping they'll be on their way very soon.' She took the umbrella and stood it in the hallway, then led her into the sitting room, noting with horror that her bare feet were gnarled with arthritis and absolutely filthy.

Settling her onto the couch, she kept hold of her bony hand. 'How did you find me, Amah?'

'Sahib Reilly told me you were here. He gave me the umbrella and money for rickshaw.'

'Thank goodness he did,' breathed Sybil. 'You couldn't possibly walk this far in such awful weather.' She paused, noting how exhausted Amah looked. 'I'll make us some tea,' she said. 'There's a bathroom through there with plenty of towels if you want to dry off or wash.'

Amah dipped her chin, her voice barely above a whisper. 'I am sorry I come to you like this, *Mem*. The shame of you seeing me this way breaks my heart. I should go.'

'You're not going anywhere, Amah,' replied Sybil, gently pressing her back down into the cushions. 'You looked after me and my girls with such love and care, and now it's my turn to help you. Sit there and rest while I make tea, and then you can tell me what happened to you after we left.'

Sybil dashed into the kitchen and fidgeted with impatience as the kettle seemed to take an age to boil. She blinked back her tears. It had come as a terrible shock to see the woman she'd come to love and trust over many years in such an awful state. She'd always had long, thick white hair twisted into a plait that hung to her waist, and her face had been smooth and serene, her movements as supple and graceful as those of a much younger woman. Now she was aged almost beyond recognition, bowed and bent, and so thin she was almost skeletal – and her feet – oh, dear God, her poor feet. What had this war done to her?

Sybil dashed away her tears knowing they would only humiliate Amah further – but what must it have taken for her to bury her pride and turn up here looking for help? Not that she would ever ask for it, but it was clear it was what she desperately needed. Hunting out some biscuits, she made the tea and carried it all on a tray into the sitting room.

Amah was curled into the cushions of the couch, fast asleep, her feet tucked into the folds of her bedraggled, mud-stained sari.

Sybil's heart ached as she quietly placed the tray on the table and sat in the chair opposite. This was the woman who'd massaged her back and combed her hair when she was feeling out of sorts or suffering with one of her pregnancies. This was the loving, patient little guardian of her babies, and the wise, gentle counsellor who'd always known how to soothe Jane's tantrums and Sarah's worries. The girls adored her, and so did Sybil – and even Jock regarded her as a much loved and respected member of the family.

They'd all been heartbroken to have to leave her behind, but the ship's captain had refused to let her on board, and the last sighting Sybil had had of her was on the docks waving goodbye before she left Jock's side and melted into the crowds.

The tea had gone cold as Amah slept, so Sybil went back into the kitchen to prepare another pot and heat up the chicken noodle soup Elsa had made the day before. Warming some flatbreads to go with it, she carried it all into the sitting room to find Amah was stirring.

'There's tea and chicken noodle soup,' she said, placing a bowl on the table in front of her. 'I'm sorry there's not much else. I got lost in the market yesterday and in a panic caught a rickshaw back here without doing any shopping.'

Amah seemed refreshed by her sleep. 'May I use the bathroom now?'

'Of course. It's through there on the left.'

Amah returned a few minutes later with her hair combed, and her feet a good deal cleaner. She put her hands together and bowed to Sybil before sitting down. 'Thank you, *Mem*. I feel very much better now.'

Sybil handed her the bowl of soup and placed the flatbreads on the table where she could reach them. So she wouldn't feel awkward, Sybil picked up her own bowl and dipped the spoon in.

Once the bowls were empty and the tea was poured, Amah smiled at her. 'That was very good soup, *Mem*. Did you make it?'

'Sadly not. Elsa Bristow put it together last night. I'm hopeless in the kitchen as you know.'

Amah smiled and said nothing as she sipped the tea.

'I don't suppose you'd like to stay and help us out, would you?' asked Sybil, dismissing the need to ask Elsa if it would be all right. 'Only with the girls about to arrive and me being so hopeless at everything, it would be a huge help. I'd pay you, of course,' she added hurriedly.

Tears brightened in the old woman's eyes and her hand shook as she carefully placed the cup back into the saucer. 'To be with you and my girls again would be enough. I do not ask for payment.'

'Oh, but I insist,' protested Sybil.

Amah looked down and it was a moment before she replied. 'To serve you, to be fed and have somewhere to live is all that I wish, *Mem.*' She looked up then and there was a world of pain in her eyes. 'I will wait with you for the sahibs to come home.'

'I wish I could promise you that they will,' said Sybil. 'But we've heard so little about what happened to Jock after he left Changi to work as slave labour on the plantation, that it's doubtful he'll ever come home.'

Amah nodded. 'Death has been with us all since the Japanese came to the island,' she said softly. 'I have seen many terrible things, and although I am small and weak, Buddha has saved me. I often asked why he should do such a thing, but now I know. He wanted me to be with you again before I die.'

'But you can't die, not now we've found you again,' gasped Sybil.

Amah's smile was serene. 'We must all go to the arms of Buddha when it is time, *Mem.* And I shall see him very soon, I think.'

Horrified at such defeatist talk, Sybil sat forward in the chair. 'Not if I have anything to do with it,' she said firmly. 'I'm going to feed you up and make sure you have any medicines you need, and you must rest and get your strength back before you even think of working.'

Amah's smile didn't falter. 'You are very kind, *Mem.*'

Sibyl realised she'd get no further with this, so changed the subject. 'Did you spend the entire Japanese occupation in the kitchens at Changi?'

'So, you received the note,' Amah said on a sigh. 'I'm glad.' She folded her hands in her lap. 'I worked for the Japanese for many months after the sahibs were sent to the plantation as slaves. They beat me for little reason, and the work was hard. When I got ill, they threw me into the street.'

She paused to gather her thoughts, and Sibyl could see how hard it was for her to dredge up these awful memories. She was on the point of telling her not to say any more when she began talking again.

'I managed to find my way to the east coast and hid there with others of my family. We survived on what we could forage or catch, but most of the time we were sick and very hungry. The Japanese came and burnt down our village, destroyed our holy temples and put us to work in the rice fields.'

Tears blossomed in her eyes and she blinked them away. 'We saw many die among the old and the very young, but with Buddha's blessing most of us lived to see the Japanese defeated.'

Sibyl moved to sit beside her and put her arms about her thin shoulders. 'It's all over, Amah. You never have to be frightened or hungry again. I'm here to look after you now.'

Much later that evening, Sybil greeted Elsa as she came in the door and quickly explained what she'd done. 'I'll pay for her keep and nurse her if necessary, but I simply can't turn my back on her after all she's meant to my family.'

'Well, of course not,' said Elsa. 'Jim told me an elderly Malay woman was asking after you, and I suspected it could have been your Amah. But it might have been polite to ask me first if I wanted another lodger. Where have you put her?'

'In the smallest bedroom at the back. The doctor's been to see her, and it appears that years of heavy work combined with the lack of proper food and dreadful living conditions has taken its toll.' Sybil kept her voice low. 'She doesn't have very long to live, Elsa, and I mean to make her last weeks as comfortable as possible.'

'Well, at least you're doing something useful at last,' retorted Elsa brusquely as she dumped a bulging bag of shopping on the kitchen counter. 'Your girls will be here tomorrow night, by the way,' she added. 'Another telegram arrived late this afternoon.'

'Oh, thank goodness!' Sybil exclaimed. 'Amah will be so pleased to see them. And is there any further news of Jock or Philip?' she asked fearfully.

'Not as yet, but there are rumours that they were rounded up in 1944 with seven thousand other prisoners deemed fit enough, and sent into Thailand as slave labour.'

Sybil covered her mouth with a trembling hand. 'Please tell me they weren't sent to work on that awful railway,' she begged.

Elsa squeezed her shoulder. 'I'm sorry, Sybil. I shouldn't have said anything. There's no hard evidence that they were sent there, and as I said, it was just a rumour – and they're as numerous as the flies around here.'

Sybil realised Elsa was trying to sweeten the bitter pill. 'How soon will we know if those rumours were true or not?'

Elsa turned her back and began to unpack the bag of shopping, but Sybil noticed that her hands weren't quite steady and her voice was hesitant. 'The teams are out there now searching the jungle between Bangkok and Moulmein in Burma for the camps. Reports coming in are brief and rather confusing, but it seems the first transport of prisoners will be flown in within the next few days.'

Sybil's pulse was racing as hope and dread battled within her. Suddenly she didn't want to be here – didn't want to know what had happened to her darling Jock. The walls of the bungalow closed in on her, the warm, damp air stifling her until she could barely breathe. She turned away swiftly to find refuge in the garden and stood there gasping for breath as the soft rain mingled with her tears.

19

The rain had finally stopped and the sun had broken through, making the wet road and sodden greenery steam in the rising heat of that early morning. The mosquitoes were out in force as were the flies, and Sybil was struggling to keep her temper as she alighted from the rickshaw and told the boy to wait for her.

She regarded the tiny sari shop the boy had recommended, which didn't look too prepossessing, being squashed between a bank and a post office. She stepped inside to be greeted by the smiling but clearly puzzled owner. 'I'd like to buy three saris,' she said. 'They are for a friend of mine and I'd like them to be very colourful as she's not feeling well at the moment.' Sybil realised she was babbling and fell silent.

'We have many beautiful saris, *memsahib*,' he replied with a bow. 'May I ask the age and size of your friend?'

'She is an elderly lady, very small and slight, and I would guess no more than five feet tall.'

An array of glorious silks in a rainbow of colours was brought out and unfurled for her to peruse, and Sybil eyed them all, unable to choose. They were so beautiful, so delicately woven, some edged with gold or silver, others bearing intricate hand-stitched designs. All the colours should have clashed, but strangely enough they didn't, and Sybil eventually chose a lime silk striped with deep purple and edged with gold; a scarlet and silver one; and a midnight blue shot through with silver and turquoise. She selected the close-fitting short-sleeved tops to go with them as well as two pairs of sandals, and waited in the blissful coolness of the shop's fans as the owner cut the lengths of silk and parcelled everything up.

Having paid him, she returned to the rickshaw and told the boy to take her to the food market. She was feeling much braver today, and determined to show Elsa that she wasn't completely hopeless.

Once she'd completed her shopping the boy took her back to the bungalow, and as she stepped down from the rickshaw she saw Amah standing in the open doorway.

'Amah,' she said, hurrying to her. 'I told you to stay in bed after your breakfast.'

'I am rested well enough,' she replied, taking the shopping from her. 'Come. I will make you tea.'

Sybil followed her into the kitchen, suddenly worried that the proud, elderly woman might be offended by her gifts and see them as charity. 'I have bought you some presents, Amah. I do hope you'll like them.'

She turned from the stove, her eyes widening. 'For me, *Mem*? But it is not my birthday, and I have done nothing to earn them.'

Sybil thought quickly. 'I thought that as we've missed so many birthdays and Christmases recently, we should catch up on the gifts Jock and I would have given you,' she said, handing over the parcel. 'Welcome home, Amah,' she said softly.

The thin fingers fumbled with the string, and the brown paper was slowly drawn back to reveal the saris, sandals and tops 'Oh, *Mem*,' she breathed, reaching almost reverently to touch the silks. 'They are beautiful.'

There were tears in her eyes as she looked up at Sybil. 'Thank you, *Mem*. You are too good to an old woman like me. I do not deserve such things.'

'Well, I think you do, so go and try everything on while I make the tea,' said Sybil. 'The girls are coming today, and we must both look our best when we go to the docks to meet them.'

307

The tea was made and Sybil had just taken it into the sitting room and sat down when Amah appeared shyly in the doorway. 'Oh, Amah, you look lovely,' she sighed, taking in the scarlet and silver sari, the matching top and delicate sandals.

'I look like old woman in beautiful sari,' she replied with a wry smile. 'But I do feel like Amah again.' She placed her palms together and bowed. 'Thank you for giving me my dignity back,' she murmured. 'Buddha will give you many blessings for your kindness.'

'Come and have your tea before it gets cold,' said Sybil, moved almost to tears by the woman's words.

'I will take mine in the kitchen, *Mem*. There is food to prepare for when my girls come home.'

'Oh, but ...'

'*Mem*, I am here to serve you. Please allow me to do my duty.'

Sybil realised that now Amah had found her pride again, she needed to return to the old ways she found comfortable and familiar, and that she had been in danger of overstepping the mark. She nodded and watched her leave the room, the sari drifting around her.

Jim had spent the day taking statements from some of the women who'd been held in prison camps since the fall of Singapore. Unlike the men, they were eager to tell their stories, to purge themselves of the horrors they'd withstood so they could regain some sense of self-esteem. As they poured out all the wrongs that had been inflicted upon them, Jim became aware of the profound anger they all possessed for their Japanese captors, and also that the same names came up time and again.

Jim had discovered early on that the men and women who'd been prisoners had lost their confidence and self-belief, and this was particularly true of the men, who felt shame at being captured when others had actively served their country by bringing the war to an end. They were mostly reluctant to talk of their experiences, but those who did haltingly revealed the depths of misery and brutality that had been inflicted upon them.

Not all the torture had been physical. There were accounts of punishments aimed at killing off the last spark of hope in men already desperate for some small sign of humanity and that they had not been forgotten by their loved ones. The cruellest had been to burn three sacks of letters from home in front of them in retaliation for an escape attempt. That had almost broken the man relating that story, and Jim had left the respite camp with a heavy heart and a bitter taste in his mouth.

For the women it had been an ongoing and desperate struggle to keep their children alive, and with each burial their spirits had dwindled. Subsisting on a diet of mouldy rice soup, they were weakened further by hard labour, malaria, dysentery, jungle sores and ulcers, and the nurses and doctors amongst them raged to Jim about the lack of medicines and the simplest things such as calcium tablets, suture needles and thread, or clean bandages.

When they'd been liberated, it was to discover that the locked storehouse was packed solid with medical supplies and Red Cross parcels filled with powdered baby milk and tinned food, the like of which they hadn't seen for four long years, and which could have saved so many lives. Their rage was bitter and profound, their stories repeated over and over as yet more women were brought in from the far-flung prison camps.

Jim had enough evidence to ensure that the men guilty of these heinous crimes would be executed – although most of the women had demanded to be left alone with them for five minutes so they could dish out their own punishment. He couldn't blame them, for they'd lost far more than any person could withstand.

He felt drained by the harrowing stories, and knew they'd live with him long after the prisoners had been repatriated.

And yet he'd come to realise, much to his surprise, that he was doing a worthwhile job that was making a difference. That he had an empathy with those men and women and the ability to listen and carefully absorb what they told him without letting his emotions get the better of him. They didn't ask for sympathy, but needed to be believed and assured that the guilty would be punished – and he was the man in a position to do that.

He bundled up the latest statements and headed for the bar. He'd railed against doing this task, but Elsa Bristow must have recognised something in him that he hadn't known he'd possessed, for he seemed to have a natural ability to put people at their ease so they found it comfortable to talk to him. And in a strange sort of way, he felt rather proud to be doing such an important job.

Suspecting that Elsa had again gone without lunch, he ordered sandwiches and a pot of tea for her, and a long glass of cold beer for himself, then followed the waiter to the office. Tiffin, as Elsa called it, had become something of a ritual at the end of each day, and they both enjoyed it.

Elsa took off her glasses, pressed her fingers to the bridge of her nose and smiled up at him. 'You must have read my mind,' she said as the waiter left the room. She glanced at her watch. 'Gosh, is it that time already? How time flies.'

Jim placed the folders on her desk and took a long drink of his beer. 'I can't stay long this evening, Elsa,' he said, watching her tuck hungrily into the sandwiches. 'I promised Sybil I'd take her down to meet her daughters.'

'Sybil's perfectly capable of hailing a rickshaw,' said Elsa. 'You shouldn't let her run rings around you, Jim. You're too soft, that's your trouble.'

'Aye,' he replied. 'I probably am, but Peggy would never forgive me if I didn't look after her and the girls.' He took another drink of the Indian Pale Ale and waited for her to finish eating before lighting their cigarettes. 'Anything concrete on those rumours yet?'

She shook her head. 'Communication between here and the search teams is very hit-and-miss, but I was told this afternoon that the first planeload of men will be arriving sometime tomorrow.'

She sat forward in her chair. 'Whatever you do, don't tell Sybil,' she warned. 'I let slip about the rumours last night, and if she knows the men are beginning to come in, she'll be here badgering me endlessly and getting in the way.'

'She's bound to hear about it, Elsa,' said Jim. 'And you can't blame her for looking to us for answers.'

Elsa gave a weary sigh. 'I don't blame her, Jim. Of course I don't. I just wish she'd find something sensible to do other than fussing over her old *amah*.'

'Perhaps once the girls are here they'll persuade her to find something,' said Jim. 'Sarah's a very practical girl, and from Peggy's letters I understand that Jane is too.'

'Mmmm. Sarah used to work in her father's office, so she could be a tremendous help here – but Jane was always treated like a child by Sybil and Jock, and behaved as such. I doubt she'd be of much use.'

Jim finished his beer. 'You might be surprised,' he said. 'According to Peggy, she held down a very important secret post with some government office during the war, and is quite the sophisticated young woman now.'

Elsa raised an eyebrow. 'That I shall believe when I see it,' she said briskly. She finished her cup of tea and reached for a file. 'You'd better get a move on. The flying boat's due in at seven.'

Jim left the office and eased his way through a large, chattering group of children who ranged in age from seven to fifteen. These were the youngsters who'd lost their mothers, and sometimes siblings, in the camps, and were now waiting to be escorted to the ship which would take them to England and the surviving members of their families.

He stood outside in the warm, rather muggy twilight and watched them boarding the bus. He knew that some of them

311

were orphans now, for their fathers had also been killed during the war, and he wondered fleetingly how they would cope in England after all they'd been through. He suspected there would be great difficulties ahead for them and their families, but at least they were being given a second chance at life.

Seeing the younger ones clamber aboard the bus, he had a sharp memory of his own boys at that age, and thanked God they'd never had to experience the same terrifying war that these youngsters had gone through.

The bus trundled off and Jim returned the children's waves until they were taken out of sight. Then he fetched the car he'd been allotted and headed for Elsa's bungalow.

Sybil was waiting impatiently for him, dressed in a pale cream silk suit, high-heeled shoes and fancy hat. Her make-up was immaculate, her hair dressed in a neat pleat at the back of her head, but the worry and stress of these last few days were evident in the fine lines around her eyes and mouth. 'I was beginning to think you weren't coming,' she said.

'I promised I would,' he replied, smiling down at the tiny Malay woman at her side. She certainly looked worlds better than she had when he'd first seen her outside Raffles, having been banned entry. 'Delighted to meet you again,' he said, not sure what to call her. 'Are you coming with us?'

'Well, of course she is,' said Sybil impatiently. 'Amah has looked after my girls almost from the moment they were born.' She closed the front door, steadied the elderly woman down the shallow steps and headed for the car. 'Amah will sit in the back,' she said, climbing into the front.

Jim raised an eyebrow but the Malay woman seemed unfazed as he held the door open for her to climb in. Making sure her beautiful sari hadn't been caught in the door, he slammed it shut and then climbed in behind the steering wheel.

As he drove away from the bungalow and headed for Singapore Harbour, he remembered the last time he'd seen

Jane and Sarah. It was while he was home on leave before he'd been posted to India. However, he'd been so preoccupied with Peggy, baby Daisy, and the others who'd come from Somerset on a short visit, that he'd barely taken notice of anyone else.

He dragged his thoughts back to the present. 'I expect you're excited to be seeing them after so long,' he said to Sybil.

'Four years is a long time to be so far apart,' she replied. 'We've had very different wars, of course, and I expect we've all changed. But they're still my daughters, and that bond can never be broken.'

'You must be missing your little boy,' he murmured as they approached the harbour.

'Yes, I am. But this is no place for him, and he's perfectly safe with his grandparents. Perhaps if Jock and Philip come through I'll telegraph my parents and ask them to bring him over. He'll need to get to know his father and sisters.'

Without replying, Jim drove through the entrance gate and headed for the flying-boat docking station. He parked the car and went round to help the women out. 'We're still a little early,' he said. 'I'll just go and check with the harbour master that they're on time.'

Sybil eyed the huge harbour with interest. There were numerous ships at anchor waiting for permission to dock, and the navy was clearly still out in force, guarding the island. 'It's all very different to the last time we were here, isn't it, Amah?'

The tiny woman nodded. 'I will always remember you being carried onto that ship with James in your arms, and the enemy planes coming in with their guns spitting death.' She shivered despite the warmth of the evening and pulled her shawl more closely over her shoulders. 'I was so afraid for you, and for the sahib.'

'I always wondered why you didn't wait with him instead of disappearing into the crowd like that,' said Sybil.

'He had important things to do,' she said. 'I would have been a burden.'

Sybil's reply was halted by Jim's return. 'It's on schedule to arrive in ten minutes. Would you prefer to sit in the car to wait?'

Sybil shook her head. 'I want to be right here where they can see me as they disembark. But perhaps it would be best if Amah sat down. She's not as strong as she once was.'

'I will stay with *Mem*,' she said to Jim's questioning glance.

Jim stood there, not sure of what to say to either woman. He was intrigued by the little Malay woman and the relationship between her and Sybil, and wondered if Amah actually had a proper name. He couldn't imagine being called by his job description all his life.

'There it is,' said Sybil some minutes later, excitedly pointing to the twin lights rapidly approaching the water, and then taking Amah's hand. 'Oh my goodness, I can hardly believe they're really here,' she breathed.

The large seaplane came in low over the water, making for the path set out with floating buoys that would keep them a safe distance from the rest of the shipping. The roar of the engines was loud and made further conversation impossible, and they all watched as the floats glided onto the water, sending up a fountain of spray on either side.

Jim was reminded of the Sutherland seaplanes that had delivered men, medical equipment, stores and machinery to remote rivers and waterways throughout Burma. The pilots had shown great bravery in landing in a war zone. Many of them hadn't made it, and he wondered fleetingly if this pilot had seen action.

The seaplane cruised to the dock and as the engines died, the propellers slowed to a stop, and the pilot climbed out with his navigator to shake the hands of his passengers who were now emerging down the steps and onto the quay.

'Sarah! Jane!' called Sybil, breaking into an awkward run along the pier towards them, her high heels in danger of sinking into the cracks between the planks.

'Mother!' the girls shrieked back in unison before scrambling out of the orderly line and running towards her. They crushed her to them, kissing her cheeks, knocking her hat askew and all of them talking at once in their excitement.

'It's so wonderful to see you again,' said Sarah. 'Did you bring James?'

'You haven't changed a bit, Mummy,' breathed Jane. 'You're still as gorgeous as ever. Have you any news of Pops or Philip? Where are you staying? And have you bumped into Jim Reilly yet?'

Sybil laughed, straightened her hat and then cupped her precious girls' faces in her hands. 'I've left James in Australia with Granny and Grandpa. There's no news of your father, or of Philip, and yes, I've met Jim. But I have a wonderful surprise for you both. Look who's here.' She stepped back and gently drew Amah forward.

Both girls gasped, clearly shocked by her appearance despite the new clothes.

Jane was the first to break the silence. 'Oh, Amah,' she said with tears in her eyes as she carefully embraced her. 'I'm so glad you're all right.'

'So am I,' said Sarah, hugging her in turn. 'We were so grateful to you for risking your life to send Mother the note about Pops and Philip. There really aren't words enough to express how much that meant to us.'

'To see you both looking so well is all the thanks I need,' said Amah, taking their hands to kiss them. 'My goodness, you are grown into fine young women – and is that an engagement ring on your finger, Jane?'

'Indeed it is,' she replied, ignoring her mother's sharp gaze. 'Jeremy asked me to marry him just before we left England. But I'll tell you all about him later.'

She looked away from Amah and grinned at Jim who was standing awkwardly a few feet away. 'Hello, Jim. My word, we're all a long way from Cliffehaven, aren't we?'

He took off his peaked uniform cap, stuffed it under his arm and shook her hand, not really knowing how to greet this self-composed young woman who bore little resemblance to the Jane he remembered.

'We certainly are,' he replied. 'How is the old place? Still standing?'

'It's a bit battered, but your Peggy has lots of plans to make it look better for when you get back,' she said, digging into her bag. 'I've got a stack of letters for you.'

She handed them over and then turned to Sybil who was looking most put out. 'There's a few for you too, Mother. Jeremy thought it was only right to ask you formally for my hand, and the others are from Peggy and Cordelia.'

'Who is this Jeremy? You've said very little about him in your letters.'

'We'll talk about everything once we've done the customs check and collected our luggage,' said Sarah, giving Jim a grin. 'Good to see you, Jim. The army and the climate have clearly suited you. Peggy will positively faint when she sees you looking so handsome in that uniform.'

Jim actually blushed beneath his tan and was thankful that the girls didn't notice as they hurried off towards the customs shed. He glanced at Amah and saw she was trembling, either from her emotions or because she'd been standing without support for too long.

'I'll take Amah back to the car and bring it closer to load up the bags,' he murmured.

Sybil was still fidgeting by the customs house as he drew the car up outside. 'Who is this Jeremy person?' she demanded the moment he'd alighted. 'Jane's been very secretive about him, and I'm not at all sure I approve of her getting engaged without her father's permission.'

'I've never met him,' Jim stuttered, rather reeling from her attack. 'But Peggy wrote that he's a very pleasant young man with exciting prospects in Washington.'

Sybil eyed him askance. 'Washington? As in America?'

'I believe so.'

Sybil's eyes narrowed. 'He's not an American, is he? Jane hasn't had her head turned by some Yank on the make?'

'I seem to remember that his mother is French and his father is English,' said Jim, somewhat rattled by her continual questions.

'Well, it's simply not good enough,' snapped Sybil. 'Jane's too young and can't possibly know her mind well enough to be getting engaged.'

Jim didn't like her tone and decided to defend Jane. 'Correct me if I'm wrong, Mrs Fuller, but wasn't Sarah engaged to Philip at the same age?'

'That was different,' she replied waspishly. 'Sarah's sensible. She knows the seriousness of getting engaged – *and* she had our approval.'

Jim had no answer to this and was relieved to see the girls coming out of the customs shed with a porter carrying their cases. He hurried away to stow the cases in the boot of the car and tip the porter.

'I get the feeling Mother doesn't approve of my engagement,' muttered Jane, lingering at his side.

'You could have your work cut out to convince her otherwise,' murmured Jim, slamming the boot shut. 'Give her time, Jane. She'll come round, I'm sure.'

Sarah and Jane climbed into the back of the car on either side of Amah and held her hands during the journey back to the bungalow.

'Oh, my goodness,' said Sarah as he parked at the kerb. 'It's the Bristows' bungalow.'

'Elsa has very kindly let us move in with her until we know for certain what has happened to Jock and Philip,'

317

said Sybil stiffly. 'Reggie died in Changi prison, but she's stayed on here to work for RAPWI.' She climbed out of the car and, without waiting for the others, marched up the path and went in through the front door.

'She's definitely on the warpath,' said Sarah on a sigh, helping Amah out of the car. 'So much for our homecoming.'

'*Mem* has many fears and worries,' said Amah. 'This is not a good place for her and the waiting is long to hear anything of the *sahibs*.'

'I'm sure it's all very worrying,' said Jane. 'But that's no excuse for being so sharp about my engagement.'

Amah reached up and lightly touched Jane's face with her fingers. 'There has been great trouble for all of us, and perhaps it is better if you let *Mem* speak what is in her heart. You do not have to agree, but it would be better to keep your thoughts inside.'

'Oh, Amah, I have missed you so,' breathed Jane, giving her a gentle hug. 'I will try, I promise. But I have to stand up to her. I'm not a child any more.'

'And I too have missed you both. Now come. I have made special dinner to welcome you back to Singapore.'

Jim left them to it and drove to his billet, rather wishing he could be a fly on the wall during the conversation Sybil would no doubt have with her younger daughter. He smiled wryly as he parked the car outside the Palm Hotel. Jane had matured and come a long way since she'd arrived at Beach View, and he had the feeling that Sybil would not find it quite so easy to get her own way with her now.

20

The first night had proved a difficult one for Jane, but with Sarah's help, she'd managed to hold her tongue long enough for her mother to run out of steam, and they'd all sat down with Elsa to enjoy Amah's delicious and very hot curry.

Over the following week, Sybil appeared to have been mollified by what Peggy had written about Jeremy, and actually approved of his formal letter asking her for her daughter's hand, and yet it was clear that she thought Jane was far too young to be tying herself down.

Jane decided the only way to convince her mother that she was no longer a child to be mollycoddled was to take charge of the chaotic filing system in Elsa Bristow's office and bring some order to it. Three weeks later, she'd organised shelves to be built from floor to ceiling on three sides, and these were now stacked with box files, each with neatly printed labels, and placed in numerical order.

Having completed that task, Jane had then turned her attention to the bewildering and often misleading data coming in from the search teams in the jungle. She began to plot maps using the information Jim had gleaned from his interviews with the returning prisoners, and the local knowledge of the natives who'd fled Burma and Thailand.

It was work she loved, and it had proved extremely useful to those searching for the thousands of hidden camps throughout Asia, and as September faded into October, even Sybil had to admit that her daughter was far more skilled and intelligent than she'd ever given her credit for. Elsa, too, had revised her opinion and often turned to her for advice on a particularly knotty problem, marvelling at the girl's ability to see things differently.

Sarah had become restless as the weeks rolled on with still no news of her father and Philip, and having seen the desperate need for help at the hospital, she'd eventually gone to the office and offered her secretarial services. She'd been snapped up immediately, and soon found herself wading through acres of paperwork that had been ignored for weeks due to the influx of so many patients.

Sybil, left alone in the bungalow with only Amah for company, felt more useless than ever, so Sarah encouraged her to go with her to the nearby convent where the nuns were looking after the orphaned native children. She'd been reluctant at first, for she'd never had much to do with nuns, wasn't a Catholic and doubted she'd have anything to offer. Yet, upon meeting the Reverend Mother and seeing the wonderful work the nuns were doing, she realised she had something to give to those little ones who needed love and care. It wasn't long before she became a valued and much-loved figure at the convent, and she happily spent her days there, coming home at night, tired but at last fulfilled.

Amah quietly kept her thoughts to herself as she watched these changes and saw how work was taking their minds off the terrible worries for their sahibs. She knew she didn't have long to be with them, but to serve, to watch them grow spiritually stronger in the good works they were doing was enough. Her babies had grown and were beautiful young women with long lives ahead of them which she prayed would be happy – although she'd sensed that Sarah was hiding a terrible sorrow behind her smiles, and that worried her deeply.

As for Sybil, her transformation had been wonderful to see. Gone was the restlessness and the need to be entertained and amused, for she'd found a huge well of compassion, and a tireless energy to bring solace to those little children – which, in turn, brought her closer to her daughters.

Amah smiled to herself as she prepared the evening meal. Whatever the outcome of the search for the sahibs, *Mem* and her girls would always have each other, for the ties that bound them were strengthening by the day.

Jim had risen early that late October morning to the raucous sound of Jumbo's snoring. His head felt as if it had been occupied by an entire band of drummers, and the shaft of glaring sun coming in through a gap in the bamboo blinds made him wince. He swallowed a couple of aspirin and then staggered out to the bathroom on the landing, hoping a cold shower might improve things.

Returning to the room some time later, he glanced at the sleeping Jumbo enviously, wishing it was his day off too and he could return to bed. The party last night had been riotous to say the least, for Myfanwy had accepted Jumbo's proposal, and the main bar at Raffles had been taken over by the celebrations which had lasted into the early hours.

Jim had danced with Sarah, Jane and Sybil as well as every one of the nurses; sung out of key to the old favourites someone was bashing out on a piano, and suspected he'd probably blotted his reputation with Elsa after pulling her onto the dance floor and then giving her a hearty kiss.

He groaned at the memory and began to dress. He had a long day ahead of him and wasn't looking forward to it, for the heat was already rising, and he had to face Elsa and Jane this morning. He could only hope that Sybil hadn't taken it into her head to call in at the office on her way to the convent, for she too had witnessed his behaviour the previous night and he could well imagine what she must be thinking of him.

Combing his hair, he pulled on his peaked cap and picked up the briefcase he'd taken to carrying everywhere. He smiled wryly at his reflection in the wardrobe mirror, wondering what Peggy would think of this very different Jim.

The traffic was the usual nightmare of blaring horns and jams as cars, trucks, donkeys, wagons and rickshaws tried to dodge pedestrians and lines of chained Japanese prisoners. The trials had begun and the first executions would take place the following week, but in the meantime they'd been put to work mending the roads and sewers, and making much-needed repairs to important buildings like the hospital.

Jim's shirt was already sticking unpleasantly to him as he parked the car and slowly headed into Raffles. If he'd learned one thing from being in the tropics so long, it was never to hurry anywhere, and to remain patient when everything seemed to take an age. The pace of life out here was necessarily slow, for they were only one degree north of the equator, and the heat could be a killer.

He tapped on the office door, steeling himself for a ribbing, then went in.

'Well, well,' said Elsa with a wry smile. 'We didn't expect to see you so early.'

'How's the head?' asked Jane, shooting him a grin.

'Still on my shoulders, but only just,' he replied sheepishly. 'Look, Elsa, I must apologise about last night.'

Elsa laughed. 'There's no need, Jim. I was actually rather flattered if the truth be known. I haven't been kissed like that in more years than I care to remember.'

Jim reddened and didn't know where to look as Jane giggled. 'I've come for the personnel files of the men I'm to interview today,' he said.

'Ah, yes,' replied Jane, getting to her feet and reaching for one of the box files on a nearby shelf. She placed it on the desk. 'These men were flown in a week ago from camps thirty-two and fifty-nine. They're all on rest and recuperation until passed fit enough to be sent back to England. I've removed the files of those who went straight to the hospital, and the files of those from Australasia, Holland and America have gone to their administrators.'

'Thanks, Jane. That all seems most efficient.'

'She's a marvel, isn't she?' said Elsa. 'I don't know how I coped before.'

Jim didn't like to point out that she hadn't coped at all, so stayed silent as he took the files out of the box and placed them in his briefcase. 'I'll see you this evening,' he said to the two heads already bowed over their work. He left them to it and returned to the car.

Driving through the crowded streets, he headed for the vast tented camps that had been set up outside the city for the returning prisoners who didn't need to be hospitalised, and were waiting to be repatriated.

A Union Jack hung limply from a tall pole beside the gate to signify this was the British camp, and Jim saluted the guards as he drove through. He parked outside the marquee which housed a walk-in clinic and an advice and counselling centre, and an area serviced by the Red Cross where the men could freely borrow books and magazines and take away writing materials, sketchpads, shaving equipment, soap and shampoo.

Jim knew the value to the men of having such things to hand after being so long without them, and also knew what sterling work the nurses and counsellors were doing in preparing the men for their return home.

The British government had also done their bit in helping these bewildered, almost shell-shocked survivors to recover from their ordeal by printing numerous leaflets on what to expect when they returned to a war-ravaged England, and the wives and children they hadn't seen for many years. Other leaflets were designed to help with looking for work or retraining, should their old jobs no longer be available. There were also generous grants on offer to help with retraining or further education.

Jim wondered if he should take a few leaflets for himself. He hadn't seen Peggy or his children for years, and the cinema where he'd worked had been bombed long before he'd even received his call-up papers. By the tone of her last letters, it seemed Peggy was getting on far too well without him, and he wasn't at all sure about her plans to renovate

Beach View. He didn't like change, and could only hope it would still be recognisable when he was finally allowed to go home, for the memory, and the affection for it, was etched in his heart.

He greeted the middle-aged nursing sister with a broad smile. 'And how are you on this very fine day, Margaret?'

'Much better for seeing you,' she replied with a twinkle in her eyes. 'How's the head, Jim?'

He groaned inwardly at the realisation that his exploits were now common knowledge but managed to keep on smiling. 'It's fine, thank you. I'm here to see Major Patrick O'Keefe and Corporals Toby Mayhew, Matthew Gresham and William Frost.'

She turned to look at the vast map pinned to a board standing on an easel. 'The corporals are all in row five, tents 435 to 437. Major O'Keefe is in row one, tent 335.'

She regarded Jim thoughtfully as he finished noting down the tent numbers. 'Be careful with O'Keefe,' she said softly. 'He's still struggling to come to terms with what happened to him and his men on that awful railway, and is finding it very hard to communicate with anyone. He's taken to writing long letters to his wife and standing for hours outside the gates looking up at the Union Jack.'

'Why's he doing that?'

'I think he needs to be reassured that he's a free man, and walking through those gates and seeing that flag up there gives him that assurance.'

Jim nodded and went outside. He would leave O'Keefe to last, he decided, for officers were far more difficult to persuade to talk – especially the ones who'd been slave labour on that evil railway.

He headed towards the corporals' tents, and on his way saw a young airman standing by an American Jeep, his gaze fixed on it in wonder as if he'd never seen such a thing before.

This strange behaviour was fairly commonplace amongst the prisoners – much like the need to just walk back and forth through the gates – and Jim understood that not all of the cruelties meted out to the prisoners were physical, and the unseen mental scars would take a very long time to heal.

He found the corporals playing a desultory game of cards outside their tents, and as he approached, they leapt to their feet to salute.

'Stand easy,' he said, noting how young and thin they all were. 'I've just come for a wee chat, nothing too official.' He pulled up a spare chair and with a nod they all sat down.

'Are you here to tell us we're on our way home at last?' asked Frost, the youngest of the three.

'I'm sorry, but no, that's not up to me.'

'But we've been here for weeks,' snapped Gresham, throwing the cards onto the table. 'I need to get home to my girlfriend before she gets fed up with waiting.'

'We all need to go home, Gresham,' said Jim patiently. 'And you will, once there's a ship free to take you there. But with so many of you coming in, the admin is a nightmare.'

'Admin, my arse,' muttered Mayhew. 'What do those pen-pushers know about anything? Can't they see we just need to get out of this bloody place and back to our families?'

'Of course they do, and I understand your frustration.' He paused. 'One of the things the admin bods are asking for is statements from all the POWs before they leave Singapore.'

Gresham folded his arms. 'With all due respect, sir,' he said with a distinct lack of such respect, 'I've been answering questions ever since I was picked up by the Nips, and I've had enough of it.'

There was a general murmur of agreement, and Jim realised they were fed up, bored and frustrated to be kept in yet another camp. 'I don't blame you,' he replied mildly. 'But there are still men missing out there in hundreds of isolated, hidden camps we've yet to hear about. All I'm asking for is help in finding what happened to them and where they might be.'

'Dead, probably,' said Mayhew flatly, concentrating on rolling a smoke. 'I helped to bury more than enough of them.'

This seemed to spark something in the other men, and soon they were remembering comrades they'd worked alongside, men they'd helped to bury, others with whom they'd shared their food and tended until they simply gave up the struggle and passed away. They talked about being force-marched from camp to camp; the guards; the senseless beatings of men too frail to stand, and the back-breaking work they'd been forced to do in a remote coal mine, despite being weak from hunger and suffering all manner of fevers.

Jim could picture it all too well, but he tamped down on the acid burn in his throat, kept his expression unreadable and wrote it all down – adding the names of the dead and the approximate position of their burial.

When the men finally fell silent, he knew they'd had enough. He thanked them, wished them a safe journey home and went to the canteen. He needed something to wash away the sourness in his throat that always came after such interviews. They were young boys – not much older than his son Bob – but they'd been turned into old, bitter men by their experiences. Would they ever be able to put those memories to the back of their minds – or would those years in the jungle taint their lives for ever?

He sat in the canteen feeling suddenly awkward, overfed and over-privileged amongst so many who'd had a much harsher war than he, for the POWs had clustered together and were ignoring him as they sat a careful distance away and talked in murmurs.

Jim knew that the ordeal they'd gone through had brought them closer than brothers – probably closer than any wife could now be – and it seemed it was only to these comrades that they felt able to talk and share their fears for the future. His presence here and the reason for it would be common knowledge, and their reluctance to talk to him was something he just had to accept with grace and understanding.

Jim finished his second mug of tea and lit a cigarette. Checking the time, he found it was already mid-afternoon, and he still had the major to talk to before he could return to the office. Gathering up his briefcase, he strolled away from the canteen and headed for row one, tent 335.

Major O'Keefe was lying on his camp bed deeply engrossed in a book and, before alerting him to his presence, Jim took this brief moment to gauge his man. He could see that although he was in his mid-thirties, he looked much older. He had big, gnarled hands and feet, brutally short black hair streaked with silver, and a six o'clock shadow on his chin.

Jim knew from his records that O'Keefe was a career soldier in the Irish Guards and had been captured shortly after arriving in Singapore. By the looks of him, he'd lost two-thirds of his body weight, and the khaki shirt and shorts hung off him.

O'Keefe looked up as Jim's shadow fell over him, and he struggled to his feet to return Jim's salute.

'I'm sorry to disturb your reading, Major,' said Jim. 'You were clearly deeply into it.'

O'Keefe shrugged and carefully placed the book on the bed. ''Tis no matter, Lieutenant. I'll easily get back into it.' He pulled out a camp chair. 'Will ye be after sitting? I find I can't stand for too long now.'

'Thank you.' Jim settled in the chair and smiled as the other man sat opposite him. 'You sound just like my father,' he said. 'What part of Ireland do you come from?'

'Cork,' he replied without returning Jim's smile. 'Though I've not been back there in a long while.' He cocked his head. 'And yourself, Lieutenant?'

'From a seaside town on the south coast of England. My father went there with his parents and sister from County Clare.'

'And what is it you'll be wanting from me, Lieutenant Reilly?' he asked quietly, glancing at the briefcase before steadily meeting Jim's gaze.

Jim explained, and then surreptitiously drew out his notebook to sit quietly and give the man time to think and decide how to answer, for he guessed he was not one to be hurried, and if he did decide to give a statement, it would be concise and insightful.

'Well now, if it will help you find those men, I will tell you what I know.' O'Keefe held Jim's gaze. ''Tis not a pretty tale, and it's painful to recall it, but I will do my best. Where would you like me to begin?'

'Where were you first taken prisoner?'

'Here, on the island,' he replied. 'I was captured after a skirmish with the invading Japs and thrown into Changi with most of my men.'

He looked off into the distance as he remembered that time and worried the thin, jagged scar on his temple with his fingers. 'There were thousands of us crammed in there alongside Australians, Canadians, New Zealanders and Americans. There were a lot of men from the local volunteer force – part-time soldiers made up from planters, bank clerks and retired military men.'

Jim's pulse quickened. 'Did you happen to hear the names of any of those volunteers?'

O'Keefe frowned, clearly annoyed at having his line of thought broken. 'Aye, one or two, but they were mostly kept apart from us – in the beginning.'

'Do the names Jock Fuller and Philip Tarrant ring any bells?'

'Oh, aye, I remember them. Fuller was a big bluff rubber planter who was most indignant at being captured. When Tarrant was brought in wounded he calmed down and took him under his wing. They stuck close together for the month or two they were in Changi, then the Japs took them off somewhere and I didn't see either of them for about two years.'

He looked at Jim questioningly. 'Are these men important to you, Lieutenant – or shall I be continuing my tale?'

'They're important to friends of mine,' said Jim hastily. 'But please carry on with what you were saying.'

O'Keefe took a deep breath before lighting a cigarette and once again massaging the jagged scar on his temple. 'I lost good men during the two years we were incarcerated in what we thought was a hellhole.' His eyes held no warmth or humour. 'But we were soon to learn there were far worse hells than Changi.'

Jim remained silent, watching the fleeting expressions on the other man's face as he recalled those dreadful days.

'We were all half-starved and sick with fevers, dysentery and a hundred other things. There was no medical help, no decent food, and morale was at its lowest. As my rank demands, it was up to me to keep order, to try and do what I could for the sick and boost morale, but it was hopeless. We were dying like flies in that place.'

He mashed out the half-smoked cigarette and lit another, his hand not quite steady. 'And then in early 1943, the Japanese told us that those who were deemed fit enough were to be sent out of Singapore to a place where the food was plentiful, and we would be given time and space for recreation in return for a little light work.'

His lip curled and a tic began to flicker beneath his left eye. 'They promised us there would be no long marches, and only the fittest would be chosen.'

O'Keefe grunted. 'That was the fantasy. The reality was far different.' He paused to agitatedly rub his scar. 'They made no distinction between the half-dead, the injured or the fit – and none of us were fit by then. They took us all, and there were thousands of us rounded up over the next few days to do the short march to the station. None of us knew what lay ahead, and it was a good thing, because if we had, we'd have given in, right there and then.'

Jim wanted to ask about Philip and Jock but remained silent, not wanting to break the thread of O'Keefe's thoughts again.

'We endured four days of being jammed into metal rice trucks without food or fresh air, and very little water, as the train took us up the Malay Peninsula. It was too much for many of the men and they never made it to the journey's end.'

He grimaced and tried to still the tic beneath his eye. 'They were the lucky ones, really, for what faced us then was a two-hundred-mile march through thick jungle. More men died along the way, and we buried them as best we could, but the Japanese were relentless and kept us moving at a terrible pace until we reached a place called Sonkrai – pronounced Song Cry – which came to mean the place of death to all of us.'

He rubbed his scar again as if to erase it along with the memories of that terrible place Jim had already heard about too often. 'I can tell you the names of the men I lost on that journey – and the names of every single man I had to bury in the years that followed. They're etched in my heart and in my mind, and I will never forget them – as I'll never forget the bastard guards and their commanders.'

Jim quickly wrote down the long list of names of those who'd died on that torturous journey, marvelling that the man had such clear recall, and thankful that neither Philip nor Jock were amongst them. The names of many of the guards and commanders were familiar from past interviews, but he noted them down anyway.

O'Keefe waited until Jim had finished writing before speaking again. 'We discovered we were there to build a monstrous railway for the Japanese which would stretch almost two hundred and sixty miles between Bangkok and Moulmein in Burma. It would traverse mountains and gorges, and almost impenetrable jungle, and the only tools we had were picks and spades.'

He took a quavering breath. 'It has been estimated since that for every sleeper laid, a man died, and I can believe that.' He hung his head and fell silent for a moment with his eyes closed. 'To be sure, the greatest writer in the world couldn't find the words to describe what we went through.'

Jim saw that the tic was throbbing harder beneath the man's eye, and his fingers were once more seeking that scar. O'Keefe was clearly suffering from having to tell his tale, and Jim wished with all his heart that it wasn't necessary.

O'Keefe rallied, took a deep drag of his cigarette and then crushed it into the ashtray. His tone of voice changed and now held profound but tightly controlled anger.

'Shortly after we were put to work, cholera broke out, killing hundreds of us as well as the Asian labourers who'd been forced to work beside us. So not only were we dying of starvation, dysentery, malaria, beriberi and jungle ulcers, we were being killed off by fecking cholera, and there was absolutely nothing I could do about it.'

He looked up at Jim. 'I took it very personally, Lieutenant, for my position as senior officer meant I had to exercise leadership and example to my men, and steer a straight, monotonous course, never showing my emotions, never letting up or giving in for a single moment regardless of what was going on around me — or to me. I was forced to cope with the horrors on my own and keep my dignity, for the morale of my men would have been broken if I'd shown one iota of what I was feeling.'

O'Keefe dipped his chin, his voice on the point of breaking. 'It was the loneliest position to be in – horribly lonely – and it was only the thought of my wife, Molly, waiting for me at home that kept me going.'

He gave a deep, tremulous sigh and ran his fingers over the scar. 'Now it's all over I'm exhausted. Exhausted by the sweat, the toil, the blood and the deaths – too many deaths – and all of them senseless. Exhausted from having to fight with every fibre of my being to stay alive, to keep my men alive, and to bolster their morale in any way I could – which was a hapless task.' He fell silent.

'Did you ever receive letters from home, or Red Cross parcels?' asked Jim softly.

O'Keefe shook his head. 'We heard nothing from anyone and thought we'd been forgotten by the world until the moment we were liberated.'

He looked up at Jim with a frown. 'It's a strange feeling to find yourself free after so long, and when the American soldiers found us, most of us just sat and waited to be told what to do and where to go. We were numbed by it all, you see, and couldn't believe it was really over and we were free.'

He began to rub his scar again, noticed what he was doing and clasped his hands tightly together between his bony knees. 'Since coming here my moods have swung from sheer elation to deep despondency, but receiving letters from my wife is a tremendous help, and I write long letters back. They seem to calm me.'

'Were you moved from camp to camp during the building of the railway?' asked Jim.

'Several times, and I've since met men here that I remember from different camps.' He took a deep breath, realised he was rubbing his scar again and gave Jim a rueful smile. 'I've found I do that when I'm feeling particularly on edge,' he explained. 'It's a habit I'll have to stop, or my wife will think I've gone potty.'

Jim realised the man had had more than enough, and as he'd given him so much worthwhile information, it was only kind to leave him in peace. He'd closed his notebook and was about to take his leave when O'Keefe touched his arm.

'Don't you want to know what happened to your friends?'

Jim's heart missed a beat. 'I'd be very grateful and so would their families,' he said carefully.

'Fuller and Tarrant were with me at camp thirty-two and survived the cholera, although they were never quite the same again. Tarrant was skin and bone when he was sent to camp sixteen which was further down the line, nearer to Bangkok. And Fuller was the same, but he remained in our work party as we were sent to camp thirty-three.' He looked at Jim, his eyes fathomless in his deeply lined face. 'He's still there. I'm sorry.'

Jim closed his eyes momentarily and digested the news he'd been dreading. 'How did he die?' he asked, his voice thick with emotion.

'He was sick and very weak, half the man he'd been when I first met him in Changi – and one day he was struggling to help two others carry a heavy sleeper. I saw his legs buckle and hurried to help him – but he was already dead by the time he hit the ground. He was buried beside the track in the jungle, as were so many others. I left a marker – it was all I could do for him.'

'Thank you for sharing your experiences with me. I do understand how very painful it must have been for you, but your testimony will help enormously in the trials to come.'

O'Keefe merely nodded, his face drained of all colour, his thin shoulders sagging from the weight of all the responsibility he'd carried throughout his ordeal.

Jim saluted him, then turned away swiftly and hurried to the car before anyone could see how deeply he'd been affected.

He sat there staring out of the windscreen, battling to contain the raging fury that was building inside him. He'd thought his war had been hard – thought he'd seen and heard more than any man should bear in one lifetime. But these men, these brave survivors, had witnessed and borne things that no man should bear. And although he'd never met Jock or Philip, he thought of them as real heroes.

Gathering his wits about him, he dried his eyes, tamping down on the awful tide of anguish that threatened to overwhelm him, then drove back to Raffles. The dread of having to face Sybil and her girls grew with every mile, and when he'd reached the hotel, he had to sit for a few minutes to prepare himself for what would inevitably be a traumatic and distressing conversation.

*

Jane looked up as Jim entered the office and knew from his expression that he was the bearer of bad news – and that could only mean one thing. Her heart began to thud painfully and her breath seemed trapped in her chest as Elsa hurried to her side.

'Who is it?' she managed in dread.

'I'm so sorry, Jane,' he replied, coming to take her hand. 'It's your father.'

'He's dead, isn't he?' she whispered.

At his nod, she felt the sob form in her throat, swiftly swelling and rising until it escaped in a storm of pain and sorrow. 'And Philip?' she wailed. 'Is he gone too?'

'We don't know yet,' said a distressed Jim. 'The teams will be out searching now we know where he was held.'

Jane turned into Elsa's embrace and sobbed against her even though she'd prepared herself for this moment – had known instinctively that it would come. But the reality of knowing he was gone, that she would never see him again, talk to him again or be held by him was stark and unbearable.

She was vaguely aware of Jim leaving the room, and hearing Elsa's soft words of comfort, but all she could see was her darling Pops – big and bluff and fully in charge during any crisis – and yet soft-hearted, loving and oh so gentle with them and their mother. Snapshots of memories flashed across her mind, and she saw him striding through the rubber trees, tanned and fit, his sturdy legs and broad shoulders giving him an aura of strength and capability.

She withdrew from Elsa's embrace eventually and pulled herself together. 'I'm sorry, Elsa, I didn't mean to let go like that.'

'You have absolutely nothing to apologise for,' said the older woman. 'It's natural to cry at times like these.'

'But I almost knew this would happen and thought I'd steeled myself against it.' Jane mopped her face. 'Oh, God,' she breathed, 'how am I going to tell Mother? This will kill her.'

'I doubt it,' said Elsa softly. 'Your mother's tougher than she looks, and I think she's already accepted that Jock would most likely not come back.'

Jim entered the room with a tray of glasses and a bottle of brandy. 'Don't ask where I got the brandy,' he said, pouring generous measures. 'Just drink it and let it do its work.'

Jane took a huge gulp which made her cough. 'Was Philip with Pops, Jim? Or had they been separated?' she managed when she'd recovered.

'They were together until the end of 1943, and then Philip was sent to another labour camp further down the line.'

Jane digested this and took a tremulous breath. 'They were both on that horrendous railway then,' she said flatly. 'Is that where Pops died?'

Jim nodded, and Jane could see he was deciding how much to tell her.

'I've heard enough from the men who survived that horror, Jim. Tell me what happened.'

Jim took a breath and told her. 'It was swift, Jane,' he finished. 'And I suspect a blessed release.'

'Poor Pops,' she murmured, the tears streaming down her face. 'At least now that we know where he is the burial teams can give him a decent resting place.'

She finished the brandy and collected her things. 'I'd better go and tell Sarah so we can face Mother together.'

Jim had driven Jane to the hospital and waited outside as she'd gone in search of her sister. He paced back and forth, smoking one cigarette after another until his head began to throb and his throat went dry.

He'd lost track of what time it was when he spotted Jumbo, who was in charge of a group of Japanese prisoners repairing the brickwork at the side entrance to the hospital clinic. He went over to tell his friend what had happened,

335

and warned him he probably wouldn't make the supper he and Myfanwy had organised for this evening.

Jane appeared with a red-eyed Sarah, and he silently opened the car door for them and then drove towards the bungalow. He glanced repeatedly in the rear-view mirror and saw that the sisters were now dry-eyed and holding fast to one another, probably preparing themselves to face their mother with their devastating news, and as they approached the bungalow, his heart sank.

Sybil was just paying off the rickshaw boy, and she turned to smile and wave at Jim as he parked outside the front gate. She looked so animated and attractive in that summer frock, that he hated the thought of destroying all that with what was to come.

He swiftly climbed out of the car and opened the door for the girls.

'Hello, Jim, what are you doing here?' she asked cheerfully before glancing behind him and seeing her daughters. 'My goodness, you are arriving in style,' she teased. And then, as she saw their expressions, her smile faded.

'What is it?' she breathed, her hand fluttering to her chest. 'What's happened?'

'Let's go inside,' said Sarah, attempting to take her arm. 'We have something to tell you, Mummy.'

'No. Tell me now,' she demanded breathlessly. 'Is it your father? Have they found him? Is he ...' Her words faltered and died and the colour went from her face as she realised what they'd come to tell her.

Jim just managed to catch her as she crumpled in a dead faint. He scooped her into his arms and carried her up the path to where Amah was waiting in the front doorway and watching it all with sad, knowing eyes.

Once he knew Sybil would be well taken care of, he left them to mourn in private and went to find a dark, quiet bar in which he could drink enough to blot out the stories and the images they'd invoked.

21

As the days went by and there was still no news of Philip, Sarah began to believe that he'd suffered the same terrible fate as her beloved father. She knew that the search and burial teams were slowly making their way down the torturous route of the Burma railway, and that more and more camps, makeshift cemeteries and survivors were being found – but having discussed it with Jim and Elsa, she realised the list of the dead was growing, and she could only hope that if he was buried out there, someone had left a marker to remember him by.

She didn't know how to feel about Philip, for he'd become a shadowy figure – a blurred memory from a past age that was gone for ever. But she had loved him once, and because of that she could mourn him and all they'd lost.

Elsa had been a stalwart supporter over those first few terrible days, and had come back the following evening with a traditional white mourning sari, incense and candles for Amah. The elderly woman had quietly and efficiently tended Sybil, who'd made a remarkable recovery. Sybil had clearly accepted that her worst fears had been realised, and although she was grieving, decided she needed to go back to her work at the orphanage.

'I need to do something,' she said a week later. 'Your father wouldn't want me sitting about here feeling sorry for myself when he gave his life so we could be free.'

Sarah had thought it was far too soon, but Jane and the others agreed with Sybil. None of them had any idea of how long they would have to wait to hear what had happened to

Philip, and there was urgent work still to be done at the hospital and in the RAPWI office.

Telegrams had been sent to Australia, and to Peggy and Jeremy, who'd now returned to England. The routine of their lives in Singapore stuttered to a start again, and they all found that it helped enormously.

The respite camps were beginning at long last to be cleared, and the men, women and children were now on their way home in the ships that came in almost every day. Raffles was slowly returning to its quiet, almost sombre self, but the hospital was still overwhelmed as prisoners were brought in from Sumatra, Java and the islands off Japan. There was a real sense that no one had been left behind or forgotten, for those who'd died were now laid to rest in cordoned-off cemeteries, their names, ranks and numbers marked on stones if known – unless they were known only to God.

It was the last week in October and Sarah was wading through the latest batch of almost indecipherable doctors' reports on patients who'd come in the previous day. The heat was stifling despite the ceiling fan, and she was looking forward to the end of the day when she could relax with a long cold Tom Collins and think about seeing the plantation house again.

It wasn't known what sort of state it was in after the Japanese had left it, but Sybil had decided they all needed a break from Singapore and that it would do them good to go back there just for the weekend, and perhaps lay a memorial stone for Jock. Sarah had been dubious, for it wouldn't feel the same without Pops, and every nook and cranny of the place would just be a sad reminder of him. There was also the fact that she hadn't heard anything about Philip, and it would be awful if she was away when news came.

Sarah had pored over the long list of the dead, and checked the names of the passengers of every plane and ship coming in. She'd even gone through the seemingly endless list of those who'd been sent home to Australia in case the authorities had heeded Sybil's pleas and sent him there. But there had been nothing, and she was beginning to accept that he must have been one of the many who'd died anonymously.

She paused in her typing and leaned back in the chair. The whole thing was tragic, for Philip had been young, virile and energetic. If anyone could have survived it should have been him. The knowledge that he must have been cut down in the prime of life and left in an unmarked grave tore at her heart. She closed her eyes and sent up a silent prayer that he hadn't suffered like so many others, and had died as her father had done – silently and in an instant.

Taking a deep breath, she pushed away from the desk and lit a cigarette. Throwing open the shutters and thereby risking an invasion of flies and bugs, she leaned on the sill to watch Jumbo patiently instructing the Japanese labourers on how to lay a line of bricks.

The sight of him made her smile, for she liked Jumbo enormously, and was delighted that he and Myfanwy had tied the knot in a simple church ceremony the previous weekend. Jim had been the best man, and given a rousing speech at the reception, which Sarah had abridged in her letter to Peggy. The celebrations had lasted long into the night and Jumbo had serenaded his bride with a stirring rendition of 'Road to the Isles' on his new set of bagpipes. Where the heck he'd found those was anyone's guess, but they certainly made the party go with a swing.

She finished her cigarette and was about to return to trying to decipher the doctors' writing when there was a soft tap on the door, and Matron stepped in.

'Hello, Matron. What can I do for you? I'm afraid I haven't finished these yet.'

'Don't worry about those, Sarah,' she replied softly.

Sarah looked at her unsmiling face and felt something lurch in the pit of her stomach. 'Philip?' she breathed. 'Have they found him?'

'Yes, my dear.' She approached the desk. 'He's just been brought in.'

'He's alive?' Sarah gasped, her pulse beating wildly.

'He is, but in a very bad way. I don't believe he has very long, so I've advised your mother and sister to get here as soon as possible.'

Sarah pushed back from the desk, suddenly desperate to see him. 'Where is he? Which ward?'

'Intensive care,' the other woman replied, reaching for her hand to stop her from leaving the room. 'But, Sarah, he might not recognise you – and you must prepare yourself for a shock when you see him. It's incredible that he's survived this long.'

Sarah nodded although she didn't feel prepared for anything. The fact that Philip was alive was a miracle in itself – which only proved to her that she'd been right to call off her engagement to Delaney and wait for his return.

She ran down the endless corridors – something strictly forbidden at all times – and finally reached the intensive care wing. Out of breath and dreading what she might find, she smoothed her hair, mopped the perspiration from her face and steeled herself to open the door.

The sister in charge met her before she'd taken more than a few steps. 'Miss Fuller?' she asked barely above a whisper. 'Matron said you were coming.'

'Is he really close to the end?' Sarah whispered back.

'I'm sorry, but yes,' she replied. 'But I'm sure that seeing you will rally him. He's in the last bed on the left.'

Sarah's legs threatened to give way as she tiptoed down the ward, trying to avoid the heart-wrenching sight of the other patients. Approaching the last bed, she hesitated momentarily, her heart in her mouth as she walked to his bedside and looked down at the man lying there.

She felt almost jubilant, for this wasn't Philip. Couldn't possibly be Philip. They'd made a terrible mistake, and he was out there somewhere still waiting to be found.

340

She turned to find the nursing sister standing by the end of the bed. 'It's not him,' she said raggedly. 'That's not Philip Tarrant.'

'I'm so sorry, Miss Fuller, but there's absolutely no doubt that it is.' She pointed to the dog tags hanging from the iron bedpost, and held out the filthy remnants of his identity papers for her to read.

Sarah's legs finally gave way and she almost fell into the bedside chair. She stared down at the old, haggard man in the bed who bore no resemblance to the handsome young man she'd known. His skin was parchment yellow and stretched across his skull so tightly she could almost see the white of the bones beneath. He'd lost most of his teeth; his head was shaven and covered in sores; the muscles of his arms now wasted flesh; his once broad, tanned chest a cavernous cage of rib and scar tissue.

Tears pricked and slowly ran unheeded down her face as her heart broke. 'Oh, dear God,' she breathed. 'What did they do to him?'

The nurse squeezed her shoulder. 'You've been here long enough to know what these men went through, Miss Fuller,' she said quietly. 'If he wakes, try not to let him see you cry. He'll find it very upsetting.'

The girl left and Sarah dried her tears before she tentatively reached for the bony hand that was resting on the sheet. It felt cold and inanimate and rather unpleasant. She flinched, but then reminded herself that this man – this stranger – was Philip whom she'd loved and had vowed to marry, and she was disgusted with herself for reacting that way. As she looked down at him, she knew she ought to be able to dredge up something of how she'd once felt for him, but there was only heart-rending pity.

She gazed at his lifeless hand and the glint of the diamond engagement ring on her finger and felt quite ill at the thought of all he must have been through. But against the odds he'd survived, and now she had to find the strength to help him fight his way back to recovery. She couldn't let him die – not now.

She leaned closer. 'Philip. It's me, Sarah. Remember me? We got engaged in Malaya and you gave me your mother's ring.'

His eyelids flickered but he made no other response, so she tried again. 'Philip, you must wake up, darling,' she murmured. 'This is Sarah. Sarah Fuller.'

His fingers twitched and he rolled his head on the pillow, his eyes opening as if with great difficulty. 'Sarah?' he sighed with a frown. 'Who's Sarah?'

A stab of shock pierced her. 'Sarah's Jock's daughter,' she said. 'You must remember Jock Fuller. He managed your family plantation.'

'Jock,' he muttered. His eyes flew open and he grabbed her hand so tightly it crushed the bones as he stared at her with haunted eyes seeing something other than her face. 'Typhoid,' he breathed. 'Sick, dying, another sleeper. Hold on, Jock. You've got to hold on. God help us,' he babbled.

And then he began to throw his head from side to side in agitation, his hands fluttering in distress. 'Stop them. Stop them. Please, please don't ...'

The nurse came hurrying over and unceremoniously pushed Sarah out of the way to give Philip an injection. 'I know it's frightening, but it takes them like this at times,' she said, emptying the syringe into the wasted flesh of his thigh.

Sarah watched through her tears as the gaunt face relaxed and the medication took effect.

'He'll sleep now for several hours,' the girl said. 'You might as well go and get some rest. You can come back at any time.'

Sarah shook her head and reached for Philip's hand again. 'I'll stay if that's all right.'

'Matron did warn you that he could easily slip away at any moment, didn't she?'

Sarah nodded. 'That's why I'd like to stay. I can't bear to think he might die alone.'

The girl nodded her understanding before going quietly to tend to another disturbed patient who was crying out for someone called Billy. Sarah marvelled at her strength of mind to be able to cope with such tragedy surrounding her day after day.

Sybil and Jane came to sit with her for a while, and then took it in turns to bring her something to eat and drink – although she wanted neither. A couple of hours later, Sarah realised they were both in shock at seeing Philip in such a bad way, and in the end she couldn't bear to see her mother's distress, and ordered them both to go back to the bungalow to rest.

Sarah sat by Philip's bedside through the long reaches of the night. She whispered to him, hoping he would hear her, and gently squeezed his hand, wanting a reaction, but he slept on.

As one of the nurses opened the window shutters and Sarah saw the first pearly grey of a new dawn and heard the birdsong, Philip opened his eyes and seemed to look straight at her.

'Philip,' she said urgently, clutching his hand. 'It's me, Sarah.'

He made no reply, closed his eyes, and with one last ragged sigh was taken from her.

22

Sybil was distraught by Philip's passing coming so soon after hearing of Jock's death, for it emphasised all that was lost. The energy she'd once had seemed to drain from her, leaving her listless and unable to face the bustle and noise of the orphanage.

The others rallied round her, but Sarah found that her mother's collapse was too difficult to cope with as she battled with her own emotions, so she returned to her work at the hospital.

She didn't really know how to feel, for one minute she was crying for her father, the next mourning the man she'd once known as Philip Tarrant, but who had become a stranger. And then there was the guilt of having betrayed him by loving another man – and the awful sense that she should have felt more than profound pity for him as he'd lain there dying.

Her thoughts and emotions were so complex and painful that she found it impossible to talk about them, even to Jane, who might have understood what she was going through. For how could she explain the terrible void that had opened up in her life? How to admit that despite everything, she longed only for Delaney – to hear his voice, see his beloved face and feel his arms about her? And how could she ever accept that he was gone from her life just as surely as her darling father, and there would be no second chance to put things right between them? Her future stretched emptily before her, leaving her lost and very much alone.

Sarah knew her mother would be shocked to the core if she'd had even an inkling of her true feelings, and the redoubtable and ultimately practical Elsa would probably have told her to pull herself together. Amah was a sad, gentle presence, who'd tried to comfort her and get her to talk about her troubles – but she would never have understood, so Sarah kept all the anguish inside, escaping to the hospital office where she had little time to think of anything but her work.

In Sarah's absence, Jane and Elsa had turned to Jim for help in organising a funeral at the rubber plantation. It was only right that Philip should be buried where he'd been born, and they decided they would also hold a short service for Jock, and place a headstone in his memory.

However, they were soon to discover that this wasn't quite as straightforward as they'd thought. Philip had been an only son, and both his parents were dead. No one knew if he'd left a will, and who the rightful owner of the plantation might be now. Elsa and Jane had approached every solicitor in Singapore in the hope of finding a will, but had come up empty-handed, so had to assume he'd died intestate. This meant that Jim had had to go through all sorts of legal red tape to arrange for Philip's body to be released from the hospital morgue and get permission to hold a burial service at the plantation – and find a vicar or padre willing to officiate.

Sarah soon realised he was beginning to feel beleaguered by it all and feeling the strain of having four women relying on him so heavily, so she'd reluctantly given in her notice at the hospital and done her best to help ease the burden by dealing with all the paperwork involved.

It was now the middle of November and they were due to leave for the plantation the following morning. It had taken all of Sarah's cajoling to persuade Amah to go and rest in her room, for she'd become very frail over the past weeks, and tired easily. They all sadly realised that she was slowly giving up and would soon leave them, and they could only hope that she hung on so they could get her home to the house in Malaya where she'd been so happy.

Sarah had finished her packing and was carrying her case into the hall when she heard a knock, and saw the shadow of someone through the glazed pane in the front door. Thinking it was probably Jim, she opened it to discover it was Jeremy.

'Oh, my goodness,' she breathed, drawing him inside. 'We weren't expecting you to make the long journey here.'

'I had to come after I got Jane's telegrams,' he said, placing his bag on the floor and taking off his panama hat. 'How is she?'

'She'll be all the better for seeing you,' said Sarah. 'But how on earth did you get here so quickly?'

'I have contacts in the RAF, and hitched several rides out.'

'Jeremy!' Jane came hurtling into the hall to throw her arms around him. 'Oh, Jeremy, it's so lovely to see you.'

Sarah left the lovebirds canoodling in the hall and went to tell Sybil of his arrival before going to her bedroom and closing the door. She didn't begrudge her sister's happiness, of course she didn't, but the sight of them together reminded her once again of all she'd lost.

Jim had had to ask his CO's permission to take some leave so he could drive the Fullers into Malaya, and because the man knew the tragic story of Jock and Philip, he'd been most understanding and helpful. He'd agreed to Jim borrowing one of the large staff cars, and even managed to find a willing army padre to travel with them and conduct the ceremony. A local funeral director had been called upon to do the embalming and provide a hearse which would go with them out of Singapore into the Malay jungle.

Jim had packed the boot with enough food and water to get them through the short time they'd planned to be away. He arrived at the bungalow very early that November morning to find a large car parked outside, and to be greeted solemnly by Jeremy. They introduced themselves and shook hands, and Jim wondered how long the other man would last in the dark suit, collar and sober tie, for the heat was already rising.

'I hired a car because I thought it might be too much of a squash with so many of us,' Jeremy explained, easing his collar with a finger.

'A good idea,' Jim murmured. 'From what I understand it'll be a long drive and take most of the day.' He peered into the shadows of the hall. 'Are they ready?'

'As ready as they'll ever be,' said Jeremy. 'I'll go and tell them you're here.'

Jim carried the cases out to the staff car and nodded to the Indian driver of the hearse which had just pulled up. The coffin, he noticed, was almost hidden by a vast spray of palm leaves and colourful tropical flowers, and the two headstones rested against its sides.

Sybil came out first, dressed entirely in black, followed by Jane in a navy dress, Sarah in grey, and Amah in her white mourning sari. They kissed and hugged a rather tearful Elsa, who would be staying behind to finish her vital work with RAPWI, and then, with a sad, lingering look at the waiting hearse, climbed silently into the two cars.

Jim settled Amah in the back with Sarah while Sybil sat bolt upright in the front. Jeremy and Jane were accompanied by the army padre in the hired car, and they set off in convoy behind the hearse.

Sarah held Amah's hand and wondered what the others were thinking as they made the long journey out of Singapore and along the winding road that cut through the jungle and eventually led to the rubber plantation. The last time they'd been this way was with Pops, and Sarah could vividly remember how jam-packed it had been with everyone fleeing from the advancing enemy.

347

The Japanese fighter planes had come in low, strafing the road with machine-gun fire, killing indiscriminately as the masses of terrified people raced into the trees and deep ditches to try to escape the deadly onslaught. So many had been killed during that flight to what they thought would be the safety of Singapore, and for one terrifying moment she'd thought her heavily pregnant mother had been one of them. But she and Amah had been safely hidden beneath a fallen tree, emerging only when Jock assured them the danger was over.

Sarah looked out of the window at the familiar scenery and found it hard to believe that it had been four years almost to the month since they'd left the plantation. So much had happened that it felt much longer.

She felt Amah's head resting softly against her arm and realised she'd gone to sleep, so shifted slightly so Amah's head was in her lap, and she could stretch out. With the windows open to garner the slightest breeze, and the deep dark shadows of the surrounding trees blotting out the glaring mid-morning sun, it was surprisingly comfortable

Even so, she was all too aware of the hearse leading the way, and the fact that Philip was making his final journey home. What they would find there, no one knew, but it was a terrible irony that both men had been forced to return as slaves to work for the Japanese, and she could only pray that Philip's soul would find peace.

The entire journey was conducted in silence as Sybil chain-smoked, sitting rigidly upright in the front seat. Sarah met Jim's gaze in the rear-view mirror and realised he was finding it as hard as she was, and her heart went out to him. He was such a good man – and Peggy was so lucky to be loved by him.

As the cars slowed and the hearse turned off onto a narrow beaten track, Sarah's pulse quickened and she sat forward, eager to catch her first glimpse of the home she'd fled all those years ago.

And there it was, standing on stilts high above the canopy of trees. She took in every detail, noting that the fly-screens over the veranda were in good condition, the shutters over the windows were sturdy, but painted a different colour, and the flight of wooden steps leading up to the single-storey house had been quite recently repaired. She gave a little sigh of relief, for it seemed the Japanese commander had taken care of it.

As Jim brought the car to a halt behind the hearse, Amah woke and looked around her with some awe. 'It's the same,' she breathed. 'And look, they have come to welcome us. We have truly come home.'

Sarah gasped as a group of Malays emerged from the neat rows of rubber trees. There were women, babies and small children amongst them, and their smiles broadened as they recognised Sybil.

'They must have returned once the Japs surrendered,' murmured Sarah, recognising one or two of the men. 'Thank goodness some of them have survived.'

She helped Amah out of the car while Jim and Jeremy unloaded the luggage and boxes of food and water to carry them into the house.

The hearse was driven deep into the shade of the trees, and the driver alighted to have a smoke and quietly converse with the padre. Sybil drifted away from the house and signalled to the two men to accompany her, unaware of everyone else as she decided on the best spot for Philip's burial and Jock's headstone.

'Do you think we should go with her?' asked Jane.

'No, leave her be,' replied Sarah. 'Let's see what the house is like inside, and if the Japs left anything useful behind.'

She left Amah happily chattering to the Malay women and climbed the stairs to the door that opened onto the broad veranda. A thin layer of dust covered the teak floor, and all the bamboo furniture was in such a terrible state, it was fit only for the bonfire. The brass lanterns hanging from the ceiling were tarnished, the two large fans were broken, and there were desiccated plants in the flowerpots.

With a tremulous sigh, Sarah followed her sister into the house and gasped in astonishment. All the furniture was still there, right down to the nest of small tables and the painted bamboo screen that had always hidden the damp patch in the corner. She peeked behind it and turned to grin at Jane. 'The damp's still there.'

'Pop's favourite painting has gone along with all Mother's silver trinkets,' said Jane. 'And there's hardly any of the crystal glasses and decanters left.' She opened the door on the intricately carved dresser and triumphantly pulled out a bottle of whisky. 'But they've left this,' she said, holding it high.

'We could all certainly do with something to bolster our spirits,' said Sybil, coming in with a wilting Amah. 'Are the beds still here? Only Amah's exhausted and needs to lie down.'

They found the bedrooms almost as they'd left them but for the mosquito nets, the clothes, pictures and rugs. The linen was filthy, so they stripped it off, discarded the disgusting sweat-stained pillows and covered the dirty mattress with a curtain. Sarah fetched a cushion from the sitting room so Amah could rest her head comfortably.

Once they were certain Amah was asleep, Sarah and Jane continued their exploration of the house with Sybil trailing along behind them. There were things missing or broken, and Pop's study had been ransacked, all his carefully collected maps and history books nowhere to be seen. The kitchen was in a terrible state, with grease coating everything, rubbish piled in the corners, and clear evidence of rat and bug infestation.

Sybil shuddered and closed the door on it. 'Jim did warn me, but I never thought I'd see it like this. We'll prepare our meals in the dining room and eat there.'

'Where is Jim, by the way?' asked Jane.

'I've sent him and Jeremy off to organise the digging,' she said. 'It's a good thing there are enough natives to help. The ground is rock hard and full of tree roots.' Somehow, Jeremy had broken down her resistance with his quiet sympathy and understanding of what needed to be done, so that she had already accepted his presence as one of the family.

Sarah and Jane exchanged knowing looks. It seemed that Sybil had eased effortlessly back into being the *memsahib*, but at least this return home had lifted her from her misery.

'I suppose I could get some of the women in to clean the place up,' Sybil went on. 'But there doesn't seem much point. We shan't be staying long, and the new owner can deal with it.'

She looked at her watch. 'I've scheduled the service for five o'clock, so there's time to have a drink and make sandwiches. I expect Jim and Jeremy will be hungry and thirsty by now.'

Sarah helped make the sandwiches and then carried some bottled water down to where the two men were supervising the sweating natives. The funeral director was sitting on a log and watching the proceedings through a haze of cigarette smoke, while the padre squatted down amongst the native children and showed them tricks with bits of string.

Sybil had chosen a quiet spot close to the office where Jock had orchestrated the smooth running of the rubber plantation. There were exotic flowers scrambling over the wooden hut now, with weeds and vines poking their way through the structure which was slowly rotting in the damp heat.

Sarah struggled to push open the warped door and stepped inside.

It smelled of heat, pipe tobacco, old paper, ink and mice – and held the very essence of her father. The big desk he'd once sat behind was as he'd left it, the leather chair now cracked and spewing its horsehair stuffing. Sarah regarded the duty rosters that were still there from 1940, the dusty diary on the desk, and the collection of pens and pipes in their various racks.

She reached for her father's favourite briar pipe and felt the silky smoothness of the wood his hands had once held, breathing in those long-remembered scents of the days she'd once worked here as his secretary – and where she'd fallen in love with Philip.

Putting the pipe carefully in her dress pocket, she opened each drawer in the desk to find old letters, paperclips, broken nibs and scraps of paper covered in Jock's bold handwriting. The ancient filing cabinet was stuffed with more paper, and Sarah smiled as she recognised many of the letters she'd typed all those years ago. And then she saw a file marked 'Tarrant. Official documents'.

She carefully drew it out and placed it on the desk, perched on the edge of her father's old chair and opened it. She found Philip's birth certificate, old school reports, and letters he'd received when he was at boarding school and university in England. There was his mother's death certificate, and reams and reams of official documents relating to the plantation and the family house. And beneath it all was a copy of Philip's will.

Sarah's hand trembled as she unfolded it to discover it had been written long before she and Philip had become engaged. The firm of solicitors was based in London, so it was no wonder they hadn't been able to trace this will. As she read through the simple last testament it became clear that should Philip die without a wife or children, the plantation was to be passed on to his father's brother or his heirs. By the address given, it appeared that the family lived in England.

Sarah folded up the will, relieved that the mystery had been solved. She would contact the solicitors by telegram as soon as she returned to Singapore.

*

Amah was woken gently from her sleep, and once everyone had eaten and drunk their fill of water, they slowly made their way to the gravesite. The curious Malays watched from a distance as the padre conducted the service and Philip's coffin was reverently lowered into the ground at the foot of the headstone Sarah had chosen. The padre then moved to the marble headstone Sybil had selected to mark Jock's passing, and said a prayer.

As the funeral director and the padre left to return to Singapore and the others began to drift towards the house, Sarah stood beside her mother, reading the epitaphs:

Philip Tarrant 1913–1945
Beloved son of Henry and Maud Tarrant
Died in the service of his country

Sarah's tears blurred her sight as she looked across at her father's memorial.

John Angus Charles Fuller (Jock)
Beloved husband and father
Killed at Sonkrai date unknown
Rest now in Eternal Peace

'Come on, Mummy, let's go back to the house and let the boys finish up here. I know Amah wants to do a short Buddhist ceremony for them both.'

'I don't think I can take much more today, Sarah. Do I have to be there?'

'It's important to Amah, and she'd be very upset if you don't show. You see, the Buddhists believe in Samsara – the circle of life – and Jock and Philip must be given the proper rites and prayers so the good deeds they have done will lead them closer to enlightenment and on to the next reincarnation.'

Sybil grimaced, but reluctantly joined everyone by the natives' Buddhist shrine which stood at the entrance to their quarters.

Amah directed the Malay women to collect flowers and fruit to decorate the statue of Buddha that they'd managed to hide from the Japanese. Once she was satisfied that all was ready, she knelt painfully, lit the joss sticks and candles she'd brought, and began to pray.

The sing-song words were unintelligible to the Europeans, but the message was clear. Jock and Philip's souls were now with Buddha, who would help them on their way towards enlightenment and rebirth.

Amah had to be helped to her feet and leaned heavily on Jim's arm as she smiled beatifically at them all. 'It is done,' she said. 'Now I must rest, for I am very tired.' She reached for Sybil's hand. 'Thank you, *Mem*, for bringing me home.'

When Sarah went in the next morning to wake her she wasn't too surprised to discover that Amah had slipped away from them during the night. She looked so peaceful, the lines of pain and weariness made smoother in death, reminding Sarah of how lovely she'd once been.

Sarah sat beside her for a while, and then closed the shutters before going to tell the others. She left the house shortly afterwards and went to inform the native women who came to decorate her room with more flowers and candles and incense before they said prayers over her and sat with her until the third day when, as is the Buddhist custom, she would be buried.

They laid Amah to rest near Jock and Philip, and covered her grave with the flowers the women had collected. Jim had discovered that her actual name was Suria, which meant sun, and so he asked the head man to make sure it was carved into the stone that would mark her final resting place.

Philip and Suria had come home, and Jim was convinced that Jock's spirit was here too.

He followed Jeremy and Jane as he drove Sarah and Sybil back to Singapore that afternoon. It had been a sad journey altogether, and he doubted any of them would return to the house in the jungle again.

'So, what are your plans, Sybil?' he asked as he crossed over the repaired causeway onto Singapore Island.

'There's nothing left for me here, so I'm going back to Australia,' she replied. 'I've been away from my little James too long and I miss him horribly. I was hoping Jane and Sarah would come with me, but it seems they have their own plans.'

Jim raised an eyebrow as he met Sarah's gaze in the rear-view mirror. 'Oh, yes?'

'Jane and I will go back to Beach View, and then she's off with Jeremy to Washington. I'm not sure what I'll do, but if my old job's still there, I'll probably take it up again and see how I feel about things in the new year.'

Jim didn't think this sounded at all exciting and he could see by the dullness in Sarah's eyes that she didn't either. The girl was clearly feeling lost and not at all sure about anything at the moment – but he suspected that had a lot to do with her chap Delaney that Peggy had told him about.

'What about you, Jim?' she asked. 'Will you be staying on here?'

'For as long as the army wants me,' he replied. 'I was hoping to be home for Christmas, but it doesn't look as if I will be.'

'You must give me anything you want me to take home for you, Jim. It's the very least I can do after you've been so good to us.' She looked out of the window. 'Oh, can you drop me here? I need to send that telegram to London.'

'I'll wait for you, so there's no need to rush,' he said.

'I actually need to stretch my legs, Jim, so I'll walk back to the bungalow.'

Jim manoeuvred through the traffic and parked.

Sarah smiled her thanks, stepped out of the car and headed for the post office. She'd already worked out what to say, so once she'd reached the front of the long queue, the task was done within minutes.

Returning to the street, she decided to stop off at Raffles to let Elsa know they were back – and perhaps treat herself to a Tom Collins in the Palm Court.

The reception hall was quiet and orderly despite the presence of so many military men, and as she crossed it, she smiled at the sight of the enormous and over-decorated Christmas tree that was standing in one corner. Christmas was a season she usually loved, but she doubted she could dredge up much enthusiasm for it this year, as it would only remind her of the last Christmas in Malaya when Philip, Amah, and her darling father had been with them.

She paused for a moment to look at the tiny coloured lights and glass baubles, wondering if perhaps she should go to Australia with her mother and stay for a while until she'd decided what she was going to do with the rest of her life. It would be lovely to meet her baby brother and to see her grandparents again, and she couldn't think why she'd been so reluctant to bow to her mother's wishes.

'Pretty, isn't it?' The man's voice was deep and tinged with a soft American accent and Sarah froze, the hairs prickling at the back of her neck. 'I do love Christmas. Don't you?' he continued.

Not daring to turn round in case she was mistaken, Sarah nodded. 'Yes,' she replied breathlessly. 'Though they've put up the tree far too early, don't you think?'

'It's never too early, Sarah, and I'd love to spend this Christmas with you.'

She turned and, with her pulse racing, gazed up into his eyes, drinking in the sight of him. 'I'd like that very much,' she managed, feeling the electricity between them in that breathless moment of wonder.

He put his arm round her waist and gently pulled her to him before softly kissing her mouth, and Sarah thought she would simply faint from the powerful feelings that were raging through her.

'Oh, Delaney,' she whispered. 'How did you know where to find me?'

'Peggy Reilly had something to do with it, but I'll tell you everything later,' he murmured, kissing the tip of her nose. 'At this very moment, all I want is to take you somewhere quiet and private so I can kiss you and hold you to my heart's content and tell you over and over again how much I love you.'

Sarah giggled and blushed. 'There's nowhere quiet and private on this island, Delaney. The hotels are full and my family are back at the bungalow.'

'Ah, well, that's where you're wrong, my love. I happen to have booked a room upstairs.'

She looked up at him with a teasing light in her eyes. 'How very convenient, but don't you think you're being a bit presumptuous?'

He grinned back at her. 'I'm an American, of course I'm presumptuous – but truth to tell, I managed to get the room when I arrived the other day. I had to have somewhere to sleep.' He reached for her hand. 'Come on, Sarah, we're wasting time,' he said softly, the yearning for her clear in his eyes.

As he led her up the stairs they were so engrossed in each other that they weren't aware of Elsa watching them from below – a soft smile the only sign that she knew their story and was delighted that they'd found one another at last.

Jane went to answer the telephone and gave a delighted yelp when Elsa told her about Sarah and Delaney. She slammed down the receiver, gave a confused Jeremy a hearty kiss and then hurried to tell her mother.

'Delaney's in Singapore,' she said excitedly. 'He's been here waiting for Sarah the whole time we've been up in Malaya. Elsa met him a few days ago, and from what he told her, I think Peggy may have had a hand in his being here.'

She clapped her hands and did a little dance. 'Now he's found her, I don't expect we'll see either of them for a couple of days.'

'Delaney?' said Sybil. 'But I thought that was all over?'

'It never really was, Mother,' said Jane, going to sit beside her. 'She only threw him over through a misguided sense of loyalty to Philip. But now they're together again. Isn't it wonderful?'

'It's disgraceful,' snapped Sybil. 'Philip's barely cold in his grave, and she's cavorting with some ... some ... American,' she finished on a hiss. 'Where are they? You must find them and bring her home. I simply won't have it.'

Jane gave a sigh and took her mother's hand. 'I'm afraid it's not really up to you, Mother,' she said quietly. 'Sarah's a grown woman with a mind of her own. Delaney has come all this way to find her and now they're together again, they'll need time to talk and discuss future plans.'

Sybil's sour expression revealed her disapproval.

Jane squeezed her fingers. 'Remember how it was with you and Pops when you were first together?' At her mother's brief nod, Jane continued. 'It's the same for me and for Sarah. So please say you're happy for us both.'

'I don't know what this world's coming to,' said Sybil stubbornly. 'My mother would have had a fit if I'd carried on like you girls. We had standards back then. We didn't sleep with someone until there was a wedding.'

Jane grinned, and then shot a glance at Jeremy who was looking very awkward as he stood in the doorway. 'Talking of weddings,' she said. 'Jeremy and I thought we might have one here before you went back to Australia.'

Sybil relaxed suddenly and her eyes glistened with tears as she looked from Jane to Jeremy. 'Oh, darlings, that would be wonderful,' she breathed.

'We'll have to go through all the usual hoops, of course,' Jane went on, 'but we thought a December wedding would be perfect.' She laughed delightedly as she looked across at

Jeremy. 'Who knows, we could even have a double celebration if Sarah and Delaney agree.'

'Now you're just being silly,' said Sybil briskly. 'I've yet to meet this American. He could be anyone for all I know, and most unsuitable.'

'He's the man Sarah has loved for some years,' said Jane. 'That's all you really need to know about him.'

Sybil was to learn that Jane had been right. Her beautiful daughter was lovelier than ever when she came back the following day to introduce Delaney to them with such love and pride. He'd come as a welcome surprise, and not at all what she'd expected from an American, for he wasn't loud and brash or flashing his money about – but quiet, thoughtful, and the most amusing and delightful company.

Although she thought Sarah was rather rushing into things, Sybil was thrilled that there would be a double wedding, and began to make huge plans with the staff at Raffles for the small but very elegant reception which would follow the service at St Andrew's Cathedral. Yet in all her excitement – and to the girls' amusement – she still made sure that Delaney returned to Raffles each night, and Jeremy continued to sleep on the couch in the sitting room.

It was two weeks before Christmas and the sisters' wedding day. Jeremy had gone to stay with Delaney at Raffles the previous night, and Sybil had been up and about since dawn to make a special breakfast for her girls before she and Elsa dashed into town to get their hair done and collect the bouquets and buttonholes. As neither man knew anyone in Singapore, Jim and Jumbo had been roped in as best men, and Sybil would break tradition and lead her girls down the aisle. The bridal dresses had been made by an Indian dressmaker that Elsa had recommended for his speed and skill, and they'd been delivered the evening before.

'I've got butterflies,' said Jane as Sarah fastened the long row of tiny buttons down the back of her simple white lace gown.

'Me too,' admitted Sarah. 'But they're happy ones.' She stepped back. 'There, all done. Jeremy's going to have fun dealing with them tonight. But don't you look lovely?' she said, admiring her sister's reflection in the long mirror.

Jane reached for her hand and they stood there for a moment regarding themselves in some awe. They'd both decided not to wear veils, but had coronets of flowers in their hair, and there were pearls in their ears and round their necks.

'I can't really believe this is happening,' said Sarah breathlessly as she ran her fingers down the white silk dress edged with gold embroidery. 'It didn't seem so long ago that I was dreading the future – and now ...' She grinned. 'Now I can't wait for it.'

Jane picked up the two glasses of champagne she'd poured earlier. 'Let's drink to Pops, and to poor Philip,' she said quietly. 'They might not be here, but I'm absolutely certain they're watching over us today.'

They clinked glasses and drank, the poignant moment broken by Sybil coming in with their bouquets and bursting into tears.

'Oh my darlings,' she sobbed. 'How beautiful you are. I never imagined that my little girls could turn into such lovely young women. Your father would have been so proud.'

She crushed them to her and then quickly pulled away with a shaky laugh to repair her make-up. 'Goodness,' she breathed. 'I look an absolute fright. Now, we must hurry. Elsa's gone on ahead, and the car is outside. As the cathedral is in the middle of the city we mustn't risk being delayed by the awful traffic.'

St Andrew's Cathedral was indeed in the heart of the city, but was surrounded by a quiet oasis of parkland which deadened the noise of the busy streets. The gracious white building had survived the war, and as the car drew up at the steps, they could see the sun shining on the columns over the entranceway and glinting in the stained-glass windows.

'I wish Peggy and Aunt Cordelia were here,' murmured Jane as her mother fussed with her dress. 'They would have loved all this grandeur.'

'We'll make sure we send lots of photographs back,' said Sarah, her heart thudding in anticipation of seeing Delaney waiting for her at the altar.

The photographer was an army man that Jim had roped in for the occasion, and the girls stood impatiently on the steps with their mother – elegant in a cream shantung dress, high-heeled sandals and a very large hat – while he took his pictures.

When he was finally satisfied he'd taken enough, Sybil took their hands. 'Are you ready?'

They nodded and grinned, and she led them through the cathedral doors to the glorious music of a mighty organ.

The aisle was long and led to an imposing altar bedecked in flowers. There were flowers everywhere, and their heady scent filled the vast, echoing space as the organ music soared to the high rafters. The cathedral was almost empty, but for Elsa, Myfanwy and a smattering of friends from the hospital and the RAPWI office. But Sarah and Jane had eyes only for their men waiting at the steps.

The vicar conducted the ceremony solemnly, but with a twinkle in his eyes as Jeremy stumbled over the vows, and Delaney nervously fumbled to get the ring onto Sarah's finger. He pronounced them married, and now permitted to kiss their brides.

Sarah melted into Delaney's arms as he kissed her. He was her future – the love of her life – and she need never be without him again.

PART FOUR

23

Cliffehaven

Peggy breathed a sigh of pleasure as she woke in the large first-floor front bedroom that December morning and regarded the spacious and attractive surroundings in which she now slept. Unlike the room on the hall floor, there was plenty of space for her big old furniture which had taken on a rather stately air since being brought up here, and it was lovely to have her elegant dressing table and stool back from Cissy's old room. She'd placed it beneath the window, so she could look out at the view as she put on her make-up.

She yawned and stretched luxuriously before dragging on Jim's dressing gown to ward off the cold as she went to open the new curtains. The sky was overcast and promising more rain, but nothing could dampen her spirits today, for the work on Beach View was finished, and Bob was finally coming home for Christmas. With that delightful prospect ahead of her, she pushed her feet into her old slippers and padded out onto the landing to Daisy's room. Opening the door, she peeked in to find that she was still sleeping, and so took the opportunity to once again admire the room that had once been Sarah and Jane's and which had been transformed by Ron's hard work.

There were two single beds so Daisy could have a little friend to stay, the floorboards had been sanded and varnished, one of the walls was painted white, the others covered with nursery-rhyme wallpaper which went beautifully with the pink curtains. The old chest of drawers and bookcase had been painted white, as had the skirting board and window frame. There were soft, colourful rag rugs on the floor and a large wooden box for her toys.

Peggy smiled and left the door ajar. Daisy loved her room, and Charlie was just as pleased with his, for now he'd taken over the double front room on the top floor, he had space for a desk and chair to do his homework, plenty of shelves for his numerous books and trophies, and a large cupboard in which to stow all his clothes and sports kit. There were two single beds up there too, for he was making friends and sometimes brought one home to stay the night.

She tiptoed past Danuta's room, not wanting to wake her after she'd been out all night tending an elderly patient, and listened at Cordelia's door before using the bathroom which had a new bath, basin, window frames, lino and a coat of paint. Danuta and Cordelia had decided to remain in their old rooms, but both had been given fresh wallpaper and paint, and Peggy had found some lovely curtain material at the Sunday market which she'd paid one of the factory machinists to run up for her for both bedrooms.

Going past the stair-lift minutes later, Peggy admired the new dark red runner and landing carpet, and the freshly re-plastered walls and ceilings which had been painted white along with the bannisters, making the whole place look much bigger and brighter.

She wandered into her dining room, which had sprigged wallpaper above the dado rail, and pretty yellow paint beneath it which went with the heavy gold-coloured curtains she'd spent a fortune having dry-cleaned. The chimney had been swept, the crack in the marble surround repaired, and Ron had found a simply gorgeous chandelier in a house clearance, the crystals of which shot rainbows of colour into the room as the morning sun came through the wide bay windows.

She gazed at the smooth varnished floor, the family photographs and brass candlesticks on the mantelpiece and her mother's ornate mirror above them. She'd had such fun going through all the things in the attic and under the stairs, and had found a great many treasures that had lain hidden there since before the war. The two armchairs had been repaired and covered with rich cream velvet, and an Egyptian rug lay in front of the brass fender, making everything look most luxurious.

However, money had become very tight after all the changes she'd made in the basement and kitchen, so there was little she could do about the battered dining table and the mismatched chairs, but a white linen cloth would hide the scratches and burns, and once it was decorated with holly and candles, no one would notice.

Peggy padded back into the hall and across the repaired red and blue Victorian tiles which now gleamed richly. In place of the rotting and pitted front door there was now a very smart one with coloured glass panes at the top which Frank had found abandoned but unscathed at the back of a bombed-out house. He'd sanded it down and painted it dark blue, then attached the lovely brass knocker and letterbox fittings he'd found in a junk shop.

Outside, the stucco walls and front steps had been repaired and painted, and the electrician had wired in the two lamps Rosie had discovered in one of the many boxes she'd stored in her cellar. They'd once graced the front of her parents' private hotel, and she'd kept them out of a sense of nostalgia, but was delighted to see them put to good use again.

Peggy crossed the hall, barely glancing into the room that she and Jim had shared for so many years, for she'd turned it into another spare room with two single beds, and the minimum of furniture, which left it looking a bit impersonal. It had proven to be surprisingly large once that huge double bed and old dark furniture had been transferred upstairs, and Daisy's cot relegated to the attic. New window frames, curtains and lino made it look fresh and welcoming.

She opened the door to her kitchen and felt the familiar thrill of pleasure she always got when she walked in here. How clean, bright and spacious it was now the old larder had been torn down, and the huge chest of drawers moved up to Charlie's room. The window had been extended to let in more sunshine in the afternoons, and spread the length of her new wooden worktops, drainer and refurbished sink. Frank had replaced the old cracked tiles with new bright yellow ones, and there were white painted cupboards and drawers beneath the surfaces that Ron and Frank had made out of wood they'd accumulated over the years – and in the place of the old corner shelves stood a sparkling white refrigerator.

It had been a surprise gift from Anne and Martin and was her pride and joy. She never tired of opening the door to see the light come on to illuminate the modest amount of food she had stored inside.

The range still sat in the fireplace, for although she would have loved a modern gas cooker, it wouldn't have been able to heat the water and radiators. But it had had a fresh coat of blacking, the hotplate covers had been replaced, and a man had come round to give it a thorough service. The two old armchairs were past it, really, but everyone had protested so vehemently when she'd threatened to throw them out, that she'd had Sally make some new loose covers for them so they didn't look quite as shabby, and she'd replaced the bulky old wireless – which Charlie now had in his room – for the modern one Cissy had sent down from London, which sat on a low table near the chairs.

Peggy filled the kettle from one of the shining brass taps over the sink and placed it on the hob. There was new yellow linoleum on the floor, and Charlie had sanded down the kitchen table and chairs in his spare time and painted them all white. Because those chairs had always been a bit hard to sit on for very long, Peggy had taken a leaf out of her sister's

book and made seat cushions with the left-over yellow ging-
ham from the kitchen curtains.

She took a deep breath of the lovely smell of fresh paint
and, with a smile of quiet satisfaction, went down the concrete steps to the basement.

She almost had to pinch herself at the transformation
down here, for gone was the old sink, mangle and boiler,
and an archway now led into what had once been Charlie's
room. This bright, white space was now home to more
worktops and cupboards which hid the new boiler and all
her mops, brooms, buckets and cleaning materials. There
was a new stone sink with brass taps – and in pride of place
beneath it was her twin-tub washing machine.

She touched it lovingly as she regarded the new linoleum,
the light switches and the floor-to-ceiling cupboard which
now housed her ironing board and fancy electric iron. The
washing machine and iron were being paid for by instal-
ments, but they were worth every last penny, for now
Saturday mornings were much freer, and she'd at last been
able to donate the hated mangle and old-fashioned irons to
the WVS.

But the real transformation was in the front basement
room which had become the repository for junk ever since
her boys had been evacuated, and Peggy still thought she
must be dreaming every time she opened the door.

The plumber had fitted a pristine white lavatory and
basin which gleamed in the sunlight pouring through the
narrow rectangular window. Frank had half-tiled the room
and painted the rest white which made the blue of the tiles
really stand out. Blue linoleum covered the floor and Danuta
and Stanislaw had very generously given her a bale of hand
towels in exactly the same colour. A blind could be rolled
down over the window, and there was a radiator to keep the
room warm and free from damp.

'Peggy? Are you down there again? Surely you know
what it looks like by now?'

She laughed and hurried back to the kitchen. 'I certainly do, Cordy, but I just can't resist looking at it all.'

Cordelia tutted and picked up the doll Daisy had just dropped. 'I don't know, Peggy Reilly, you're like a child in a sweet shop. I dread to think how much it all must have cost.'

Peggy kissed her cheek. 'Not as much as it might have done if I'd had all the changes I wanted,' she said lightly before hugging Daisy. 'Good morning, darling. Isn't it a lovely day?'

Daisy frowned and hitched her doll under her arm. 'It's raining, Mum.'

'Is it?' She glanced out of the window and giggled. 'I suppose it is, but it feels as if the sun's shining in here now it's all so lovely and bright.'

She quickly poured some cereal into a bowl as Daisy clambered onto the kitchen chair and added just enough milk to make it edible. The rationing was really beginning to bite now, with potatoes and bread at a premium because of the wet summer and autumn they'd had, and even though there were fewer of them to feed, it was becoming more and more difficult to be imaginative with what she could get in the shops. Christmas was only two days away, and she'd been fretting over how on earth she'd manage to put a decent meal on the table even though the others were helping out with food stamps and odds and ends.

While Cordelia made the pot of tea, Peggy grabbed an umbrella and went outside to see if there were any eggs this morning. The hens had been a godsend all through the war, but recently they hadn't been laying as well, and it was becoming a real worry. She found three brown eggs in the laying box, scattered some food about and locked the coop before dashing back inside.

'The hens only gave us these this morning,' she said, placing the eggs carefully in a crock on the drainer. 'I'm wondering if they're getting old and past it.'

'Well, we have had them for a good many years,' said Cordelia, briskly stirring the tea leaves in the pot. 'Perhaps they need another cockerel to liven them up?'

'No fear,' replied Peggy. 'Adolf was a holy terror, and I'm not risking my hens getting mauled about again.'

Cordelia thumped the teapot on the table and sat down. 'Talk to Ron,' she said. 'He'll know what to do.'

Peggy looked at her sharply. 'Are you all right, Cordy? Only you seem a bit put out this morning.'

'I'm fine,' she said dismissively. 'It's this cold, damp weather getting into my bones which makes me cross. Things are difficult enough without the arthritis flaring up in my hands again – and we're only in December. I dread what the next few months will bring us.'

Peggy accepted her explanation, but suspected her being out of sorts had more to do with the loss of her nephew and Philip than with her arthritis – although it did always flare up at this time of year.

'Will you be all right looking after Daisy while I go shopping?' she asked tentatively. 'Only, with Bob due to arrive today, I need to finish stocking up on things for Christmas.'

'I'm neither senile nor helpless, Peggy,' Cordelia retorted. 'Of course I'll look after Daisy. But instead of you standing in queues for hours, you should get Charlie to help you.'

'Organising my Saturday morning for me, Cordelia?' teased Charlie as he came in looking still half-asleep. He slumped into a chair and eyed the rain which was lashing across the garden. 'It's not going to be much fun on the rugby pitch this afternoon,' he said gloomily.

'It won't be much fun queuing either,' said Peggy. 'But if we do half the list each, it shouldn't take too long.' At his reluctant nod, she went through her list. She'd do Alf the butcher, Fred the Fish and Sam the greengrocer because there was always a chance that these old pals might slip her something extra from under the counter. Charlie could do the bakery and the Home and Colonial.

She found the appropriate food stamps and counted out enough money to cover his share of the shopping. 'There should be enough there, but if there isn't forget a couple of the tinned stuff,' she said. 'I can just about manage without them.'

Charlie nodded, his mouth full of cereal.

Peggy arrived back at Beach View almost three hours later, cold, wet and thoroughly fed up. The car had refused to start for some reason, and she'd had to lug her shopping home after standing about in the teeming rain for half the morning only to discover there were to be no surprises from under the counter, and little choice in the meat and fish. Sam the grocer was charging an arm and a leg for potatoes which she really begrudged, but then Ron's spuds had rotted in the ground, so she'd had little choice in the matter.

She pulled off her sodden hat and coat, shook them out and left them on the coat rack in the basement with her umbrella. Trudging up the steps with her shopping, she hoped the kettle was on as she was gagging for a cuppa and a fag after that ordeal.

'Hello, Mum,' said Charlie cheerfully. 'I managed to get nearly everything on the list, but was a halfpenny short for the tin of baked beans, and that new chap at the Home and Colonial wouldn't let me off it although I promised to go straight back and pay it.'

'Tight as a tick that one,' said Cordelia with a grimace, looking up from Daisy's colouring book. 'Doris's Ted might have been a gambler and womaniser, but he was always fair with his customers.'

Peggy began transferring the butter, cheese, fish and meat to her new refrigerator, placing the bottle of Daisy's free orange juice next to the milk in the door compartment. The fresh vegetables and five-pound bag of potatoes went into her new rack on the worktop. She lifted the lid on the bread bin to find Charlie had managed to get two loaves.

'I hope you got more packets of tea and cereal, Charlie. The speed we get through them is astonishing.'

'They're all in the cupboard with the marmalade and tins of Spam and pilchards.' He grinned at her as she sat down to her cup of tea and lit a cigarette. 'I'm still trying to find my way round this kitchen, and keep forgetting we don't have a larder. We're so posh now; poor Dad will think he's come to the wrong house.'

'I doubt that,' said Peggy wearily. 'He'll be so glad to be back with his family he probably won't notice. It's us he won't recognise,' she added thoughtfully. 'If Bob's changed as much as you, then he'll have a hard time of it. And of course Daisy was just a babe in arms when he left for India.'

'What time is Bob due to arrive?' asked Charlie. 'We kick off at two-thirty, so if he's early enough he might come and watch me play.'

'Well, he might,' said Peggy doubtfully, 'but he's not in until three and if it's still raining hard I expect he'll come straight here.'

Charlie snorted. 'Bob's used to being out in all weathers, so a bit of rain won't bother him.' He pushed back from the table, grabbed his gabardine mac and tweed cap, and picked up his holdall containing his rugby kit. 'I'm having lunch with Grandad and Rosie, so I'll see you after the match.'

He clattered down the steps and banged the back door behind him, making both women roll their eyes. 'It's like having Ivy and Rita in the house again,' said Cordelia with a soft smile before she bent once more to help Daisy colour in her picture.

'Wasn't there any post this morning?' asked Peggy, feeling somewhat refreshed by the tea and the sit-down. 'And where's Danuta? She can't still be asleep, surely?'

'She went off to Cliffe to be with Stanislaw as he's got his first physio session without the walking sticks today. The only thing in the post was an electricity bill.'

373

'Oh well,' sighed Peggy. 'I expect Jane and Sarah are busy dealing with things in Singapore, and Rita will have only just reached Australia. As for Ruby, if the weather's closed in as badly as she feared, I doubt any post will be able to get through. I do hope all of them are all right, Cordelia. They've each of them had huge changes to deal with just lately.'

The afternoon post came just as they'd finished their lunch of onion soup and toast, and Peggy hurried back from the hall. 'There's a letter from Rita to both of us; one from Ruby, and one from Jim,' she said excitedly, placing them on the kitchen table.

Cordelia relaxed back into the armchair with a drowsy Daisy on her lap. 'You read Rita's out to me, Peggy. I don't want to disturb Daisy by hunting for my glasses.'

Peggy eagerly tore open the letter which had been posted over a week before. 'Their address sounds very exotic,' she said. 'Pandanus House, Warratah Road, Ravenshoe, Queensland.'

She scanned the first few lines to ensure that Rita wasn't as depressed as Ruby, and then began to read it out to Cordelia.

Dearest Peggy and Grandma Cordelia,

Well, here we are in Australia at last, and it's all so wonderful, I hardly know where to begin. We docked in Brisbane which is a lovely small city between the sea and a wide river, with huge parks full of silvery-barked trees called ghost gums which have leaves that shimmer and shiver in the slightest breeze. There are parrots of every colour, black swans, and long-legged ibis strutting about, and some of the birdsong in the morning is so beautiful it almost brings me to tears.

Pete arranged for our luggage to be sent up to his parents' place by road train – that's what they call the enormous lorries hauling numerous trailers that go at huge speed all over the country carrying everything from freight to cattle – so we could

ride our motorbikes along the highway which runs parallel to the
coast all the way to Cairns.

We stopped along the way to explore deserted, palm-fringed
beaches, some of which ran for mile upon empty mile, and swam
in a sea that was every bit as blue as Pete had promised. We drove
through rainforests and cane fields, and saw mountains soaring
out of vast ochre plains. We explored dirt roads which led to
isolated settlements that were no more than a few houses, a pub
and a church, and watched the kangaroos bounce away at the
sound of our engines.

I heard the laughing kookaburra on my second day here, and the
gorgeous piping of the magpies, and saw a huge wedge-tailed eagle
hovering above us in search of prey. There are termite mounds as
big as houses, and enormous black bats which hung from the trees
near the waterholes – yuck and double yuck. They stink!

I've also seen my first snake – a horrid brown and orange
thing Pete said was a deadly taipan. It was basking in the middle
of the road and as Pete thinks the only good snake is a dead one, he
ran over it, poor thing. He warned me all the snakes here are
lethal, and so are a lot of the spiders and skinks, so I'll have to
watch where I walk.

But none of that can take away the sheer joy of being here. The
scenery is breathtaking, the weather absolutely glorious, and the
sheer size of the place is quite overwhelming. I do wish you were
here to see it all.

We stopped off in Ravenshoe to look at the place his dad
thought we should buy, and fell in love with it immediately. The
house is what they call a Queenslander, propped on stilts and
made of wood. It has a deep wrap-round veranda, three bedrooms,
a kitchen, bathroom and sitting room. It needs a lot of work doing
to it, but with almost a hundred acres of fields and pandan forest
surrounding it and several large outbuildings, it's utterly perfect.
Our offer was accepted, so now we're eager to get the paperwork
done and start making it our own.

We explored the whole area, which is between the outback and
the sea, and although the town itself is very small, the people are

friendly and welcoming, especially as Peter is a returning
serviceman. We rode out to visit Pete's family on their farm – or
station as they call it here – and I couldn't believe how vast it is,
and how utterly peaceful beneath that big sky. Pete's parents are
really welcoming, but I've yet to meet his sisters and their families
as they live hundreds of miles away on the outer edge of the
property, and are busy with the shearing.

There are Aborigines working on the station who kept the place
going throughout the war when so many of the men went to
enlist, and Pete spent a long time with them talking about his
experiences. I hadn't realised that some younger Aborigines had
enlisted, and one of them actually became an ace fighter pilot and
was much decorated.

Pete took me camping under the stars one night, and told
me some of the local Dream Time stories which simply explain
the mysteries of the world's creation. Looking up at the Milky
Way, it felt as if I could reach up and touch the stars. I have
never seen anything quite so awe-inspiring, and it makes you
realise how very insignificant we all are in the vast scheme of
things.

I know I've rattled on a bit, but I've been so longing to tell you
how excited and happy we are to be here. We'll be starting work
on the house soon, and hoping to be in by Christmas, but the Wet
has arrived, so it might take a bit longer. We're lovely and snug in
a caravan at the moment because the house isn't really habitable,
but the sight of the parrots hanging upside down in the trees to
clean their feathers in the rain makes me laugh. In fact, I can't
stop smiling, I'm so very happy.

I've written to Dad and tried to keep it less enthusiastic,
because I know he must be feeling deserted, but I knew you'd
appreciate knowing how we are and what we're feeling. I hope all
is well with you, and that you have a wonderful Christmas. Pete
and I have sent a big box of goodies over, which we hope will
arrive in time to help the celebrations go with a swing.

Much love, hugs and kisses,
Rita

'Well, there's no doubt someone's fallen on their feet,' breathed Cordelia. 'My goodness, she sounds as bright as a lark and not missing us at all.'

'It's such a relief to know she's taken to it. I just hope her father won't get dejected if his letter is anything like this one,' said Peggy.

'Jack's mature enough to be thankful that it's all turned out well and his girl isn't pining for home. It would be awful if she was feeling the same way as poor Ruby.'

Cordelia eased Daisy's head to a more comfortable spot against her shoulder and eyed the other letters on the table. 'What does Ruby have to say, Peggy?'

Peggy opened Ruby's letter to discover it wasn't very long at all. Scanning down the single page, she realised little had changed for poor Ruby.

'She's written in haste because the weather is closing in and she wanted to catch the post,' she said. 'She thanks me for the baby clothes I sent, and Mike's mother, Claudine, is teaching her to knit and sew in preparation for the baby's arrival in March.'

She scanned the rest of the short letter, her spirits plummeting. 'Mike and his father have now gone up to the logging camp, and probably won't be back until after the baby is born – which means Ruby will spend her first married Christmas with just Claudine.'

'Oh, dear,' murmured Cordelia. 'That poor girl. I do feel for her.'

Peggy returned to the letter and read the last of it out to her.

The snow is starting to fall and although it looks as pretty as a Christmas card, it means getting into town for me doctor's appointments is really dangerous – even with heavy chains on the truck tyres. Claudine's stockpiled food and emergency supplies to see us through until the thaw, and she's promised me that if this baby comes early, she'll know what to do.

I ain't happy about it, Aunt Peggy. When I were married to
Ray, I lost two babies cos of his beatings, and I don't know what
sort of damage he might have done to me insides. I wish I could
move into the hotel in town, but Claudine won't hear of it, so I'm
stuck here.

Peggy turned over the page. 'She apologises for moaning, bless her,' she said. 'And wishes she could be with us for Christmas. She'll write again when the snow starts to thaw and the mail can be delivered again.'

Peggy folded the letter and gave a deep sigh. 'I'm really finding it hard to forgive Mike in all this. Whatever was he thinking of to take her there and then leave her with his mother for months on end?'

'I'll be very surprised if that marriage lasts,' replied Cordelia sadly. 'Not many women would put up with such behaviour, and our Ruby isn't cut out for that sort of life, especially now she's expecting.'

'I didn't know she'd had two miscarriages,' murmured Peggy. 'No wonder the poor girl's so frantic to have a proper doctor to hand.'

'It's all very distressing,' said Cordelia. 'She'll probably hate the place even more if something goes wrong.'

Peggy nodded. 'And I wouldn't blame her, Cordy.' She set the sad little letter aside and lit a cigarette. 'I so wish she'd found the same happiness as Rita, for I know she loves Mike and was utterly determined to make a success of things out there after her disastrous marriage to Raymond.'

'Well, there's nothing either of us can do about it, unfortunately,' said Cordelia. 'As my mother would have said, "She's made her bed, and now she must lie in it."' She grimaced as Daisy's weight shifted on her arthritic knees. 'Can you take her, dear? Only she's heavy on my legs.'

Peggy lifted Daisy from Cordelia's lap and kissed her forehead in the hope she'd wake. Too much sleep at this time of the day usually brought on grizzling moodiness, and with Bob due to arrive within the hour she didn't want the distraction.

However, Daisy stirred and woke in a good mood, and once she'd had a cup of her orange juice and a digestive biscuit, she played happily at the table with her soft toys while Peggy quickly scanned Jim's letter in case it contained anything which might upset Cordelia.

Darling Peggy,

A great deal has happened since I last wrote to you – a lot of it very sad – but some very pleasant and quite surprising. Jeremy turned up in Singapore and we drove Sybil and the others up to the rubber plantation for Philip's burial and to place a memorial stone for Jock. I don't know if either girl has written to tell you, but both men had been slave labour on the notorious Burma railway, and it's not known when Jock died, but a witness I spoke to helped bury him and left a marker.

Philip survived less than a few hours after arriving at the hospital in Singapore and Sarah was with him at the end. He never came round enough to recognise her, and from what I heard from Sybil and Jane, his death was a merciful end to his terrible suffering. Poor Sarah didn't know how to feel, but I think she mourned the memory of the man she'd once loved, rather than the stranger who'd returned. Coming so soon after losing Jock, it was a very difficult time for them all.

It was almost a month after Philip's death when we made that sad and rather poignant journey to the rubber plantation in Malaya. The house was still standing, but for Sybil and her girls it was too full of memories, so they didn't stay long. On our return to Singapore Sarah discovered that Delaney had come looking for her, and to cut a very long story short, Jumbo and I are to be the best men at the double wedding.

'Oh, my goodness,' Peggy squeaked, startling Cordelia. 'Delaney and Jeremy went to Singapore, and there's to be a double wedding.'

'They're getting married so soon?' breathed a shocked Cordelia.

Peggy nodded. 'It seems so, Cordy. But I agree it does seem a bit hasty – although waiting wouldn't really have changed anything.'

'Maybe not. But it would have been the decent thing,' huffed Cordelia.

Peggy read down the page and quickly turned it over, absolutely thrilled that Delaney had clearly gone straight to Singapore after dropping in here – luckily, Cordelia had been out that morning, so she had no need to know of the part Peggy had played in getting those two together.

'They decided to hold the ceremony two weeks before Christmas because Sybil had already been in Singapore for three months and wanted to get back to little James in Australia.' Peggy sighed. 'Oh, that means it's all done and dusted, and it's too late to send a telegram congratulating them. I do wish they'd written to warn me.'

'I think the whole thing's disgraceful,' grumbled Cordelia. 'Sybil should be ashamed of herself for allowing it so soon after those men died.' She folded her arms. 'As for Sarah carrying on like that … I would never have believed it of her.'

'You know as well as I that Delaney was Sarah's true love,' said Peggy quietly. 'And as Jim has rightly pointed out, Philip had become a stranger to her, and it was the memory of how he'd once been that she was really mourning. So of course when Delaney turned up, she had to follow her heart.'

'It's all romantic tosh if you ask me,' retorted Cordelia huffily. 'Are they coming back here? Because if they are, I shall tell them straight that I do not approve.'

'Oh, Cordy,' sighed Peggy. 'Just be thankful that everything turned out all right in the end, and try to be happy for them.'

Cordelia scowled. 'My poor nephew must be turning in his grave at his daughters' lack of respect,' she muttered.

Peggy wasn't at all sure that Jock would be doing any such thing, but as Cordelia seemed determined to disapprove, she said nothing and quickly read the last of the letter.

'Well, you'll be glad to hear they aren't coming back to Cliffehaven,' she said when she'd finished. 'They left for Australia after the wedding and will stay there over Christmas. Jeremy and Jane will then go to Washington, and Sarah and Delaney will travel to Texas so she can meet his family, but there are no plans as to what they will do next.'

'So they'll both be in America,' muttered Cordelia. 'I doubt we'll see either of them again – but what about the things they left behind? What are we supposed to do with them?'

'There's nothing of Jane's, and only a few bits and pieces of Sarah's. I'll pack them up and put them in the attic should she ever want them.' She folded Jim's letter and slipped it into her apron pocket. 'It would be nice if the girls can get to see Rita while they're in Australia,' she murmured. 'Didn't Sarah say her mother lived near Cairns?'

'I believe she did,' said Cordelia, her mind clearly on something else. 'Does Jim give any details of how both men died?' she asked. 'Only the telegrams they sent were very brief and not at all informative.'

Peggy carefully relayed what Jim had written, and then perched on the arm of the chair to comfort her as she wept once more for the two men she'd never known but for whom she'd prayed would beat the odds and return safely.

Bob Reilly donned his cap and grabbed the two heavy hold-alls as the train ground to a stop at Cliffehaven Halt, sighing great clouds of steam and smoke. He climbed out, his chin tucked into his coat and the peak of his cap almost touching his nose to shield him from the rain which was coming from the sea as straight and hard as stair-rods. He could barely see where he was going, for although it was only three in the afternoon, it was already dark, and the weak light of the two platform lamps was shrouded by the gloom.

'Jim! Jim, is that really you?'

Bob looked up to find the stationmaster beaming back at him. 'Hello, Uncle Stan,' he replied. 'Sorry to disappoint you, but it's me, Bob.'

Stan grabbed his arm and pulled him into the lee of the remains of the old waiting room where a dim light filtered down from a lantern. 'Well, as I live and breathe,' he gasped. 'So it is. My goodness, boy, you're the very image of your father.'

Bob grinned. 'So I've been told. How are you, Uncle Stan? You're looking well, but I see the old place took a bit of a battering.'

'Aye, it did that,' he said on a sigh. 'And by the New Year, all of this will be gone.' He went on to tell him about his enforced retirement. 'When your father does come home, he'll have to get off at Willingham and catch the bus.'

'Yes, I was told it was closing when I bought my return ticket,' said Bob. 'But now you'll have lots of time to work on your allotment, Uncle Stan, and I'm sure you'll be glad not to have to get up for the milk train every morning.'

'I've been doing it for years, so will probably still be up with the lark anyway,' he replied gloomily.

Bob could feel the unpleasant iciness of the rain dripping down the back of his collar. 'I'd better get home. Mum's expecting me, and I promised Charlie I'd go and watch some of his match.'

Stan shook his head. 'I don't know how those rugby boys do it. Out in all weathers, they are.' He grinned at Bob. 'But young Charlie seems to thrive on it.'

Bob wished him a happy Christmas, promised to pop by during his stay for a longer chat, and headed down the High

Street. He'd always liked Stan, for as a small boy, he had sneaked up here for a rock bun and a cup of tea to listen to the old man's stories, and wave the flag when the trains left the station. He also had fond memories of Cliffehaven, for he'd been almost thirteen when he'd left, but now he was shocked to see how dilapidated and run-down it looked on this miserable day.

He paused to watch the workmen battling the wind to decorate the large Christmas tree in the centre of town, then continued past the huge bomb site which had once been Woolworths and the Odeon Cinema, thinking again how lucky his father had been to escape uninjured from the blast. Grandad Ron had made much of the fact in his letter that he'd been left without a stitch of clothing on, and he'd had to carry him home on his back.

Grinning at the image that evoked, Bob glanced at the heaving grey sea, then turned into Camden Road and out of the wind. There was the fire station and the factory where his mother had worked, and the funny little café opposite the hospital where Grandma Cordelia sometimes used to treat him and Charlie to afternoon tea. But where there had once been an enormous block of flats was a gaping hole.

He walked on to discover that the houses at the end of the street had been blasted to smithereens, although the Anchor had clearly survived, and a new school had been built in the footprint of the old one. He crossed the road to stop and stare at the ruins at the end of Beach View cul-de-sac, which he knew had come about as a result of a gas explosion, but as he splashed his way through the muddy puddles of the twitten, he saw the remains of the house behind Beach View and was forcibly reminded of how close his mother and little sister had come to being wiped out completely.

He'd had little idea of what his mother had been through, for she'd kept her letters light-hearted, but seeing the devastation all around made him feel guilty for the easy time they'd all had down in Somerset.

Bob took a firmer grip of the heavy bags and pushed his way through the gate, to see that the shed, the Anderson shelter and the outside lav had gone, and in their place was a sodden vegetable plot which he suspected had yielded very little this autumn. The hens were huddled inside their nesting boxes, gloomily squawking at the muddy mess in their run. He remembered those chickens being given to them by a bunch of Australian soldiers, but that was years ago, so the old birds were probably past laying, and good only for the pot.

Eager to be out of the rain, he pushed open the back door and came to an abrupt halt. His mother and Charlie had written to him about the changes she was making to the house, but he hadn't expected this.

Aware that he was dripping rainwater and would leave muddy footprints on the pristine lino, he quickly eased off his boots onto the doormat, and bundled his coat over his arm. As no one seemed to have heard his arrival, he left the bags and coat on the concrete steps and had a nose about.

He was utterly amazed by the transformation, and could hardly believe that he, Charlie and Grandad Ron had actually slept down here – and that they'd shared the once damp and cramped space with Harvey and the ferrets. As he tried to take it all in, he heard footsteps on the kitchen floor above him, and quickly gathered up his things.

Running up the steps he pushed open the door, ready to greet his mother, but the words never came as he took in how different the kitchen was.

'Bob!' Peggy leapt from her kitchen chair and threw her arms round him. 'Oh, Bob, it's so lovely to have you home, even if it is just for a little while.'

He was in a daze as he hugged her and let her fuss over him. Charlie had warned him in a letter that he wouldn't recognise the place – and he didn't – but it was the change in his mother that was so startling. Her soft curves had gone and she seemed thinner and much smaller than he remembered. And there was a brisk efficiency about her that hadn't been there before, which revealed itself in the way she took his coat to dry by the fire, put on the kettle and pressed him into a chair. She was also very smartly dressed, even though it was the middle of the afternoon – and he found that a bit shocking.

'Cordelia will be down in a minute.' Peggy gazed at him adoringly. 'My goodness, Bob, I thought Charlie looked like your father, but you ... You're the very image of him.'

'That's what Stan said, and I'll take it as a compliment.' He grinned at her. 'I thought I was in the wrong house at first. You have been busy, Mum. Is the rest of the place this posh?'

'It's all lovely and clean and fresh,' she replied, quickly filling the teapot and giving it a good stir. 'I was fed up with how dreary it looked, and now I'm earning good money, I decided to spend a bit of it on doing up the place. I do hope you like it, Bob,' she said anxiously.

'Having a downstairs toilet is definitely a bonus,' he replied. 'I always hated having to go outside at night. And this kitchen looks really nice, and much bigger than I remember. I'm glad you kept the chairs, though.'

'I didn't want to,' she admitted, 'but everyone made so much fuss, I didn't have the heart to chuck them out.'

'Well, well, well,' said Cordelia, coming into the room with Daisy. 'Look who's here, and isn't he handsome, Daisy?'

Daisy stared at Bob in confusion. 'Charlie?'

Bob laughed and squatted down in front of her. 'Hello, Daisy. I'm your big brother Bob,' he said. 'And I've come to spend Christmas with you.'

'Bob,' she said solemnly, her big brown eyes wide with interest as she regarded him. 'I'm four now,' she said proudly. 'How old are you?'

'I'm eighteen,' he replied

Daisy frowned. 'That's old,' she said thoughtfully. 'But Gangan's eighty-one, and that's really, really old.'

'Daisy!' admonished Peggy. 'That's enough.'

Bob laughed, turned to Cordelia and gave her a gentle hug. 'You're looking very well for someone who's really, really old,' he teased, although she wasn't really, and he suspected she might have recently been crying. 'It's good to see some things haven't changed round here,' he added with a wink at his mother.

'Sit down and drink your tea before it gets cold,' said Peggy, trying to be stern, but failing to hold back a smile.

'I promised Charlie I'd look in on his match if I could,' he replied, glancing at the clock on the mantel. He drained the cup of tea, patted a wide-eyed Daisy on the head and then reached down for the heavy bags. 'Before I go, I'd better give you this lot,' he said.

'Presents!' shouted Daisy, clapping her hands.

'They're not really presents,' explained Bob, delving beneath his clean clothes to bring out several tins, numerous jars and a dozen carefully wrapped parcels. 'Proper presents are for Christmas, so you'll have to wait a bit longer.'

He turned to his mother. 'Vi and I thought you'd appreciate a little extra over Christmas as the rationing is so tight now.'

Peggy and Cordelia gasped at the bounty. There was a home-cured ham and rashers of bacon; jams, chutneys, tins of cakes; home-made pork pies, apple pies and meat pies, and canisters of butter, cream and honey. There were even packets of tea, coffee and sugar, but the crowning glories were the iced Christmas cake and fruit-filled plum pudding.

'Oh, Bob,' said Peggy through her tears. 'What wonderful, generous gifts. We shall certainly make great use of them, but I do wish Vi was here to join us for Christmas.'

'I tried to persuade her to come, but she's settled at Owlet Farm, and now there are children about the place again, she's planning on a real family Christmas.'

'We'll be having one here too,' said Peggy delightedly. 'Frank's coming with Betty and Brendon and their little boy, Joseph. Your grandad will be here with Rosie – and probably the dogs. And then there's Jack Smith who's on his own, and Danuta who is bringing her chap along too. I'm hoping Cissy will come down, but I'm not holding my breath.'

'What about Anne and Martin?'

'They're spending the day in their own home with the children and then coming over here on Boxing Day. Suzy and Anthony are coming down to spend Christmas with Doris and John and they'll be bringing little Teddy and Angela, the new baby, so it'll be a full house here on Boxing Day.'

'It's a good thing I brought extra supplies, then,' said Bob. 'Sounds like you'll be feeding the five thousand as usual.' He grinned, pushed back from the table and retrieved his coat from in front of the range fire where it was in danger of getting scorched. 'Enjoy putting it all away in that posh fridge, Mum, and I'll see you later.'

24

Doris was in the same euphoric state as her sister, for like Peggy she'd been living with upheaval, dirt, dust and inconvenience for weeks, and now the work on the two bungalows was finished just in time for Christmas. She parked the car, but instead of retrieving her shopping and going indoors, she just sat there admiring the result.

There were dormer windows in the roof now, for the vast attic had been reconfigured into a double bedroom, bathroom and dressing room with a flight of stairs coming down into what had been the two entrance halls, and which now had a single front door. The walls between the bungalows had been knocked through and a graceful archway led into a spacious sitting room where John's spare bedroom and bathroom had once been. Another two arches behind the staircase led into a kitchen that ran right along the back of the house and overlooked the combined gardens.

The front room and part of the spare bedroom on Doris's side had been knocked through and was now an elegant dining room, and her old bedroom had been enlarged and now had an en-suite bathroom to cater for visitors. Deep cupboards had been built beneath the stairs to house John's golf clubs, the Hoover, and all the usual junk one accumulated, and in her lovely new kitchen there was a washing machine, refrigerator and an AGA which heated the water and the radiators and kept the whole house cosy.

Doris sighed with pleasure, for the house had fulfilled the dreams she and John shared, and every time she walked through that front door she was reminded of how lucky she was.

As the rain drummed on the car roof and the wind buffeted against it, Doris snapped out of her thoughts and gathered up her shopping baskets and numerous packages. She was about to struggle out of the car hampered by the strong wind coming up from the sea when John came hurrying towards her with his large golfing umbrella.

'I was looking out for you,' he said, taking the baskets, and shielding her from the rain as they scurried up the garden path. 'Let's get you inside. You must be exhausted.'

They entered the quiet, warm luxury of their beautiful home and John took her packages and helped her off with her coat and hat. He kissed her damp cheek. 'The kettle's on. I thought you'd appreciate a cuppa after trawling round the shops most of the day.'

She took his hand and softly kissed his lips. 'Whatever would I do without you?' she murmured.

'I sincerely hope you never have to,' he replied, giving her a brief hug. 'Come on, let's have that tea and you can show me what you bought.'

Doris took off her wet shoes and left them on the doormat. Slipping her feet into her slippers, she followed him past the stairs and into the kitchen, which despite the gloomy day looked wonderfully bright and welcoming with its pale cream walls, white cupboards and the original blue and red floor tiles the builder had managed to match up with some he'd found in his shed.

She sat at the scrubbed pine kitchen table and lit a welcome cigarette. 'The queues were horrendous, but I didn't manage to get everything I was after,' she said. 'The shops are half-empty and there's very little choice, so Christmas lunch will be very much a case of making do with what there was. But I found a wooden fire engine for Teddy, a smart tie and cufflinks for Anthony and a very pretty blouse for Susan. I splashed out a bit on the new baby and found a silver rattle for her in one of the antique shops. I'll have to clean it thoroughly, of course – heaven knows the germs that might be on it.'

John was smiling as he stowed away the bread, vegetables and tins, and put the meat, eggs and fish in the fridge. 'It sounds as if you had a successful day. I'm afraid I've been very lazy really and only managed to put together a vegetable pie for supper.'

'It's a shame the weather's so awful. I know how much you enjoy your weekend golf,' she sighed.

She sipped the tea he placed in front of her and relaxed. 'The town's looking pretty with lots of lights everywhere, and the shop windows all dressed for Christmas. The council workers were decorating the tree in the High Street, and having a hard time of it with the wind and rain. There hasn't been one there since 1940, so it's lovely to see it again. I expect Peggy will be taking Daisy down there once it's all decorated – just as our mother used to take us when we were small. It became quite a Cliffehaven tradition over the years.'

'Then we must take Teddy and baby Angela down to see it if the weather's clement,' said John. His smile was warm and full of love as he looked at her. 'I'm really looking forward to Christmas this year,' he said. 'I'm sure Anthony and Suzy will be amazed by what we've had done, and there'll be lots of room for Teddy to race about on the tricycle I bought him.'

Doris smiled although she dreaded the thought of her new parquet floors being scratched by a small boy on a tricycle. 'It will be a real family Christmas for both of us,' she said. 'Christmas Day here, and Boxing Day with Peggy and all her brood. Bob's due home today, you know, and Cissy might even come down from London.'

She stopped babbling when she noticed that John had stopped smiling and there was a terrible sadness in his eyes. She reached for his hand. 'There's always a chance that

Michael's had a change of heart, and will turn up sometime over the holiday.'

'I doubt that very much,' said John. 'He might be my son, Doris, but after the way he's behaved towards you, I have no wish to see him again. He'd have to have a radical change in character before I allowed him to step one foot in our home.'

Doris knew in her heart that this awful rift between father and son was not of her making, but she still felt guilty about it. However, if he did turn up unexpectedly it could cause a ghastly atmosphere and ruin everything they'd been so looking forward to. She silently hoped they'd seen the last of him.

It was now Christmas Eve and it had at last stopped raining. Thankful for the weak sun glinting on the puddles, Peggy looked out of her kitchen window to watch Bob and Charlie cleaning out the chicken coop.

Ron was busy digging up the rotten vegetables and turning over the ground of the vegetable plot, hoping it would dry out enough for him to plant his winter seedlings. Harvey and Monty were exploring the compost heap, and Daisy was getting in everyone's way by tramping about in her wellington boots and issuing orders.

Peggy leaned on the new sink and rested her chin in her hand as she watched the activity. She still couldn't get over the fact that Bob was a man – a tall, handsome man just like his father, with the strong arms and big, capable hands that a farmer needed, and the weathered complexion of someone who spent his days out of doors.

She bit her lip as she watched her sons leave the coop and start fooling about with the dogs. They were as tall as each other and had the dark hair and bright blue Reilly eyes, but as big and grown-up as they were, it seemed they still possessed their grandfather's aptitude for mischief.

Ron stopped forking the ground to turn his back to the wind and fill his pipe, and she giggled as Bob surreptitiously removed the fork and hid it behind the coop. Ron began patting all his pockets, looking puzzled, for he'd left his tobacco pouch on the garden wall, and hadn't seen Charlie slip it into his own pocket. Both boys were trying very hard not to laugh when a bewildered Ron stared at the spot where his garden fork had been and turned a complete circle in search of it.

'Ach, to be sure, you're a couple of wee divils,' he roared, more for effect than from any real anger. 'You wait until I get hold of you, then you'll be laughing on the other sides of your wee faces so you will.'

'You've got to catch us first, Grandad,' said Charlie.

Ron made a grab for him, but he vaulted over the back wall, and Bob shot out of the gate. The dogs barked and chased after them, leaving Ron shaking his head as they disappeared up the hill. ''Tis grand it is you can run,' he shouted after them. 'But I'll get me own back, you see if I don't.'

Daisy was laughing so hard she lost her balance and plumped down onto the path.

Charlie's cheeky face appeared round the corner. 'Lost anything, Grandad?'

Ron just caught the roll of tobacco that came sailing over the wall, and shook his fist good-naturedly before settling his rump against the wall to fill his pipe and get it lit. He cupped his filthy hands around the match and caught sight of Peggy watching him through the window. Shrugging his shoulders and grinning broadly, he followed tell-tale Daisy to the back of the coop to retrieve his fork.

Peggy turned from the window and went to check on the chicken stew which was bubbling away in the slow oven. Ron and Bob had agreed that the hens were now too old to be productive, so they would use them for stews, soups and stock. This was the first of eight, and although it was sad to see them gutted and plucked, it did mean they'd provide good, filling meals for quite a while – and would be a welcome change from the usual rabbit.

She sat at the kitchen table with a cigarette, poised to stop them all coming into her lovely basement with their muddy boots, and wondered if it might be an idea to get a porch built over the back door where boots, wellingtons and wet coats could be stowed instead of bringing them into the house. She smiled at the idea and decided she'd tackle Ron and Frank about it tomorrow after they'd eaten and had a few drinks.

The weeks of worrying over how to feed everyone over the Christmas break had been allayed by Vi's generous bounty and the three food parcels that had arrived this morning. There had been two from Australia, each filled with tinned ham, salmon and jam; bags of lemons, dried fruit and nuts, as well as sugar, tea and coffee, and Christmas cards from Sarah, Jane, Sybil, Rita and Peter – it seemed they were all planning to meet up over the holiday period.

Cordelia had received a parcel from her family in Canada, and this had been full of tins of gorgeous biscuits, short-bread, more dried fruit, knitting wool and neatly wrapped small gifts. Peggy's cupboards were groaning with it all, and the turkey from Ron and Rosie was so large, it would probably feed everyone for a week.

The knowledge that Jim would miss yet another Christmas was sobering, but he'd sent a lovely parcel of presents for everyone, and a long letter to tell her how much he was missing her and longed to be with them all. It wasn't the same as having him here, but his loving words had warmed her, and she could start to tentatively believe he would be home before another Christmas loomed.

The house was peaceful for a change as Daisy and the boys were outside with the dogs. Danuta was on duty and would be spending the evening with Stanislaw, who was slowly and painfully learning to walk unaided again. Cordelia had gone out with Bertie and would be home soon, for she didn't want to miss Doris's drinks party this evening and the chance to nose around the transformed bungalow.

Doris was very proud of the house, and Peggy knew her sister well enough to realise the drinks party was her chance to show it off. Peggy had already been round there, and had been amazed at the transformation, but she still preferred what she'd had done here, for the essence of the old house was still evident.

She stubbed out her cigarette and checked that Ron was still with Daisy, then wandered into the dining room. There was a large tree now gracing the bay window, bedecked with the tinsel, glass baubles and tiny coloured lights she'd found in her attic. A pile of presents would be placed beneath it once Daisy was in bed and asleep, and her stocking was already hanging from the mantelpiece waiting to be filled.

The table looked lovely with a white linen cloth set with brass candlesticks, home-made crackers and a centrepiece of holly and ivy laced with scarlet ribbon. She'd unearthed her grandmother's heavy silver cutlery from a case in the attic and had spent an entire evening polishing it to a gleam, and it looked wonderful set against the scarlet placemats and napkins she'd made from the remnants of an old damask curtain.

There would be fourteen of them sitting down for lunch tomorrow, plus baby Joseph who would be using Daisy's old high chair now he was big enough. She hadn't heard from Cissy recently, and as she'd been reluctant to make a firm decision about coming down for Christmas the last time they'd spoken on the telephone, Peggy doubted she would come. She understood that it was probably a very busy time for the taxi company and the attractions of London would be far more tempting than a family Christmas in Cliffehaven.

Peggy gave a sigh, adjusted a fork and spoon and went back to the kitchen just in time to stop Ron and his muddy dogs from going into her basement.

'Oh no you don't,' she said. 'Get those dogs out of here and your boots off. I spent half the morning polishing the lino, and I don't want to do it again.'

Ron puffed out his cheeks and looked at her mournfully. 'To be sure, Peggy girl, you're getting too house-proud. A bit of mud never hurt anyone and I'll be cleaning up after them.'

Peggy relented, but very reluctantly as Bob and Charlie appeared in the doorway, mucky as mud-larks and grinning from ear to ear. 'See that you do,' she retorted. 'And I don't want any of you upstairs until you're clean and that floor is spotless again. The mop and bucket are in the scullery cupboard.'

Daisy came excitedly into Peggy's room at five o'clock on Christmas morning with the stocking Santa had left at the bottom of her bed. She clambered into bed with her and chattered away non-stop as she showed Peggy the spinning top, the set of doll's clothes and the packet of sweets.

Peggy drew the covers around them both and groggily admired everything, until Daisy finally ran out of steam and snuggled up for a little snooze. Peggy drifted off again, but she was aware of the heavenly smell of the turkey she'd put in the oven to cook overnight, and the huge amount of work she'd have to get through before lunch could be served. But it was lovely cuddling her little girl on this special day.

They were woken by a knock on her door. 'Yes? What's the matter?' Peggy called, quickly disentangling herself from Daisy and pulling on Jim's dressing gown.

'We thought we'd bring you breakfast in bed,' said Bob, pushing the door open as Daisy scrambled off the bed to hug his legs. 'And to take this one downstairs,' he added with a chuckle, swinging her up onto his hip.

'Oh, darlings, how lovely,' she breathed as Charlie came in with a loaded tray.

'I want breakfast in bed too,' demanded Daisy, wriggling in Bob's arms.

'Yours is downstairs, pipsqueak,' he said firmly as Charlie placed the tray on the bed. 'And if you keep making a fuss, there won't be any more presents.'

This threat had an immediate effect, and Daisy quietened.

Peggy looked in amazement at the breakfast. There was a plate of bacon, egg and fried bread, a big mug of tea and a sprig of holly bright with red berries in a small vase. 'Gosh,' she murmured. 'That's a man-size meal.' She looked up at her two strapping boys, tears of love threatening. 'But thank you, it's such a lovely, lovely treat. You are good boys.'

'We decided you needed feeding up, Mum,' said Charlie, going a bit pink as she kissed him. 'So you've got to eat it all.'

'Happy Christmas, Mum,' said Bob, planting a kiss on her cheek. 'And don't worry about Daisy, we'll keep her busy until you're ready to come down.'

They closed the door behind them and Peggy nestled against the pillows to tuck into the delicious breakfast, wondering if they'd given her this treat because they remembered their father doing the same thing every Christmas and birthday morning, and wanted to somehow make up for his absence.

She smiled at Jim's photograph on the bedside chest. 'Happy Christmas, darling,' she murmured, blowing him a kiss and raising her mug of tea. 'Here's hoping we'll be together long before the next one.'

Almost an hour later Peggy was bathed, dressed and ready to join the fray. She was wearing her favourite yellow dress with a thick white knitted cardigan, the gold filigree necklace and earrings Jim had sent her from India, and the garnet ring he'd entrusted to Ron to give her on the first wedding anniversary they'd had to spend apart. She'd added a dash of lipstick and some powder as it was a special occasion, and hurried down to see what was happening in her kitchen.

The turkey was very nearly cooked, and the boys had prepared all the vegetables. Cordelia was clearly in charge of the Christmas pudding which was now steaming nicely on the hob, and Danuta was instructing Daisy on how to wrap the sausages in rashers of bacon to put in with the roast potatoes and parsnips which would go in an hour before dishing up.

Peggy found that she had very little to do, so she lit a cigarette, made tea for everyone and then tuned the wireless in to the church service being transmitted from Winchester Cathedral. As the lovely sound of the choir filled the warm, deliciously scented room, it really began to feel like Christmas, and Peggy relaxed, determined to enjoy every moment so she could write and tell Jim all about it.

The morning sped past, with Stanislaw arriving by taxi armed with some of the bottles of champagne that Martin and Roger had smuggled over from one of their flights to France. Frank brought a huge pot of winkles and whelks for tea and looked very smart in a tweed jacket and twill trousers, and Peggy noticed he'd had a haircut and was looking rather chipper for a man whose wife had deserted him.

Betty and Brendon brought bottles of wine and had dressed baby Joseph in a scarlet and white knitted romper suit with a matching bobble hat which made him more adorable than ever. Bertie Double-Barrelled brought a box of cigars for the men, a lump of cheese and two bottles of very good port. Ron and Rosie arrived armed with beer and gin, the collars of the two dogs adorned with red and green ribbon bows. And last but never least, Jack Smith brought a cooked joint of beef for the Boxing Day buffet, a sack of potatoes and two pounds of carrots and two cauliflowers.

All the presents had been placed beneath the tree in the dining room, and Daisy was in a fever of excitement as she sat by them and tried to guess which ones were hers and what could be in them.

Ron had just begun to carve the turkey when the telephone rang. Peggy dashed into the hall and had to plug one ear against the noise coming from the dining room where Stanislaw was regaling them all with one of his tall stories.

'Hello?'

'Happy Christmas, Mum,' said Cissy. 'I'm sorry I can't make it down, but I just wanted you to know I was thinking of you all.'

'Oh, darling, thank you. We miss you, but do understand you must be very busy up there.'

'It's absolutely hectic,' she replied. 'With all the parties going on, we're non-stop from morning until very late. I'm exhausted, if the truth be told, but it's all so exciting, Mum. London really is spiffing at this time of year.'

Peggy smiled at her daughter's plummy tones. 'Did you get the present I sent? I'm sorry it's not much, but there's so little choice in the shops.'

'The blouse is absolutely lovely,' Cissy enthused. 'I'm actually wearing it now with a black skirt and jacket.' She paused for breath. 'I'm terribly lucky, because I've had some really super presents this year, so really feel guilty about not being with you all. Dad sent me the most amazing red and gold silk wrap from Singapore which will look quite stunning with the new dress I bought in Harrods.'

Peggy raised an eyebrow. Harrods indeed. Her daughter certainly knew how to spend her hard-earned money.

'Will you thank Grandad and Rosie for my lovely earrings – and Anne for the absolutely spiffing gloves. They're all beautiful, and every time I wear them I shall think of you all.'

The pips started. 'I have to go, sorry, Mum. Have a lovely day and give my love to everyone.'

Peggy smiled as she replaced the receiver. Cissy was happy with her new life – that was all that really mattered

– and she'd cared enough to make the call, so she wasn't lost to them, just on loan to the bright lights of London for a while.

The lunch was a noisy, very jolly affair as they ate the delicious food, drank copiously, pulled crackers and wore the paper hats Peggy and Danuta had made. Baby Joseph joined in the racket by banging a spoon on the high-chair tray, his paper hat over his eyes. Harvey and Monty had been surreptitiously treated to bits of turkey, sausage and ham by Ron, and when it was clear there would be no more, flopped down on the rug in front of Ron's seasoned applewood fire which Bob had lit earlier.

After lunch the presents were handed out and soon the floor was littered with paper and string and bits of ribbon which Joseph crawled through in great delight. Daisy had been given a doll's pram and she had to be forestalled from trying to put Joseph in it, and to avoid a temper tantrum, was distracted by Charlie showing her how to spin her top properly.

Bob and Ron pushed back the table and chairs and Frank started the gramophone so everyone could dance. Ron grabbed Rosie and swung her onto the floor, as Bertie led Cordelia in a stately foxtrot. Charlie jigged about with Daisy in his arms as Bob took Danuta onto the floor for a jive. Brendon danced with Betty, their son between them, while Frank and Jack kept Stanislaw company over the remaining cheese, crackers and port.

Peggy's heart was full as she gazed with love and pride at the sons she and Jim had made together. Seeing them enjoying the first Beach View Christmas for years was something she'd dreamed about, and although Jim couldn't be here, it was as if he was present in those two boys who looked so very like him.

25

The festive season had been exhausting, but great fun as Beach View rang with the sound of children, music and the happy voices of friends and family each day. Peggy had been in her element, delighting in being mother and grandmother again, and catching up with everyone's news. It had been a real treat to see how motherhood had made Suzy blossom, and her new baby girl was utterly adorable and looked just like her.

The day after Boxing Day there had been an excited telephone call from Robert to say that Fran had just delivered a son, Peter, and mother and baby were doing very well. And then on New Year's Eve, Gloria had rung from the Crown, almost incoherent with joy as Ivy and Andy were now the proud parents of Eve, who'd come early that morning. Peggy felt as if she'd become a grandmother all over again now two of her precious chicks had little ones of their own.

The celebrations were now over and January was its usual anti-climax, for the new year of 1946 had dawned with the same dreary wet weather as the old one, with nothing much to look forward to since February and March would no doubt be just as depressing. The household bills had come in, work had begun again, the schools were back, and all in all, Peggy was feeling rather deflated.

She watched the rain come down from her kitchen window that mid-January Sunday lunchtime and wondered if it would ever stop, but at least now she had her twin-tub washing machine, she could guarantee her washing would be dry and ready for ironing every Saturday.

She turned from the window and finished her solitary lunch, thinking sadly how much she missed Bob now that he'd returned to Somerset. Daisy and Charlie missed him too, for he was a very dear, thoughtful, caring young man, and they'd all loved having him here. He would come back one day – probably to welcome his father home and stay a while – but she knew his heart was really with the farm, and that was where he would make his life.

Peggy washed up her soup bowl and mug with the wireless on for company. It was peaceful in the house, for Anne had taken Daisy off for the day to play with Rose and Emily at the cottage; Charlie was upstairs doing his homework now the new term had started; Cordelia was out to have lunch with Bertie, and Danuta was with Stanislaw. Danuta's workload had been eased considerably now a third district nurse had been taken on, and she'd been looking much brighter and less tired lately.

Peggy smiled while she dried the china and stacked it away in her lovely new cupboards. She guessed this healthy glow was down to the way Danuta's strong feelings for Stanislaw were reciprocated, but she did worry that the girl would be taking on rather a lot if she married him. Stan wasn't the easiest of men to persuade to take things slowly and be patient, but at least he'd cut down on the drinking, and was looking healthier for it.

As yet, there had been no engagement announcement, but Peggy suspected it would come as soon as Stan was released from Cliffe and could lead a more independent life. His ability to walk unaided was improving by the day, so much so that he'd taken Danuta to a dance on New Year's Eve and managed a short turn round the floor which had thrilled them both. There was little doubt he adored Danuta, but how on earth would he be able to provide for her? Surely he wasn't really contemplating getting back into a cockpit again?

Peggy set these worries aside when she heard the knock on the front door. Whipping off her apron, she hurried to see who was calling on this murky Sunday afternoon. When she saw the telegram boy on the step and the brown envelope in his hand, she felt light-headed and had to steady herself against the door jamb. She'd been here before, and really didn't know how she'd cope if it was bad news from Jim.

'Sorry, missus,' the boy said, the rain dripping from his cap. 'Is there a reply?'

She took a deep breath and ripped open the envelope. Reading the few words, she gave a screech of joy, grabbed the startled boy and hugged him. 'Thank you, thank you,' she babbled, tears of happiness rolling down her face. 'You can't possibly know what this means to me.'

He looked at her warily as he disentangled himself, straightened his cap and dug in his bag for his notebook. 'Is there a reply, missus? Only I got to get on.'

'Yes. Tell him, "I can't wait, stop. Love you, stop. Peggy, stop."' She scrabbled for her purse which she'd left on the hall table and found the appropriate money. Adding a few coppers as a tip, she grinned as the boy dashed off down the steps and disappeared round the corner. 'He must think I'm absolutely potty,' she giggled.

She closed the front door and read the telegram again, hardly daring to believe it could be true. But there it was, as clear and definite as it could be.

*Home by May * Love you * Jim*

'Oh, Jim,' she breathed, sinking onto the hall chair. 'Such wonderful, wonderful news. You must be over the moon.'

Realising she didn't have to keep this to herself, she leapt from the chair and bounded up the stairs two at a time, ran along the landing and raced up the second flight.

'Charlie! Charlie!' she called breathlessly.

He shot out of his bedroom, his face drawn with anxiety. 'What's the matter, Mum?'

She didn't know whether to laugh or cry, but had the breath for neither. 'Your dad's coming home,' she managed to gasp, clutching at his sweater. 'He's coming home in May, Charlie. Isn't that wonderful?'

'Whoopie!' Charlie grabbed her round the waist and danced her along the landing before swinging her off her feet and planting a kiss on her cheek. 'Did he say what date? Which port will he be coming into?' He set her back down and had to steady her.

Peggy felt quite giddy with it all and, unable to speak, handed him the telegram.

'This calls for a celebration,' he said decisively. 'Get your coat, Mum. We're going to the Anchor to tell Grandad.'

'I'll leave a note for Cordy to let her know where we are and why,' she said, already halfway down the stairs. 'And I should really telephone Frank, Anne and Doris.'

'We'll do all that from the Anchor,' said Charlie, thumping down the stairs behind her as he dragged on his heavy school winter coat.

Peggy left a scribbled note for Cordelia and Danuta on the kitchen table, dragged on her coat, outdoor shoes and hat and snatched up an umbrella before following Charlie out into the teeming rain.

She ran as if she had wings on her heels, her heart so light and full of happiness, she barely noticed the rain any more. It wasn't until she arrived breathlessly at the side door of the Anchor that she remembered she could have driven here, and burst out laughing.

'Are you all right, Mum?' Charlie asked, frowning.

'I'm absolutely fine,' she assured him, 'but if we don't get indoors we'll both drown.'

Charlie pushed through the door, and they were greeted by the two delighted dogs. 'Grandad! Rosie!' he shouted up from the dark, narrow hall.

'What the divil's the matter?' Ron appeared in the upstairs doorway looking dishevelled as he tucked his unbuttoned shirt into his trousers and blocked their progress.

'Jim's coming home,' said Peggy excitedly, and then realised in horror that they must have disrupted Ron and Rosie's canoodling. 'Sorry if we've disturbed you, Ron,' she babbled. 'But it's such fantastic news we had to come and share it.'

Ron's disgruntled expression disappeared into a broad grin. 'Ach, to be sure that's grand, so it is. Come up, come up and dry off by the fire.'

He fumbled to fasten his shirt properly and shouted to Rosie. 'Come away and hear this, Rosie, me darling. Charlie and Peggy are here with news of our Jim.'

Rosie appeared wrapped in a thick dressing gown, her hair mussed, face clean of make-up. 'What on earth's going on?' she asked, attempting to tidy her hair.

'It's our Jim,' said Ron, taking her hand. 'He's coming home in May.'

Rosie gathered Peggy to her and gave her a hug. 'Oh, Peggy, that's the best news ever.' She drew back and tightened the belt on the dressing gown as she noticed Charlie admiring her cleavage. 'You'll have to excuse my appearance, but we were having a lie-in as it's Sunday.'

'Go and get dressed while I fetch everyone a drink,' said Ron with a loving pat on her bottom. He grinned and winked at Charlie. 'Come on, wee boy, let's raid the bar.'

'Before you do that, can I telephone the others to let them know?'

'Of course. You didn't have to ask, Peggy girl,' he said expansively before clumping down the stairs with Charlie and the dogs.

By the time Cordelia arrived with Bertie, Danuta and Stanislaw, the party had moved down to the bar and was in full swing. Daisy and her little cousins were dressing the patient and rather long-suffering dogs in doll's clothes while

Joseph slept in his pram. Betty, Rosie, Anne and Doris had taken over the bar stools, while the men tried to outdo each other with their war stories as they huddled over their beers in the corner by the inglenook. Rosie had thought to ring Gloria so she could celebrate not only Jim's homecoming but the new baby, and she'd bumped into Jack who'd been on his way to Beach View, so of course he'd joined in.

Peggy was delightfully squiffy from all the gin she'd had as she tried to maintain her balance on the bar stool and sing along to Gloria's enthusiastic piano playing. She loved these people so much, her heart was full. And soon – very soon – her Jim would be home and life would be complete again.

Doris woke that Monday morning with a thumping headache. She groaned as she climbed out of the empty bed and went into the bathroom in search of some aspirin. John was already up and about and didn't appear to be suffering at all, but drinking in the afternoon had never agreed with Doris, and she regretted having got rather too much into the swing of things yesterday.

She stared at her reflection in the mirror – an unedifying sight – and splashed cold water onto her face in the hope it might improve things. It didn't, but by the time she'd cleaned her teeth, brushed her hair and dressed for the day, the aspirin had started working and she'd begun to feel somewhat better.

'I'm sorry, John, but I really can't face a fried egg this morning,' she said, pushing the plate away. 'I'll just have this tea and a slice of toast.'

John grinned and set about demolishing her breakfast, despite the fact he'd already eaten his own. 'It was a good party, wasn't it? I'm sorry you're not the full ticket this morning.'

'It's my own fault, John. I should never have tried to match Gloria drink for drink. That woman must have the constitution of a navvy.'

John chuckled as he cleared the dishes. 'She's been in the pub trade for years, so you shouldn't be surprised.' He patted her hand. 'Stay at home this morning, Doris. I can cope in the office on my own.'

'But you have that appointment in town this morning,' she reminded him. 'And actually, I think I'd rather go into work than mope around here. The walk there should blow some of the cobwebs away.'

'Well, if you're sure, my dear,' he murmured, finishing the washing-up. 'I shouldn't be too long at the solicitor's, and paying in the rental cheques will take a matter of minutes. I'll buy something nice to eat at our desks for lunch.'

Doris looked out of the window at the threatening sky. 'You'd better take the car,' she murmured. 'It looks as if it's going to rain again.'

'I need the exercise,' he said. 'We've been cooped up indoors since before Christmas, and with all the rich food and drink, my waistband is getting rather too snug.' He patted his flat stomach and then bent to kiss the top of her head. 'I should be back by midday.'

Doris carried her cup of tea into the hall and watched him don his raincoat and hat and pick up the large golfing umbrella. He kissed her lovingly on the cheek and opened the front door. 'See you later.'

She stood in the doorway and watched him stride away until he was out of sight, and then went back into the kitchen to finish her tea, tidy up and get ready for her walk to the office.

The heavy grey clouds were scudding across a gloomy sky as the bitter wind came up from the sea. Doris wedged the velvet hat firmly on her head, pulled up her coat collar and walked briskly towards the factory estate, glad it wasn't raining, for not even the sturdiest umbrella would survive this wind.

She waved to Jack Smith who was working on a car, and hurried up the steps to the office that overlooked the estate.

Closing the door behind her, she plugged in the kettle, hung up her things and switched on the two-bar electric fire. Once she'd made the tea, she sat down to go through the morning post.

John had spent an hour with his solicitor, discussing the recent changes he'd made to his will, and coming to the conclusion that it was the fairest way to deal with the thorny problem of his estranged son. Once it had been signed and witnessed by two members of staff, the old boy insisted they had a glass of sherry and a slice of Madeira cake.

John knew the elderly man had all but retired from the law firm which was now in his son's capable hands, but since he'd been widowed, he preferred coming into his office rather than sit alone at home. So, being a patient man, John spent another half an hour he couldn't really spare chatting about the Lake District and drinking rather good sherry.

John left the solicitor's office satisfied that he'd done his good deed for the day, and hurried to pay in the rental cheques for the leased factory units. There was a long queue as usual on a Monday morning, but time passed quite quickly as he chatted to a golfing pal and fixed up a game for the following weekend if the weather improved.

He checked his watch, saw it was almost midday, and quickly headed for the Home and Colonial to buy something for lunch. There was a long queue of gossiping housewives which stretched along the pavement, so he changed his mind and went to the bakery instead. Here was yet another queue, but much shorter, and he was soon happily heading back up the High Street clutching lovely warm pasties.

The large black Bentley came careering down the hill, clearly out of control. It swerved, the tyres screeching in protest as cyclists and other cars tried to avoid it. It hit the far kerb, narrowly missed a lamppost and threatened to overturn as the elderly woman driver yanked on the steering wheel but kept her foot on the accelerator.

John froze as he watched it sway and skid across the road, heading straight for a woman with a pram. He could see she was frozen in shock and quickly moved to push her out of the way, but the Bentley hit a deep pothole, turned turtle and spun in a different direction.

John saw it coming but had no time to get out of the way. As the front fender clipped him hard and tossed him into the air, he could hear screams and shouts and the terrible sound of tearing metal and splintered glass. He hit the ground, the breath punched from him as everything suddenly went black.

The morning had sped past as Doris worked solidly through the pile of letters and answered telephone calls. It wasn't until her stomach gurgled with hunger that she looked up at the clock on the wall. Surprised to find it was after one o'clock, she wondered where on earth John had got to, and then remembered that old Mr Clarke enjoyed a chat over sherry and cake.

She put the kettle on for more tea in the hope that John had remembered to buy something for lunch. She was feeling very much better now and was looking forward to having something to eat after her meagre breakfast, so she treated herself to a biscuit from the packet in the tin.

The telephone rang just as she'd poured the tea, and everything was forgotten in the horror of what the woman was telling her. Slamming down the receiver, she abandoned the tea and biscuit, grabbed her coat, keys and handbag, locked the door behind her and charged down the stairs. She had two choices. Waste precious minutes by fetching the car to drive down – or just run.

She ran faster than she'd ever thought possible and arrived at the Cliffehaven General out of breath and terrified. She raced up the steps into the reception area and headed straight for the accident and emergency department.

'Mrs White,' she gasped to the sister in charge. 'My husband ... my husband.'

'It's all right, Mrs White,' the woman soothed. 'He's in good hands. The doctors are with him. Sit down and catch your breath while I get you a cup of tea.'

'I don't want tea,' Doris said fiercely. 'I want to see my husband.'

'I'm afraid that's not possible just yet. Please, Mrs White, sit down.'

Doris felt light-headed and the room began to swim round her, so she let the young woman help her to sit, and tried desperately to regain her wits. 'What happened?' she asked eventually.

'He was knocked down by a car in the High Street,' she replied. 'He has several broken bones, and a very nasty bump on the head, I'm afraid.'

'But he'll be all right, won't he?' she rasped. 'He'll pull through?'

'I'm sorry, Mrs White, I really can't say anything until the doctor has finished examining him. Is there anyone you'd like me to call to be with you?'

'Are you saying his injuries are serious?'

The nurse's expression said more than any words could convey, and she pressed her hand on Doris's shoulder in sympathy as she asked again if there was someone she could call.

'My sister,' she managed. 'My sister, Peggy Reilly. She's at work, but ... but ...' Doris burst into tears.

'It's all right, Doris. I'm here,' said a breathless Peggy. 'I saw you running hell for leather away from the factory and knew something must have happened.'

She put her arm about Doris's heaving shoulders and tried to soothe her as the nurse explained about John. 'I'll stay with her for as long as she needs me,' she promised.

Doris eventually dried her eyes, but she was shivering with shock, her heart heavy with dread. 'I can't lose him, Peggy,' she said tremulously, clasping her hand tightly.

Peggy gripped her arm. 'No one said anything about losing him, Doris,' she said firmly. 'We just have to believe he'll come through this. John's a fit man for his age and broken bones can heal. Please try not to think the worst.'

They sat there, hand in hand and shoulder to shoulder, for what felt like hours until a doctor came out to see them.

'Your husband has come round momentarily, but he was very groggy. We're taking him down to theatre to repair his broken pelvis and the fractures in his left leg. I must warn you that all surgery carries certain risks, but it's vital we repair the damage as soon as possible.' He handed her a clipboard. 'You need to sign this consent form.'

Doris stared up at him, her whole body trembling with fear. 'But he's a very fit man for his age,' she managed tearfully. 'Why should there be complications and risk?'

'It's the way it is with even the simplest operation, Mrs White,' he said rather impatiently. 'Please sign the form so the surgeon can get on.'

Doris signed the form, her hand shaking so much it was all but illegible. 'How long will he be in theatre?'

'For several hours,' he replied, taking the form from her. 'Perhaps it would be better if you went home, and I'll get someone to telephone you once it's over.'

Doris shook her head. 'I'm staying here.'

He nodded curtly and strode away, leaving Doris numb, icily cold and unable to think straight. Her world was crashing around her, and there seemed to be nothing she could do to stop it.

'Do you think we ought to try and contact Michael?' asked Peggy hesitantly.

'I don't want him here,' hissed Doris, clutching Peggy's arm. 'And there's no need. John's fit and strong and a few broken bones won't kill him.'

'I'm sure that's the case,' said Peggy. 'But Michael has to be told, Doris. He's enemy enough without you keeping something like this from him.' She shifted in the hard chair. 'Do you have a telephone number for him?'

Doris shook her head. 'I only know he's a major at Catterick – or he was before Christmas.'

'Then that will have to do. Will you be all right on your own while I pop across the road to the Anchor to make the call?'

Doris nodded, too upset to speak.

Time passed slowly as she sat there huddled into her misery and fear, and although a probationer had brought her a cup of tea it was sitting on the floor at her feet untouched.

'Well, now, Doris,' said Ron, plumping down and putting his arm round her shoulders. ''Tis awful about John, but we must stay positive. The doctors here are ruddy marvels, and your man is as fit as a flea. He'll pull through, I've no doubt of it.'

'I wish I could be so sure,' she murmured, glad to see him even though they'd never really got on. 'Did Peggy manage to get hold of Michael?'

'She left a message with some chap at the barracks. It turns out he's been sent to West Germany as part of the British Army security presence. I suspect he'll be flown home immediately.'

Doris closed her eyes. It was bad enough knowing that John was at this moment under the knife, without the added pressure of his unpleasant son turning up.

Peggy hurried away from the factory in Camden Road, relieved that Daisy would be kept on at the crèche and fed if necessary, and that Solly had been so understanding of her leaving her post at the factory so abruptly. Knowing Ron was keeping Doris company, she quickly drove home, made some potted meat sandwiches and a flask of tea, and told Cordelia what had happened.

She'd had to be rather firm with Cordelia, for the arthritis was particularly bad today and Peggy didn't want her going out in the appalling weather, or sitting around in draughty hospital corridors. Promising she'd telephone the minute she had any news, she drove back to the hospital to discover that Doris and Ron were now in the relatives' room, but there was no sign of Michael. John was still in surgery, and probably would be for several more hours, but the surgeon was evidently pleased with his progress.

Peggy hugged her sister, appalled at how she'd aged in the last hour or so, and how small and defenceless she looked suddenly. Coaxing her into drinking some tea, she offered her a sandwich and wasn't surprised when she pushed it away.

'Rosie said not to worry about tonight, as it's always quiet on a Monday and she can cope on her own.' She offered Ron a sandwich which he took and ate hungrily. 'I've also left a note at home, asking Charlie to pick up Daisy from the crèche after her tea and put her to bed.'

The door opened and they all looked up expectantly. 'I heard about what happened,' said Danuta. 'I am very sorry, Mrs White. Is there anything I can do for you?'

'Thank you,' she replied weakly, 'but there's nothing really anyone can do but wait.' She looked at Danuta as she sat down beside her. 'The nurse said he was hit by a car in the High Street. Have you any idea of how it happened?'

'I saw only the ambulance drive away and a car on its roof, all smashed up inside Plummer's shop window. I went to see if I could help and someone told me what had happened.' She bit her lip, clearly wondering how much to tell her.

'Please, Danuta. I need to hear it all,' said Doris.

'The driver of the car is an elderly lady and she put her foot on the accelerator instead of the brake. She would have killed a woman and her baby if the car had not hit a hole in the road, turned over and changed direction.'

Danuta paused and took Doris's hand. 'The lady I spoke to said John would have been safe if he had stayed where he was, but he went towards the woman with the pram to get her out of the way, and the car hit him.'

Doris covered her mouth with her hands, her eyes bright with unshed tears.

'What about the driver?' Ron rumbled.

'She has only scratches and bruises, but is very shaken.'

'I hope they arrested her for dangerous driving,' snapped Doris.

'I expect it will be so,' murmured Danuta. 'Someone said she'd been taken to the police station once the ambulance men said she was well enough to be questioned.'

She looked at the watch pinned to her uniform. 'I am sorry, but I have other patients to see. I will come back later.'

'She's a nice girl, isn't she?' said Doris into the silence once Danuta had left. 'I didn't realise. I always thought she was a bit aloof. But then she is foreign.'

Nobody dared reprimand Doris, but the already tense atmosphere became almost unbearable. Ron left shortly afterwards to have his tea and make sure Rosie was managing all right in the bar, and as the time slowly passed, Peggy was relieved to see him back, accompanied by Frank and Anne, who'd left the girls with Martin.

It was almost eight in the evening when the doctor appeared in the waiting room to tell them that John was now in the recovery ward. 'You may see him for just a minute, Mrs White, but you will find he's very sleepy and probably won't really know you're there.'

'But he's all right, isn't he?' asked Doris. 'There are no complications?'

The doctor smiled. 'Apart from his injuries, he's a very fit, healthy man for his age, which has helped him through the operation. There is always the possibility that he will suffer from concussion, but we'll keep a close eye on that.'

'How soon will he be able to come home?' asked Doris.

413

'Not for some time yet, Mrs White. It will take several weeks of recuperation and physiotherapy before he is able to walk again, but once we deem him fit enough, we'll be sending him to the Memorial.'

'Thank you, Doctor,' she said meekly. She gathered up her things. 'I'd like to see him now, if I may.'

'Not before I do,' said Michael, who'd come in unnoticed and in full army uniform.

The doctor raised his brows. 'And who are you?' he asked.

'Major White, Colonel White's son,' he replied curtly. 'And as I've just been flown in from Germany I demand to see my father.'

Peggy and the others shifted uncomfortably in their seats at this rude intrusion.

'I'm sorry, Major,' the doctor replied coolly. 'But only the next of kin may visit tonight.' He looked at Doris who'd gone ashen and took her arm. 'Come, Mrs White. I'll show you the way.'

The colour drained from Michael's face as he clenched his fists at his sides. 'If my father dies before I get to see him, I shall blame you,' he hissed at Doris.

There was a sharp gasp of disgust from Peggy who stood to defend her sister.

Doris faltered and drew her arm from the doctor's grasp. 'Perhaps it would be better if Michael saw him tonight,' she said fretfully. 'I'll come back in the morning.'

The doctor looked from her to Michael, clearly sensing the tension that was building in the room. 'Why don't you both come?' he said to forestall any more trouble.

'I have no wish for this woman to accompany us,' said Michael stiffly.

'Then you will stay here,' retorted the doctor.

Slipping her hand into the crook of the doctor's arm to steady herself, Doris studiously ignored Michael who was incandescent with fury at being snubbed, and made as dignified an exit as possible.

'How *dare* you speak to my sister like that,' snapped Peggy.

Michael looked down at her in disdain. 'I'll speak to her in any way I want,' he replied icily. 'Not that it's any of your damned business.'

Ron and Frank got to their feet, eased in front of Peggy and stared Michael down – two monolithic and immovable forces.

'We don't hold with talk like that in front of our women,' said Frank.

'I'm thinking you should apologise, and then leave,' said Ron, his fists curling.

Michael glowered at the two men, turned on his heel and slammed out of the room. In the silence that followed, they could hear his heavy footsteps down the corridor.

'He's a nasty piece of work,' muttered Frank.

'Aye, that he is,' said Ron. 'But we've not seen the last of him, you can be sure of that.'

Peggy scrubbed her face with her hands. 'Oh, lawks,' she sighed. 'I wish now I'd never called him back. Poor Doris has got enough to deal with without him being such a beast.' And then an awful thought struck her. 'I hope he won't be lying in wait for her back at the house,' she gasped. 'She'll have no defence against him, and it would be simply awful if he insisted upon staying with her.'

'You don't really think he'd do that, Peggy? It's obvious he loathes her,' said Frank.

'It would be a fine act of revenge, though,' murmured Ron. 'Probably best if she comes to the Anchor with me and Rosie.'

Doris had fought back her tears as she'd looked down at John who was incarcerated in thick plaster casts. But he'd woken enough to assure her he was feeling fine, and once the nurse had given her his wallet, keys and watch, she'd gone back to the waiting room in some trepidation, fearing Michael would still be there.

Horrified by Peggy's suspicions, and accepting that Michael could very well do such a thing, she'd gladly accepted Ron's invitation to stay at the Anchor. It meant only crossing the road to the hospital, and she felt safer with Ron than she would have on her own all day at Beach View with only Cordelia for company.

She rose early that Tuesday morning, dressed in the crumpled clothes she'd been wearing the day before, and tried to do justice to the lovely breakfast Rosie had cooked for her. At some point she would need to go home to fetch her car and pack a small bag of essentials, although Rosie had lent her a nightdress and some underwear. But John was her priority now, and as the doctor had given his permission for her to visit out of the usual hours today, she wanted to be with him for as long as possible before Michael turned up – as he inevitably would.

She arrived at the hospital shortly after breakfast had been cleared away and made the long trek to the men's surgical ward. The sister in charge had been notified of her visit and showed her where John's bed was. 'He's had a little breakfast and is sleeping again,' she said quietly. 'It will take time for the heavy medication to wear off, but don't worry, it's quite usual.'

Doris sat in the armchair by the bed and regarded him lovingly. His beloved face was a much better colour today but for the dark bruise on his forehead. The left side of him had taken the impact, for that arm was in plaster, as was the leg, which was raised up by a set of pulleys. The sheet and blanket covered his body, but she knew his broken ribs were tightly bound and there was another plaster cast surrounding his hips which, according to the doctor, would stay on the longest.

She eyed the needles in his arm and the drips above the bed, managing to resist stroking his lovely silver hair from his brow, and sat patiently waiting for him to wake.

Halfway through the morning there was a bit of a kerfuffle outside the ward door, and Doris thought she heard Michael's hectoring voice and braced herself for another confrontation. However, the noise soon died down, and she forgot about it when John finally woke.

'Hello, darling,' he murmured, his bright blue eyes rather unfocused with the effects of the heavy medication. 'I'm sorry to be such a nuisance.'

'You silly, sweet man. Of course you're not a nuisance,' she assured him, carefully holding his hand. 'I'm just so relieved I still have you.'

He smiled at her. 'It'll take more than a runaway car to get rid of me.'

'Now, you're not to worry about the office,' she said. 'I telephoned the secretary we employed over our honeymoon and she's coming to collect the keys later today. I'm staying at the Anchor for the time being, by the way, so I can come to see you more often.'

He frowned at this, but let it pass. 'Promise me you'll take care of yourself, Doris,' he murmured, his eyelids drooping once more.

'I will, my love,' she whispered back before softly kissing his brow.

Lunchtime came and went, but John slept on, so Doris nipped out for a sandwich from the Lilac Tea Rooms and was back by his side when the bell rang for visiting time. She braced herself for the inevitable as the visitors poured in, and Michael marched towards her, his expression set.

He ignored her completely as he stared down at his father for a long moment, and then went to talk to the nurse. Returning minutes later, he sat down on the other side of the bed and glared at her. 'Where were you last night?'

'I was with friends,' she replied, meeting his gaze and refusing to be cowed.

'I suppose it didn't occur to you that I would need somewhere to stay? And by rights, it should have been in my father's house.'

Doris refused to be drawn into an argument and remained silent.

'It was most inconvenient,' he went on. 'I had to book into a hotel.'

Still Doris said nothing, but she could see it was really irritating him, and he was itching for a fight – and yet she couldn't think of a thing to say to him.

He leaned forward, checked that his father was still asleep and eyed her coldly. 'I see you've spent my inheritance by having all that work done on that ridiculous house,' he hissed. 'Well, don't get too comfortable, you gold-digging harpy, because if anything happens to Father I will see you back on the street with nothing.'

Doris suddenly felt very calm. 'Why do you hate me?' she asked, genuinely curious. 'I've done nothing to you to deserve such spleen.'

'My mother was the most wonderful, caring woman with grace and beauty, real class and great charm. You aren't fit to walk in her shadow, let alone take her place.' He eyed her with a sneer. 'You've inveigled your way into my father's affections, catching him while he was still grieving for her and worried sick about me. All you really wanted was a meal ticket – and it shows in the amount of money you made him spend on that house.'

'We shared the costs equally,' she said flatly. 'Your inheritance has not been touched – and I find it appalling that you should carry on like this when your poor father is lying there helpless and in pain.'

'Father knows my feelings,' he countered. 'I'm not saying anything he hasn't already heard.' He glanced across at John before turning his cold gaze back to Doris. 'Sooner or later, he'll realise what a fool he's been and send you packing – you'll see.'

'Michael.'

They were both startled by John's rasping voice, and Doris could feel the heat in her face at the realisation he must have heard some – if not all – of their conversation.

'Michael, you will apologise to my wife,' John managed. 'And then leave. I do not wish to see you again.'

'I'm not apologising to her, and I'm staying right here,' retorted Michael.

John made a tremendous effort to grasp Michael's jacket sleeve. 'When I die, and I'm telling you now, it won't be for a long while yet – you'll get your share of the proceeds from the family home I sold. I've arranged for you to receive the lump sum from your mother's estate on your next birthday, on the proviso you make no further trouble. The home I share with Doris is already fully in her name, so you can't touch it. If you contest the will, or threaten Doris in any way, your inheritance will go straight to an army charity.'

His hand slipped from Michael's arm and flopped onto the bed. 'Just go, Michael,' he said wearily. 'I have nothing more to say to you.'

Michael's face was so bloodless Doris thought he was about to faint, but he rallied enough to scrape his chair back and loom over his father. 'You're a fool,' he hissed. 'Mother must be turning in her grave at how easily you've been duped.'

He stormed out of the ward, startling patients and visitors alike as he slammed through the double doors, leaving them swinging wildly behind him as he marched away down the corridor.

'Oh, John,' said Doris tearfully. 'I do wish you hadn't heard any of that.'

'Well, I'm glad I did,' he said on a sigh. 'And although it breaks my heart that my son should be so bitter and unforgiving, I can see him now for what he really is.' He reached for her hand. 'I'm sorry he distressed you, my love. But I don't think we'll see him again, so dry your eyes and give me a kiss.'

Doris softly kissed his cheek, overwhelmed with love and sorrow for him at the loss of a son he'd once adored, and who'd utterly betrayed him.

26

It was now March, and with the coal shortages, it was a battle for Peggy to keep the range fire burning so she could cook and keep the radiators working. Beach View was a large house, and with so few people living in it at the moment it felt colder than usual, so she'd shut off the dining room and the spare bedrooms and, like the war years, the family now spent most of their time in the kitchen – the only truly warm room in the house.

Compounding this misery, the cold and wet had rotted the winter harvest, so the price of bread and potatoes had soared, and it took all of Peggy's ingenuity to put a decent, filling meal on the table every night. Frank helped by bringing some fish now and again, and Ron brought home the occasional rabbit or pigeon, but now all the old hens had been used for stock, stews and soups, there was precious little meat to be had and only one egg each once a week on the ration.

Peggy was bundled up in layers of cardigans and sweaters beneath her overcoat, with a woollen scarf around her neck, gloves, hat, and thick socks inside her boots to keep her feet warm. She climbed out of the car and was immediately blasted by the icy wind coming off the sea, so she gathered Daisy into her arms and ran up the front steps, shielding her from the bitter elements. It had been a long and tiring day at the factory with everyone moaning about the cold despite the bank of electric heaters Solly had provided, and Peggy was looking forward to putting her feet up with a cup of tea and a fag.

The hall was relatively warm as she closed the door behind her, and she hurried into the kitchen where the heat was positively blissful, and the aroma of rabbit stew came from the oven.

'Hello, Cordelia,' she said, noting how the elderly woman was sitting so close to the fire she was in danger of singeing the blanket over her knees. 'Would you like me to make you a hot-water bottle for your poor hands?'

'No thank you, dear,' she replied. 'Charlie's just done one for me. There's fresh tea in the pot too.' She regarded Peggy over her half-moon glasses. 'You look tired, Peggy. Busy day?'

'Every day's busy, Cordy,' she said, helping Daisy off with her layers of clothing. 'It's the cold that's getting everyone on edge and grumpy.' She poured cups of tea for herself and Daisy and sat in the other fireside chair to light a cigarette. 'I'm glad Charlie's been looking after you, but where's Danuta? Shouldn't she be back by now?'

'Charlie's been a godsend,' sighed Cordelia. 'There's no way I could have managed to put the stew together without him. As for Danuta, she's been popping in all through the day to make sure I've wanted for nothing, so I expect she's having to catch up on her nursing duties.'

Peggy closed her eyes, finally relaxing to let the warmth flood through her. 'May seems so far away,' she murmured. 'It's strange, isn't it, but now I know Jim's coming home the time seems to be dragging even slower than before. When I think how many years it's been, a few months is nothing at all really – but it feels like an absolute age.'

'You've got the winter blues,' said Cordelia. 'Once spring comes, the time will go much faster.'

Peggy roused herself and went to check on the potatoes which were on the point of boiling dry. 'I sincerely hope so,' she replied, adding some more water to the pot. 'But if the winter's this bad here, how on earth is poor Ruby coping over in Canada? I do wish we had more news from her

– that baby's due around now – but the mail is clearly not getting through yet.'

'She'll write when she can,' said Cordelia, lifting her cup with both cruelly swollen hands and taking a sip. 'By the way, Doris telephoned earlier to say that John will be transferred to Cliffe Memorial at the end of the week to begin his course of intensive physiotherapy. They're both hoping he'll make as good a recovery as Ron did when he had that operation on his spine. But of course it's still early days yet.'

'I'm just glad John sent that rotter of a son packing,' said Peggy, testing the potatoes with a fork. 'It's tragic, really, but Michael only has himself to blame.'

'The whole episode was most unsavoury,' said Cordelia with a sniff. 'But it did prove that John has Doris's best interests at heart by signing the entire house over to her.'

Peggy grinned. 'Yes. It came as quite a shock to her that he'd do that, but at least it means she's secure and I don't have to worry about her.'

Charlie came thudding downstairs just as Peggy was about to lift the heavy stew pot out of the oven. 'Let me do that,' he said, taking it out and placing it carefully on a trivet to protect the new worktop.

'You're a good boy, thank you,' murmured Peggy, leaving him to dish it up while she drained and mashed the potatoes.

The back door slammed and Danuta pushed her way into the kitchen carrying her nursing bag and a large, bulging holdall. She dropped the holdall on the floor, clearly not in the best of tempers. 'Sorry I'm late, but Stanislaw asked me to fetch this from Cliffe, and we had a long disagreement which took up much time.'

Peggy frowned. 'He's not been drinking again, has he?'

Danuta shook her head and began to peel off her scarf, hat and gloves. 'It is worse than that,' she said darkly. 'He is leaving Cliffe first thing tomorrow to go on a retraining course at Biggin Hill.'

'But that's—'

'Exactly,' snapped Danuta. 'He is not anywhere near ready to fly again, but he has the head of a mule and will not listen to me. I tell him he is a fool – that he cannot even climb into the cockpit without help – and is a danger to everyone. But he laughs at me and says I must trust him as he knows best.'

'Most men think they know best,' said Cordelia acidly. 'But it's all a bit sudden, isn't it? Why the urgency?'

Danuta took a shallow, quavering breath. 'Phoenix Air needs another pilot now Kitty is very pregnant and Charlotte cannot fit in much flying with having to cope with the twins. There is too much work for Roger and Martin, and Stanislaw is convinced he is the man for the job.'

'Oh dear,' sighed Peggy. 'But if he's that keen to prove he can fly again, surely we should support him?'

Danuta's lips thinned, her face drawn with anxiety and real fear. 'He will do too much – show off and make danger,' she hissed. 'I know him very well, and he will kill himself trying to prove a point.'

Charlie placed the bowls of stew and mashed potato on the table. 'If you don't mind me saying, Danuta,' he said carefully. 'Stan has always had a mind of his own, and he needs to prove to himself that he can still fly – that he's still useful.'

'I know and I understand this, Charlie,' she replied, sinking into a kitchen chair. 'But I fear he is a man who thinks he cannot come to harm and will take terrible risks. He is proud Polish man with much spirit – and that is very dangerous combination.'

'The instructors won't let him fly until they're absolutely sure he's ready,' said Charlie. 'He'll have a lot to prove before he's even allowed into a cockpit, believe me.'

'I would like to believe this,' she said on a sigh. 'But Stanislaw can be very persuasive.'

'Persuasive or not,' said Charlie thoughtfully, 'he won't get very far if he can't actually climb into the cockpit.' He must have seen the stricken look on Danuta's face, for he awkwardly patted her shoulder. 'Sorry, but it had to be said,' he mumbled.

Peggy took Danuta's hand. 'I know he won't be easy to live with if things don't go right for him, Danuta, but at least you'll have him back safe and sound.'

Danuta shot her a watery smile. 'But which is worse, Mama Peggy? A Polish man with bruised pride – or a Polish man determined to do or die? I am thinking neither is going to be easy.'

'If Stan's well enough to go off like that, then he must have been discharged from Cliffe,' said Peggy. 'Has he found somewhere to live?'

Danuta nodded. 'He has already spoken to Frank, and will rent one of the small houses from him in Tamarisk Bay.'

'But that's right out of the way of everywhere,' Peggy gasped. 'How's he going to get about?'

'He bought a car and it is being adapted for him at special factory in London. Until it is ready, I will be driving him.'

'Good Lord. He has been busy, hasn't he? Honestly, Danuta, you have the patience of a saint,' sighed Peggy, dipping into her stew. 'I hope he realises how lucky he is.'

Danuta laughed. 'I love him, but I am not afraid to tell him how I feel when he goes too far. Patience might be for saints, Peggy, but a hot temper can also work wonders.'

It was the first week in April and Stanislaw had been away at Biggin Hill for almost a month. Danuta had received a few letters from him, asking if his car was ready and if Frank and Ron had finished working on the little house in Tamarisk Bay. However, she'd noticed there were few and only very vague references to what was going on with him at Biggin Hill, which was most unusual, for Stan wasn't known for keeping things to himself, and she was beginning to wonder if he was in fact keeping his distance, unable to face her as he'd failed the course.

Danuta had gone up to Cliffe airfield to talk to the others, but it seemed they hadn't heard much from him either, and Roger had even hinted that they'd soon have to find someone else to share the flying hours, as by law there had to be a pilot and co-pilot on each flight. Dispirited, not only for herself but also for Stanislaw, she'd buried herself in work, and gone in her off-duty hours to check on how the repairs were going in Tamarisk Bay.

The cottage was right at the end of the short row and tucked into the natural curve of the low cliff that shelved down to the shingle beach. Frank had rented out the other two cottages to returning servicemen and their families as they waited to be rehoused, but this third and rather dilapidated little dwelling had slowly mouldered during the years it had been vacant, and it had taken time and a great deal of effort to make it habitable again.

That Saturday morning, Danuta parked her car alongside two others in the lee of a stand of bushes to one side of the steep track which led down to the beach, and gazed out to the sea which was sparkling in the bright sun. It was all very pretty, but utter madness for someone with Stan's disability to decide to live here. And yet that was typical of Stan.

She climbed out of the car and discovered that despite the sunny day there was a sharp wind. Wrapping her scarf round her neck, she made her way down the track, carefully avoiding the water-filled potholes which would have to be filled in if Stan had any chance of getting out.

There was no sign of Frank, but she assumed he was sleeping in after a night's fishing, so she walked along the paved path, past the outhouses to the last cottage. Finding it unlocked, she stepped inside and smiled. Frank had clearly been very busy these past few days, for the painting was finished, the wooden floors sanded, and the old cooking range had been given a fresh coating of blacking. All she had to do now was to find furniture, curtains, rugs and kitchen equipment to make it homely.

The cottage consisted of just three rooms with a lavatory, tin bath and hot water boiler in the outhouse that was tacked on at the front. The bedroom was on her right, the tiny kitchen on the left and the sitting room ran across the back, its large window giving a magnificent view of the sea and bringing light into the whole cramped space. Frank had painted the walls and ceilings white, the floors gleamed with fresh varnish, and the new windows were sturdy enough to keep out any draughts.

Danuta wandered from room to room, wondering how quickly Stan would find it claustrophobic, for he was a big man and needed lots of space around him. Yet she could imagine them sitting cosily in the sitting room of an evening to watch the moon slowly rise over the water before they snuggled up into the lovely big bed Rachel Goldman had promised them. Blushing at the thought, she dug her hands into her coat pockets and stared out of the window, not really seeing anything.

Stanislaw had yet to ask her to marry him, for he wanted to secure a future for them first. Neither had they had the chance to sleep together – not that they hadn't wanted to, but circumstances so far had made it impossible. But she sensed he would be a wonderful lover, for he was a passionate man who not only had the capacity for great gentleness, but a deep respect for her moods and feelings.

She wrapped her arms about her waist as she watched the sea lapping at the shingle. It had taken all her courage to tell him why she couldn't give him children, for he'd begun to talk about them having a son together. But he'd surprised her by tearfully taking her into his arms and telling her he'd rather live without children than lose her.

Remembering that she'd promised to fetch Cordelia's prescription from the chemist before it closed at lunchtime, she stepped outside and heard Frank talking to someone. She was about to greet him when she realised who was with him and quickly shot back behind the door to watch them getting into Frank's truck which was parked outside his house.

'Well, well, well,' she murmured with a giggle as Frank drove up the track and disappeared from sight. 'Now there's a surprise.'

She arrived back at Beach View with the cough medicine to find Peggy and Cordelia in a complete tizzy.

'Thank goodness you're back,' Peggy said the moment she stepped into the kitchen. 'We've got to go up to the airfield. Now hurry up.'

'But why? Is there an emergency? Will I need my medical bag?'

'I shouldn't think so,' said Peggy distractedly as she helped Cordelia on with her coat and handed her the walking stick. 'But it is very important, and if we don't get a move on we'll be too late.'

'Late for what? You are not making any sense.'

'It will all be explained soon enough,' Peggy replied, chivvying her into the hall. Peggy helped Cordelia down the steps and into her car. 'Do get a move on, dear,' she urged Danuta.

Danuta shut the front door behind her and ran down the steps to climb into the back seat, utterly confused. 'Where's Daisy?'

'She's with Charlie,' said Peggy. She started the engine and drove at reckless speed out of the cul-de-sac and up the road which would eventually take them to the airfield.

'I know you have a lot of questions, Danuta, but I need to concentrate on my driving,' she said firmly.

'Cordelia, do you know what all this is about?' she asked, leaning towards her.

'No dear, I haven't got gout. The arthritis is bad enough without that,' she replied calmly.

Danuta flopped back into the seat and folded her arms in frustration. It was clear Cordelia had switched off her hearing aid and Peggy was determined to keep her lips sealed about why they were now hurtling past the Cliffe estate and turning into the airfield so fast the tyres squealed in protest. The only thing she could think of was that Martin and the others had found another pilot and wanted to show him off.

Peggy brought the car to an abrupt halt by the office shed, and Danuta frowned as she saw almost the entire complement of crew and maintenance staff gathered there along with their families, Charlie, Anne and all the children. The only person missing seemed to be Kitty's husband Roger.

She helped Cordelia out of the car and regarded her steadily, for there was definitely a naughty twinkle in her eyes. 'What are you all up to, Grandma Cordy?'

'I couldn't possibly say,' she replied, hobbling off to sit on a chair Anne had brought out for her.

Danuta looked across at the single DC-47, and her heart sank. It looked as if they really had found another pilot, and Stanislaw had missed out. She turned to Peggy to ask again what was happening, but she just smiled back at her and pointed to the east.

'Look,' she said, 'Phoenix Air's right on time.'

Feeling sick at heart, Danuta watched the small speck in the sky take shape, and soon the sound of the powerful DC-47 engines drowned out any further possibility of talking as it circled overhead twice and then came in to land with a gentle bump before taxiing towards the end of the long runway.

The man in the control tower rushed down the steps as the engines were switched off and the propellers slowly stopped turning. The ground crew ran forward to place the chocks in front of the wheels and open the cargo door which was behind the wings. A set of steps was quickly placed beneath it, and everyone made their way towards it across the runway.

'Come on, dear,' said Peggy, taking her arm. 'You don't want to miss this.'

Reluctantly, Danuta went with her, wondering why Peggy couldn't see that this whole outing was turning into the most bitter of disappointments. *Poor Stanislaw*, she thought as she waited at the back of the eager crowd by the steps. *He'll be devastated to know he won't be part of all this.*

There was movement in the dark interior of the plane, and Roger ran cheerfully down the steps, and then all the men suddenly stood smartly to attention and saluted, making Danuta think that this new pilot must be someone very important indeed to warrant such attention.

Stanislaw walked awkwardly out of the shadows to stand in the doorway. His face was flushed and he had the broadest of smiles as he saluted back and everyone whistled and cheered.

Danuta nearly fainted. She couldn't believe what she was seeing. But there he was. Her Stanislaw – as large as life and twice as handsome in his Phoenix Air uniform, the peaked cap at a rakish angle over sparkling brown eyes, the gold bands of braid on his sleeve winking in the sun.

She met his gaze, felt someone nudge her forward and walked towards him in a daze. The rest of the world seemed to disappear until there were only the two of them, and as she climbed the steps and he reached for her hand, she was quite overwhelmed by love and pride.

'My darling little Danuta,' he managed through his tears of joy. 'I have done it. And it is all for you, my love – my dearest love.' He took her hands and kissed them. 'For us too,' he murmured, holding her gaze. 'I hope you will forgive me for not kneeling, but I've yet to learn how. But now I have good job, will you marry me?'

'Yes,' she breathed. 'Oh, yes, yes, yes.' She threw herself into his arms and almost knocked him off balance as a huge cheer went up from those watching down below.

He clung to her, laughing with such joy he didn't realise his face was wet with tears. 'I've come home, Danuta,' he finally whispered to her, placing a diamond ring on her finger. 'And together we will make a good life. I promise you.' He grinned. 'But first I must get down these steps.'

The men waiting below didn't wait for her to help him, but swept both of them up and carried them to the office hut on their shoulders. Stanislaw roared with delight. 'I have champagne,' he shouted. 'We must celebrate.'

Peggy was glad it was Sunday, for she was feeling the effects of too much champagne and excitement. The party had carried on long after she'd come back with Cordelia and Daisy, and she thought she'd heard Danuta stumbling in with Charlie at about two o'clock.

She tutted at the thought of her son drinking too much, and then concentrated on getting dressed and ready for the day. It had been the most romantic and heart-melting moment when Stanislaw had asked Danuta to marry him, and she wasn't ashamed of the fact that she and Cordelia had sobbed their way back to the hut to get stuck into the champagne.

Daisy was awake and playing quietly with her toys in her bedroom, so Peggy helped her to dress warmly and took her downstairs for breakfast. Cordelia was snoring quite happily, so she'd leave her to wake slowly and come down in her own time.

'Good heavens, Danuta. I didn't expect to see you this early,' she gasped as she saw the girl sitting at the table with a cup of tea.

'I was too excited to sleep,' she confessed, getting up to fetch the teapot. 'Stanislaw stayed the night with Anne and Martin because our house has no furniture. He is flying to France tomorrow with medical supplies, so we are going to the big market in Dover to see what we can find to make the place ready and comfortable for him.'

'I've got some old curtains and spare sheets and blankets,' said Peggy. 'But not much else, I'm afraid.'

'That is very kind, Mama Peggy. We are most grateful. Rachel has promised us a beautiful bedroom suite, but the room is so small, only the bed will fit in it. I hope Stanislaw doesn't feel too cooped up there. It's a very cosy little house.'

'I'm sure it will be fine for starters,' said Peggy comfortably, putting out cereal and orange juice for Daisy.

Danuta sipped her tea. 'By the way, there is something I meant to tell you yesterday, but in all the excitement it went out of my silly head.'

'Oh yes?'

'I think maybe it is secret, so you must promise not to say anything.'

Peggy was instantly alert. 'What is it?'

'I saw Frank yesterday, and he had a visitor.'

'Go on,' urged Peggy shifting to the edge of her chair. 'I promise I won't breathe a word, Danuta, but do get on with it. The suspense is killing me.'

'It was Brenda from the pub. They were holding hands and he kissed her cheek before driving off.'

Peggy sat back. 'Well I never,' she breathed. 'Good for Frank. It's time he saw a bit of life, and Brenda's a lovely woman – very loyal and hard-working, with a good sense of humour too. He'll be all right with her.'

Danuta frowned. 'When I first came to Beach View I'm sure someone told me she was married.'

Peggy nodded. 'She was. He signed up for the navy, working in the engine room, and got killed when the *Ark Royal* was sunk by a U-boat off Gibraltar, back in late '41.'

She gave a sigh. 'He was a nice man, and it was a shame they'd had no children. It took a long time for her to get over his death, but she found it a great distraction to work at the Anchor for Rosie, and she's almost become part of the fabric of the place.'

'Then I hope they will be happy. But isn't it a bit soon after Pauline left?'

'There's been little love between Frank and Pauline for years, and now their divorce has come through he's free to do as he pleases. If Brenda can give him what he's been missing all these years, then good luck to them both, I say.'

Danuta grinned. 'You never liked Pauline very much, did you?'

Peggy grinned back. 'Let's just say life is far more pleasant without her, and leave it at that, shall we?'

PART FIVE

27

Singapore

Jim swung the car into the Raffles driveway that April afternoon and parked in the shade of the palm trees. He climbed out, adjusted his hat and took the steps in two strides. Upon reaching the entrance foyer, he quickly made his way to the bar, ordered two Singapore Slings and then carried them to Elsa Bristow's office.

'Tiffin time,' he announced, kicking the door shut behind him.

'You must have read my mind,' said Elsa, turning from the now empty shelves with a smile. 'My goodness, you look pleased with yourself today, Jim.'

'That I am,' he said, handing her the glass frosted with condensation. 'Here's to the *Empress Aurelia* and all who sail in her.' He raised his glass and drank thirstily.

'So, your ship has finally come in,' she murmured. 'I'm glad for you, Jim. When do you sail?'

'Tomorrow on the early tide. We should be in England by the end of May, then it will take another half-day to get from Portsmouth to home – unless the trains haven't improved since I left, and there are the usual hold-ups and delays.' He grinned at her. 'I've prepared so many times for this day, that I won't actually believe I'm going home until I'm on the ship and sailing.'

'Well, I'm glad for you, Jim. You've been away from home for too long. Here's to a safe journey.' She sipped her drink and then lit a cigarette. 'I'm off at the end of the week too,' she said as they settled on either side of the empty desk. 'As you can see, my work here is all but done, and I'm missing my daughters.'

'Won't you miss Singapore?'

'Not really,' she admitted. 'I lived here for years when my husband was alive, but it's changed, and with the unrest simmering between differing factions as the elections loom, it doesn't feel like home any more. Besides,' she added, 'I much prefer the climate in Sydney. There are four seasons, and the humidity is much more bearable.'

'It'll be spring when I get back,' Jim said, 'but that's no guarantee that the weather will be nice. My Peggy said they've had a wet winter, and it doesn't look at all hopeful for a good spring or summer.'

'Ah, the famous English weather everyone moans about,' she said on a laugh. She shifted in her chair. 'I don't know why we're sitting in here. Let's go into the bar where it's comfortable, and I can buy you a drink for a change.'

'I'm sorry, Elsa, but I can't stay long. Jumbo will be boarding his ship soon, and I wanted to say goodbye to him.'

Her disappointment was clear, but she quickly covered it up with a smile. 'Oh, that is a pity, but of course, I quite understand. How come he isn't on the same ship as you?'

'He's going straight to Scotland on the *Stradivarius* to prepare a proper home for Myfanwy on the Isle of Skye. She'll return to Wales and stay with her family, and once he's sorted out somewhere decent to live, he'll go to fetch her and take her back there.'

He grinned. 'I don't think it's hit him yet that being married involves a huge amount of organisation and cost if he wants to keep his wife happy.'

'And what about you, Jim? What will you do when you get back?'

'Well, I was working as a projectionist in the local cinema, but that was blown up, and by the sound of it, there are no plans to build a new one, so that idea's out. Peggy tells me an old pal has started up a motor repair shop and is desperate to find a decent mechanic to help with the workload. But I'm not sure I want to do that.'

Elsa cocked her head and frowned. 'Why ever not, if it's something you're good at?'

Jim was thoughtful for a moment, as this particular subject had been worrying him for some time. 'I've learned a great deal about myself these past few years, especially during my time here in Singapore, and feel that I'm capable of doing much more than just mucking about with engines or selling second-hand cars. The plight of those men and women I interviewed has really struck a chord, and I'd like to find some way in which I could continue to help them.'

Elsa regarded him evenly. 'From what I understand, there isn't much help being offered by the governments for the Far East prisoners of war, or for their families. But if you really want to do some good, you should apply to the Royal British Legion. They've been helping servicemen and women since the previous war with all aspects of their repatriation. My husband was a staunch supporter of the work the Legion does, and I'm sure I could put in a good word for you.'

Jim shifted in his chair. 'That's kind of you, Elsa, but as the Legion is a charity, I'd still need to find a job that pays.'

'Not necessarily,' she replied briskly. 'There are positions within the charity which pay a salary.' She began to write on a slip of paper. 'If you're really serious about continuing your work with the prisoners of war, then this is the man you should get in touch with, and this is my Sydney address so you can keep me up to date.'

She handed him the slip of paper. 'Write and tell him what you've been doing here and give my name as a reference – we're old friends,' she added with an enigmatic smile.

He felt the weight of indecision lift from him as he tucked the note safely in his top pocket and got to his feet. 'I'll certainly give it a go,' he said, reaching for her hand. 'Thanks for everything, Elsa. It's been a pleasure knowing you. If you're ever in England, you must come to visit. I think you and Peggy would get on well – you're very alike.'

'I'll take that as a compliment, Jim,' she replied, shaking his hand warmly. 'And thank you for all the hard work you've done for us here. You've shown great compassion and understanding, and it has been a pleasure to work with you – but I shall miss our daily tiffin.'

He winked at her and settled his hat over his head. 'So shall I, Elsa. Have a safe journey home.'

Elsa sat back down and gave a wistful sigh as he closed the door behind him. Jim Reilly was not only handsome and charming company, but he'd brought colour and a delightful frisson of pleasure into her rather dull life – and in that one silly moment when he'd kissed her on the dance floor, she'd dared to hope it would lead to something more intimate.

She smiled at her foolishness and finished the drink. Jim might slip now and again, but she knew he would never really stray, for it was clear that Peggy was the light and love of his life. 'Lucky, lucky woman,' she murmured as she picked up her bag and headed for the bar.

Jim was also smiling as he left Raffles, for he knew Elsa would have liked to move things on between them, and it would have been awkward if she hadn't been worldly enough to realise it would have spoilt the friendship they'd forged over the months they'd worked together.

He liked her very much, for she reminded him of his Peggy, both in looks and character, and could be just as fierce when thwarted. If he hadn't been married to Peggy, then he might very well have taken things further, for he'd enjoyed kissing her that time. However, life was full of lovely women and it could get hazardous when his flirting was taken seriously and he had to talk his way out of difficult and often embarrassing situations.

He left Raffles for the last time, his hopes high that there really would be a position for him with the Legion, for it was work he knew he'd be good at, and at the same time he would gain enormous satisfaction from doing something worthwhile.

He drove back to the billet to find the place in chaos with men doing their last-minute packing and dashing in and out for one final drink or shopping expedition.

Jim ran up the stairs, hoping he wasn't too late to catch his old pal Jumbo before he left. Going into the room they shared, he saw Jumbo, resplendent in his kilt, filling yet another suitcase with linens and bolts of material.

'Good grief, Jumbo, you must have bought up the entire market,' he exclaimed.

'Well, I'll need all this and more to make a proper home for Myfanwy, and everything is so much cheaper here than at home,' he replied, tying a label to the handle.

'Typical penny-pinching Scotsman,' teased Jim, digging him in the ribs. 'Why not parcel it all up and post it back?'

Jumbo looked at him in wide-eyed horror. 'D'ye ken how much that would cost, Jim?'

Jim laughed. 'I have a fair idea, as I've posted enough stuff back home to fill a ship.' He slapped the other man's shoulder. 'Come on, you've time for a couple of beers before you have to leave for the port. I'm buying,' he added with a wink.

'Och, Jim, you go too far with your teasing. But I'll happily drink with ye one last time.'

Jim helped him load everything into the back of the army truck which would take it all to the docks. There was a bustle of pent-up excitement in the air as the Scottish contingent prepared to leave, and Jim warmly shook their hands and wished them a good journey as he probably would never see them again.

Jumbo refused to let his precious bagpipes out of his sight, so he carried them under his arm as they set off for the bar on the corner. They settled at a small table in the dark little bar that was cooled by several large fans hanging from the low ceiling. They drank beer with whisky chasers; talked about the good and bad times they'd shared over the past few years; toasted the comrades who hadn't made it back, and then discussed Jumbo's plans for a house-warming party once he and Myfanwy were settled.

'It's a bit far for me and Peggy to get to,' said Jim, downing his fourth whisky. 'But I promise to look into the price of train tickets.'

'Och, now who's counting their pennies, eh, Jim?' teased Jumbo. 'You'll have saved a fair whack of your wages and there's your demob money to come – so don't pretend you cannae afford it.'

'If my Peggy's done half the alterations to the house that she threatened to do, then I'll have very little money left,' Jim said gloomily before downing the cold beer in three large gulps.

Jumbo grinned, finished his beer and then reached for his bagpipes. 'How about one last tune before we say goodbye?'

'Aye, why not?' said Jim, wondering what on earth the Indian owners of the bar would say to having that racket in this confined space.

Jumbo blew air into the bag and the pipes whined and screeched for a bit and then he began to play a lovely, lilting Scottish tune that was unfamiliar to Jim.

The enormous Scotsman got to his feet and went outside as the owners and other customers covered their ears. He stood on the street corner, the sound less intrusive in the open air, but stirring enough to stop passers-by and still the other Scots who were now clambering into a fleet of army trucks.

The tune came to an end and Jumbo hitched the bagpipes under one arm as he flung his other round Jim's shoulders and squeezed him to his side. 'For a Sassenach, you're all right, Jim. It's been an honour and a privilege to know you. Keep your powder dry, my friend, and have a safe journey home.'

'I'll see you again, you old rogue,' replied Jim gruffly, 'even if it does cost me an arm and a leg to get to you.' He lightly punched Jumbo's muscled belly, feeling foolish to be so emotional about this parting. 'You'd better get a move on. The trucks are starting to leave.'

Jumbo grinned and strode off, kilt swinging, to clamber into the back of the last truck, showing off a good bit of hairy and very sturdy legs. As the truck pulled away, he saluted Jim before striking up a lively reel on his bagpipes.

Jim saluted back and stood in the street until the truck was out of sight and the sound of the bagpipes no longer drifted back to him. Turning away finally, he climbed back into the car to do one last circuit of the island before he had to return it to the motor pool.

Standing on the deck of the *Empress Aurelia* at sunrise on the next day, he leaned on the railings to say a last goodbye to the part of the world that had been his home and his hell for too many years. And yet there had been good times too, and he knew he had much to be grateful for.

He was the fittest he'd ever been, strong and healthy, his battle-scars merely fading reminders of how lucky he was when so many had not been as fortunate. And he'd surprised himself at his ability to do a job he'd never in a million years have applied for. It certainly boded well for the future, and the letter he'd posted last night to Elsa's friend in the Legion was the first step, for he knew now that he was capable of so much more than being a grease monkey for the rest of his life.

As the deep bass of the ship's hooter blasted out and they sailed through the Straits of Malacca, Jim said a final farewell to Jock and Philip and Amah – and all the men, women and children who would never return home.

443

He remained on deck in the blistering noonday heat until the coastline of Thailand was merely a blur on the distant horizon and the ship began to head into the Indian Ocean. He made his way to the bow, and as the troopship ploughed through that vast, glittering stretch of blue water his spirits soared.

'I'm coming home, Peggy,' he breathed. 'At long last, I'm coming home.'

28

Cliffehaven

Peggy was in a complete tizzy that April morning, for she'd received Jim's telegram telling her he was at long last boarding a ship for home, and he should be docking at Portsmouth in five weeks. However, beneath that happiness was a deep worry that simply wouldn't go away, for she hadn't heard from Ruby since before Christmas.

'I just don't know what to make of it,' she said to Cordelia as they sat at the kitchen table. 'Surely the snow must have melted by now, so why hasn't she written?'

Cordelia took off her glasses and set aside her newspaper. 'I don't know either,' she murmured with a frown. 'And it's very odd she hasn't let us know if the baby arrived safely.'

'That's what's really worrying me,' said Peggy fretfully. 'I have this awful feeling that something's gone horribly wrong over there, and she's afraid to tell us.'

'There's no point in speculating, Peggy dear, for it will drive us both mad.' She gave a sigh. 'I'm sure that if anything has gone wrong, she would have told us as soon as possible. She and Mike are probably having a honeymoon of sorts after he's been away throughout the winter, and looking after a baby is exhausting as well as time-consuming. I expect she's simply settling in at last and hasn't had time to write.'

Peggy nodded, feeling marginally reassured. 'You could very well be right, Cordy,' she said. 'And after all, it's what

445

we both wanted, isn't it – for her to find her feet and settle down in Canada?'

'It certainly is,' said Cordelia. 'So I suggest you stop worrying and imagining all sorts, and learn to be patient. We'll hear from her soon, I'm sure.'

She must have seen that Peggy was still to be totally convinced, for she patted her hand and softened her tone. 'Let's just be thankful our Jim's on his way home, and that we have Danuta's wedding to look forward to, and concentrate on them today.'

'Of course I must,' said Peggy, 'but the lack of news from Ruby has sort of taken the shine off everything.'

Cordelia clucked her tongue and looked up at the mantel clock. 'Aren't you supposed to be going to Sally's for a last fitting?'

'Lawks, I completely lost track of time,' Peggy gasped, rising hurriedly from the chair to pull on her jacket and collect her handbag. 'Daisy will be over at Anne's all day, so you don't have to worry about her, and Charlie's gone out with Ron before his last rugby match of the season this afternoon. Danuta's down at Tamarisk Bay, so there's no need to think about doing much for lunch, as it will only be us two.'

'Stop fussing and just go,' said Cordelia affectionately.

Peggy kissed her quickly and dashed out of the front door, thankful that Sally and John lived only three streets away at the bottom of the hill.

The terraced houses were over a hundred years old, and had once been cramped, single-storey fishermen's hovels. They sat at the eastern edge of the seafront facing the shingle beach where Frank and Brendon kept their trawlers, and the front doors opened directly onto the rough track that acted as a pavement.

The entire terrace had gone through many changes over the years as the fishermen left and young families had moved in and converted them into more habitable dwellings. Each one was now two-storeyed, with a bathroom tacked onto the back in the walled courtyard gardens.

Peggy always thought of them as dolls' houses, and in her many visits to Sally that impression remained, for the rooms were small and low-ceilinged with very little space to store anything. It wasn't really surprising that it had become impractical for a growing family, and Peggy knew that now Sally was expecting, she and John were trying to sell up so they could move somewhere with more room.

She waved to Ernie and Harry who were playing on the beach, and her rap on the brass knocker was quickly answered by Sally, who was looking extremely well in her first months of pregnancy.

'Hello, Auntie Peggy,' she said, giving her a hug before leading her into the front room. 'You'll have to excuse the mess, but I ain't had time to tidy up this morning.'

Peggy smiled, for this radiant, happy girl had come a very long way from the slums of London where she'd been sole carer for her crippled brother Ernie, and her future had seemed so bleak. 'I don't mind,' she said, looking round the rather cluttered space which John had converted into a sewing room.

Shelves on one wall held the carefully folded piles of fabric Sally had harvested and laundered from old ballgowns, cocktail and wedding dresses, evening capes, skirts and coats. The lace, fur and beaded trimmings she'd carefully snipped from them were neatly wound over squares of cardboard.

A rail took up another wall and held the dresses, suits, skirts and blouses she'd made which were waiting to be picked up. A tailor's dummy stood in the corner, sheathed in a length of white sheeting, and was reflected in the long mirror at its side. And under the window were her cutting table, sewing machine and chair, with two small chemist cabinets beneath that held cottons, needles, pins and all the other small bits and pieces she needed to make her clothes look special.

Peggy eyed the tailor's dummy with barely contained inquisitiveness. 'Is that Danuta's wedding dress?' she asked eagerly.

'No. I put that somewhere you can't see it,' replied Sally, shooting her a grin. 'Honestly, Auntie Peggy, you are terrible.'

She looked out at her brother and son who were now throwing pebbles into the sea, and pulled the blind over the window before removing the sheet to reveal the deep sapphire dress and bolero that Peggy would be wearing to Danuta's wedding next weekend.

'It looks lovely,' breathed Peggy, quickly stepping out of her skirt and taking off her blouse to reveal her patched petticoat and rather grey bra, which reminded her she really should go and buy some decent underwear before Jim came home.

Sally held the dress for her to step into, and once she'd fastened the long zipper at the back, Peggy looked at herself in the mirror. The square neckline was flattering, the short sleeves hid her rather untoned upper arms and the colour enhanced the dark of her hair and eyes and brought light to her tired face.

The dress had once been an evening skirt; now it skimmed over her small breasts and was elegantly draped over her narrow hips to reach to just below the knee in a tulip-shaped hem.

'It looks wonderful, Sally,' she said in delight. 'I just wish I could put on a bit of weight and be five years younger.'

'We'd all like to be younger, thinner, fatter, taller or smaller, Auntie Peggy,' Sally giggled as she got down on her knees to pin the hem. 'Us women are never satisfied, are we? Now, how high would you like this hem?'

'Keep it mid-knee, dear, if you wouldn't mind. My legs are too skinny to show off.' She stood very still as Sally measured and pinned. 'How's this pregnancy going, Sally?'

'The doctor's happy I'm over the first three months. He thinks I should carry this one full term as long as I don't do nothing daft.'

'That is good news,' Peggy murmured in relief. 'I know how cut up you were last time.'

'Things are very different now,' she replied, getting to her feet again. 'I'm at home with John, relaxed and happy and not living in fear of bombs dropping on me 'ead.' She checked the level of the hem again with a long wooden ruler. 'There, how's that?'

'Perfect,' said Peggy. She pulled on the bolero and turned this way and that to regard the effect. 'It's all absolutely lovely.' She gave the girl a hug. 'You are clever.'

Sally grinned impishly and helped Peggy out of her finery. 'I've come a long way from that first day at Solly's factory, ain't I? And I'm ever so pleased, because it means John and I can afford a bigger place once we sell this.'

'How's that going?' Peggy asked, buttoning her blouse.

'We've accepted an offer,' she said, 'and are hoping to be moving in about six weeks' time if the solicitors get a move on, and the buyers don't change their minds. We've had our offer accepted on a house close to Betty and Brendon on the old Chumley estate.'

Sally gave a contented sigh. 'Ever so lovely it is, with four big bedrooms, three receptions, kitchen, bathroom and a big garden for the kids. I never thought in a million years I'd 'ave a place like that, and won't really believe it until we move in.'

'Gosh, I didn't realise any of them were for sale. They were only built last year.'

'Yeah, we was lucky, cos Brendon tipped us the wink that their neighbours wanted to move back to Derby to be nearer their daughter and grandchildren, so we jumped straight in the minute we knew we 'ad a buyer.'

'It'll be a bit of a journey to school each day for Ernie and Harry,' said Peggy.

'They can come in on their bikes if the weather's good, and if not, John will drive 'em in on his way to work as the school's only opposite the fire station.' She smiled happily. 'They're ever so excited to 'ave a room each at last, and I can't wait to get my sewing room all kitted out. So as long as nothing goes wrong, we're all sorted really.'

'Charlie and I will come and help John and Ernie with the packing,' said Peggy. 'I don't want you lifting heavy things and getting overtired.' She dug in her handbag and pulled out her purse. 'How much do I owe you, Sally?'

'Nothing, so you can put that purse away,' she replied, steering Peggy towards the door.

Peggy dug her heels in. 'I'm not leaving without paying, Sally. You've put a lot of work into that outfit, and I wouldn't feel right wearing it if I haven't paid the proper price for it.'

'You'll have to go to the wedding in your old clothes then,' she replied on a giggle. 'Cos I ain't taking a penny from you after all you done for me and Ernie.'

Peggy realised the girl wouldn't budge, so deliberately ignored her jacket and went out into the hall as if she was about to leave. 'Oh dear, I don't know where my head is today. I seem to have left my jacket in your sewing room.'

As Sally turned back to fetch it, Peggy slipped some money into the pocket of the girl's jacket which was hanging from a hook in the hall, and dropped her purse into her handbag.

Sally returned with her jacket. 'Oh, thank you. dear. I'd forget my head if it wasn't screwed on today. You see, I got a telegram from Jim this morning to say he was finally on his way home.'

'Oh, Auntie Peggy, that's brilliant news,' Sally exclaimed, giving her a hug and kiss.

'Yes, it is,' she agreed, returning the affectionate embrace. 'The Reilly family have got a lot to look forward to what with the wedding and Jim coming home.'

She left the house just as Ernie and Harry rushed up the beach, no doubt in search of something to eat. Ernie was a strapping lad of thirteen now who no longer needed the callipers, and young Harry was growing like a weed too, she noticed, slipping them each a threepenny bit before heading home.

Walking up the hill she began to wonder if she'd put enough money in Sally's pocket. And yet it was more than Solly's machinists would have earned for the hours taken to make that lovely outfit – and this did ease her conscience a little. With a new baby on the way, they would need all the money they could get if they were about to move up to the Chumley estate.

Returning to Beach View, Peggy found a note from Cordelia who'd left with Bertie to have lunch at the golf club. Realising she had the rest of the day to herself, she made a quick cup of tea and then headed into town to buy new underwear, and then go up to see Stan and April at the stationmaster's house.

It had come as a terrible shock to everyone in Cliffehaven when it was announced that the station was to close, for being a seaside town the local businesses relied heavily on the trains to bring in the tourists.

Rosie, who was on the council now, knew that if they lost this vital link the town would die, and she had immediately started up a fierce campaign to stop the closure, by gathering hundreds of signatures, talking to the press and generally making herself a thorough nuisance to the railway company. When it seemed she was getting nowhere, she went with the mayor and half the town council to both Downing Street and the railway company headquarters to present the petition and plead their case.

She'd been partially successful in that the trains would still come to Cliffehaven, but the station would no longer be manned. Poor Stan had been forcibly retired on a good pension, and the people of Cliffehaven had thrown him a huge party to thank him for the years he'd spent looking after everyone. The railway company gave him a gold pocket watch, demolished the signal box and the remains of the booking hall and waiting room, and that had been that.

Stan had been desolate to think he was no longer useful, but with his niece April's encouragement, his allotment was now flourishing, and he'd begun to sell his produce to Sam the greengrocer, which gave him some extra pocket money.

Danuta had worried about wearing white on her wedding day, for she'd borne a child with Jean-Luc and was far removed from the innocent young girl who'd fled Poland all those years ago. However, Stanislaw seemed to expect her to be dressed like a traditional bride as they were marrying in St Cuthbert's church, and after discussing it with Peggy, Danuta had bowed to her wisdom and chosen white lace, which wasn't rationed.

She'd always hidden her ugly scars and had dreaded Sally seeing them and asking difficult questions when she'd gone for her initial fitting. But Sally had been discretion itself as she'd measured her and then pinned the fabric around her, and the subject never arose.

Now, at last, it was her wedding day, and Danuta shivered in anticipation as the cool lining of her beautiful dress slithered over her skin. She stood patiently in front of the long mirror as Peggy fastened the concealed zipper at the back, and fussed over the froth of lace which fell from the knees to swirl around her satin shoes into a sweeping train.

She couldn't believe how different she looked, and felt a thrill of excitement at how Stanislaw would react when he saw her.

'You look stunning,' breathed Peggy as she stood behind her and gazed at her reflection. 'Stan's going to faint when he sees you.'

Danuta giggled. 'I hope not, because if he goes down it will take four men to get him on his feet again.'

She took Stanislaw's gift of crystal earrings and necklace from the velvet-lined box, and once they were in place, she turned this way and that to see the effect of the sun shining on them and the tiny sequins stitched into the column of lace that moulded to her slender body, and the way the froth of lace swirled around her feet. Sally had padded and wired the close-fitting, heart-shaped bodice so it stayed firmly in place and didn't really need the support of the wide satin straps.

'Beautiful,' sighed Peggy, her eyes bright with tears.

'We must be careful to pin the veil very tightly,' Danuta said. 'For if it falls and I look back, it is a very bad luck for Polish bride.'

Peggy took the gossamer veil and carefully fixed the sparkling comb into Danuta's glossy dark curls, anchoring it firmly with hairpins. Fluffing it out around the girl's shoulders to her satisfaction, she stepped back and handed her the sweet-scented posy of early white roses and lily of the valley that young April had made from her uncle's allotment.

'Perfect,' she sighed. 'You really are the most beautiful bride, Danuta, and I'm so proud and happy to be with you on this special day.' She softly kissed her cheek. 'I'll tell Ron he can come up now.'

'Wait, one more moment, Mama Peggy.' She set aside the posy and took her hands. 'I want to tell you that I love you with my heart. You have given me so very much, and I will never forget that. And although I am to be Stanislaw's wife, I will always be your daughter.'

'Oh, Danuta, I never for a moment thought I would lose you.' Peggy blinked rapidly on her tears to stop them ruining her make-up. 'We have a saying in England, that a son is a son until he gets him a wife, but a daughter's a daughter for all of her life – and I firmly believe that's true. Now, I must fetch Ron, or we'll be in danger of arriving late at the church.'

Danuta's heart was full as Peggy left the room, for although her Polish family were gone, she knew they'd be watching her now, happy in the knowledge that she'd been truly blessed in the loving second family she'd found here in England – and in the man who was soon to be her husband.

Peggy had to take a moment to repair her make-up before she went down to tell Ron he was needed and to make sure Cordelia and Rosie were ready to be driven to the church. Daisy, Rose and Emily were to be bridesmaids and they had gone ahead with Anne. Martin was best man, and was probably having a hard time of it to keep Stanislaw calm, but knowing the emotional Pole, Peggy suspected there would be many happy tears shed before the day was out, so she made sure she and Ron had plenty of handkerchiefs.

The drive out to St Cuthbert's was very pleasant as the sun was shining, the blossom was bursting out in all the trees, and the grassy banks on either side of the road were jewelled with bluebells, anemones and bright yellow crocus.

She parked the car, noting that Anne was waiting with the children by the ancient church's steps, the new priest chatting happily with every guest as they arrived. The grumpy old priest Ron had sparred with over many years had finally retired, and Father Finlay was a breath of fresh air, for he'd served as a padre in the navy throughout the war and had a terrific sense of humour.

Peggy took Cordelia's arm and followed Rosie into the cool, dark church which had stood here since Saxon times. The ancient stained-glass windows glowed with the sun, emitting a rainbow of colour into the small church to chase away the shadows and bring a sense of warmth. The altar was dressed in white, and April had once again come up trumps by decorating the church with beautiful flowers. She and her Uncle Stan, the now retired stationmaster, smiled a welcome as Peggy walked down the aisle to the soft organ music and low murmur of the wedding guests.

Everyone had made a terrific effort, Peggy realised, as she saw the smart suits, big hats and pretty dresses. Charlotte, Kitty and Roger sat with their three small toddlers; Sally was with John, Ernie and Harry; Solly and Rachel were sitting with Doris, and a large contingent from the airfield had turned up with their families, as had the district and hospital nurses from both Cliffe and the Memorial.

Peggy guided Cordelia into the front pew and caught sight of Frank, who looked back at her rather sheepishly as he sat cosily next to Brenda who appeared to be extremely happy to be there. She grinned at him to let him know she approved and then sat down.

'Danuta told me they were seeing one another ages ago,' she confided in a whisper to Cordelia. 'But this is the first time they've been seen together as a couple.'

'Well, it's about time,' said Cordelia, turning to wave and smile at them. 'I guessed weeks ago.'

They settled down to wait for the bride, and Peggy watched Stanislaw and Martin who were sitting in the front row of the crowded choir stalls and quietly talking together. They looked very handsome in the Phoenix Air uniform which closely resembled that of the RAF, and had pinned on their medals in honour of the occasion.

The old oak door creaked alarmingly and Father Finlay came up the aisle with a beaming smile.

Stanislaw and Martin got to their feet as he approached, and Peggy noted that Stanislaw had gone the most interesting shade of green. She hoped fervently that he wouldn't faint, but it seemed Father Finlay was well prepared for nervous grooms, for he surreptitiously dug a brandy flask from his pocket. Once both men had taken a restorative nip, he hid it back beneath his white cassock and turned to the congregation.

'If you would, please rise to welcome the bride.'

The organ music soared to the rafters as Danuta slowly came down the aisle on a very proud Ron's arm. Her beautiful dress glittered and shimmered as she moved, and her lovely face was positively radiant beneath the veil that drifted around her shoulders.

Peggy glanced away to Stanislaw whose look of adoration spoke volumes as tears began to fill his eyes and slowly trickle down his face, but Martin had clearly come prepared, for he handed him a handkerchief.

Danuta floated past on Ron's sturdy arm, her gaze never leaving the man who waited for her. The little girls were wearing the same dresses they'd had for Rita's wedding, their coronets of lily of the valley firmly pinned in place. It seemed they were getting the hang of being bridesmaids, for they behaved perfectly.

'I never realised how beautiful our little Danuta is,' said Cordelia, mopping up her tears.

'Beautiful inside and out,' murmured Peggy tearfully, watching the groom meet his bride at the steps to lovingly kiss her hand.

The service was a long one as is the Catholic tradition, with hymns and prayers and the couple taking communion, and Peggy noticed that Danuta had surreptitiously let the hem of her dress cover the top of Stanislaw's shoe, which according to Polish superstition would give her prominence in the partnership. This made Peggy smile, for they were both as fiery and stubborn as each other, and she'd be most interested to see who emerged the stronger.

Father Finlay surprised everyone by conducting the vows in Polish, and once they and the rings had been exchanged, he encouraged Stanislaw to kiss his bride, which he did with such alacrity, he had everyone chuckling.

Peggy, Ron and Cordelia had been fully advised on the etiquette and tradition of a Polish wedding so weren't at all surprised when Stanislaw's fellow Poles showered them with small coins along with the confetti as they emerged from the church.

Photographs were taken on the steps and by the lychgate, and then the happy couple followed the priest into the cemetery to lay flowers on the graves of Aleksy and Katarzyna, and bow their heads as he said a prayer for them in Polish.

The wedding party finally moved to the Officers' Club where the reception room had recently been updated and extended to twice the size with a sprung dance floor and huge windows overlooking the coastline. Everyone crowded in to wait for the bride and groom, and when they arrived, they were presented with a specially baked loaf of bread sprinkled with salt, as was the tradition. The bread was to ensure they never went hungry; the salt a reminder of life's difficulties and the importance of learning to cope.

Ron stepped forward with two glasses – one filled with water, the other with vodka. It was the bride who had to choose which one to take first, for whoever had the vodka would be the dominant one throughout the marriage. Danuta looked at Ron for a clue, but he merely grinned and refused to say anything.

Stanislaw roared with delight as he drank the vodka. He lifted his glass high, and Danuta followed suit, and then, to protect the new floor, they wrapped them in napkins and smashed them beneath their feet.

The vodka was now flowing and the guests presented the happy couple with envelopes containing money before they sat down to enjoy the first course of cheeses and cold meat which Phoenix Air had flown in the day before from Holland. As the vodka continued to flow and the second course arrived, there were constant shouts of 'Gorzko! Gorzko!' urging the couple to kiss, which they did very happily.

'We're in for a very long session,' Peggy warned Cordelia, who was really getting into the swing of things. 'So take it easy with the drink.'

Cordelia just laughed and knocked back her third vodka.

The imported food kept on coming, the vodka kept on flowing, and by midnight, Cordelia was asleep in an armchair, and Anne had taken the girls home to bed, so they missed the moment when Danuta's veil was removed to be replaced by a wedding cap to signify her passage from girlhood to wife. It was traditionally given by the bride's godmother, but Peggy had been given that honour and she'd placed the cap Sally had made on the girl's shining curls and kissed her cheek, wishing her all the luck in the world.

All the single men and women were lined up at each end of the dance floor, and Stanislaw took Danuta into the centre. He threw his tie to the men while she threw her veil to the women, and like the English custom of catching the bouquet, whoever caught the veil and tie would be married within a year – although not necessarily to each other.

The wedding cake was cut, and then the band struck up and Stanislaw took his bride into his arms and managed a full turn of the floor before they were joined by everyone else. From that moment on the party really got going, and the eating, drinking, dancing and endless toasts continued until the sky grew light and breakfast was served.

29

Ruby stubbed out her cigarette as the train chugged slowly to a halt at Cliffehaven station that Sunday afternoon. She returned her silver cigarette case and lighter to her leather handbag and stood to check her appearance in the small mirror below the luggage rack. Her eyes told of her profound sadness, but otherwise she looked reasonably calm and ready to face whatever happened next – although inside, it was a different story altogether. Adjusting her hat and touching the pearls at her neck, she pulled her expensive overcoat on over her two-piece costume, slung the strap of her handbag over her shoulder and gathered up her suitcases.

This was the sort of homecoming she'd never dreamed she'd make, and as she stepped down from the train, memories of the last time she'd been here came flooding in and made her falter. She'd been so happy then – so in love and excited about the future – a future that had ultimately betrayed her and brought her back.

Gripping the cases, she determinedly began to walk down the platform, noting that the damaged buildings and old signal box had been removed, and there was no longer a Nissen hut for the left luggage, but a large car park and bus stop had been constructed in their place. Peggy had written to tell her the station was no longer manned, and she could only feel relief that she wouldn't bump into Stan and have to answer his numerous questions, for there was only one person she wanted to talk to, and that was Peggy.

However, she missed not seeing him in his customary place on the platform, for he'd been her saviour on that night four years ago when she'd arrived here, bruised and battered with nowhere to go and no one to turn to. And now she was back, once again in need of comfort, but this time her bruises and scars were hidden deep inside her, and she doubted they'd ever fully heal. Glancing towards the stationmaster's cottage, she quickly turned away to walk down the quiet Sunday afternoon High Street, her high-heeled shoes tapping on the pavement.

She reached Camden Road, but to avoid having to pass the Anchor where she might be seen, she went down to the promenade and sat in one of the renovated Victorian shelters. Dumping the cases at her feet, she pulled up her collar against the chilly wind and stared out over the grey waters of the English Channel.

All the while she'd been in Canada the hours had felt like days, the weeks like months, but in reality it hadn't been very long at all, and nothing much had changed here. But she had changed, the inner steel she'd always relied upon coming to the fore again and proving to her that whatever fate threw at her, she was a survivor. And yet it had taken huge courage to find that strength of purpose when her world had collapsed to leave her floundering in a sea of pain, the likes of which she'd never experienced before – and hoped to God she never would again.

Ruby watched the sea glisten in the hazy sun, not yet ready to face Peggy and Cordelia, even though it was to them that she'd returned in search of love and warmth and unfailing support. This was home, and Peggy's Beach View the one place in the world where she might be able to begin again and look to the future – a future that until now had seemed so very bleak. She lit a cigarette and allowed the memories to return, of that moment when her life had begun to disintegrate.

The snow had been falling steadily ever since she'd kissed Mike goodbye and waved him off with his father as they'd set out for the logging camp. She'd known she wouldn't see him until the spring thaw, and the silent white world had seemed to close in around her as the tree branches bowed beneath the weight of the snow, and icicles hung from the eaves of the log house.

If she hadn't been so frightened for the baby she was carrying, she might have acknowledged how pretty it was, and how cosy it could be inside the house with the range fire glowing. But all she could think of was the fact the doctor was miles away, and if things went wrong, he might not be able to get to her, and she'd have to rely on Mike's mother, Claudine, for help.

Christmas came with Mike's gift of pearls, and a rare two-way radio call from him and his father to wish them a happy day, but the atmospherics made it difficult to hold anything more than a very brief exchange, so it had been most unsatisfactory, leaving her feeling more isolated than ever.

As the New Year had approached, she'd been almost six months pregnant, but suffering from what Claudine called 'cabin fever', so she'd wrapped up in thick coat, boots, gloves, hat and woolly scarf to go outside and fetch some small logs for the fire.

The air had been crisp and dry, but so cold it almost took her breath away, and as she'd glanced at the barometer hanging outside the door, she'd seen it was twenty-nine degrees below freezing – and yet the sky was the clearest blue, the sun making the snow blinding white in the glare.

The stack of wood the men had cut to see them through the winter was piled against the house at the end of the veranda which had been heavily gritted by Claudine just that morning. She'd edged carefully along, but suddenly her feet skidded and slipped on an icy patch, and before she knew it, she'd fallen awkwardly and hit the railing hard before tumbling down the steep flight of steps to land face first in the snow, the wind knocked out of her.

She'd thought at first that the soft landing might have saved her baby, but she was suddenly wracked by a terrible stabbing pain and she'd begun to scream for Claudine, her cries echoing in the dull, dead silence of the thick snow and surrounding trees.

Ruby blinked and tried hard to dispel the horrific memory of that day, but she knew it would live with her always. It had taken six hours for the doctor to arrive by husky-pulled sled, but by then her precious little girl had been stillborn. Ruby still felt the inconsolable pain of losing her, which merely stoked her abiding hatred for the white wilderness that had brought it about.

She stubbed out her cigarette, got to her feet and squared her shoulders, ready now to face Peggy, and explain her reason for coming back.

Peggy had been feeling the after-effects of the wedding for most of that Sunday, even though she'd brought Cordelia and Charlie home shortly after one o'clock in the morning. The copious amounts of rich, imported food and vodka meant that neither Peggy nor Cordelia were very hungry, and even Charlie had been satisfied with just soup and sandwiches for his lunch before he went off with Ron to visit Frank.

As it was the Easter school holidays, Anne was keeping Daisy with her until the morning, so the kitchen was peaceful that late afternoon. With the radio playing softly in the background, Peggy and Cordelia sat by the fire drinking tea.

'I hope the happy couple aren't feeling as tired as we are,' Peggy said.

'I shouldn't think so,' Cordelia replied. 'They'll be far too busy enjoying their honeymoon in the Cotswolds. Stanislaw told me he was going to fly them up there, but thank goodness Roger refused to let him and did the honours himself. The amount Stanislaw drank yesterday was enough to sink a battleship.'

Peggy giggled. 'You didn't do too badly yourself,' she teased.

'Well, it was a wedding, Peggy, and I got to rather like the taste of vodka.'

Peggy was about to reply when there was a knock on the door. She glanced up at the clock and frowned before dragging herself reluctantly out of her chair. 'It's a bit late in the day for visitors,' she muttered.

She opened the door and was momentarily lost for words at the sight of Ruby standing there looking extremely well-to-do but exhausted, with dark circles under her eyes.

'I'm ever so sorry to turn up like this so unexpected, Auntie Peg. Would it be all right if I stayed for a while?'

Peggy put her arms about her and held her close. 'Oh, Ruby, darling, of course you can stay for as long as you like.' She looked into her wan little face, noting the dullness of her eyes, and felt a pang of dread. Clearly the girl was deeply troubled. The questions were numerous, but they would have to wait. 'Come in,' she urged, taking one of the heavy cases.

Ruby stepped into the hall, put down her case and gazed round in astonishment. 'Blimey,' she breathed. 'You really did do the place up, didn't you? I thought it looked right smart outside, but this is really posh.'

Still fretting that Ruby's solitary arrival boded ill, Peggy nevertheless shot her a smile. 'You wait until you see the rest. But first, let's get your coat off, and then we can sit down and have a cup of tea. Have you eaten?'

'I 'ad a plate of pie and mash in London,' she replied. 'But a cuppa would go down a treat, Auntie Peg.' She shrugged off her good quality coat to reveal a smart two-piece skirt and jacket, with a white silk blouse beneath it and a string of pearls around her neck.

Peggy made no comment on the expensive clothes, for they were merely another puzzle to be solved later. She led the way into the kitchen. 'Look who's here, Cordy,' she said brightly. 'Isn't she a lovely surprise?'

'Well, goodness me,' gasped Cordelia, returning Ruby's affectionate kiss of welcome. 'Don't you look the bee's knees?'

Ruby smiled. 'Not 'alf as smart as this kitchen,' she replied, taking it all in. 'But I'm glad it ain't changed too much and you kept them old chairs.' She perched on the edge of a kitchen chair, her pencil-slim skirt inching back to reveal slender, shapely legs clad in nylon stockings.

She opened her leather handbag and offered Peggy a cigarette from a silver case. Having lit them both with a matching lighter, she must have seen the others eyeing these expensive accessories with confusion, for she shrugged. 'Yeah, smart, ain't they? But they come at a cost, so don't be envious.'

Peggy placed a cup of tea at her elbow and sat down next to her. 'What happened, Ruby? Why haven't you written back to us?'

Ruby took a sip of tea. 'I didn't write cos what I 'ad to say weren't something to be told in a letter. I'm ever so sorry if you was worried, but things were happening so fast, I barely had time to breathe these last few months.'

Peggy took her hand, sensing that despite the girl's outward show of calm, it hid a world of pain, and she needed to talk. 'I'm just thankful you're home, Ruby. Do you want to tell us what happened?'

Ruby sipped at the tea, the cup rattling in the saucer, her unsteady hand revealing her inner turmoil as she told them how she'd lost her baby. 'Mike and I had decided on a name should the baby be a girl, so I called her Louise,' she said finally. 'Claudine and I buried her in the family plot behind the house, and said prayers for her as the vicar was too far away to get to us until the thaw.'

'But surely Mike was with you, wasn't he?' asked Peggy sharply.

Ruby shook her head. 'They had dogs and sleds, but there'd been an avalanche which they couldn't get round.' She took a shallow breath. 'I really resented him for not being with me, and ranted and raved against him, the snow and the logging camp for keeping him away. All we 'ad to stay in touch were the two-way radio, and the signal were that bad, it were almost impossible to talk proper or hear what he were saying.'

She dipped her chin. 'I'm ashamed to admit that I said a lot of hurtful things to him, even though I knew it weren't his fault, but I was hurt and in terrible pain – I just needed him with me.'

'Of course you did,' murmured Cordelia, coming to sit on her other side. 'You must have felt quite abandoned. But what I don't understand is why he's not with you now?'

Biting her lip, Ruby ground out her cigarette. 'There was an accident at the camp. His dad reckons he was distracted cos of what were happening with me, and didn't check the chain he'd used to hold a stack of timber they was hauling up on a crane to lift it to the riverbank. The chain snapped or came loose and the timber fell right on him.' She took a quavering breath and closed her eyes. 'He didn't stand a chance,' she finished softly.

'Oh, Ruby, my dearest girl,' gasped Peggy, clutching her hand. 'I don't know what to say.'

Ruby managed a fleeting smile which didn't reach her eyes. 'There ain't nothing anyone can say, Auntie Peg. It's what 'appens in a place like that.' She clenched her fist, her expression hardening. 'And I've never hated a place so much. It took everything I loved, Peg, and I couldn't wait to get out of there.'

Peggy had no words to ease her awful pain but knew instinctively that Ruby needed her love and warmth and the assurance that now she was home, she'd never have to leave again. She drew the girl to her, expecting tears, and was surprised when Ruby remained dry-eyed during their long embrace.

Ruby finally drew back. 'I ain't got no more tears left,' she explained. 'But I knew I was right to come back to Beach View, cos it's where I can start to make sense of it all and begin again.'

She brushed her dark skirt with her fingertips and gave a sigh. 'Nothing and no one will ever replace them, but Mike left me with more than enough money to make my life much easier, so the days of working in a factory are over.'

'Well, it's good you can be financially independent,' said Cordelia, drying her eyes. 'But you'll need to invest it wisely. I can put you in touch with the chap who advises me, if you'd like.'

'Thanks, Grandma Cordy. I might take you up on the offer once I get me bearings again.'

'I didn't realise Mike had much to leave you,' said Peggy, pouring more tea.

'He didn't before we was married,' she replied. 'But 'is dad made him a partner in the family business as a wedding gift. It's big and very successful, with the logging, pulping, timber and paper mills and fleet of heavy lorries, so when Mike were killed, I inherited his third share.'

She reached into her handbag, pulled out a silver brandy flask and added a tot to each cup. 'To help keep out the cold,' she said lightly. 'The freezing winter is still in me bones, and I reckon it'll be a while before I ever really feel warm again.'

'So you're part owner of a huge business in Canada,' murmured Peggy as she appreciatively sipped the alcoholic tea. 'Won't it be difficult to keep tabs on it from over here?'

'I didn't want nothing to do with any of it,' Ruby said flatly. 'So the minute the thaw come, I went to Quebec City and got advice on how much it were worth, and then sold my share back to Gerard and Claudine.' Her smile was wry. 'I think they was relieved, cos they knew I were never going to stay on without Mike, and it would 'ave complicated things.'

'You're very wise for someone so young,' said Peggy.

Ruby shrugged. 'I've had to think on me feet since I were a nipper, so it made sense to clear things up once and for all so I could come 'ome and start again without being tied to the past.' She gave a deep sigh. 'Though there's still a tiny part of me in Canada, lying in the family cemetery – and it was very hard to leave them behind.'

'Well, you take your time deciding what you're going to do, Ruby,' said Peggy. 'You're home now, so you can be a lady of leisure for a while and really think things over. You don't want to be rushing into anything while you're still grieving.'

Ruby smiled. 'Oh, but I already know what I'm going to do,' she said. 'Mike and I talked about it when he realised how much I hated living in Canada, and before he left for the winter, he promised he'd talk to his dad about it.'

Peggy looked at her questioningly. 'So you were planning to come back, even then?'

Ruby nodded. 'We thought that if the Anchor were still for sale, we'd take it on.'

'But you wouldn't still do that, would you?' gasped Peggy. 'Not without Mike?'

Ruby grinned. 'Rosie ran it on her own for years, and made a huge success of it. So why shouldn't I follow in her footsteps?' She squeezed Peggy's fingers. 'I need a challenge, Auntie Peg – something to take me mind off all what's happened and be part of the community here again.'

'Well, it will be all that and more,' said Peggy. 'And Rosie will be delighted to know you'll be stepping into her shoes.' She eyed Ruby's leather high heels. 'I see you're already very well equipped in that department,' she teased.

Ruby giggled and gave her a hug. 'I'm ever so glad I'm 'ome at last, Auntie Peg,' she breathed. 'I've missed you something awful.'

Ron had gone out early with the dogs and Rosie was getting ready for the bank holiday rush at lunchtime that Monday morning, her thoughts on Ruby as she dried the last of the glasses and set them on the shelf below the bar. Peggy had telephoned the previous evening and told her of the double tragedy that had befallen Ruby, and had hinted that the girl had an interesting proposition to make to her.

It hadn't taken Rosie long to guess what that proposition might be, but if Ruby was really serious about taking over the Anchor, then she deserved to know that the pub trade was in the doldrums, with shortages of rationed beer and spirits, the like of which hadn't been seen since the Depression.

She heard the rap on the window and saw Ruby peering in at her from the pavement. As it was still some time before opening, she signalled to her to come through the side entrance and went to greet her. 'Hello, love, Peggy told me you were back,' she murmured, giving her a hug.

'I expect she also told you why I wanted to see you,' said Ruby.

'Only in the vaguest terms,' said Rosie tactfully. 'Come into the bar so we can talk privately before I have to open up. Do you want a drink?' Ruby shook her head and Rosie sat down. 'So, what's this proposal, Ruby?'

'I'd like to buy the Anchor,' she said without preamble. 'I've worked here, so I know it's a good, profitable pub with a steady local trade that increases over the holiday periods. What's your asking price?'

Rose grinned, pleased the girl was so quick in coming to the point. 'Two thousand pounds, including goodwill, the freehold, bar fixtures, fittings and furniture,' she replied. 'The stock would be extra, of course, and the upstairs furniture is something to discuss at a later date, but I'm willing to let it go for a fair price.'

'That's a bit more than I'm prepared to pay,' said Ruby thoughtfully. 'I was in London over the weekend and did a bit of poking about. The pub trade's struggling at the moment, what with all the rationing and restrictions, and I'd need to see the books before I firmed up any offer.'

She eyed Rosie speculatively. 'Would you consider one thousand five hundred?'

Rosie shook her head. 'This place is worth more than that for the freehold alone.' She regarded Ruby thoughtfully. 'But as it's you, I'd take one nine.'

Ruby grinned. 'One six. Can't say fairer than that, Rosie, seeing as 'ow it's been up for sale since before I left.'

Rosie chuckled, admiring the girl's nerve. 'One thousand eight hundred, or we forget the whole thing.'

'Tell you what, Rosie, why not split the difference? One seven and we've got a deal.' Ruby stuck out her hand.

Rosie knew it was a fair price, so she shook Ruby's hand. 'It's a deal – and remind me never to negotiate with you again. You're way too hard-nosed.'

Ruby laughed. 'It takes one to know one,' she replied. 'How about that drink now to celebrate?'

'And what is it you're celebrating at this time of the morning?' asked Ron, coming into the room with the panting dogs.

'Ruby's just bought the pub,' replied Rosie, pulling three bottled beers from beneath the counter and collecting glasses.

'Well, that's grand, so it is,' he said, sitting down and grinning at Ruby. 'Has she told you the pitfalls of running a place like this, young Ruby? It won't be easy on your own, you know.'

'I'm hoping Brenda will still be around to help out,' she replied. 'If not, then I'm sure I can manage to find a part-timer who I can train up.' She poured the beer expertly into the glass and raised it in a toast. 'Here's to the Anchor, and your retirement.'

The toast was echoed, but Ron didn't look too happy about it.

'Ach, retirement's for old folk with nothing better to do, wee girl,' he grumbled. 'Rosie's on the town council now and there's talk of her becoming leader next year after the sterling job she did to keep the railway open. As for me, I shall no doubt be too busy doing up the wreck of a place Rosie's had her eye on to be lazing away the days.'

Rosie smiled. 'Ignore him, Ruby. You know how he likes to have a good moan about everything and anything.' She glanced up at the clock as someone impatiently rattled the front door handle. 'No peace for the wicked in this place, Ruby, as you'll soon find out. Fancy lending a hand over lunchtime to get the feel of the place again?'

Ruby swiftly downed the last of her beer and picked up her handbag. 'I thought you'd never ask,' she said in delight.

Ron quietly sat in the corner of the bar with the dogs slumped at his feet and watched the two women working in harmony behind the bar. They made a pretty picture, he mused, noting how Ruby was like a younger, darker-haired version of his Rosie as she smiled, pulled pints and chattered to the customers. She was more than capable of taking over the reins from Rosie, and although Ron knew she'd have her work cut out at times, she would make a success of this new venture.

The minute he returned from walking the dogs on Tuesday morning, Ron found himself being chivvied back outside to walk with Rosie to Havelock Road. She'd been to the estate agency and collected the keys to the property she'd thought she'd never have the chance to buy.

'To be sure, I can't see the need for all this rush,' he grumbled, having to keep pace with her. 'And why are we coming here? I thought you were after that house up by the Memorial?'

'I realised it's far too big, and has been empty too long,' she replied. 'A developer's put in an offer for it anyway and will probably tear it down to build a couple of dozen houses on the site. This one's far more practical, *and* they've dropped the price for a quick sale.'

She came to an abrupt halt and looked up at the detached house on the corner of Havelock Road and the High Street, which had escaped the devastation of the V-2 that had flattened Doris's house and the three at the other end of the cul-de-sac.

The early Victorian house was set back from the pavement and faced Havelock Gardens which were only just returning to their full beauty after being used as a communal vegetable plot during the war. The back of the house overlooked the end of the promenade and the sea.

'How come this place is for sale?' Ron asked, frowning up at the roof which needed fixing and the windows which looked as if they were about to fall out. A wisteria had gone berserk all over the front of it and was entangled in rampant ivy which was making its way under the roof tiles and dragging the guttering down. The rotting garage door was leaning drunkenly on one hinge, and the driveway shingle had been all but washed away by the years of heavy rain and neglect.

'The owners left before the war and decided they wanted to stay in Devon,' Rosie replied, leading the way up the short drive to the front door. 'The asking price is very fair, but I'm sure I can beat them down, for they're keen to be rid of it and it does need a bit of work.'

'To be sure, it's more than a *bit* of work.' Ron followed her gloomily into the house which was a mirror image of the one Doris had owned, but smelled damp and musty from being empty for so long. There was a cloakroom, dining room and staircase leading off from the hall, the kitchen and

471

scullery were at the back and the sitting room with its large picture window looked down on an overgrown and tangled garden to the sea.

Rosy wrinkled her nose at the smell and opened a window which promptly fell out and landed in the weeds and brambles of the flower bed beneath it. 'Oh. Oh dear. Can you sort that out while I have a look upstairs?'

Without waiting for a reply, she bounded up the stairs, and as Ron tried to haul up the metal-framed window, he could hear her hurrying footsteps above him. He managed to ram the old hinges back in place and eyed the soot fall in the hearth, wondering if the chimney was safe, then went up to join her.

He'd never been upstairs in Doris's house, but wasn't surprised to find four good-sized bedrooms as well as a bathroom – but each and every room had peeling wallpaper, cracked ceilings, flaking plaster and rotting window frames.

His heart sank as Rosie excitedly went from room to room, making all sorts of plans as to how it should be decorated and where to put the furniture she'd yet to buy. The place would probably need rewiring and plumbing on top of renewing the roof and all the guttering. It was going to take months to get it habitable again and would probably cost a fortune – but if it was what Rosie wanted, then he'd have to knuckle down and get on with it.

He left her rummaging around up there and returned to the sitting room to gaze out to the sea, thinking that he could live with a view like that, and there was plenty of room for the ferret hut and his tool shed. The dogs would like it too, with all that lawn to play on, and the beach so close.

He dug his hands into his pockets, his smile wry as he thought of Doris, and how she'd react to him living in this posh side of town. Havelock Road had never been a place he'd considered living in – but it would certainly be a step up from the pub, Peggy's basement and the old fisherman's cottage where he'd started out. But then Rosie was a lady, and it was only right she should have a fitting home.

Rosie came back and slipped her arm about his waist. 'It will cost a bit, but it'll be worth it just for the view, won't it?' she said on a sigh. 'Oh, Ron, we're going to be so happy here, I just know it.'

His sour mood fled as he saw the light in her eyes and the yearning for him to love it as much as she did. He kissed her softly. 'Aye, wee girl. We'll be as happy as turtle doves, so we will. As long as I don't put my back out with all the work that needs doing.'

She slapped his arm playfully. 'I have a remedy for bad backs,' she murmured with a twinkle of mischief in her eyes. 'Let's return the keys and put in an offer, then I'll show you my magic cure.'

30

Jim shivered from the cold wind as well as in the anticipation of seeing home and Peggy again within a matter of hours. He felt excited and strangely nervous about being thrust back into civilian life, for although Peggy and the rest of his family had written regularly and sent lots of photographs, he knew it would take time to settle down, get used to a slower pace, and reacquaint himself with his wife and children.

As in his brief First World War participation, his time in the army had been structured and tightly regulated, with there always being somewhere to go or something to do, and he'd become used to living in a rough, tough male environment until he'd been sent to Singapore. And that had been quite an eye-opener, for it had proved to him that his Peggy was not the only woman who'd spread her wings during the war and found independence in doing a fulfilling job outside the home.

Jim knew that his experiences during the Burma Campaign and in the aftermath of the Japanese surrender had changed him irrevocably. He was more sober and thoughtful, less likely to return to the ducking and diving of his youthful days, but more ambitious to forge a good future in which he too would be fulfilled. What that future might hold was as yet unknown, but he meant to grasp it with both hands, and be the man Peggy deserved.

He stood on the deck of the *Empress Aurelia* bundled up in his army greatcoat as the dawn mist swirled around him and the ghostly outline of Portsmouth Harbour began to slowly emerge and take shape. The *Empress Aurelia* had once been a cruise liner, but it had been commandeered during the war and stripped of all its luxuries and refinements to be used as a troopship. It carried not only the remaining troops of SEAC, but the last few returning prisoners of the Japanese who'd finally been deemed fit enough to be repatriated. These men stood alongside him, eagerly waiting for the ship to dock, and searching the quayside for sight of any loved ones who might have come to meet them.

Jim knew Peggy wouldn't be there, but waiting for him at home, no doubt as excited as he now their long separation was finally at an end. He watched the ship edge into its berth, heard the shouts of the sailors calling to their counterparts on the dock, and then the rattling grind of the chain as the anchor plunged into the murky water.

He peered through the mist, frustratingly unable to see much at all, then picked up his heavy kitbag and slung its straps over his shoulder before hefting up the equally heavy holdall. There were several other bags in the hold which would be sent on by rail, and Peggy should have received the numerous parcels he'd posted before he'd left Singapore.

As the troops and POWs had now been officially demobilised there was to be no further hanging about. Jim joined the long queue waiting to disembark, bitterly disappointed there was no quayside welcoming party, no flags or military band – just a handful of nervous relatives, some disinterested dock workers and a couple of nurses to watch them step onto English soil again.

He wasn't really surprised, for the war in Europe had now been over for a whole year, and his commanding officer had warned all the men that the war in the Far East had been so distant, it had been out of sight and was now mostly out of mind. It was galling to Jim to realise that all that blood, sweat and loss had already faded from memory, but then you had to be there to know what it was like and to appreciate the brutal cost so many men had paid.

He followed the others down the ramp and walked through the vast sheds that housed customs and immigration. He paused to have his passport stamped, nodded his thanks to the official who gruffly welcomed him home, and stepped outside. The sun was finally breaking through the mist, and it looked as if it was going to be a beautiful day.

Jim hitched up his kitbag, gripped the holdall and headed for the station. If all went as planned, he'd be home for tea.

Peggy hadn't been able to sleep, for she was too excited, and her mind too active with all the things she wanted to do to make Jim's homecoming special. It wasn't quite dawn when she finally climbed out of bed, impatient to be getting on with her day. Daisy had crawled in with her around midnight, as she often did when she knew there was something exciting afoot, and was now curled up fast asleep.

Peggy left her there, closed the door softly and went into the bathroom to prepare for the day. She would have a strip-wash now, she decided, and then just before she went to the hairdresser's, she'd treat herself to a lovely bath with the scented oil Jim had sent from Singapore. Her new underwear was folded within tissue paper in a drawer, and her lovely blue dress and bolero was hanging up in the wardrobe, all ready to step into nearer the time. She wasn't absolutely sure when Jim would arrive in Cliffehaven, but if the ship came in early, it would probably be around six this evening.

She was grinning with happiness as she went downstairs to put the kettle on and check that she had everything ready for tonight's dinner. Ruby, Danuta and Charlie had helped her and Cordelia dress the dining room; Ron had rigged up bunting and balloons out the front to welcome him home, and she'd gone through the house yesterday like a dose of salts making sure everything was spotless so he'd approve of all her changes.

She hugged her delight to herself, for Solly had given her two weeks off work, and it felt as if half of Cliffehaven wanted to ensure that Jim's homecoming was as welcoming as possible. Alf the butcher had kept a leg of lamb aside for her; Fred the Fish had supplied some lovely smoked salmon for starters; Sam the greengrocer had sold her cabbages, potatoes and carrots at half price, and Julie had insisted she paid nothing for her hairdo and manicure today.

She sat down with a fag and a cup of tea to watch the rising sun chase the shadows from the back garden. Martin would be back in time for dinner from the latest delivery into France; Rosie and Ron were providing the drinks. Cissy was due to arrive from London at some point in the day, and Frank had asked rather shyly if it would be all right if he brought Brenda along to the dinner. Of course she'd said yes, for she was thrilled they were getting on so well, and that Brendon seemed quite happy about it. Brendon, Betty and Anne would come straight from school with the children, and John and Doris would get here after John's physio appointment at the hospital. There was an open invitation to all the others to pop in whenever they could, and although it would mean feeding the five thousand, everyone had willingly chipped in, so there would be enough of a spread to make a good show.

Peggy thought about Jack who was still struggling to get through all the work he had now he was also selling cars as well as mending them, and could only hope that Jim would realise what a fine opportunity it offered for a stable job and income. However, that was for another day. Jim had to settle in first and get used to them all again.

The only dark cloud on Peggy's horizon was the possibility that Bob wouldn't be here, although he'd promised he'd do his very best – and surely Jim would understand that the farm seasons waited for no man, and as he was now a full partner with Aunt Vi, it was his livelihood and his future.

'Morning, Mum,' said Charlie cheerfully, plonking down into a kitchen chair. 'What's for breakfast?'

Peggy chuckled. 'Trust you to bring me down to earth on a day like this,' she teased. 'Go and see if those new chickens have laid anything. If they haven't, it's toast and cereal as usual.'

He came back a few minutes later with three brown eggs. 'Bob said it'll take a bit of time for them to settle in and start laying properly, but this is a start.' He put them carefully in the crock by the range. 'Any news from him by the way?' he asked, sitting back down.

'No, but I expect he'll telephone tonight to speak to Dad.' Peggy popped one of the eggs in to boil and loaded the new toaster with bread slices. 'Don't hang about after football practice,' she warned. 'It would be awful if you weren't here when your dad arrives.'

Charlie rolled his eyes. 'As if I'd not be here. Honestly, Mum, I'm as excited as you to see him again. And I bet he's getting impatient on that slow old train.'

Peggy smiled. 'I expect he is,' she murmured, remembering how quickly he could get fed up if made to hang about for anything too long.

Jim had found the journey home to be achingly slow, for the train stopped at every station and halt along the way. He'd shed his overcoat as the day had warmed up considerably and was now feeling cooler in his tropical whites, but his impatience was rising as the last part of the journey seemed to take an age, and the only way to relieve the nervous tension was to get up and pace back and forth along the corridor, which earned him a few mutters of annoyance from the other passengers.

The day wore on, and it was almost six o'clock when, at last, he saw the familiar rolling hills, the chalk cliffs and the sea. He leaned out of the window as far as he dared as the train slowly chugged into Cliffehaven Halt, and breathed a sigh of relief as it came to a stop.

Grabbing his bags, he jumped down, and through the steam saw a blur of blue rushing towards him.

'Jim! Oh, Jim!' Peggy cried, throwing herself into his arms.

Jim dropped the bags, catching her just in time to hold her close. He lifted her from her feet and kissed the very breath from her until he realised they had a laughing, cheering audience. The pair of them giggling and blushing like school children, he set Peggy back onto her feet and grasped her hand, almost afraid to let go of her now she was by his side again.

'Welcome home, Jim,' shouted Stan above the cheers of the disembarking passengers.

'Thanks, Stan. It's good to be back.' He nodded and grinned in acknowledgement of the welcoming smiles of the other passengers, and slipped his arm around Peggy's narrow waist. He bent low to whisper in her ear, 'I didn't realise there'd be a welcoming committee.'

'Of course there is,' she murmured back, her love for him lighting up her eyes. 'But you wait until you get home, Jim. Bob and Cissy are both waiting for you with all the others.'

Jim shook Stan's hand, grabbed his bags and walked with Peggy out of the station, which he noted had changed beyond recognition since he'd left. 'Good to see you've got the old car going again,' he said, dumping the bags into the boot and settling happily into the passenger seat.

Peggy cupped his face and kissed him softly. 'Welcome home, my love, my darling man. I've missed you more than words can say.'

He hugged her to him, noting how small and delicate she'd become, but how radiant and beautiful she was. 'I've dreamed of this day for so long, I can hardly believe it's real,' he murmured against her lips. Then he sat back and grinned. 'Let's get home, Peg. I can't wait to see everyone – especially Daisy and my boys.'

Peggy drove down the High Street pointing out the new Woolworths, W.H. Smith, Boots the chemist and bingo hall which now filled the site of the old Odeon Cinema where Jim had worked before the war. Jim noted that the ancient Mermaid Inn was gone, and an ugly three-storey block of flats was going up in its place, but the Crown was still there, looking very smart in its fresh coat of paint – and Gloria was her usual flamboyant self as she waved an enthusiastic welcome from the doorstep.

He returned her wave, and as Peggy turned into Camden Road, he felt a shiver of pleasurable anticipation as they passed the new school and the Anchor pub. He was almost home.

Peggy slowed to a halt as they reached the line of shops, and there was Fred the Fish, Alf the butcher and Sam the grocer with their wives and children all waving flags and calling out to welcome him home. He climbed out to shake hands and receive kisses, his heart so full of love and gratitude for their welcome he could barely speak.

Peggy slowly drove the car towards the junction, and although he could see the evidence of war all round him in the bomb sites, he had eyes only for Beach View. The stucco was freshly painted white, the door a shining dark blue, and there were unfamiliar lanterns gracing the pillars at the bottom of the steps – it looked lovely in the sunshine, and thankfully hadn't really changed all that much. But what made his heart miss a beat and brought tears to his eyes was the bunting and balloons, and the large, hand-painted sign above the door, welcoming him home.

'It looks like we've been spotted,' murmured Peggy, her voice trembling with emotion as everyone came pouring out of the house to wait for them on the front steps.

Jim was out of the car almost before Peggy had brought it to a halt, and immediately swamped in loving arms and smothered in kisses, the two dogs leaping up, desperate to welcome him as he was slowly drawn up the steps and into the house.

'Hello, Dad,' said Bob, flinging his arms round him. 'It's so good to see you.'

'Oh, son,' he replied, holding him tightly. 'It's the very best thing in the world to see you – and looking so grown-up, too.' He pulled back eventually and caught sight of Charlie grinning at him. 'Charlie?' he gasped. 'Is that really you?'

'It certainly is, Dad,' he replied, giving him a bear hug. 'Welcome home.'

Jim was unashamedly tearful as he regarded his two handsome sons. 'I can't believe how you've both grown,' he said in awe. 'What the hell has Vi been feeding you in Somerset to make you so big?'

'Better food than Mum and the others got here,' said Bob on a chuckle. 'But Mum's laid on a proper feast in honour of your homecoming, so you won't go hungry.'

'Hello, Dad. Remember me?'

Jim could only stare at her. 'Cissy?'

'Well, of course it is, silly,' she giggled, giving him a smacking kiss which left lipstick on his cheek. 'It's lovely to have you home, Dad, really it is. And don't you look handsome in your uniform? I bet you had all those nurses positively drooling.'

He grinned bashfully. 'Well, I don't know about that, Cissy,' he replied. 'I was a bit too busy fighting off the Japs to take much notice of nurses.'

Cordelia pushed her way through and clasped Jim's hand. 'Welcome home, Jim. I'm so very glad you made it through, even if you have lost a bit of your ear.' She grinned up at him. 'Doesn't this old woman get a kiss, then?'

'Ach, to be sure, Cordelia, you're my favourite girl. Of course you get a kiss.' He softly kissed her lined cheek, his heart saddened by how old and frail she'd become during his absence.

And then he was being embraced by Anne who introduced his shy grandchildren, before Martin pumped his hand. Frank and Brendon hugged him fiercely and he finally met Betty and baby Joseph.

'This is Daisy,' said Peggy, leading her to him by the hand. 'Daisy, this is your daddy.'

Daisy looked up at him thoughtfully for a moment and then shook her head. 'He's not my daddy. He's got legs,' she said firmly.

Jim frowned and looked to Peggy for an explanation, but received only a shrug of confusion, so he squatted down to Daisy's level, noting how very pretty she was with her dark curls and big brown eyes. 'Why do think your daddy has no legs, Daisy?

'Cos I seen my daddy's picture.'

Jim realised she was talking about the studio photograph he'd had taken as a memento for Peggy before he'd left for India. 'Ahhh,' he breathed, and gently took her hand. 'But I was sitting down for that, and I'm sure that if you look very closely you'll see that I really am your daddy.'

Daisy inspected his face minutely, and then smiled. 'Mummy said you were coming home. Are you going to live here now?'

He resisted hugging and kissing her, sensing that she wasn't yet ready for that sort of intimacy. 'Yes. I'm home for good and this is where I shall live from now on.'

Daisy still didn't look totally convinced. 'Will you live in the spare room? Mummy made it very nice.'

Jim chuckled and shot a glance at a giggling Peggy. 'Well, I was rather hoping I could share Mummy's room,' he said.

Daisy shook her head. 'I share with Mummy. You'll have to sleep downstairs.'

'Well, we'll see about that,' he said, ruffling her hair and earning a scowl. He stood and grinned at the others who were trying hard to muffle their laughter. 'It seems I've been put very firmly in my place – and will have to negotiate my position in this house from now on.'

Peggy hugged him. 'Don't mind Daisy,' she whispered in his ear. 'She'll get used to you sleeping in my bed.'

He looked down at her, holding her loving gaze and wishing they were alone, but the moment was broken by his father.

'Well, to be sure, 'tis grand you're home, wee Jim,' Ron shouted before charging through the others to get to him. His hug took Jim's breath away.

''Tis grand to see you too, Da,' he managed, fending off Harvey's rapturous welcome. 'You're looking well. Marriage obviously suits you.'

'Aye, it does that,' said Ron, gazing at his son as if he couldn't really believe he was finally here. He gathered Bob and Charlie to him, nudged Harvey out of the way and grabbed Jim, his blue eyes bright with unshed tears. 'My boys. My precious boys. 'Tis glad I am I've lived to see you all home again.'

'Get away with you, Da,' laughed Jim through his own tears. 'You'll probably outlive us all, you old rascal. How's the poaching going? Salmon for tea, is it?'

'Maybe,' replied Ron with a twinkle in his eye. He turned to Peggy. 'Is there a chance of a wee drink, Peg? To be sure, a man could die of thirst in this house today.'

Jim was quite overwhelmed with their rapturous welcome, and although he only had a brief moment to admire the stair-lift contraption Rita and Peter had made for Cordelia, he could see that the hall had indeed been given a complete overhaul with new carpet, paint and paper, which made it look very smart. And yet, when he walked into the kitchen to find there was a much bigger window, new lino and cupboards, it was still familiar enough to maintain the homeliness he'd remembered, and he was grateful that Peggy hadn't gone overboard on the refurbishment.

Peggy must have seen him looking around, for she tucked her hand in his arm. 'Come and see the rest of the house while Frank sorts out the drinks. I do hope you like what I've done, Jim, but I have tried to keep the essence of the house the same – just given it a bit of a facelift, really.'

He grinned down at her and went down to the basement to admire the laundry room and cloakroom, avoiding asking her how much all the changes must have cost. Then he went out into the back garden, saw the ugly bomb site on the other side of the twitten and pulled Peggy to him. 'You didn't tell me you were that close to trouble,' he murmured.

'There was little point in worrying you, Jim,' she replied, 'and we were all quite safe, as you can see.'

Jim kissed her cheek and kept his arm round her waist as he quelled the stab of fear and viewed the garden. The back wall had been repaired, the Anderson shelter removed along with his father's shed and the outside lav. The chickens were happily pecking in their coop, and his father's vegetable garden was clearly flourishing.

'Do you think we could sneak up and have a look at the upstairs without anyone noticing?' he asked with a wink.

'I doubt it,' Peggy giggled, nudging him gently in the ribs. 'You'll just have to wait for what you've got in mind, Jim Reilly.'

Jim grinned down at her before going back inside, where he was immediately escorted through the rest of the house by everyone in their eagerness to show him all the work that had been done.

'It's all grand,' he said truthfully. 'My goodness, Peggy, you've certainly brought the old place alive again. You are clever.'

'It's Ron, Frank and Charlie who are clever,' she replied happily. 'They did most of the work – and saved us a pretty penny too.'

He hugged her to him, and then took a turn on Cordelia's stair-lift with all three little girls on his lap, which slowly broke the ice between him and Daisy, who decided it was great fun to have a daddy in the house.

Returning to the chaos in the kitchen as the women began to dish up the dinner, he quickly went through the mound of post that was waiting for him on the mantelpiece. Swiftly reading the cards and telegrams welcoming him home, he left the official-looking letter until last in the hope it would prove to be what he hoped it was. Scanning the two pages, he smiled and folded it back into its envelope. He'd wait until later to tell Peggy what it was all about, he decided.

Jim had eaten his fill, and now he was sitting at the table in the beautifully refurbished dining room, listening to the happy chatter and laughter going on around him. His heart was full with love and thankfulness that he'd made it home to these wonderful people when so many hadn't been given that blessing. The feast Peggy had laid on was magnificent given how restrictive the rationing was now there were so many shortages, yet it seemed everyone had chipped in, and he was profoundly grateful for their kindness.

He watched Peggy and their eyes met repeatedly across the table, holding promises for later that would be fulfilled once they were alone, and Jim was content to wait, for this was the homecoming he'd dreamed of for many years.

As he ate and drank and listened to his da's tall stories, his gaze flitted from face to face, marvelling at how they'd changed – and yet were still recognisable because of all the photographs Peggy had sent to him over the years. He'd been shocked to hear about Pauline's desertion, but his brother didn't look as if he was too concerned, appearing very happy with Brenda. Rosie was looking as glamorous as he'd remembered, Doris was as neatly groomed as always and he definitely approved of her husband, who'd wrought such a change in her that she was actually being pleasant to him for once.

As for Anne, she was now a mature woman and mother with another baby on the way, and her little girls – his grand-daughters – were quite lovely, if a bit of a handful. He was relieved that Anne and Martin had survived the trauma of Martin's wartime experiences, and were making terrific progress both in their marriage and in their future.

Jim watched the children playing together on the rug in front of the fire. He'd never considered himself old enough to be a grandfather, and yet the proof that he'd aged was there in Rose and Emily, as well as in his little Daisy, who was going to turn into another Cissy if she carried on as she was – but that was all right. Cissy certainly hadn't turned out so badly after those tempestuous early years, even if she did now talk as if she had a plum in her mouth.

Brendon and Betty seemed very happy together and little Joseph was a joy – but it was his two strapping sons who were a forcible reminder of the years that had passed since the last time they'd all sat together, and he was finding that hard to digest.

Jim bathed in the gloriously warm glow of love and pride as he watched his extended family joyfully celebrate this longed-for homecoming. The love he felt was quite over-whelming, for although each and every one of them had changed, and there were new faces, it was as if he'd never been away. He let his gaze wander to each of them in turn, and then decided it was time to let them know how very proud he was of them all, and how much he loved them.

He pushed back from the table and tapped his knife against his glass. 'I look around me and my heart is full,' he said into the ensuing silence. 'I see my boys grown hand-some and strong, with bright futures ahead of them, and to both of you, I wish you all the success in your chosen careers on the farm and in the RAF.'

He searched out his daughters. 'As for my beautiful girls – Anne, you're strong of heart and mind and the most loving wife and mother, and I'm very proud of the young woman you've become. Martin's a lucky man, and so am I to have such a lovely daughter.'

He grinned at Cissy. 'Cissy, you've got the Reilly spirit, and have shown a strength of purpose in following your own path – rather like your grandad. May all your dreams come true, wee girl, and make sure you come to visit more often now your mum and I are getting on a bit.'

There was much laughter at this, and Jim waited for it to die down before he turned to his father. 'Da. What can I say to thank you for all you've done over these past few years? You've been my Peggy's rock, and knowing you were always here for her eased my mind considerably and helped me concentrate on the job I had to do. I salute you for being stout of heart and truly the bravest man I know, for although you keep it to yourself, I know you've risked your life many a time in defence of this country.'

His gaze fell on Peggy. 'And you, my darling girl,' he said softly. 'I've seen enough to know how hard it must have been for you over the years, but you've soldiered on; kept the home fires burning; raised our daughter and looked after all your chicks with such love and patience that they will always call this place home.'

He glanced towards Ruby, April, Sally, Danuta and Kitty before looking back at Peggy. 'I love what you've done to the house, Peggy – and I love that through all the bombing, the rationing and shortages, you've found the strength to carry on without me and most of our family, and have found fulfilment in your work, and in the joy our children and grandchildren bring.'

Jim grinned at his older brother Frank and tipped him a wink before raising his glass. 'I propose we drink to the precious gift of family – to those we love without question, and who we can now watch flourish in this new era of peace.'

Much later, when everything had been cleared away and the house was once more peaceful now everyone had gone to their beds, Jim took Peggy's hand and led her outside to sit on the front steps as they used to do before the war. It was a clear, warm night with a new moon rising and a myriad of stars twinkling above them.

He put his arm round her shoulders and held her to his side as they listened to the silence broken only by the distant sound of the waves lazily breaking on the shingle beach. He looked out to the chimney pots and roofs of the town, beyond the twinkling lights from the many windows towards the dark, almost sensuous undulations of the surrounding hills, and breathed in the familiar salty air.

'It's so good to be home, Peggy,' he murmured. 'And I'm so proud of everything you've achieved.'

'Oh, Jim,' she replied softly. 'I didn't do very much at all. It's you who should be proud. Without men like you, this world would still be at war.' She rested her head against his shoulder. 'I'm just so very thankful that you made it through in one piece, when so many have terrible burdens still to bear both physically and mentally, and I pray that your experiences over there won't haunt you.'

She looked up at him and touched his damaged ear. 'This is the first night of the rest of our lives, Jim, and now you're home, you must rest and take your time deciding what you're going to do.'

Jim kissed the tip of her nose. 'I know you and Jack were hoping I'd go into business with him, but I told him tonight that I won't be taking up his offer.'

Peggy looked back at him, her face lit by the golden moonlight, her eyes wide. 'Would that have something to do with that letter from the Royal British Legion?'

He nodded, and swiftly told her about Elsa Bristow's help in providing a senior contact within the organisation, and his heartfelt need to use his experiences and do something worthwhile.

'They've offered me the post of Southern co-ordinator for the Far Eastern Prisoners of War. I shall be responsible for making sure they get the medical help they need, the grants and pensions they're entitled to, and that the right people are put in place to organise any other needs they or their families may have.'

He hugged her to him. 'They're offering a good salary, and I shall have the use of a car so I can get about, but I shall always come home at night, Peggy. I'm never leaving you again, I promise.'

'Are you sure this is what you want, Jim? I know how badly affected you were by the awful stories you had to listen to.'

'I've never been more positive,' he said firmly, before kissing the top of her head. 'Those men need all the help they can get, and I can think of no better way of repaying them for all the sacrifices they've made.'

'You're a good man, Jim Reilly,' she said softly. 'I'm so very lucky to have you love me.'

He cupped her face and gently kissed her lips, her eyes and the tip of her nose. 'I'm the lucky one, Peggy Reilly,' he murmured. 'You're my heart and my home – my everything – and we will walk into the future knowing the world is finally at peace and a better place for having one another to share it.'

She placed her hand against his heart and looked into his eyes with such love he felt like weeping. 'One heart, one mind, one love above all others to bind us,' she whispered. 'We are truly blessed.'

WELCOME TO

Cliffehaven

ELLIE DEAN

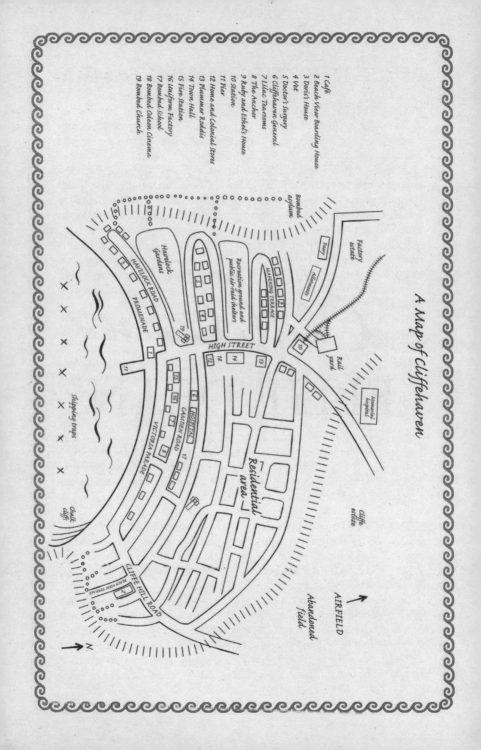

A Map of Cliffehaven

1 Café
2 Beach View Boarding House
3 Doris's House
4 Vet
5 Doctor's Surgery
6 Cliffehaven General
7 Lilac Tearooms
8 The Anchor
9 Ruby and Ethel's House
10 Station
11 Pier
12 Home and Colonial Stores
13 Plummer Roddis
14 Town Hall
15 Fire Station
16 Uniform Factory
17 Bombed School
18 Bombed Odeon Cinema
19 Bombed Church

Bombed
asylum

Factory
estate

Dairy

Allotments

Havelock
Gardens

HAVELOCK ROAD

PROMENADE

Recreation ground and
public air-raid shelters

MAFEKING TERRACE

HIGH STREET

Rail
yard

Cliffe
estate

Memorial
hospital

Shipping traps

VICTORIA PARADE

CAMDEN ROAD

HOSPITAL

Residential
area

Chalk
cliffs

BEACH VIEW TERRACE

CLIFFE HILL ROAD

Abandoned
field

AIRFIELD

N

MEET THE CLIFFEHAVEN FAMILY

PEGGY REILLY is in her early forties, and married to Jim. She is small and slender, with dark, curly hair and lively brown eyes. As if running a busy household and caring for her young daughter wasn't enough, she also runs the local uniform factory and still finds time to offer tea, sympathy and a shoulder to cry on when they're needed. She and Jim took over the running of Beach View Boarding House when Peggy's parents retired. When war was declared and the boarding house business no longer became viable, she decided to take in evacuees.

Peggy can be feisty and certainly doesn't suffer fools, and yet she is also trying very hard to come to terms with the fact that her family has been torn apart by the war. She is a romantic at heart and can't help trying to match-make, but she's also a terrible worrier, always fretting over someone – and as the evacuees make their home with her, she comes to regard them as her chicks and will do everything she can to protect them.

JIM REILLY is in his mid-forties and was a young engineer in the last days of the First War, where he served alongside his elder brother, Frank, and father Ron. Now he's fighting for king and country in India and Burma.

Jim is handsome, with flashing blue eyes and dark hair, and the gift of the Irish blarney he'd inherited from his Irish parents, which usually gets him out of trouble. He enjoys the camaraderie of being a soldier, but the conditions and dangers he's encountering in the jungles have somewhat dampened his enthusiasm, and he treasures the letters and cards from home.

RONAN REILLY (Ron) is a sturdy man in his sixties who often leads a very secretive life away from Beach View now that his experience and skills from the previous war are called upon during the hostilities. Widowed several decades ago, he has recently married the luscious Rosie Braithwaite who owns the Anchor pub.

Ron is a wily countryman; a poacher and retired fisherman with great roguish charm who tramps over the fields with his dog, Harvey, and two ferrets. He doesn't care much about his appearance, much to Peggy's dismay, but beneath that ramshackle old hat and moth-eaten clothing, beats the heart of a strong, loving man who will fiercely protect those he loves.

ROSIE REILLY is in her fifties and has recently married Ron, after her husband died following many years in a mental asylum. She took over the Anchor pub twenty years ago and has turned it into a little gold-mine. Rosie has platinum hair, big blue eyes and an hour-glass figure – she also has a good sense of humour and can hold her own with the customers.

HARVEY is a scruffy, but highly intelligent brindled lurcher, with a mind of his own and a mischievous nature – much like his owner, Ron.

DORIS WILLIAMS is Peggy's older sister and for many years she has been divorced from her long-suffering husband, Ted, who died very recently. She used to live in the posh part of town, Havelock Road, and look down on Peggy and the boarding house.

But her days of snooty social climbing and snobbishness are behind her. Having lived with Peggy at Beach View Boarding House after bombs destroyed her former neighbourhood, Doris has softened and although she's still proud of her connections to high society, she's also on much better terms with her sister and the rest of the family. But despite all this, Doris is still rather lonely, especially with her only son now married and moved away. Could her recent change of heart also lead to a new romance?

FRANK REILLY has served his time in the army during both wars, but now he's been demobbed due to his age and is doing his bit by joining the Home Guard and Civil Defense. He's married to Pauline and they live in Tamarisk Bay in the fisherman's cottage where he was born.

CORDY FINCH is a widow and has been living at Beach View for many years. She is in her eighties and is rather frail from her arthritis, but that doesn't stop her from bantering with Ron and enjoying life to the full. She adores Peggy and looks on her as a daughter, for her own sons emigrated to Canada many years before and she rarely hears from them. The girls who live at Beach View regard her as their grandmother, as does Peggy's youngest, Daisy.

ANNE is married to Station Commander Martin Black, an RAF pilot, and they have two small girls. Anne has moved down to Somerset for the war, teaching at the local village school.

CICELY (Cissy) is a driver for the WAAF and is stationed at Cliffe aerodrome. She once had ambitions to go on stage, but finds great satisfaction in doing her bit, and is enjoying the new friendships she's made. She has fallen in love with a young American pilot, Randolf Stevens, but now he's been sent to Biggin Hill, they rarely see one another.

BOB and **CHARLIE** are Peggy's two young sons, who are also living in Somerset for the duration. Bob is serious and dedicated to running the farm, while Charlie is still mischievous, and when not causing trouble, can be found most of the time under the bonnet of some vehecle, tinkering with the engine.

DAISY is Peggy's youngest child, born the day Singapore fell. She can sleep through air raids and simply adores pulling Ron's wayward eyebrows. She and Harvey are best of friends, but she has yet to truly know her father, or her siblings.

RITA SMITH came to Beach View after her home in Cliffehaven was flattened by an air raid. Rita is small and an energetic tomboy who is a fully qualified mechanic, having been taught from an early age by her father. She can usually be seen in heavy trousers and boots, and a First World War leather jacket and flying helmet.

FRAN is from Ireland and works as a theatre nurse at Cliffehaven General. She has been living with Peggy since before the war, and has become an intrinsic part of the family. She plays the violin at the Anchor for the sing-songs, and has fallen in love with Robert – an MOD colleague of Anthony Williams.

SARAH FULLER and her younger sister, **JANE**, came to England and Beach View after the fall of Singapore. They are the great-nieces of Cordelia Finch who has welcomed them with open arms. Sarah works for the Women's Timber Corps, and Jane has now left Cliffehaven for a secret posting where she's deciphering codes.

IVY is from the East End of London and was billeted for a time with Doris where she was expected to skivvy. She's stepping out with Fire Officer Andy, who is the nephew of Gloria Stevens who runs the Crown pub in Cliffehaven High Street. She and Rita are best friends and the untidiest pair Peggy has ever met – other than Ron and Harvey.

Lose yourself in the

There'll be Blue Skies
Ellie Dean

Far From Home
Ellie Dean

Keep Smiling Through
Ellie DEAN

Some Lucky Day
Ellie Dean

While We're Apart
Ellie Dean

Sealed With a Loving Kiss
Ellie Dean

Where the Heart Lies
Ellie DEAN

Always in my Heart
Ellie Dean

All My Tomorrows
Ellie Dean

Find Love. Find Hope.
Find Cliffehaven.

world of Cliffehaven